CRIMSON UNDER THE MOON

BY
FANTASY NELSON

Dedication Page

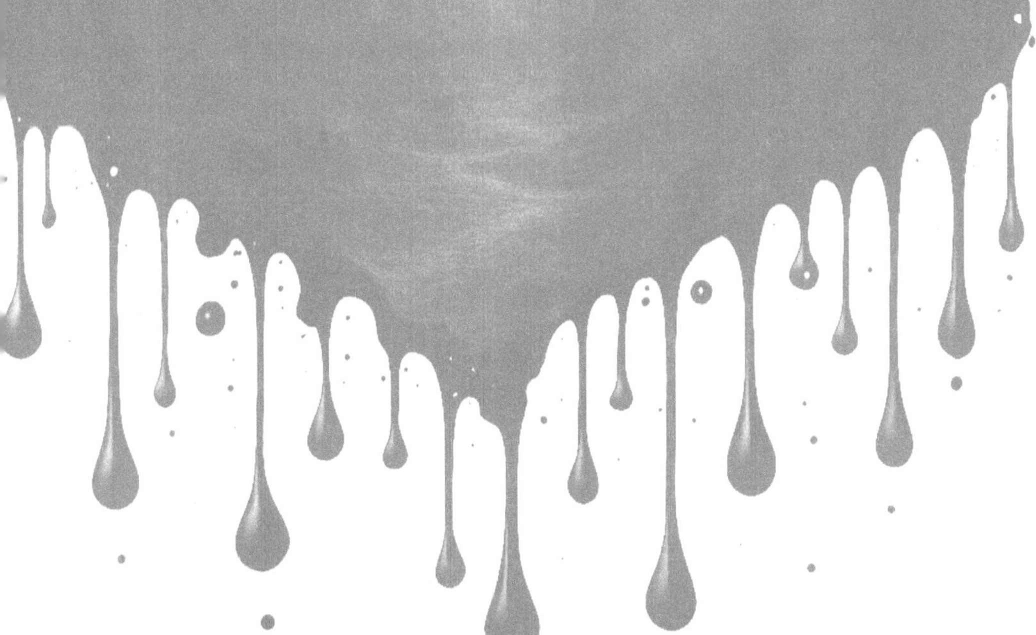

Thank you to my best friend who encouraged me to write this book after so long. I'd stopped writing for a long time because I didn't feel it was good enough. Not only did she encourage me to write again, but she was my sounding board through this whole process.

Thank you for believing in me!

This book contains SA, spice, death, and mentions of
self-harm, miscarriage, and depression.

Chapter 1

"Uh, Dominique, I know we're in this machine together, but why does it feel like the world around us is tilting off its axis? Are you sure they can handle both of us being in the same world together?" Melissa's voice trembled.

Dominique swallowed. Her stomach fluttered as the world around them blurred. Flashes of images flickered in and out, disorienting them. The road beneath their feet cracked apart, shifting until they nearly lost their balance.

For a dizzying moment, it felt like everything might collapse. Then, just as quickly, the pieces knit themselves back together. The world stilled.

Dominique gave Melissa a sheepish grin.

"Sorry. I've been thinking about the dreams I've been having lately. They keep replaying on a loop."

"Can I see one?" Melissa asked, curious.

"Sure," Dominique replied as she began to manipulate the machine so it created the dream.

***

A young girl walked down a dirt road, a wooden pail of water swaying at her side. Suddenly, a horse burst from the trees. She fell back, the bucket slipping from her hand and splashing water over her dress.

Cursing, she stood and shook out her skirts, mud clinging stubbornly to the fabric. Her scowl deepened as she yelled at the rider, who had wheeled his horse around to face her.

The knight hadn't noticed her until he saw something fly as he broke through the woods. Now he saw her clearly: a peasant girl, furious, standing in the sunlight. His blood rose at her insult, but his eyes lingered. Despite the mud streaking her dress, her golden hair gleamed. The wet fabric clung to her curves. She glared at him as if she were allowed to.

"I apologize, my lady," he said, his voice edged with warning. "I rarely encounter anyone on my rides. But you should mind your tongue when you don't know who you're speaking to."

She gave a sarcastic bow. "My apologies, good knight. Forgive my insolence. My tongue runs away with me when my temper rises."

A smile tugged at his lips. Only his father dared speak to him so boldly. She had forgotten her place. Perhaps he should remind her.

"Your apology doesn't sound sincere. Perhaps your father should hear of this insolence."

Her face paled. He extended his hand. She refused it, stepping back. Irritation flared in him. With a sharp move, he urged his horse forward, reached down, and caught her arm. A spark jolted through him at the contact. His hand slid to hers, tightening as he hauled her closer.

"You're getting on this horse," he growled. "Either throw your leg over, or I'll throw you across my lap."

She swallowed hard, then nodded. With awkward grace, she climbed up behind him, her skirts riding high enough to bare her thigh. Improper. Tempting. He didn't complain.

Her arms circled his waist, her cheek pressing to his back. The heat of her body bled through him, dangerous and distracting.

"Where do you live?" he asked, steering the horse.

She told him the name of the village, guiding him toward the road that led to her home. As they passed through the streets, heads turned. Villagers bowed low, for they knew him; the heir to the castle and its lands. He spurred the horse faster once they left the village behind.

As her home came into view, he rested a hand on her thigh. "When we stop, I'll get down first. Then I'll help you."

"Sir knight," she said, steadying her voice, "I thank you, but I ride often. I know what is proper and what is not. And it is not proper for a man to touch a lady as you are now."

His lips curved. "What is your name, girl?"

"R-Rose."

"Well, Rose," he murmured, halting the horse, "you need to learn to hold your tongue."

He dismounted, then yanked her down roughly, pulling her against him. His breath brushed her ear as he whispered, "And I'm more than happy to teach you that lesson."

***

The world dissolved into white, the dream tearing apart at the edges until nothing remained.

Melissa's voice broke through the haze. "Did you get to finish it? Or is it time?"

"The dream wasn't finished. It seems we've pushed past the safe limit. Post is forcing us out."

They closed their eyes and let their minds go blank. When they opened their eyes again, the visors of the helmets were reflecting back at them. They each stepped out of the booths, breath unsteady, as if they had truly lived the dream.

"Well, you've seen one of the dreams now, so what did you think?"

Melissa let out a low whistle. "Damn, girl. That felt real. Like I was standing right there, watching it all unfold. Your machine works, and your imagination's wild. Are all your dreams like that?"

"Not all," Dominique admitted. "Some are longer. Some are rougher. They feel too real sometimes. And the strangest part? I never see his face. I can only assume it's because I'm not dreaming about anyone in particular. I can feel the girl's desire, though." She hesitated, almost whispering. "It's overwhelming."

Melissa smirked. "Makes you wonder."

"Well, how did we do?" Dominique asked her brother, Post as they approached.

"Pretty good, actually. A few more tweaks and it'll hold steady for the full two hours. Two going to be enough?"

"It'll have to be. I can't risk pouring more money into this until we know it'll succeed. The bar's doing well now, but that could change overnight. If these machines flop, I'll be buried in debt."

Post grinned. "Trust me, they won't flop. You've built something people crave. Whatever they imagine, they can live. And let's face it, half of those fantasies are dirty ones."

Dominique chuckled, but her gaze lingered on the machines. "So many people want what they can't have. The question is… if they can taste it for just a little while, is that better than never at all?"

Dominique noticed the time, and they all rushed downstairs to set up the bar before opening.

Dominique took pride in her bar. It was two stories of dark elegance. The main floor held the bar, a stage for the band, and a wide dance floor. Upstairs, another dance floor glowed under colored lights, and a VIP lounge promised private decadence for a price. Beside it, tucked away and locked, her machines waited for the first brave customer.

She didn't know what she would do without Post and Melissa. They were everything: bandmates, coworkers, friends, family. When Post wasn't working on the machines or doing maintenance, he played the drums. Melissa played the guitar and waitressed for her. Dominique did it all, from singing to keyboards, to bookkeeping, to filling in behind the bar.

There were open mic nights for the people who liked to sing. Most nights, they played a mixture of R&B, country, pop, and rock. There was something for everyone.

Dominique was getting ready to replace Teddy, her bartender, as she was getting married, and her soon-to-be husband wanted her to stay home. She hated losing her, but Teddy had also just found out she was pregnant. Dominique couldn't blame her for not wanting to be in this type of environment while pregnant.

Don, her bouncer, was walking through the door as she reached the bar. She waved to him, walked up to the stage, and set the playlist to make sure everything was working properly. Dominique sighed as she finally sat down, thankful everything was set for the night to begin.

At the end of the night, Dominique sat in her office going over the tallies for the night. It had been busy, and the exhaustion from checking on everything came over her. Closing her eyes, she sat back, and sleep overtook her immediately. Once again, the dreams started.

Chapter 2

Rose lifted her chin, glaring at Nathaniel. "I will not let you do anything without a fight. I refuse to be a concubine. Not even to the great Sir Nathaniel. Punish me for speaking my mind if you will, but I will not lie down like a dog."

"You do not understand your place in this world," he said, his voice cold. "Or perhaps you simply wish to die. Either way, I think it will be… interesting to have you around."

He seized her arm and began leading her toward the small house she shared with her father. She followed with unflinching defiance, refusing to open the door, forcing him to open it. Knowing he wouldn't relent, she called out to her father, her voice tight with frustration.

Her father's weak voice answered from inside. He hobbled into the front room, his warm smile fading as he saw the knight.

"Sir Nathaniel! Welcome to my humble home," he said, bowing deeply.

"Thank you. I've come to discuss your daughter," Nathaniel replied.

"Please, have a seat, Sir. What has my daughter done?"

"This afternoon, during my ride, I came out of the woods at a speedy pace. Your daughter was knocked down, and her tongue was sharp. Arriving here, there was no improvement."

Her father's brow furrowed. This was not the first time Rose had spoken out of turn, but now it was far more dangerous. Punishment for insolence toward a knight could be severe.

"I must apologize for my daughter. Pray tell me what I can do to correct this grievance?"

Nathaniel's eyes were unyielding. "I am taking your daughter. She will work for me and learn humility."

"Please, I can not leave my father. He is ill!" Rose pleaded.

"Rose! You do not speak unless spoken to. Leave the room. Now!"

Rose looked at her father, whose cold eyes met hers. She glared at Nathaniel and then obeyed, leaving the room.

"Sir Knight, I humbly apologize for my daughter. But I beg of you not to take her. I have no one else to help with the farm. Is there no other way to appease this wrong?"

"I will not have her whipped. It would be a shame to mar such beautiful flesh. She will serve me, and whatever else I deem necessary. This is not a request. You have one week to prepare before I return. If she is not here, you will face consequences."

Her father's shoulders slumped. "I have no one to help. The farm was to be her dowry. Rose has never been with a man. Her tongue is too sharp. There is a suitor, but she begged me not to marry her off. I've been too lenient since her mother passed."

Nathaniel considered him, expression cold. "I do not want the land, only the girl. I will send a farmhand to replace her while she learns her place. Afterward, I shall return her."

"I fear I will never see her again," her father said quietly. "She is stubborn, like her mother."

Rising, Nathaniel said, "One week from today, I will return."

Rose stood in the hallway, riding gear now replacing her usual attire. She wore a man's shirt and pants, daring and unexpected. Her frown deepened as Nathaniel's gaze wandered over her. He grinned, his mind already plotting how her defiance would serve him later.

Without another word, he pivoted, storming out the door. Swinging himself upon his horse, he made straight for the woods. Her attitude was a new challenge; he couldn't wait to see what she did next. For some unknown reason, the brat intrigued him.

***

Groaning, Dominique awoke stiff in her chair, a sharp crick twisting her neck. She rubbed her shoulders and frowned, trying to make sense of her dreams. Why did they hit her so hard? She chuckled softly, a little bitterly. Was she going crazy… or dreaming of a past life? After everything she'd survived in her twenty-five years, now this?

Sighing, she stretched and gathered her things, stepping out the back door. The sunlight stabbed at her eyes, forcing her to squint. Checking her phone, she realized it was noon. Seven hours in the chair. No wonder her neck protested. Finally, it was time to go home.

She liked her privacy, away from nosy neighbors, which was why she'd bought five acres and a modest house. Not huge, but enough for just her.

She headed straight to her room. The shower called her name, promising relief. After a few minutes under the hot water, she felt some of the tension ease. Dressing quickly, she settled at her desk, trying to focus. The bartender's job needed to be posted, and the hiring process had to begin.

Her eyelids felt heavy, her eyes gritty, like sandpaper. The dreams had stolen her rest, vivid and relentless, as if she had lived them for real. Was she half asleep, half awake? Could that be why they felt so real?

Hours passed as she worked. Finally, she allowed herself a quick nap before returning to the bar. Hoping to stave off the dreams, she jotted down everything she could remember. But it was no use. Their torment began again almost immediately.

***

Nathaniel hid in the woods, watching the girl. Women did not behave like her. He had never seen a woman dress as a man to ride a horse. How did she even know how to saddle it? She had so much spirit.

He remained silent behind a redwood tree as she sat on the ground and spoke aloud, her voice tinged with grief. Her mother's grave. Nathaniel knew that longing for a mother's love. He had visited his own mother's grave often after her passing two years ago.

He listened carefully, though much of what she said made no sense. How could her mother leave a Duke's side? Peasants did not marry Dukes, and Nathaniel himself was forbidden from marrying one, next in line for a dukedom.

Nathaniel wanted her as any man would, but there was something there that made him want more from her. Could he really break her? *Did he want to?* He stayed hidden as she cried, laying her head on the grave. So she was not all spitfire; there were other emotions as well. He wanted to see them all.

Satisfied that he had seen enough for now, Nathaniel left her to her sorrow and rode back to the village to make inquiries.

Most villagers knew little beyond the fact that she and her father lived on the small farm. Her mother had been kind, they said, and had visited an old woman on the edge of town. That was where Nathaniel headed.

Arriving at the old woman's hut, the door was ajar. He called out, and a raspy voice beckoned him inside. Walking to the small table near the fire, shuffling sounds filled his ears. The old woman came into view, gnarled hands clutching her skirts.

"Hello, good knight. I've been expecting you. Took longer than I thought, but Nanny sees all… and some things take longer than others."

"What are you talking about, old woman?" Nathaniel demanded.

"You seek answers about a certain young woman. I knew her mother well. She paid me to watch the future, always fearing her past might catch up with her… and her daughter."

"Her past? What do you know?"

"I know much, good knight. I was paid to remain silent, but for the right price, I may talk. And do not think to threaten me. I can do more than see things," she said, fixing him with a sharp gaze.

He exhaled and tossed a bag of gold coins on the table. He needed answers. She gestured to a chair beside a cauldron, where strange vapors swirled into a shifting scene. Nathaniel watched, fascinated.

A young man brought flowers to a little girl. They were just children. He was the son of a farmhand, forbidden to speak with her, yet she always snuck out to play.

As they grew older, she came to him in tears. She was to be married to an old man she did not love. He held her close and promised to help her escape. Days before the wedding, she met him at the river with a bag of jewels. Two horses waited, and they rode hard, fleeing.

The next day, they traded for new horses, keeping a two-day lead. She traded jewels to buy supplies. Eventually, they settled, half a world away, finding safety.

After a year, she gave him a jewel to buy their own land. A seer had assured her the future was secure. The Duke of Levies would not find her. In fact, he had broken a treaty with her father and attacked, but her father's army had prevailed. The Duke of Shirely never sought her, leaving her essentially dead to him. Her mother had never stopped hoping she might return.

The girl gave birth to a daughter. Nathaniel watched the years skip by, seeing the baby grow into a young girl, then finally, Rose at her mother's grave, clutching a necklace with a royal insignia.

The vision shifted, showing Nathaniel meeting Rose. He emerged from the trance, breath held.

"It will do no good to search for the Duke. He's long dead, slain many moons ago. The Duchess lives, but what use is it to seek her with Mary gone?"

"Peasants can not marry royalty. Perhaps I would simply like to know more about Rose," Nathaniel replied.

"You seek to own her," the old woman replied. "She will not bend to your will. Her mother raised her strong, ready to flee if necessary. Mary feared discovery, and Rose inherited her sharp tongue. Daniel, her father, is too soft-hearted to control her fully."

"I do not wish to own her. I am intrigued by her story, nothing more," Nathaniel replied.

The old woman laughed and walked away. He called after her, but she vanished. On the table, a scrap of paper caught his eye. He picked it up and read:

Your future has already been written. Tell Rose not to fight hers. Fight it, and it will end badly.

Chapter 3

Dominique had interviewed half a dozen people for the bartender position that week, but the last interview was the one she dreaded most: her ex-fiancé. Two years had passed since she'd seen him. Why had she agreed to this? She could've refused outright, but knowing Tim, he would've twisted it, claimed discrimination, and dragged her name through the mud.

Stepping out into the bar, she froze. Her blood ran cold at the sight of the son of a bitch who had broken her. It had taken everything she had to rebuild her life. When their relationship had crumbled, she'd nearly gone down with it. If not for Post and Melissa helping her keep the club afloat, she would've lost it all.

Dominique sat across from him, her glare sharp enough to cut. He hadn't changed much, same blond hair, green eyes, and the same smug grin. She'd tried to forgive, to move on, but one look at him and the wound bled fresh. She opened her notebook and glanced at his resume.

"Mr. Lithe," she said coolly. "I've reviewed your application. Frankly, your work record doesn't speak well."

Tim smirked. "Dominique, it's been a while. How have you been?"

"Mr. Lithe, this is an interview. I'd appreciate it if you remained professional."

"Aw, come on. Just making small talk. Playing catch-up, you know? It's been two years. I want to know how you've been."

Her laugh was sharp, bitter. "How have I been? You didn't stick around to find out when you decided we were over. When you decided to screw that whore of yours. How's that going, by the way?"

His grin faltered. He looked at his hands, then looked back up. "She wasn't permanent. Just… a bit of fun."

"So she left you, too, huh? Not surprising." She slammed her notebook shut. "Since this isn't really an interview anymore, I'll tell you how I've been. After you destroyed me, I broke. I drank until I couldn't think. Then I found out I was pregnant. Three months along, I lost the baby from the stress and the drinking."

Tim's head snapped up, eyes wide. "Was it mine?"

Dominique's blood boiled. She nearly vaulted the table and strangled him.

"Yes, you jackass. I'm not a whore like you!" Dominique spat.

He flinched. "I didn't mean that. I just… didn't know. Dom, I'm sorry. I never meant for things to go that far. I was stupid. But I really am looking for a job. I didn't apply just to screw with you. Honestly, I figured this would ruin my chances."

She bit back the truth—the darkest truth—that after losing both him and the baby, she had tried to end her life. No. She would never give him that power.

The air between them felt suffocating. Dominique pushed back her chair and stood. "Thank you for coming in, Mr. Lithe. I'll consider every applicant before making my decision."

He stood too, hesitant. "Why didn't you tell me? About the baby?"

"What difference would it have made?" Her voice cracked with restrained fury. "At the time, I never wanted to see you again."

"That's messed up, Dom. No matter our issues, you should've told me."

Her spine stiffened. "Don't call me that. You have no right to use pet names anymore."

Tim nodded. "All right, Ms. Reed. Thank you for your time."

He held out his hand. Reluctantly, she shook it, then escorted him to the door and locked it behind him.

The silence that followed was unbearable. Dominique staggered to her office, collapsed into her chair, and sobbed. How could the man who'd reduced her world to ashes still have this much power over her?

She tugged the necklace from beneath her shirt, fingers trembling. Inside was all she had left of her baby. Ashes of her daughter, Lily Rose.

Tears blurred her vision as she imagined the child she'd never meet. Would she have had Dominique's raven hair, that shimmered blue in sunlight? Tim's green eyes or hers? Would she have been strong-willed, toddling around the office, laughing?

Sighing, she got up to splash water on her face to keep anyone from knowing she'd been crying. It was no one's business but her own. She'd been managing her depression until today, but was now set back in her progress. Maybe Melissa was right. Maybe she needed to get back out there, date, and try to find happiness.

Did she really want to put herself through that again, though? Was she willing to wade through the bullshit to find someone? And what if she didn't? What if there wasn't someone out there for her?

Shaking her head, Dominique decided that if she reached thirty still single, she would simply have a baby by herself. There was always artificial insemination. *'Yeah, right,'* she muttered to herself and got back to work.

***

Once Dominique finished testing the machines, she couldn't shake the thought that they might be causing her dreams. Only now, she didn't even need to sleep to see them. The visions seeped into her work, her life, everything.

Shoving the thought aside, she headed down to the bar. The stage lights were warm on her skin as she joined Post and Melissa for their set. Halfway through a song, movement in the crowd caught her eye—a man weaving his way closer to the stage.

When he finally reached the front, she saw him clearly. He was stunning.

Dark brown hair, long enough to brush his shoulders. Eyes so shadowed she couldn't tell if they were deep brown or black. A neatly trimmed goatee framing a chiseled jawline. Lean, muscular build that carried itself with quiet confidence.

And every time she glanced at him, his gaze was locked on her.

Their eyes met, and Dominique felt heat coil low in her stomach. She hadn't been drawn to anyone in years, but this was different. His stare pulled her in, made her feel as if she were singing just for him. He never looked away.

By the time the set ended, her body was flushed and restless. She switched the music over so the crowd could keep dancing, then stepped off stage. The man was still there.

Melissa appeared at her side, tugging her toward the bar.

"That guy hasn't stopped staring at you," Melissa murmured.

"I know. I can't tell if I should be flattered or creeped out. Do I know him?"

Melissa smirked. "If you don't, you should. He's gorgeous. Go talk to him. You deserve some happiness. If nothing else, it'll keep me off your case about online dating."

"Ugh. You are impossible. I'm not about to flirt with some total stranger."

"Scaredy cat!" Melissa grinned as they slid onto barstools.

Dominique had just gotten her drink when the stranger sat beside her. She caught him from the corner of her eye, tall, self-assured, but he didn't order anything. Instead, he turned toward her, resting a hand lightly on her shoulder. A spark shot down her spine.

"Excuse me," he said, his voice smooth, low. "Am I right in thinking you own this bar?"

"Depends on who's asking," Dominique replied carefully.

His smile nearly blinded her. For a moment, his eyes looked impossibly dark; black as midnight. Her pulse jumped.

Did he think she was checking him out? *Aren't you checking him out?*

He extended his hand. "Nathaniel."

Dominique hesitated. The name rattled through her like déjà vu. She'd never seen him before, yet… had she dreamed of him?

A spark jolted up her arm the moment his hand closed over hers, quickening her breath. Instead of shaking, he lifted her knuckles to his lips, brushing them with a kiss. *Oh, he's good.*

"I asked around," he said, voice low and deliberate. "The locals said you own this bar. Is that true?"

"Depends on who's asking, Mr…?" Dominique prompted.

"Black. Nathaniel Black." His smile was devastating, the kind that could melt defenses in seconds. "And yours?"

"If you already asked around, then you should know my name," she countered, though her pulse betrayed her calm tone.

That smile again—devastating. "I only asked if the owner was here. They gave me no names. So…?"

"Dominique. Dominique Reed. Nice to meet you, Nathaniel."

"A pleasure." His voice lingered over the word. "Now, about my other question."

"What other question are you referring to?"

"Are you the owner?"

"I figured we had already established I'm the owner since my regulars told you I was."

"I see. Are you looking for anyone else for your band?"

"Do you play?"

"Guitar," he said, "mostly to relax. I'm a businessman first. Investor, really."

"Have you ever played in a band before?"

"Not yet. But I'd like to try. Let me audition. If I'm terrible, you can say no." His grin was magnetic, daring.

Heat curled through her again. Sexy, charming, and fully aware of it; a bad combination to have around.

"Fine. Come Tuesday. We practice at seven."

"Alright. I'll be here."

"Good. Now, if you'll excuse me."

"One last thing." His voice softened, drawing her back. "Do you dance?"

"Sometimes. Why?"

"Because I came to check out this club. And while I've danced with others tonight, you're the one who caught my attention. Save me a dance?"

Her throat went dry. "If I'm not busy, maybe."

"I'll be here all night," he said, lifting her hand once more to kiss it.

She slipped away toward her office, Melissa intercepting her with a grin wide enough to split her face.

"Sooooo… I see you had a pretty lengthy conversation with Mr. Sexy back there. Going to see him again?"

"Tuesday. He's auditioning."

"Seriously? That's it? I thought he was checking you out. You didn't flirt with him even a little?"

"No, Melissa. He asked for a dance, and I said maybe."

Melissa folded her arms. "You're going to say yes."

"Probably not. He's just after a spot in the band. Besides, I told you, I'm not interested in dating."

But the voice in her head was merciless. *Liar. You're lonely. You crave touch. Ever since Tim, you've been drowning in the past. You want someone—anyone—to break through that emptiness.*

Melissa leaned close, smug. "Dance with him, or I'll nag you for the rest of your life."

Dominique glared, but finally relented. "Fine. One dance."

Before Melissa could celebrate, dizziness hit like a wave. Dominique staggered, barely managing to excuse herself before she bolted upstairs. She locked the office door just as another vision seized her.

***

Rose was cleaning Nathaniel's room when a maid came to fetch her. She told her she had orders to take her to her room. Rose didn't like that. She had been ordered around by Nathaniel for months now. She'd tried to play the broken girl, but she never managed to do it. He would order her to do something, and she would always say something sarcastic or be defiant. He'd recently started ordering her to draw his bath and then would order her to bathe him.

He'd embarrassed her, but her will remained unbroken. She cleaned his room, changed and washed his bedding, and washed his clothes. She cleaned out the horse stalls and took care of the horse. She'd found a way to escape for a time when she stated she was going to exercise his horse. She took the horse into the woods and rode him.

The maid took her not to her room but to the bath. There was a gown laid out and scented soap. Her brush lay on the small table. The bath was full. Why did she bring her here? And why was there a nightgown there, along with scented soaps? Was she to bathe a woman for Nathaniel now? Was this her next punishment to break her?

"You are to bathe and then I will help dress you," the maid said.

"What? Why would you need to help dress me? And what am I to dress in?"

The maid nodded to the nightclothes and said, "Nathaniel requested this, Rose. I am only doing as requested. Now, please undress and get into the bath."

Rose didn't like this one bit, but she did as she was told. She bathed with the scented soap and let the maid wash her hair. When it was done, she dressed her in the nightclothes, brushing and braiding her hair. Once that was done, she put on a dress coat and made her way back to Nathaniel's room. The maid forced her into his bed, threats of what would happen if she disobeyed, dancing on her tongue. She left her there, alone, leaving her to wonder what was happening.

Later, when the door creaked open, Rose tried to feign sleep, but her heaving chest gave her away. His eyes on her were like fire trailing down her body as the bed dipped, and his hand traced down her body. She tensed. He stopped on her breasts and untied the gown so he could shove his hand under. He leaned down and whispered in her ear for her to open her eyes and look at him.

She slowly opened her eyes and looked at him. There was no fear there, just defiance. He smiled at her, and it made her angry. She tried to sit up, but he pushed her back down.

"Do you think you will be defiant, and I will let it continue? You are mine to do what I wish with."

"I told you before, M'Lord, that I would not lie down like a dog and let you do as you wish."

He chuckled as he said, "But you will."

Pulling her to her feet as he stood, bodies colliding together, and kissing her, had her heart pounding against her ribs. Turning her head so his lips grazed a cheek caused his arm to tighten, forcing her body impossibly closer. Grabbing her chin with the other hand, forcing their eyes to meet, he kissed her harshly. Biting his lip forced a grunt as blood flooded his mouth.

He pulled back and said, "You'll pay for that. Take my boots off."

At first, she didn't, but when his hand started towards her face, she bent down to avoid the slap. She took his boots off and stood up. Being instructed to undress him slowly left a sour taste in the mouth. Moving quickly instead, she pulled his shirt over his head and untied the breeches, hesitating to take them off.

Nathaniel grabbed her hands and pushed them under the breeches, forcing both her hands and the breeches down. Rose knew this would end badly, smelling the mead. Knowing he was drunk, fighting would cause her to be hurt worse.

Pulling his breeches the rest of the way down, his cock was in her face. Face hot from a deep blush, the breeches were removed from his feet. Never having been with a man or seeing one completely naked, as Nathaniel had never made her wash that part of him, had her intrigued.

The fear of the unknown was there, but she had often wondered what it would be like to lie with him. Her stomach was in knots, but also butterflies were beating their wings in it. Nathaniel jerked her up and against him, every inch of him known to her through the thin nightgown.

He kissed her again, thrusting his tongue in her mouth. She had never kissed a man, especially not like this. Nathaniel's kisses were rough, bruising her lips. He fumbled with the buttons on the back of the gown. A growl vibrated against her neck, then her body jerked as the gown ripped, and the buttons hit the floor.

Rose pushed against his chest as the gown was pulled down to her waist. Grabbing her hands and pinning her arms to her sides, he pulled back. His cock jerked against her, and a flush hit her face. His lips kissed her neck. Her body thrashed as his mouth found her breast.

She moaned as her body betrayed her. The more she struggled, the tighter his grip became, until pain flashed up her arms. Releasing her and grabbing the gown, Nathaniel ripped it off, causing her to stumble.

Pushing her onto the bed, his calloused hands moved over her body as he climbed on top of her. Thrusting his fingers inside of her caused her to gasp and slap him. He slapped her back, sending a shockwave of disbelief down her spine. No man had ever hit her.

"Do not do that again. I do not wish to hit a woman, but I will not tolerate you hitting me either."

Shaking her head, she closed her eyes against the tears. Ever so slowly, his fingers began moving again as his other hand squeezed her breast. A strange sensation grew between her thighs.

"Open your eyes, Rose. Look at me," Nathaniel commanded.

Rose forced her eyes open as a wave of pleasure crashed down on her. Trying to wriggle away, her body denied her.

"Touch me, Rose," Nathaniel demanded.

Her trembling hands ran over his chest, along his arms, and then to his back.

Taking her hand, Nathaniel placed it over his cock. Her face flushed, and her stomach tightened as her fingers glided over him. He groaned, and it emboldened her to move a little faster.

Nathaniel wrapped her fingers around his cock and began to move her hand up and down. She shyly began doing as he had shown her.

His fingers were moving faster now as his mouth bit and sucked on her breasts. It was painful when he bit her, but somehow it made her want more. Rose let out a loud moan as she felt a shudder run through her, her body clenching around his fingers.

Nathaniel moved up her body and lay on top of her. He kissed her lips as he thrust himself inside of her. She screamed against his mouth, her nails raking down his back, causing him to grunt.

At first, he did not move, but when he did, a sharp pain moved through her. She held her tears back as best she could. Letting out a growl, he spilled his seed inside of her.

She felt no pleasure from his actions, only pain. She hadn't been prepared enough for what he'd done. When he finished, he lay on top of her. She felt as though she was suffocating. After a few minutes, he rolled off and pulled her onto her side, against him.

Nathaniel put his cheek on hers and whispered in her ear, "You are mine. No other man will ever have you."

When his arm grew heavy and his breathing evened out, she slipped off the bed. Grabbing the nightcoat and wrapping it tightly around herself, she sat in front of the fire. The soft rug called to her. Curling into a ball on it, she cried herself to sleep.

***

Nathaniel woke to an empty bed. A dull ache throbbed behind his eyes from too much mead, his back sore from the night before. He hadn't meant to drink that much—hadn't meant to come to her in that state.

Had Rose slipped out while he slept?

He glanced around the room. Her torn nightclothes lay in a heap. By the dying fire, something small and still was curled on the rug.

Nathaniel rose, feeding the fire until flames flickered again. When he turned, the sight stopped him cold. Rose.

Her face was marred with bruises, the mark of his hand stark against her pale skin. Shame knifed through him. He hadn't been gentle—far from it. Cursing himself, he knelt and gathered her into his arms.

She moaned softly, eyes still closed, and instinctively nuzzled into his chest. Her body was ice against him. He carried her to the bed and laid her down, but the moment her back touched the mattress, she startled awake.

He caught her by the waist and pulled her back, his voice low, urgent. "Calm down, Rose. I have no intention of hurting you."

She turned to him, wide-eyed. The fear there gutted him. Once, her fire had matched his own. Now, she looked at him as if he were a monster.

And he realized, with a hollow ache in his chest, that he had broken her. His Spitfire was gone.

Chapter 4

Dominique came to on the floor of her office. She had passed out, hit the floor, and now her body screamed in agony. The pain Rose had gone through echoed inside her. She began to cry. *Why was this happening to her?*

When Dominique stopped crying, she glanced at the clock. One-thirty. She'd been out for at least two hours. Going into the bathroom connected to her office, she looked in the mirror. When she pulled her hair back, there was a bump on her head. The visions had become more than just a nuisance. What would happen if she were driving and one hit? This couldn't go on. She had to find a way to stop this.

She opened the office door. Melissa stood there, mid-knock, frowning. Dominique quickly masked her distress.

"Are you okay? You've been gone a while and just took off while we were talking!" Melissa said, her voice sharp with worry.

"I'm fine, Melissa. Just haven't been sleeping well. I guess it's affecting me more than I realized," Dominique replied.

"Have things gotten worse since… you know who came around?"

"Some. It set me back a little, realizing I haven't truly forgiven him or moved on. Maybe I should go back to therapy."

Melissa smirked. "Or maybe you should just go find that hot guy and get under him."

Dominique frowned. "Fucking someone isn't going to help me move on. I need to work through this myself."

"I didn't say it would heal your wounds, but maybe dancing with him could help. He's been playing pool with people for the past hour, but keeps looking around."

Sighing, Dominique agreed to go find him. With only thirty minutes until last call, what harm could it do? She wasn't planning to go home with him, just a dance.

At the pool table, he was taking his turn against a blonde-haired woman. The moment he noticed her, he handed the stick to someone else and began moving toward her, scanning the crowd. He seemed more predator than man, sensing her presence even from behind someone who towered over her. Stepping past the man, Nathaniel smiled, a predatory smile that sent a shiver through Dominique. She was startled by her own reaction.

He grabbed her around the waist and pulled her close. "Ready to dance, Dominique?" he whispered.

His voice, with a slight, unplaceable accent, made her pulse quicken. The way he held her was possessive, as if he always got what he wanted. She nodded, unable to refuse, and wrapped her arms around his neck.

Their bodies moved together. His hands glided along her back, his reaction pressed against her belly, unabashed.

Dominique had never danced like this, not even with her ex-fiancé. She barely noticed the songs changing until last call echoed through the bar. Breathless, she stepped back. His wide smile darkened his eyes, sending another shiver of desire down her spine.

"Thank you for the dance. I have to close down the bar now," she called over the music.

Nathaniel took her hand, kissed it, and said, "The pleasure was mine, Dominique. Hopefully, we can dance again."

"Maybe," she said, smiling.

At the bar, Dominique asked Shane to fix her a drink. No. What she really needed was a cold shower. Melissa appeared, smiling, but Dominique shook her head.

"Don't even try it. We *will* talk later." Melissa walked off with the last drink of the night.

Dominique downed her drink and helped see patrons out. Don managed the crowd well, but she always stayed attentive to prevent injuries. Once the bar was empty and cleanup was done, she headed to her office with Melissa following.

"You really aren't going to let this go, are you?" Dominique asked as she sat opposite her friend.

"Nope. Spill. Was Mr. Sexy talkative? Did he try to take you home? Did you like dancing? Is he coming back?"

Dominique laughed. "No, he wasn't talkative and didn't try to take me home. But the dance… amazing. I've never moved like that with a man before. Normally, I don't let strangers touch me, but there was something about him. The way he looked at me… intense. He's coming back on Tuesday to audition for the band."

Melissa smirked. "I was asking if he's coming back for you, not the band."

Dominique's heart fluttered at the thought. Why did a stranger affect her like this? She shook the image from her mind: Nathaniel's dark brown eyes, almost black, staring into hers, his forehead against hers as they just… stared.

"He's coming back to audition. That's all."

"Is that the only reason you want him to come back?"

"I don't know if I want him to come back at all. He's...intense. I can't describe him any other way."

Dominique considered telling Melissa about the dreams, the visions invading her life. Wouldn't it be better if at least someone knew and could check on her?

Melissa leaned back. "Girl, you're deep in thought. Either this guy really got under your skin, or you zoned out again. That happens a lot lately."

"What do you mean?"

"There have been times you'll be talking and suddenly stop, like you're on another planet. One time, it took me an hour to get you back."

"It's the dreams; they're taking over. They're happening while I'm awake now. I didn't want to worry you or seem crazy."

"Oh, Dom… of course I'd worry! But I'd never think you're crazy. I don't know what's happening, but I'll always listen. Maybe talking would help."

"I don't know what to say. The dreams, visions, whatever, they hit all the time. I feel dizzy. I see them in my sleep, and I don't feel rested. And… the guy I dream about is Nathaniel. Then tonight, a man named Nathaniel walks into my bar, and it's like I've never felt before. It's almost like we've known each other a long time. I know it sounds crazy."

Melissa nodded thoughtfully. "My mom had dreams like that. If she didn't do certain things, they came true. Maybe it's the same with you?"

Dominique shook her head. "I don't remember her ever having anything like this happen, and definitely not getting hurt." She showed Melissa the bump on her head.

"Ouch. How did that happen?"

"I passed out earlier when a vision hit. I woke up on the floor, and every time it happens, I feel exactly like Rose did. It's starting to freak me out."

"Okay. I'll drive you home tonight, pick you up tomorrow. Or you can stay home and rest."

"You know I'm here every night. Something could always happen."

"You have more than one car. If anything happens, I'll call you. It's Saturday. Take the night off. Relax at home."

Dominique sighed and agreed. Melissa drove her home, and she sat on the porch for a while before bed. Peaceful. Stars bright above, a gentle breeze cooling the air. She loved the seclusion. The hairs on her neck prickled; someone was watching. But no one was there. The woods weren't close enough. Still… she glanced around, unnerved.

"It's possible you are going crazy, girlie," she giggled to herself.

She leaned back in her chair, watching the sky until sleep overtook her.

Once she was deeply asleep, a man moved silently through the woods. He came onto the porch, staring at her for several minutes before lifting her and taking her to her room, lingering until near dawn.

***

Rose hadn't been the same since that first night with Nathaniel. Her defiance, once sharp and unwavering, had vanished. She moved through her days in quiet obedience, eating little, drinking less, and performing her daily chores as though she were already a ghost. Nights were the hardest. Her belongings had been moved into Nathaniel's room, and the privacy of her own quarters was gone. She bathed him nightly, and they lay together afterward. She waited for him to take her again, but he never did.

Instead, he spoke with her, gently coaxing her words. She responded in short bursts, careful, reserved. Her thoughts always drifted back to that first night, to the reality of what had happened. She'd imagined intimacy as a tender, shared thing, a dance of mutual affection and trust. Nathaniel had offered none of that. He didn't love her, nor did he desire to marry. Yet he wanted her here, in his room, in his life. Why?

"Calm down, Rose. I have no intention of hurting you," Nathaniel had said that morning.

"You already did," she whispered. "Why even say that? I will never forget. I would rather die than remain here. Please, return me to my father."

His face hardened. She shrank back, refusing to meet his gaze. He reached for her, and she turned away. Yet he pulled her close, steadying her against his chest.

"My intention was never to come to you drunk," he said quietly. "I came to claim you as mine. You will not be sent home. Your place is here, with me."

He left moments later, leaving Rose curled on the bed, weeping. The sound of the bath being drawn brought her out of her misery.

The maid guided her into the soothing water and retreated from the room. The gentle heat eased the aches and bruises that claimed her body. For a brief moment, she felt some measure of comfort, though shame lingered, knowing others had seen the evidence of what had happened.

When Nathaniel's hand touched her shoulder, she tensed instinctively. He was gentle, washing her carefully, apologizing when his hands grazed a tender spot. Confusion churned within her. Why this tenderness now? Why care for her as he did?

The heat, the touch, the subtle care, it began to make her body respond in ways she hadn't expected. Done bathing her, he joined her, holding her close in silence.

She eventually requested to leave the bath. The remnants of her own frantic defense on his back caught her gaze. Guilt blossomed in her chest. Taking the rag from him, she washed his wounds carefully, applying salve once he stepped from the water. He thanked her, pressing a kiss to her lips that made her startle, but he released her gently, leaving her with a dress to wear.

Rose was brought out of her remembrance when Nathaniel crawled behind her, undoing her nightgown. She froze, tension rippling through her body. He whispered, reassuring her.

"I will not hurt you, Rose. Tonight you will feel nothing but pleasure."

He kissed her, exploring her lips with a gentle rhythm. His hands cupped her, softly grazing her skin, eliciting shivers she couldn't control.

Nathaniel broke the kiss and gently pulled the gown off. His mouth found her breasts, then made his way down her stomach. His hands ran over her body, worshipping her. Fear and anticipation mingled, yet she responded, letting herself experience sensations she had never known.

Glancing down his body, intense heat bloomed across her face.

"Do you like what you see, Rose?"

"Yes, M'Lord," Rose whispered.

"I want you to touch me as I touch you."

Rose's hands trembled as she touched Nathaniel, stroking his arms, chest, and back, feeling every line of his muscles.

His hand stroked between her thighs as his mouth again found her breasts. He sucked and nipped her nipples. Heat curled in her belly.

His fingers gently pushed inside her, coaxing her to relax. Heaviness grew in her belly, causing her to moan when he removed his fingers. His mouth trailed fire down her body.

He licked her folds, tongue finding that small nub, eliciting a sigh of pleasure from her lips. That heaviness began to grow again. He continued the onslaught of his tongue, moving faster, as her body began to quiver.

Rose's thighs squeezed Nathaniel's head as her hands clenched the sheets. Intense pleasure swirled down her spine, forcing a cry from her lips as her orgasm ripped through her.

Nathaniel moved back up her body, pressing against her opening as he kissed her. She tasted herself on his lips. He nudged her as if asking permission. Rose's nails sank into his arms, her heart stampeding in her chest.

Slowly lifting her hips, her legs slid up so her knees pressed against his hips. Nathaniel slid himself inside of her, slowly, filling and stretching her to her limits due to his girth. The lovemaking was slow as he kissed down her neck.

Wet heat pooled between her thighs, stomach tightening. His hips rolled as the pace quickened. His hand caressed her thigh, pulling it further up his body and opening her further. She moaned, and a responding growl pressed against her throat.

"Don't be afraid, Rose. Touch me. I won't do anything to hurt you, I promise," Nathaniel whispered, encouraging her to engage in the lovemaking.

Rose's body responded to his voice even as her mind screamed he was lying. She caressed his chest, tracing the lines of his muscles. Moving down his stomach, feeling his hard abs. Stroking his arms upward, her hands pushed into his soft hair.

His pace became aggressive. "Open your eyes, Rose."

She gazed into his eyes as her body soared to the sky. Wrapping her legs around him, her body clenched him tighter.

Sweet nothings whispered in her ear. Crying out, her stomach unclenched, heat and fluid rushing down to coat him.

Nathaniel echoed her pleasure, spilling his seed.

Afterward, he held her close, their skin pressed together, her fingers tracing the warmth of his hair. She discovered a strange comfort in his weight, the heat of his body, the rhythm of his breathing.

"Why are you keeping me here?" she asked, trembling but defiant. "I'm broken. You have won, yet you broke your promise to my father."

Nathaniel gazed at her, lips twitching before becoming a full-blown smile.

"You are not broken, woman, your strong will remains. You tremble, yet your spirit flares. I feared I had lost you forever. At first, I sought only to break you. But now... I care. You are mine."

His eyes darkened as he proclaimed her to be his, his concubine forever.

"Rose, all will be well. You will be taken care of and protected. I will see to it."

"Will I be loved? Will I forever be your concubine as you are married off? Will I always compete for affection once you have a family of your own?"

Nathaniel remained silent, eyes darkening.

Tears pricked her eyes as she shook her head. Her blood had run cold from the thought of being kept here. Defiance filled her as she lay down, feigning sleep.

***

Dominique woke from the dream, heat and anger pulsing through her veins. Her eyes snapped open, and she realized she was in her bed. How had she gotten here? Had she fallen asleep outside? Had she sleepwalked without realizing it?

Exhaustion made the explanation seem more likely. She must have dozed off and barely had enough awareness to drag herself to her room. Her clothes from the night before were still on, sticking slightly to her skin. As she swung her legs over the side of the bed, that familiar ache between her thighs reminded her of Melissa's advice, and of a certain Nathaniel who occupied her thoughts far too often.

Chapter 5

Saturday was dragging on as Dominique stayed home. She tried to sleep but kept having dreams of Nathaniel and Rose having sex. She decided she was going to go out; anything was better than just sitting home bored out of her mind. Dinner and a movie sounded like a good plan.

She put on a dress, did her hair, and applied makeup. She couldn't remember the last time she'd dolled herself up.

Standing before the full-length mirror, she studied her reflection. The black V-neck dress hugged her curves perfectly. Loose waves of hair tumbled down her back. Her eyes popped under carefully applied makeup, and the deep red lipstick added a hint of danger. She skipped heels, opting for strappy sandals instead.

Even though she wasn't well rested, Dominique felt better than she had in a while. Maybe taking some time off from work was a good thing. Perhaps she was just pushing herself too hard, and this story she was dreaming was part of the stress.

She'd written several novellas from her dreams as her imagination had known no limits. Maybe it was just taking her over until she finished the story?

Dominique headed to La Nobles. Their steak was unbeatable.

The high-class restaurant was always packed, and she rarely came because it was expensive. But tonight, she decided she deserved it. A nice evening just for herself.

The waiter sat her at a table and she picked up the menu. While looking it over, she heard a familiar voice say her name. *Evening officially ruined.*

Dominique looked up as Tim asked, "Is this seat taken?"

"Yes. I'm waiting for my date. And frankly, I don't want to chat."

"Oh, come on, Dominique. It's not like I plan to take your date's place, but by the looks of it, you're here alone," Tim replied, sitting down.

"You never were good at taking no for an answer. My date is running late. Now, would you please go away?"

Her voice dripped with hatred, even as she tried to stop it. Two years of simmering rage were ready to boil over. She didn't want to make a scene, but how could she escape the trap she'd set for herself?

"No, I never was good at that. I see something I want and I go for it. I want you. Why don't you let me buy you dinner, and we can talk?"

"No. I don't want to talk to you, and I damn sure don't want to feel like I owe you anything. When my date gets here, he won't appreciate it either."

Tim laughed as he said, "You and I both know you're lying. No waiting for him to arrive before ordering. Plus, you only have a placement for one here."

Dominique's words died on her lips when she heard a man's voice say, "I believe the lady told you to leave."

Relief flooded her, chased by curiosity. She turned to Nathaniel. He looked devastatingly handsome in dark slacks and a royal blue button-down that made his eyes look nearly black. His slicked-back hair curled just at his shoulders. Her stomach flipped.

"Who the hell are you?" Tim asked.

Nathaniel replied coolly, "My name is Nathaniel. Dominique is my date for the evening, and you're in my seat. Now get up and leave the lady alone. Clearly, you're bothering her."

Nathaniel bent down, kissing her lips ever so lightly. "I'm sorry I'm so late. My meeting ran longer than I thought it would."

Nathaniel glared at Tim as Tim glanced at Dominique. Smiling shyly at Nathaniel, Dominique's lips tingled. Nathaniel sat in the chair that Tim had now vacated.

"Maybe we can catch up later, Dominique," Tim said, walking off.

"I have to say, I'm grateful," she said, voice low. "But where did you come from? And how did you know what I said?"

Nathaniel smiled. "I just finished dinner and noticed you. I came over to say hello… and overheard part of the conversation. I apologize if the kiss was too forward."

Dominique blushed thinking about that kiss. She wondered what it would be like to kiss him for real, to have him touch her in other ways. She glanced at him, and his facial expression had changed. His wicked smile and twinkling eyes said he knew what she was thinking. Dominique cleared her throat, trying to get the dirty thoughts out of her head.

"It's okay. It's a little weird, but I appreciate the save. I would say I'd buy you dinner, but you've already eaten."

"How about another reward then?"

"Depends. What do you want?"

"I'd like a conversation. You can still eat dinner. I'll sit with you, and we can chat, get to know each other a little better."

Dominique laughed, but stopped when she saw his face. "Oh, you're serious. I'm afraid I'm pretty boring. I go to work and home."

"Dominique, you know that's not true. You have hobbies, people you talk to, a whole past that has led you to where you are today."

Dominique loved the way he said her name with that slight accent.

"Ok, I guess. But why you'd want to get to know me is beyond me. What's your first question?"

"Why were you really here tonight?"

"Well, that one's simple. I haven't taken a day off from work in about a year. When the club wasn't open, I was working on a project. The stress was getting to me, so my best friend made me take a night off. Since I couldn't sleep anymore, I decided to go out and treat myself."

The waiter came over and she ordered. It was odd eating in front of him, but he assured her that he had already eaten.

"So, you came out by yourself. Who was the man sitting here?"

"A ghost from the past, one I wish would've stayed there."

Nathaniel's brow arched, a frown lining his lips, letting her know the answer wasn't good enough. Dominique sighed.

"He's my ex-fiancé. We broke up two years ago. He wasn't ready to be a husband, and I obviously wasn't what he wanted."

"Then he's a fool," Nathaniel replied.

"You don't know me well enough to say he was one. I broke it off."

"I know enough to say he's a fool. He wants you back in his life. Anyone can see what he wants. May I ask what he did to make you end your engagement?"

"He cheated. I wasn't enough for him, I guess," Dominique said, pushing her food around on her plate.

Electricity ran up her arm as he placed his hand over hers. "He's a fool to let such a stunning woman go. You're very beautiful and a hard worker. I'm sure you put just as much effort into your relationships."

"*Relationship*. It was just him. I was always shy as a kid and didn't start dating until I was eighteen. We were together for five years. At the end, he was drinking and partying a lot. Loose women and alcohol became his addictions."

"I'm sorry, Dominique. No one deserves that. A woman should be cherished and made to feel like a queen. She will then, in turn, treat you like a king."

"You sound like you have a queen in mind when you say that. Do you have a girlfriend? A wife?"

"The queen I speak of was my wife. Our start was rocky, but after a year or so, things smoothed out. We had a beautiful life together until she passed away. You remind me of her."

"You don't look old enough to be a widower. What happened to your wife?"

"Sadly, she passed from a disease that ate away at her body until there was nothing left."

Dominique studied him as he zoned out. Curiosity about his wife flowed through her.

"I can see your mind is flooded with questions. However, I would request that you not ask them. Perhaps at a later date, I'll be able to talk to you about it, but not now. Ok?"

"Ok. I can understand. There are things I would prefer not to talk about, my ex being one of them."

"Fair enough. Do you have any children, Dominique?"

Subconsciously, she touched her necklace. "No. I don't have any children. What about you?"

"No, I have no children. What's the necklace that you keep touching?"

"That subject is off-limits."

Nathaniel leaned across the table and stroked his hand down her face. That electricity was there. Why did her body react each time he touched her?

"I apologize if I brought up bad memories. I merely wish to get to know you better."

"It's fine. So, are you just getting to know me so you have ammo for Tuesday? Because I'll be honest, it won't help you get into the band. I'll judge you on your playing only. Then if you suck as a person, well, I'll probably kick you out."

Nathaniel smiled. "Maybe I'm interviewing you to see if I want to join the band."

"Sure, whatever you say. Well, I'm ready to go. It's been nice chatting with you, but I have somewhere else to be."

Nathaniel waved the waiter over. Dominique leaned down to grab her purse. When she looked back up, Nathaniel was handing the waiter his card. She frowned.

"Why'd you do that?"

"I merely paid for your dinner. You could look at this as a first date, as we did get to know each other. May I ask where you have to run off to?"

Dominique murmured, "A movie."

"Will anyone be meeting you there?"

"No. I told you before I was treating myself."

"Would you mind if I joined you? I could drive us there and bring you back to your car. We could continue to get to know each other."

"I don't think that's a good idea. You could be a serial killer for all I know."

Nathaniel laughed. "Then let's take your car, and you can bring me back to mine. You can even pat me down for weapons if you wish."

Dominique blushed. She would thoroughly enjoy touching him. What was wrong with her? Was she really this in need of a good lay? Or was she just so attention-starved that anyone would do? No. That wasn't true. She'd had options before tonight. There was just something about him.

"I don't think I'd be comfortable with that."

"It was just an offer. I have no weapons on me, but I want you to be comfortable."

"Um, ok. I really did intend to be alone."

"You're dressed for a date. Let me be that date."

Dominique stared into his eyes, caught in a strange trance. His words didn't sound like questions but like quiet commands. Before she realized it, she was agreeing to spend the rest of the evening with him.

They went out to her car. He opened her door, but then stood in front of it. She glanced at him. He winked and grinned.

"Aren't you going to make sure I don't have any weapons?"

"Umm… no. I think I'll be okay. I don't see any bulges anywhere I should worry about."

"If you're sure," Nathaniel replied, stepping out of the way.

At the theater, Nathaniel insisted on paying.

Once the movie was over, they got up and walked out.

Getting back into the car, Nathaniel asked her to drive them to a field.

"I'm not going to hurt you, Dominique. This is the perfect place to dance under the stars. Will you please get out of the car?"

Dominique bit her lip and thought about it. Finally, she got out.

"Would you like to play some music? Something slow would be preferable," Nathaniel suggested.

Dominique kept an eye on him as she got back in the car and pulled up a playlist on her phone.

Nathaniel simply smiled as she got back out.

Drawing her close, he murmured, "Dance with me."

Nodding to him, they began to dance.

The evening air was warm, a soft breeze carrying the scent of night-blooming flowers. Dominique tilted her face to the sky. The full moon gleamed bright, stars glittering across a velvet backdrop.

"It's breathtaking," Dominique whispered.

"Yes, it is."

Dominique's gaze met Nathaniel's. Heat moved through her. The way he looked at her was so intense. She lay her head on his chest. He pushed his face into her hair.

"You smell good. Almost good enough to eat," Nathaniel commented.

"Umm… thanks, I think. Just don't turn into the big bad wolf, and we'll be okay. Although I don't think the big bad wolf would smell so good. Or have a gorgeous smile. Or have a body like yours."

"So you think I'm gorgeous?" Nathaniel murmured in her ear, making her shiver.

Dominique's body burned with embarrassment. Why had she said all that? The man knew he was gorgeous. He had to, but she hadn't needed to tell him she thought so, too. Worry struck her. Allowing herself to feel anything for anyone… and it not working out, she wasn't sure she would survive it.

"I guess it's too late to say no?"

Nathaniel laughed. They slow danced for a long time before Nathaniel kissed her. His hands slid down her sides, grazing the curves of her breasts, then her hips, slipping around to her butt. He pulled her tight against him, deepening the kiss. Dominique's body was on fire, aware of the bulge in his slacks. Reluctantly, he broke the kiss and let her go.

"I think we should go before I turn into the big bad wolf. I apologize, Dominique. It wasn't my intention to take advantage of you. But I must say I'm not sorry the kiss happened."

Dominique was practically panting. Damn, the man was good. Her blood was boiling, and her lips were tingling. Apologizing for what he'd done took her aback. He hadn't taken advantage of her, especially not the way she wanted him to.

"The way you talk, the way you act, isn't what I'm used to. How old are you?"

"I'm thirty. I have an old soul."

"Indeed. Well, I guess I should get you back to your car then."

"Yes, I think that would be best."

Dominique drove them back to the restaurant. Pulling into a parking space, Nathaniel got out. Coming around to her door, he opened it. She slid her hand into his and got out. He gazed into her eyes as his lips brushed across her knuckles.

"May I kiss you goodnight, Dominique?"

Dominique smiled shyly, nodding. Nathaniel gave her a sweet, gentle kiss.

Pulling back, he smiled. "Thank you for allowing me the pleasure of your company."

"Thank you for a wonderful evening."

Dominique got in her car and drove home.

It'd been one hell of a night. Smiling to herself, she went inside her house. Sitting on the bed and taking her shoes off, she noticed the clock read twelve-thirty. She couldn't remember the last time she'd gone to bed so early. She got up, took her makeup off, and changed into a nightgown. Lying down, sleep immediately overcame her.

***

The man waited outside Dominique's house. He watched as she turned off the light in her room.

An hour passed before he slipped inside. He watched her for a little while. When he felt she wouldn't wake up, he lay down beside her, running his hands over her body. She moaned when he began playing with her breasts.

She mumbled in her sleep, letting him know she was dreaming. Her mumblings matched his actions. He wouldn't take her. Not yet. He wanted her to want him first, to know it was him causing her pleasure. Instead, he slid his fingers inside of her, sucking her breasts through her nightgown.

She moaned and writhed for him. He felt her release around his fingers as she let out a loud moan. He brushed his lips against hers as her breathing evened out and she lay still, her dream over. He watched her sleeping peacefully just a little longer and then slipped out as quietly as he'd come in.

Chapter 6

Dominique woke up the next morning more refreshed than she had been in months. She'd slept straight through the night. She was going to work on the machine some today, but that could wait until later when Post was awake. He didn't sleep much. Four hours of sleep, and he woke up feeling refreshed. Must be nice. If she got less than eight, she was cranky as hell.

Instead, she worked on her story. Rose and Nathaniel were very interesting to her. She wondered if she would dream of the ending or write one herself? She typed the dreams she'd had so far. Before she knew it, a new story was being written.

Dominique sat back and looked at what she'd written. Had she dreamed that last night? She vaguely remembered having a dream involving *her* Nathaniel, but hadn't remembered it, or so she thought. *Her Nathaniel?* Where had that thought come from?

Shaking her head, she saw the time. She went to the club, calling Post on the way. She was going to push the machine and see if it would withstand the two-hour limit. If it did, then she only had one more test, syncing them together so two people could be in, and "feel" what the other was doing. She and Melissa had gone in together, but it wasn't the same. They didn't touch, kiss, or anything of that nature.

"Alright, Post. Are you ready?"

"Yep. I think we've got all the glitches out, so go for it. I'll sit right here and make sure nothing goes wrong. And don't worry, I have something to do."

"Alright. Here goes."

Dominique got in the machine, put the helmet on, and closed her eyes. She let her mind go blank and then started thinking of a scene, putting herself into Rose's story.

***

Rose began making plans to escape the day after Nathaniel had proclaimed she would bear his heir. Over the next month, she hid supplies, taking a coin here and there. Nathaniel was going to be furious, so she had to warn her father about her plans.

When everything was ready, she waited until Nathaniel fell asleep. She gazed at him for a while, heart clenched, and caressed his cheek one last time. Then she changed into a pair of Nathaniel's breeches and a shirt. Her long hair was twisted into a bun and wrapped in a cloth.

She grabbed the bag with the few clothes she was taking and moved quietly through the halls. In the barn, she saddled Nathaniel's horse. Once everything was loaded, Rose walked the horse to the woods. There, she climbed on and rode toward her father's home. It had been six months since she had seen him.

Rose rode all night, stopping only long enough to use the bathroom. By the time she reached the farm, she was exhausted, and so was the horse. She dismounted and went inside.

"Who's there?" her father called out.

"It's me, Father."

"Rose?" he asked, shuffling into the front room.

She started to cry when his frail frame came into sight. He touched her face and then hugged her. Standing back, he looked her over.

"I feared I would never see you again. But why are you dressed like this?"

"I—I ran away, Father. I begged you once not to marry me off, but I was wrong. I want love in my life, just like you and Mother had. I do not wish to be Nathaniel's concubine."

"Oh, my Rose! Has the knight mistreated you? Has he dishonored you?"

"He… Well, he has treated me fairly, except for one instance. But I do not wish to remain in his bed and die unloved."

"Rose, you must go back and beg his forgiveness. He will surely kill us both for your insolence."

"How can you tell me to go back to that, Father? I did not think you would want your daughter to be any man's concubine."

"I do not wish that for you, but I do not wish harm on you either. His hand that was sent here was very clear that if you were to return, the knight would punish us both. And he will be here soon. You will rest for a while, and then you shall return."

Rose's body tensed as her father's words sank in. She went and lay in her old bed, exhaustion taking over. She had come to get her father to run, not have him send her back. She planned on running and not stopping until she felt safe.

But how far would she have to run for that?

While Rose slept, Nathaniel awoke to find her gone. When she did not return after an hour, he searched for her. No maid had seen her. He went to the barn, though it was not her usual time for a ride. His horse was gone. Fury coursed through him. Gathering several men, he rode out, instructing them to find Rose and bring her back with the horse.

His tracker found a trail hours old. They followed it straight through and rested only near the village. After sending his men to search, Nathaniel headed for her father's house, hoping she had gone there.

When he arrived, Peter approached, unsurprised.

"M'Lord, what brings you? Your visit isn't due yet," Peter said.

"The girl," Nathaniel demanded, his voice clipped. "Is she here?"

"She was, M'Lord. I thought you sent her home. She claimed it was just a visit, stayed a few hours, mostly sleeping. Her father sent her back. Did you not see her?"

"No. I did not give her permission. I doubt she is returning."

"Apologies, M'Lord. If she comes back, I will send word."

"No need. She will not return."

Nathaniel's blood boiled as he stormed to the barn. His horse stood there, groomed and fed. His gaze landed on the saddle. Paper lay there. He pocketed it and asked Peter about the horse. Peter had only seen Rose when he arrived; he had not entered the small stable.

So Rose had stolen his horse, yet cared for it, swapping it for her own. Shaking his head, Nathaniel rode to the old woman's hut.

Arriving, the door was open. Stepping inside, she came into the room, welcoming him.

"M'Lord," she bowed, "I was wondering when you would return. I did not think it would take this long."

"Why would you think I would return?"

"I saw it. I gave you a message for Rose, but you delayed. You made her feel desperate and unloved. She is your destiny. But you will have to go far to make her your wife."

"I do not wish for that. She is already mine. I want to know if she is here."

"No, M'Lord. She has left. She fears losing herself. The past has a way of catching up with us."

"Your men are foul. One will have her before he returns. Don't let him."

"Show me the future, old woman. I have to know."

"You will not like it."

She sat Nathaniel down, stirring a brew. Its aroma hit him; his body felt heavy. He saw his man catch Rose, taking what did not belong to him. Later, his father whipped her for stealing the horse. Rose, impregnated by the knight, eventually took her life and the child's.

The scenes shifted, showing an alternate version: Nathaniel returned Rose. His father tried to kill her, Nathaniel killed his father, and war broke out. Winning the war, he reigned with a dark shadow over him.

"I can not kill my father. It brings war, not peace. Also, why does it not show what the darkness is?"

"Yes, there will be war, but peace will follow. Rose is of the people. She will help you. Times will resemble when your mother lived. Your father has burned villages, made enemies; these paths will lead to that. The darkness is unseen."

"Rose is of noble blood. Take this ring. It was Mary's father's. Rose wears Mary's coming-of-age necklace. Bring her to Shirely; the Duchess will accept her and aid you. Beware her son. He will not welcome her. Rose is in the next village."

The old woman handed him the ring. Nathaniel sent the knights back with the horse, under orders to tell his father nothing, then rode off to find Rose. He stopped to rest and pulled the paper from his pocket:

Nathaniel,

I apologize for stealing your horse and pray your hand will return him. I will not live as a concubine and bear bastard children. I may be a mere peasant, but I wish for love and happiness that you will never provide. I can never truly be yours, so I will find peace in knowing you will be set free of me.

Love,

Rose

Shaking his head, he pocketed the note and mounted his horse. He had to catch her before the next village.

Nathaniel reached the river outside the village and spotted a familiar horse tied to a tree. He waited in the grove. A scrawny figure approached the horse, movements too delicate for a man. Closer, he recognized his breeches and shirt.

He rode forward as Rose mounted and turned to leave. Hearing him, she spurred her horse. Dusk fell as he shouted, "Stop!"

Catching up, he grabbed the reins. Her horse bucked. She clung to the mane, lying low to avoid being thrown. Eventually, the horse slowed. Nathaniel dismounted and hauled her off.

"What were you thinking running away like that? Do you know what could have happened? Do you know what will happen when we return?" he asked, anger flaring.

"I know. I will not go back. Kill me now if you intend to. I know your father's cruelty will lead to death. Either way, I will see my mother again and leave this wretched place," Rose spat.

"You would choose death over me?"

"I would choose death over being your slave. You have said I am yours, but you wish to own me as your castle slaves. I am a mere peasant. I have no place but to be your whore."

"You are no mere peasant, and you know that, do you not?"

"I do not know what you speak of," Rose said.

"You do know. I saw it in your face, surprise, when I mentioned it."

Nathaniel grabbed the chain under her shirt, pulling out the ring. Holding them together, he showed her. Her eyes widened; she bit her lip.

"Where did you get that, M'Lord?"

"The old woman. She said your mother visited her often. This belonged to her father; the necklace to your mother. I watched you the day I ran into you, followed you to your mother's grave. What did she tell you about herself?"

"My mother told me many stories; stories of grand balls, people dressed in costumes, beautiful gowns, fine foods, and Dukes and Duchesses. There were knights, farmhands, and mean old men, too. They were merely stories, M'Lord."

"You do not believe that, or else you would not have mentioned being punished for her sin. Tell me the story your mother told you," Nathaniel commanded.

Rose sighed. "My mother told a story of a Duchess in a faraway castle. She was meant to marry a cruel old man thrice her age, but she loved another. Forbidden love. She ran away with him, taking treasures she needed. They had a daughter, Rose, and lived happily ever after. Just a story, M'Lord."

"The old woman showed me a vision of your story. I doubted her, yet you describe it. How could she have the ring and you the necklace? Such trinkets that bear a Duke's insignia."

"M'Lord, I am a peasant. You have seen my home. I do not wish to be a slave. Even if noble, it would not matter. You said you do not wish to marry me; there is no love."

"I will not have another man touch you. You. Are. Mine." Nathaniel stepped closer.

He pulled her against him, kissing her hard. Hands slid down her sides, tugging her shirt from her breeches. He fondled her. Breaking the kiss, he carried her to the trees, pressing her against one, untied her breeches, which fell to the ground.

"M'Lord, we are out in the open!" Rose exclaimed.

"There is no one around, Rose," he said, spreading her legs and entering her.

Her body reacted instantly. He moved fast and hard, he kissed her, felt her tighten, and she cried out into his mouth. He mirrored her pleasure.

Nathaniel gave her a few minutes to recover and redressed. Rose pulled up the breeches, loosely tucking in her shirt, then tying them. He glanced at the dark sky and moved to the horses.

"We will stay in town tonight. Tomorrow we return. I need to take care of matters," he said.

"Your father will not allow me back without punishment, M'Lord. Would you still have me return?"

"No. I will leave you with your father for now. By our return, those I sent to find you will have told my father. I pray he does not send them after me. I need to gather supplies to take you to Shirely. You will be safe; it will take time to get there."

"Why Shirely?"

"That is where your mother was from. Your grandfather has passed, but your grandmother is alive. She will accept you as her granddaughter, giving you nobility."

"You wish to leave me there while you do what, M'Lord?"

"Nathaniel. Call me Nathaniel. Yes, I will leave you there. My father will not allow my betrayal. Few knights are loyal to me; most to him. I must kill him to take my place and reign."

"Nathaniel, I do not wish you to fight your father. Can you not stay with me in Shirely?"

"No. My rightful place is in Athalon. You will be by my side once the war ends. I will send for you."

Rose stayed silent as they entered the village.

***

Dominique pulled herself out of the story, breath quick and skin warm. Putting herself inside the program had worked; it hadn't been like watching anymore. She had *lived* it. Every rush of emotion left her body reacting, turning the dream into something far more real. With a small, embarrassed laugh, she tugged the helmet off.

Stepping from the machine, she called, "So, how did we do? How long was I in?"

"Everything ran smoothly. No glitches at all. I was going to pull you at two hours, but I wanted to see how the system held up. You made it three. Congratulations! Your machine's officially glitch-free."

"That's great, Post! Just one more test and we're ready."

He raised a brow. "What test? I thought we were done."

"We need to make sure two people can link. So both actually *feel* what's happening."

"Didn't you try that with Melissa?"

"Not really. We were in the same scene, but she didn't feel what I did. Either something's off in the code, or the user has to immerse completely with the other person."

"Okay… when are you running this test? And with whom?"

"I'll run it."

Post gave her a look. "And your partner? Because it's not going to be Melissa. Best friends or not, what kind of 'story' could you two run that wouldn't get weird? You know some of the clients will want freaky stuff."

"I don't know. As long as both people feel it's real, that's what matters. And no, I don't plan on testing anything freaky. I'll figure it out. Then I'll talk to Melissa about it."

"Whatever you say, boss," Post teased.

"Boss? I *like* the sound of that. Especially from my older brother," Dominique shot back with a grin.

"Don't get used to it," Post chuckled.

She stuck her tongue out at him and waved him off. "Go on, take the rest of the day. Sundays are slow. I've got it covered."

Chapter 7

Tuesday crept in, nerves knotting Dominique's stomach. She hadn't seen Nathaniel since Saturday night. No numbers were exchanged, no second date, not even a promise of one.

By seven, she kept stealing glances at the door. Still no Nathaniel. They started practice, but when the door swung open at seven-thirty, Nathaniel strolled in. The music halted as every eye followed him toward the stage.

Looking sheepish, he said, "I'm sorry I'm late. A business call ran later than I thought it would."

"If you can't be on time for an audition, how do I know you'll be on time for the show?" Dominique asked.

"I won't schedule anything that would make me late for the show."

"So, you might miss practice then?"

"Possibly. But if you already know the set, I can practice at home. I can also listen in and join once I hear the opening chords," Nathaniel replied.

"What do you think, guys? Let him audition?" Dominique asked Melissa and Post.

"Why not?" Melissa grinned. "Let him amuse me."

"Yeah, let's see if he backs up his claims," Post said.

"Alright, Mr. Black. The stage is yours," Dominique said as the others stepped down and grabbed chairs.

Nathaniel set up his guitar and began to play. The chords were unfamiliar, haunting, shifting seamlessly between rock, pop, and softer notes.

"He's not only hot but a musician too. Dom, if you don't go for him, I will!" Melissa whispered, making her laugh.

"What if I told you he took me out Saturday night?" Dominique asked.

"I wouldn't believe you. You'd have told me already."

"Well, I was taking myself out when he bumped into me at the restaurant. He even ran Tim off. Bonus points."

"You and I need to talk later, girlie. You've been holding out on me."

Dominique laughed, then climbed back onstage. Nathaniel paused, watching as she slid behind the keyboard. A moment later, he caught her rhythm and joined in.

Damn, he really could pick up chords on the fly. Impressive. With Melissa and Post joining in, they ran through the covers. Every time, Nathaniel slid right into the tune. Melissa was right. He was hot, and he could play.

After another hour of practice, Nathaniel packed up and crossed the stage with Melissa and Post trailing.

"Well? Think he can join our little house band?" Dominique asked.

"He's good. I say yes," Melissa replied.

"I agree," Post added.

"Looks like you're in, if you want. Fair warning, though. We don't get paid. Just for fun. Twice-a-week practices, Friday night gigs."

"I don't need the money. I told you, I'm here because I love to play. It helps me relax," Nathaniel replied.

"Then welcome to the band. And to Club X."

"Why Club X?"

"Because X marks the spot. And who doesn't want to be at the spot?" Dominique laughed.

"Didn't think of it that way," Nathaniel smiled. "I'll be back Thursday. Since it's usually dark when I leave home, would it be alright if I came a little late to practice?"

"As long as you're here by seven-thirty. That's when we run the Friday set," Dominique said.

"Thanks. I'll do my best not to disappoint. Mind if I stay until you open?"

"Uh…sure, as long as you stay at the bar."

"I'll stay at the bar."

Nathaniel flashed that brilliant smile, kissed her hand, and walked off. Dominique didn't mind watching him go. Shaking her head, she slipped into her office with Melissa close behind while Shane handled the bar.

"Ok, girlie. *Spill.* What happened Saturday night? And why didn't you tell me?" Melissa pouted.

Dominique laughed. "I actually took Saturday off like you suggested, but I got stir-crazy. So I dressed up and went to La Nobles. Tim showed up at my table, wouldn't leave even when I told him no. I faked waiting for someone; he called my bluff. Then Nathaniel walked up, kissed me, and pretended to be my date. Tim left."

"Hold up! He kissed you? He doesn't even know you and just did that?"

"It was just a peck for show. But then he asked me out. We saw a movie, then he took me to some random field and we danced under the stars. It was… a good night."

"So… Did he kiss you goodnight?"

Heat crept up Dominique's cheeks.

"That blush is a yes! Dish girl! Was it amazing? Was it a long kiss?"

"The field kiss was long, with some touching, nothing too inappropriate. The goodnight kiss was lighter. But the only word I can think of for him is… intense. I don't even know him, yet he's driving me crazy."

"You don't believe in soulmates, but I do. Maybe he's yours," Melissa said.

Dominique laughed until she saw Melissa's serious face. "Wait. You're serious?"

"Hell yeah. I believe in soulmates. I'm just waiting to meet mine. Even if he isn't yours, you could still have fun. Maybe it'll lead somewhere," Melissa teased, wiggling her brows.

Dominique laughed. *Leave it to Melissa to turn it into sex. Best friends. What can you do?*

***

Dominique drifted through the club, chatting with her "frequent flyers." When laughter tipped into rowdiness, she caught Don's eye, and a subtle nod had him steering them toward the door. Every time she glanced at the bar, Nathaniel's gaze was already waiting for hers.

A warm hand settled on her shoulder. She looked up to see Nathaniel, palm outstretched. After a beat, Dominique excused herself from the table and slid her hand into his. He led her straight to the dance floor.

"I thought I'd try my luck at that dance you promised," Nathaniel murmured.

"You were serious? I figured once you made the band, the charade would be over."

"No charade, Dominique. I do want to know you better. For now, I can come to the club. Or you can let me take you out on a real date."

"Why? What's so interesting about me? I really am boring. I'm a workaholic, and don't do much outside of work."

"Perhaps I see myself in your situation. I worked very hard to get to where I am today. You also remind me of my wife. I lost her, but she would want me to be happy. If I found true happiness with her, why wouldn't I jump at the chance of finding it again?" Nathaniel said.

Dominique's brow furrowed. "Not sure how I feel being compared to your wife. Feels like I can't compete with a memory."

Nathaniel exhaled slowly. "I'm not comparing. I'm chasing the same happiness I once had. Have you ever felt that? True happiness?"

"Yes, my music. Music is my life. I can find a song that fits every mood."

"Well, imagine you lost that. If you found something else that made you just as happy, would you not pursue it?"

"Good point. I suppose I would, but honestly, I'm not looking to date. Once burned, twice shy."

"I understand you're hesitant. Just get to know me first. I'll be your friend. We can see where it goes from there."

"Ok. I can deal with that. So, newfound friend of mine, what would you like to talk about?"

"What are your hobbies? What do you do for fun?"

"I play music. *All the time*. It's background noise when I'm writing."

"What do you write?"

"I mainly write short stories. I've written a book or two."

"Are any of your works published?"

"No. I just write for me. Whatever my mind dreams up, I put it down. I have to do something with all the material my mind thinks up. It's a good way to deal with my emotions. I think some are good."

"Do you ever let anyone read them?"

"No. Well, I did let Melissa read one of my short stories. She liked it. But… she may have lied to spare my feelings." Dominique laughed.

"I'm sure she liked it. Maybe I can talk you into letting me read one sometime."

"I won't say never, but I will say it's doubtful. Do you mind if we sit down?"

"I like holding you close, but we can sit."

Dominique sat at a table in the corner so she could keep an eye on everything while they talked.

"So, you said you're an investor. What do you invest in?"

"I own a few properties, but mainly I have a stockbroker that does my investing for me. Some investments are overseas. That's why I work later into the night. Different time zones from me."

"I see. So, you never leave your house unless it's dark?"

"Rarely. I prefer the night. It's always been more alive to me. During the day, you have the hustle and bustle of everyone working. During the night? People come alive."

"Did you major in philosophy or something?"

"No." Nathaniel laughed. "I studied and still study life. I never went to college. I read a lot, though. Mostly, I've been lucky. I'm very comfortable with what I have."

"So, you didn't come from money?"

"My family had money. We weren't millionaires, but comfortable. I never lacked for anything material."

"Material? The way you say that sounds like you lacked something else you needed."

"My mother was a sweet woman. Strict when needed, but I never lacked love from her. She died when I was seventeen. My father became a drunkard after that. He was never a good man anyway. He died when I was twenty-two. I took over his company, not mourning his passing. I met my wife not long before my father passed. She was my family until her passing."

"How long were you together? If you don't want to answer, you don't have to."

"We were together for nine years. We had our ups and downs, but it was worth it."

"You must've met at a young age."

"Yes, we did," Nathaniel said, not elaborating.

"Sounds like she was the love of your life. I can't imagine that type of love. My relationship was so crappy, I don't think I ever want to get into another one."

"It couldn't all be bad. You were engaged, were you not?"

"At first, he was sweet… flowers, texts, the little things. Then the late nights started. Drinking. Excuses. Broken plans. Eventually, even forgetting I was there." Dominique's voice wavered. "He hit me once… and I found out he hadn't been working where he said he was. I followed him, watched him leave a bar with other women. I wanted to believe I was wrong. Naive, I know, but I desperately wanted him to still be the man I fell in love with." She brushed at the tears streaking her cheeks.

"He denied cheating during the confrontation. I saw it, though. Things ended."

"I'm sorry, Dominique. No one deserves to be treated like that. Thank you for telling me. The other night, you didn't wish to discuss it. I don't want to push you, but as time passes, I want to know you."

"Yeah, maybe."

"So, are your parents still alive?"

"No. They were involved in a car wreck when I was eighteen. I met Tim right after my parents died. Being in a vulnerable state, I didn't want to talk to him at first. Melissa got his number and gave it to me. And of course, she gave him mine." Dominique rolled her eyes. "I was actually furious about that at first."

"What does she think of me?"

"I don't think she has an opinion of you yet. She wouldn't give you my phone number if you asked for it. Never again will she do that." Dominique grimaced.

"So, you'll give me your number then?" Nathaniel smirked.

"Are you asking me for it? Or just assuming that I'll give it to you?"

"We're friends now, aren't we? Why wouldn't you give your friend your number?"

"You're funny. Do you have something to write it down with?"

Nathaniel handed her his phone. Surprised, she tapped her number in and passed it back. A buzz in her pocket.

"You already texted me?" she laughed.

"Now you've got my number too, whether for the band or… anything else."

Dominique nodded. "I appreciate it. I'll text you sometime."

"Do you not like to talk on the phone? Texts are so impersonal."

"I don't talk on the phone unless I have to. I won't call you, but I will talk if you call me."

"I'll keep that in mind. So, what do you do during the day?"

"Sleep mostly. I'm a total night owl. Being out under the stars is my preference. I stay here until early morning, then go home. Sometimes I stay up until it's almost dawn. Sleep, tinker for a while, nap, repeat."

"I love the warm nights with a slight breeze. I was outdoors a lot in my youth. Hard to tell from my paler complexion now," Nathaniel said, gazing at his hands.

"You aren't that pale," Dominique laughed. "Not like me. I'm pretty fair-skinned for having such dark hair. Not ghost-white but still."

Nathaniel laughed. Dominique couldn't help but smile. He had a great laugh. Chatting with him was so easy. He seemed genuinely interested in her, but so was Tim when they first met.

"You seem to have drifted away. Do that a lot?"

"I'm sorry. I didn't before. Been having some messed-up things going on lately. My ex triggered some things. Not handling it very well. I seriously thought my past was behind me."

Dominique gazed at Nathaniel. His eyes were trained on her neck. Realizing the necklace was being played with, she slowly put her hand down.

"One day, you'll have to tell me the importance of your necklace." He threw his hands up at her glare. "I know, I know, it's off-limits, I remember. Let's move to another subject. You said music was a big part of your life. What type of music do you like?"

"*Types*. Just about everything but bluegrass and classical. It isn't really what type of music it is. It's about what speaks to me."

"I love that answer. I often find that if something speaks to you, you should continue to do it. Or in your case, listen to it. Do you write songs? Seems like you would."

"I don't. I guess I don't know how to put feelings into a three-minute song. Do you write as well as play?"

"No. I just enjoy the music. I love to feel the guitar vibrating as I play… the music drumming through my body."

"It's amazing what music can do, isn't it?"

"Yes, I must agree."

"Well, Nathaniel, I've enjoyed getting to know you better. I have to attend to some things now. I'll see you on Thursday?"

"Yes, I'll see you then."

When Dominique rose, Nathaniel stood too, taking her hand. He brushed a kiss across her knuckles, collected his guitar, and left. She lingered a moment, hand tingling, before turning back to the business of closing her club.

***

Later that night, Dominique curled up on the porch, the night air cool against her skin. The conversation with Nathaniel replayed in her mind like a song she couldn't shake. She had told him things. Personal things, like Tim, that she usually locked away. Why him? Why did his presence loosen her guard and make her feel… alive?

He was undeniably sexy, but that wasn't the reason. The pull ran deeper. Her dreams had whispered his name long before she ever saw his face. Coincidence? Or something else? Something Melissa would call fate. Dominique had always laughed at the idea of soulmates, but now the thought lingered like a dangerous hope: *What if he was hers?*

She tilted her head back, eyes tracing constellations. Music drifted faintly from inside, blending with the hush of the night. Sleep tugged at her, heavy and insistent, but she refused to move. The porch chair creaked beneath her as she sank into it, trading comfort for the wide, glittering sky. It wouldn't be the first time she'd wake sore from sleeping out here. For now, it was worth it.

***

The man crouched in the shadows of the woods, eyes fixed on Dominique's porch. Hours had passed since he arrived; watching her nightly had become a ritual. Some nights lingered longer than others, but he always slipped away before dawn.

Soon, he thought, she would invite him in willingly. Tonight, she had lingered on the porch longer than usual, eyes tracing the horizon. What thoughts had held her captive so late?

Dominique's deep breaths carried the rhythm of sleep. Twitches and murmurs marked her dreams, and he welcomed every movement.

He slipped from the shadows, lifting her effortlessly into the house. In her bedroom, he sank onto the mattress and drew her close, savoring the heat of her body against his. Tonight, she curled against him. A rare occasion. He pressed a gentle kiss to the crown of her head. Her arm curled around him, and he held her as if she might vanish.

Hours slipped by with her in his arms. Finally, he kissed her lips softly, whispering he'd see her later. He left before dawn broke, craving more than nightly shadows could give. Patience was key; he wouldn't force her, not like before. She would want him. He would see to it.

Homeward, he sank into his bed, letting the day stretch away. She was his, and he would claim her fully when the time was right. The challenge now: making Dominique understand that her place was with him. Sleep took him until dusk, fueling the night to come.

Chapter 8

Dominique stared at her phone, the image of a single rose glowing on the screen. Her thumb hovered over the keyboard before typing "Hi." Her chest fluttered. She wanted to know him, but a tight knot of fear coiled in her stomach.

What if she let herself fall, and he tore her heart apart? The memory of her first heartbreak still ached like a fresh wound. What if she gave him her trust, her heart, and he couldn't return it? His wife lingered in his words. Could he ever truly move on, or would she always be chasing a shadow? Dominique shivered at the thought of living in someone else's ghost.

Dominique shook her head as if she could physically knock the thoughts loose. She barely knew him, yet her mind insisted otherwise. Pushing off the chair, she left for the club. Post would throw a fit if he discovered she had used the machine alone. She didn't care. Dreams had consumed her lately, and now Nathaniel had woven himself into them.

She activated the machine. Auto-shutoff set.

Dominique slid into the machine and closed the door with a soft click. Helmet in place, she drew in a deep breath, then let it out slowly. Her mind was a whirlwind, impossible to quiet. She pictured a white, empty room. Slowly, deliberately, she planted herself in its center, closing her eyes, forcing every stray thought into silence.

***

Rose awoke with a start, unsure where she was. Nathaniel's weight pressed against her, and she slid out from under his arm. After using the bathroom and dressing, she went to the horses, feeding them and grabbing some bread from her saddle.

"Thinking of running again?" Nathaniel's voice cut through the morning calm.

"No, M'Lord. Just feeding the horses and grabbing some food," she said, turning to face him.

"Call me Nathaniel. If you are to be my wife, you will need to remember that. Now, change into a dress. Those clothes are dirty and unbecoming."

"Your wife? You have said you did not want to marry me. Why now?"

"I care for you, Rose. On my way to find you, I thought of nothing else. I was angry you left, but I worried for your safety. I have denied wanting you as my wife, but I can not anymore. You belong with me, by my side. Now, call me Nathaniel." He growled, pulling her close.

"Nathaniel," Rose whispered.

His body trembled, lips crashing onto hers.

Nathaniel broke the kiss. "Go change into a dress. I will fetch food."

"I can not hide being a woman in a dress, Nathaniel. This village is your father's land. I do not want to be noticed."

"No one here reports to my father. He is many things, but not a good man. Tax collectors will not be around for at least a week. We will be safe. Change, please."

Rose scowled and went inside. When Nathaniel returned, he had laid out eggs and a slab of meat. Rose cooked as he watched.

"What was your plan, Rose? How did you expect to survive?"

"I planned to run as far as I could. Eventually, I would need to work. Men do not see women as capable on a farm, but maybe someone needed help at home. Room and board would have been enough. I had not thought it through, Nathaniel. I just could not be a man's slave forever."

"Do you care for me, Rose?"

Rose gazed at Nathaniel. "Yes, I care. Is that what you are truly asking of me, Nathaniel?"

"You seem to know my thoughts. Maybe the old woman was right… You are destined for me, and I for you. Do you love me?"

Rose hesitated. "Yes. Does it please you to hear that?"

"Yes, very much." He pulled her onto his lap, kissing her.

"You say you care. Do you care for or love me?" she asked, eyes downcast.

Gripping her chin, he forced her gaze upward. "I love you, Rose. I apologize for making you feel like a slave. I sought to break you… But you broke me instead."

Rose threw her arms around his neck, tears of joy falling as he soothed her. Once she dried her eyes, she made them plates to continue their journey.

Mounting the horse, her dress rode up. Nathaniel's eyes flicked up her thigh before meeting hers. Her gaze was fiery, a mischievous grin daring him to comment. He only laughed and spurred the horse toward her father's home.

When they rode into the village, Thomas ran ahead, forcing Rose to halt her horse.

"Rose, you are alive! Thank God! I thought they had killed you!" Thomas exclaimed.

"What are you talking about, Thomas?" Rose asked.

"The knights came last night. I overheard one saying they would kill the girl who ran away. They raided homes, describing you. Everyone knew it was you, but no one saw you. Your father... he..." Thomas trailed off.

"What about my father?" Rose asked, frowning.

"I can not, Rose. It is too horrible."

Rose spurred Winter into a full run toward her father's home. Thomas yelled for her to wait, but she didn't listen. Nearing the house, she slowed, hesitating.

Nathaniel rode up beside her. "Rose, your father is not home. Thomas told me what happened. We need to leave. I need to get you to safety."

Rose spurred her horse on. Tears streamed down as her sight landed on the ash that was once her home. Nathaniel dismounted, pulling her off the horse. Holding her tight, running his hands over her hair, he tried to calm her.

When the tears stopped, Nathaniel pulled back. "I am sorry, Rose. It was never my intention for this to happen."

"I caused this. I cause everything to go wrong because I cannot mind my tongue," Rose whispered.

"No, Rose. My father caused this," Nathaniel said firmly.

"Where is my father?" Rose whispered.

"Please, let us leave this place."

"No, not until I have seen my father. Where is he?"

"In the village."

When they reached the village, Nathaniel led her to the old woman's hut. He helped her off the horse and walked her inside. Rose stopped at a thin sheet covering something on the table, blood-soaked. An old woman shuffled in, surprise on her face.

"M'Lord, she should not see him like this," the woman said.

"Show him to me. I have to know," Rose demanded.

"Child, please… remember him as he was," the old woman pleaded.

"If you will not show him, I will look," Rose said, stepping toward the table.

"No. I will show you. Prepare yourself, child," the woman said, pulling back the sheet.

Rose gasped. Her father had been whipped nearly to the bone. She screamed, fell to the ground, and wept. Nathaniel held her, running his hands over her hair, shushing her.

Once she calmed, Nathaniel placed her father's body across her horse, mounted behind Rose, and took them to her father's land. There, he buried him beside her mother. Afterwards, he returned Rose to the village, where the old woman promised to hide her until Nathaniel returned.

He kissed the top of her head, promising to come back. Rose stared at the empty table, silent.

At the castle, a knight informed Nathaniel that he needed to see his father. In the great hall, he waited.

"Where have you been?" his father demanded.

"I searched for the thief who stole my horse. She's dealt with now," Nathaniel replied.

"Has she? Did you bring her back for punishment? I do not see her."

"No. I wanted to handle it myself," Nathaniel said.

"I think you lie to your father. Perhaps you should be punished as well."

"Do as you see fit, Father," Nathaniel said, barely concealing his anger.

"My son, you are finally learning. I will let the punishment go since I had my bit of sport regarding the matter. The girl's father lied about his daughter's whereabouts; I made an example of him. Fear has spread." He laughed, an evil glint in his eyes. "We will take the land, and a knight will occupy it."

"Let me go there, Father. It will teach me humility," Nathaniel said.

"My throne is not yours yet, boy. You need humility. Build another hut on the land. I will see what you can do," his father commanded, dismissing him.

Nathaniel packed their things, waiting for darkness.

Slipping out, he moved among the shadows. His father, asleep in the chair, mead still in hand, made him pause. Slowly, he made way to the treasury where he took coins.

Still moving in the shadows, he saddled the horses and left the castle.

At the old woman's hut, he found Rose in a fitful, tearful sleep. Shaking her awake, she swung at him.

"Rose, it is Nathaniel. We have to go. I will keep you safe," he said.

She finally allowed him to carry her to the waiting horses. He thanked the old woman and mounted Rose's horse.

***

Dominique stepped out of the machine, relieved. It had worked perfectly, no side effects. She smiled, proud that her hard work had paid off. One more test, and she could put it on the market.

Maybe if she relived the dreams, she could control them, get some normalcy back. Gathering her things, she saw her phone flashing with messages. It was already after seven.

Melissa had texted, asking where she was and saying the bar was open. Dominique hadn't realized she'd been in the machine so long. She replied, letting Melissa know she was in the building and in her office.

Soon after, Melissa walked in, scowling as she sat across from Dominique's desk. Dominique just stared back. Melissa had opened the club for her before, but usually with some warning.

"I'm sorry, Melissa. I was playing with the machine and didn't know what time it was. I kind of got wrapped up in my own head."

"So not funny. You know I worry about you. With everything that's gone on lately… well, I thought the worst. If you pull something like this again, at least text me first."

"Yes, mother," Dominique replied.

"Don't do that. Don't patronize me like it's no big deal," Melissa snapped.

"It isn't a big deal, Melissa. I was here the whole time. My car's parked around the side."

"That's not your normal spot, so I didn't see your car when I came in. And it is a big deal with your history. Are you seriously texting someone while I'm fussing at you?" Melissa demanded.

Dominique nodded without looking up.

"Yes, I'm texting Nathaniel back. Apparently, he thought something was wrong when I didn't text him back right away.

Guess it's okay for him not to text me back for hours. How messed up is that?"

"Well, he'll have to get in line. But, it's nice he worries, isn't it?"

"I guess, but he doesn't really know me like that."

"Give it some time, and he will. You just have to open up."

"Easier said than done. Let's get back to work. I'm fine as you can see."

Melissa nodded, leaving with a final, "I'm still mad at you."

Dominique smiled and shook her head.

Chapter 9

Months passed with Dominique and Nathaniel texting nightly. Behind a screen, she found it easier to hide fear and anxiety, slipping into a version of herself that felt safer. His messages always came late, which had her staying up into the night and sleeping longer during the day.

When Nathaniel came to the club, he lingered—playing pool, coaxing her into dances. Easygoing fun, though the air shifted when they danced. Even when apart, she could feel his gaze anchored on her.

Her phone rang, pulling her from her thoughts. She frowned at the caller ID.

"Hey, Becky. How have you been?"

"I'm good. Sorry to bug you, but you should check the news."

"What's up?" Dominique asked.

"I can't say because of HIPAA. Just turn on the local news. It's bad."

"Hold on."

Dominique flipped to the news. A crash filled the screen. Two cars collided, one T-boned on the driver's side, crushed beyond recognition. The anchor said victims were being airlifted to the hospital.

Why had Becky wanted her to see this? The camera pulled back, showing the cars more clearly. Dominique dropped her phone.

She snatched the phone back up. "Becky, please tell me that isn't Shane's car. It looked like his, plates and all."

"I can't confirm, but I had to show you."

"Thanks, Becky. I just wish it were for another reason."

"I know how you are about your people. Just…don't call anyone right away, okay?"

"I won't. I'll wait, but it's going to kill me."

"Give it time to air, then you can say you saw it on the news."

"Alright. I'll wait. Thanks, Becky. See you at the club."

"Bye."

Dominique sank back, stunned. That had to be Shane's car. Why else would Becky call? Had he survived?

After an hour of agonizing waiting, Dominique called Shane's wife, Lisa. No answer. She left a message: please call back, just checking in after seeing the news. She did the same for Shane's phone.

***

At the club, Shane didn't show up. Her worry spiked. Dominique took over behind the bar, eyes on her phone. When it finally rang, she answered. "Lisa, hold on, I need to step into my office."

"Lisa, are you okay?" Dominique asked, closing the office door.

"Shane…he's gone," Lisa choked out.

"I'm so sorry, Lisa. Shane was a good man. I'll do anything I can. Tell me what you need."

"I just need time. I don't know what to tell Danny. The other driver ran a red light and hit Shane on the driver's side. They tried to save him, but…" Lisa broke off.

"I hate that all I can say is sorry. Let me know about arrangements. I want to cover the funeral, if you'll let me."

"I wasn't thinking about that yet. Thanks, but I can't let you pay," Lisa said.

"You have a son, Lisa. Funerals aren't cheap. Let me help."

"Alright. I'll let you know. I need to get to Danny now."

"Take care."

Dominique hung up and returned to the bar. Melissa sat her down. Dominique couldn't speak at first. Shane had been fine hours ago, alive and well. How could this happen?

She finally told Melissa, then braced herself to make the public announcement. Onstage, she silenced the music and crowd, announcing Shane's death. All profits for the night would go to Lisa and Danny.

The tragedy reopened wounds—her parents' fatal crash caused by a drunk driver. She thought of Tim, his reckless drinking, and why she enforced strict cutoffs at her own bar.

Dominique returned to the bar, juggling orders. Post handled the grill well, waitresses got beers, and strangers donated to the jar. She was surprised and touched.

It felt good to see humanity shine. Nathaniel had arrived, sitting at the bar, asking if she was okay. When she told him, he broke protocol, coming behind the bar, hugging her.

She couldn't scold him, needing the hug. She cried on his shoulder, then pulled back, thanked him, wiped her tears, and returned to work. For Lisa and Danny.

Chapter 10

The next day, Dominique called her applicants to replace Shane. She hated it, but the bar couldn't close. It'd been a while since they applied; she hoped someone was still available.

None were available: either they moved on or took other jobs. Only one applicant remained, the one she least wanted to call.

Dominique sighed, picked up the phone, then set it down. Could she really call him? Bring him into her bar? Was she crazy? Still, she had no choice.

She dialed, hit his voicemail, and winced at her voice. Definitely not professional.

"Tim, this is Dominique. It's been a while since our interview, but I need to know if you're still looking for work. Call me back at this number."

The phone rang quickly. Dominique jumped. Caller ID: Tim's number. She answered slowly. "Hello?"

"Hey, Dominique. Sorry, I was in the shower," Tim said, voice husky.

Dominique closed her eyes. Tim's looks were never the issue. Six feet tall, spring green eyes, wavy sandy-blond hair, close cut, all muscle, always fit.

"Tim. Can I assume you're still looking for work?"

"Yeah. Been doing odd jobs, but need full-time. How you been, Dominique?"

"Not calling for niceties here. I need a bartender, fast. Are you available?"

"How soon?"

"Yesterday. When can you start?"

"I have a prior job tonight. If you needed someone yesterday, why didn't you call then?"

"I didn't know my bartender died until after opening. You wanted to know how I'm doing. There it is."

Dominique was angry. Why did he have to ask so many questions? Why couldn't he just answer yes or no? Why was he always trying to talk to her? She didn't want him back. Hadn't wanted him for years. She'd almost died because of him.

"I'm sorry. Just checking on you. I'll see if I can cancel my job and call back."

"Forget that. When can you come in?"

"Tomorrow. Want me to come in early?"

"Yes. Come early. I'll show you around, and we'll discuss pay. Don't like it? Walk away."

"Doesn't matter, I'll take it. See you tomorrow, Dom. Sorry, Dominique."

Dominique rolled her eyes, hung up, and braced herself. Was her nightmare returning? No… he was just here to work. Nothing more. She would not let him destroy her again.

Chapter 11

Dominique waited for Tim to arrive. When she heard the knock, she opened the door and let him in. She guided him to a table, sat, and motioned for him to do the same. He looked her over as he sat.

"Here's the deal. Eleven dollars an hour, plus tips. We're open daily. Need a night off? Request in advance. Sick leave, paid vacation—approval required. Fridays and Saturdays, we stay open later; other days, we close at midnight. Interested?"

"Still straight to the point, huh?" he asked.

"With you, yes. This isn't an ideal situation. Do you want the job or not?"

"I said yesterday I'd take it. But Dominique… you gonna ignore me the whole time? We'll have to talk eventually."

"No. You're here for a job, nothing else. I don't want anything to do with you, Tim. You lost your place long ago. I loved you, gave everything, and you gave me a black eye and a broken heart. You destroyed me. That ends now. Let's go over your job responsibilities."

Tim grabbed her hand. "I don't deserve another chance. I did horrible things. No excuse. I hope one day you'll let me explain what happened to me. It affected my life badly, and I didn't know how to handle it back then."

"It doesn't matter. You chose your path; I chose mine. Come on, I'll show you around."

Dominique showed him the club and explained his duties. By the time she finished, Post and Melissa arrived. Melissa grabbed her arm, pulling her into the office.

"What the hell is Tim doing here?" Melissa demanded.

"He's the new bartender," Dominique said.

"What? Are you kidding me? Why in the hell would you hire him of all people?"

"I need a bartender. No one else was available. He was last on my list. I didn't want to hire him." Dominique shrugged. "I can't run the bar and bartend every night. I have responsibilities."

"I can't believe this. I'll be watching you. No way that bastard breaks you again."

"Melissa, I love you, but I'm grown. I can handle myself. He's here to work, nothing else. I told him that."

"Yeah, yeah. He knows how to push you. He did it before, and that body… better than ever. But you have Nathaniel now. He can keep Tim away."

"I don't *have* Nathaniel," Dominique said, making air quotes. "He doesn't belong to me. We're just friends."

"Sure. That man wants more than your friendship. I don't understand why you haven't gone for it."

"I don't want a relationship. Nathaniel's a friend. Nice guy. Enjoy his company, but nothing more. We haven't gone out, I've kept my distance. Point made."

"You're so frustrating. I'll be watching you." On her way out, Melissa pointed her fingers at her own eyes and then at Dominique.

Dominique kept a watchful eye on Tim that night. He worked, but women flocked to him. She overheard him give two drinks on the house upon approach to the bar.

"Keep that up, and you'll be out of a job by the end of the night. Either pay for the drinks or make them pay."

"I already paid. They're friends of mine."

Dominique rolled her eyes and walked off.

Chapter 12

Tim eyed the two women. If they kept returning, they'd ruin this for him.

"After your drinks, you leave. I'm working. Tell Jacob this place is off-limits. And you, stay away from me."

"Oh, come on, honey. You never had a problem before. We just want to have a little fun," Roxy cooed.

"No. I mean it. Cause trouble again, and I'll handle it. Now get out. Remember what I said," Tim said.

He shook his head, scanning for Dominique. She sat with a man. He quickly realized it was the guy from her date. No way Dominique was with him. They didn't even touch. He had to get to her first.

Dominique kept checking that table all night. He caught her glance and smiled, but she just shook her head. Later, seeing her dance with the man, a low growl escaped him.

"Don't even think about it," Melissa said, approaching the bar for drinks.

"I don't know what you're talking about," Tim replied.

"You know exactly what I mean. Stay out of Dominique's life. I was there when you broke her. You have no idea the hell you caused her."

"I know what I did, Melissa. Trust me, I know."

"No, you don't. Did she tell you what happened after she ended things?"

"I know about the baby. She drank heavily and lost it. She had no problem telling me off after that."

"So, she didn't tell you everything. It's more than just that. The fact that she started drinking heavily was bad. She was trying to drown her pain… almost completed that task. So, stay away from her."

"Almost completed it?"

"I've said too much. Ask her if you want details."

"I will. I'm different now, Melissa. I've grown a lot in the past two years. I would never intentionally hurt Dominique."

"Yeah, sure. Heard that one before," Melissa sneered, walking away.

Tim sighed. Yeah, he had too. He'd promised to love Dominique and protect her forever. Had even given her a ring. He meant it then and still meant it now. He'd fought his way out of the life he had back then, literally. His anger had come in handy there.

Chapter 13

Nathaniel held Dominique while they danced. Eyes on them drew his attention to the bar. Her ex stood there. She hired him? The look on his face showed displeasure with Nathaniel talking to, let alone touching, her.

"Dominique, may I ask you a question?"

"Sure. You've never asked before. Why start now?" Dominique replied.

"Is that your ex-fiancé?"

"Yep," she sighed.

"Why is he bartending?"

"My bartender died. None of my other applicants were available. Gotta do what you gotta do sometimes. It's not ideal. But I can't be in several places at once. Do you have a problem with it?"

"Would it matter if I said yes?" Nathaniel asked.

"We're friends, so yes, it matters. Not to the point of firing him, though. First day. He hasn't done anything to warrant it. I hired him for a job, not to get him back in my life."

"I like you, so I'll admit… I'm jealous. I see something I want, I go for it. Not giving up on that date either, but I don't want to compete for your affections."

"You're sweet. But nothing to be jealous of. Tim had his chance and blew it. I don't want a relationship now. I need to take care of myself first."

"I understand, but sometimes it's good to let someone take care of you."

"Thanks, but I need time. Maybe later, I'll take you up on it."

"I'll be here," Nathaniel said, kissing her hand, twirling her, pulling her close.

When they finished dancing, Nathaniel went and sat at the bar.

Tim approached Nathaniel. "You want something?"

"Yes. Dominique. I see how you look at her. Don't. I don't want a fight with you or your people. Leave her alone so she doesn't get caught in your mess."

"I do what I want. You don't have dibs. She's single. I wouldn't involve her without her knowing. I know about you. I smell it all over you. Does she?"

"Not yet, but she will. She isn't ready. She belongs with me. She feels it, but denies it."

"Whatever. Just admit that she doesn't want you. Because she damn sure doesn't believe in soulmates."

"We'll see. She hasn't seen enough yet, but she will. Then you won't stand a chance. Bow out while you still can," Nathaniel said, standing and leaving the bar.

Chapter 14

Dominique ran into her office, throwing herself onto the couch. Convulsions wracked her body like a seizure. Why now? Melissa promised to check on her, but would it be soon enough? Fear gripped her tight as the vision started, her eyes wide open. What was happening?

***

The first winter storm trapped Nathaniel and Rose in a small cottage. Since her father's burial, Rose had been silent; cooking, cleaning, even sharing his bed, but always distant.

Unable to bear her silence, Nathaniel caught her as she passed, pulling her onto his lap. She resisted, but he held her still, kissing her lips. She stayed motionless, her distance cutting deeper than any blade.

"Rose, I cannot take this silence. You told me you loved me. Do you still?"

She only stared. He shook her gently, her breath hitching, eyes wide. Pulling her against him, he stroked her back, voice breaking.

"Please, Rose. I know your heart is broken, but mine breaks too without your voice. Do you still love me?"

At last, she whispered, "Yes. I love you."

"Then don't give up on me, on us. I cannot give your father back, but I would gladly give my life for you. If you do not want me, I will accept it, but I will die without you."

Rose broke down again, tears that seemed to never end these past weeks.

"I am sorry," she wept. "I have punished you with my silence, but punished myself more. My father is dead because of me. If I had not run, he would still live."

"No, Rose. This blame is not yours. You cannot see it yet, but time will heal this wound."

She rested her head on his shoulder. He held her, fingers combing through her hair, breathing her in.

"It is late. We should rest. We leave in the morning. The storm has passed."

In bed, Rose surprised him by nuzzling his neck. He kissed her gently, cautiously, but she didn't pull away. When her hands slipped beneath his shirt, he slowly unlaced her dress. That night, they made love and finally fell asleep, tangled in each other's arms.

***

They wandered the countryside in a rhythm of road and rest, village inns when fortune smiled, hard ground and canvas when it did not. Winter clung to the air, snow nipping at their cheeks, but Nathaniel always pulled Rose into the shelter of his arms, their shared warmth fending off the chill.

At the last village, armored knights bearing the Duke's insignia blocked their way. Nathaniel approached with steady confidence, asking for an audience with the Duchess. But when he revealed the ring, suspicion darkened the knight's face. Steel hands seized them, accusations of theft flying before they could defend themselves. Within the hour, Rose and Nathaniel were wrenched apart and thrown into the castle dungeons.

Days blurred together in the damp, echoing dark. Then came muffled voices, bootsteps, and the clink of keys. Rose's breath caught as the guard stopped at Nathaniel's cell and hauled him away. Left alone, she paced until her legs trembled, then froze as footsteps returned. Panic clawed at her chest. She shrank into the farthest corner, pressing herself small against the stone, shivering with dread.

"Rise, child. Let me look at you."

Rose forced herself up on shaking legs, edging closer to the bars. The woman drew back her hood, and Rose froze. Golden hair spilled over her shoulders, and her eyes, piercing blue, sharp yet wet with unshed tears, locked with hers.

"Heavens…" the woman whispered, voice trembling. "You are the mirror of her."

"M'Lady, I do not know who you speak of," Rose said quickly, desperation sharpening her voice. "But I beg you, listen. Nathaniel is no thief. The ring he showed your knight was not stolen. It was given to him. Please tell me you have not harmed him?"

"Nathaniel?" the woman echoed. "The knight? No, he has not been harmed. My men await my command. Were he lying, he would already be dead. Guard! Unlock the cell. Escort her to the great hall."

The woman swept back up the stairs. The guard obeyed, jerking the door open and yanking Rose forward. She stumbled hard, her palms scraping raw against the stone. Blood spotted her skin, but she pushed herself up, trembling. The guard shoved her toward the steps, the iron tip of his blade grazing her back.

As they entered the great hall, Rose's eyes immediately found Nathaniel, kneeling with a sword pressed against his throat. Instinctively, she tried to rush forward, but the guard's strong hand stopped her.

The woman from the dungeon sat high upon a throne, radiating authority. Beside her, an older man scowled, brow furrowed and lips pressed tight. The guard shoved Rose before the throne, forcing her to kneel.

"My knight tells me this man presented him with a ring after seeing the insignia on his armor. Where did he obtain it?" the woman demanded, voice sharp as steel.

"There was an old woman, a witch, I presume, in my village. She gave Nathaniel the ring," Rose answered, voice shaking but steady.

"This Nathaniel, as you call him, claims to be a knight from Athalon. I have my scholars' maps; it is far from here. Why would you come?" Her gaze bore into Rose. "Speak the truth, or that man dies."

"Mother, this is absurd. Kill them and let us be done," the man beside her growled.

"Hush, Michael. I will hear her out," the Duchess said firmly.

Rose bowed her head. "The old woman in my village told Nathaniel to bring me here. He believes my mother came from this place. I apologize, M'Lady, but I cannot explain more, other than Nathaniel is trying to protect me from an untimely death. He believes you can help."

"Why should I risk my throne for a stranger's tale? You say your mother hailed from here. Who was she?"

"Mary Dumont. She was married to my father, Daniel Dumont. Her maiden name was Mary Dupree," Rose whispered, eyes downcast.

"You lie!" Michael bellowed.

Rose lifted her chin, voice calm but resolute. "I have no reason to lie, M'Lord. I do not know you, nor wish to. The only remnants of my mother are her name, her temperament, and this necklace she gave me."

"Bring me the necklace, child," the Duchess said gently, her tone softening.

"Duchess, I beg your pardon. Please allow me to bring you the necklace," the guard said.

"No. I wish for her to bring it to me. She has no weapons. You have made sure of that. Come, child, bring me the necklace."

Rose lifted her head with quiet dignity and approached the throne where the Duchess sat. Carefully, she removed the necklace, the only remaining keepsake from her mother, and extended it toward the Duchess.

"I have not seen this in many years," the Duchess murmured, fingers brushing the delicate piece. "My daughter, Mary, received this necklace at her presentation at age thirteen. Three years later, she was promised to a Duke, but she ran away, and her father banished her. It sparked a war between our kingdoms. You resemble her so strongly. Michael is next in line for the throne. He will not yield it, and he shall not. But you, child, shall not be banished nor sentenced to death. You are too young to have taken this ring and necklace. Tell me, what happened to your mother?"

"My mother fell to illness. She withered and died when I was very young. She gave me this necklace on her deathbed. I have worn it ever since. Please, I beg you, allow me to keep it," Rose implored.

"You do not demand anything from the Duchess," Michael snapped.

"Michael, control your temper," the Duchess replied calmly. "She asks nothing for herself. She desires nothing from your throne, correct child?"

"No, Duchess. I desire nothing of a throne. I only seek Nathaniel's safety and vengeance for my father," Rose stated with measured clarity.

"Release the knight. Let him approach the throne and kneel," the Duchess commanded.

Nathaniel rose slowly and moved to kneel beside Rose. She rested her hand lightly on his shoulder. When he looked up, their eyes met, and a shared smile passed between them.

"Rose Dumont," the Duchess said, voice softening, "you are truly my granddaughter, Mary's daughter. Tell me, what does this man mean to you?"

"He is my future husband, my protector. I would plead for his life if needed. I seek nothing from you save safe passage. I do not claim a birthright or treasure. I ask only for your protection until we can face his father, who killed my own," Rose explained, her gaze steady.

"I shall grant you safe passage, child. You will remain here, and in time, we shall grow acquainted. When the moment comes, if vengeance is sought, you shall have my army. A treaty with Athalon will be established," the Duchess declared.

"Thank you, Duchess. I will honor a treaty with you. We shall govern in peace, and I pledge myself to your service if you so wish," Nathaniel said, still kneeling.

"No pledge is required. As my granddaughter's husband, you join our family. My blessing ensures the army you will need. Come, child, let us prepare, and then we shall speak earnestly," the Duchess said, rising to lead them down the hall, guards flanking them.

She showed them to a chamber and left them alone. Maids soon arrived, filling a warm bath. Rose and Nathaniel entered together, holding each other as the heat and water relaxed their tense muscles.

Once bathed and dressed, the guards escorted them to a sunroom where the Duchess awaited. They sat across from her as a maid poured tea. After dismissing the staff, the Duchess set her cup down.

"So, Rose, tell me about your mother," she said gently.

"My mother was extraordinary. Sharp-tongued, yet the kindest soul. She loved my father and me fiercely. She taught me to read and write, and shared the most enchanting tales of balls and distant lands. Even facing death, she showed no fear," Rose recounted, tears glimmering in her eyes.

"Before she passed, my mother expressed regret that she would not witness my growth into the woman she envisioned," Rose continued, her voice faltering slightly.

"One of my greatest regrets is not seeing my daughter married and as a mother myself. We shall have more talks about her, I promise," the Duchess said warmly. "But for now, let us discuss your engagement. Do you plan to marry before returning to Athalon?"

Rose shifted uneasily, wringing her hands until Nathaniel covered them with his own.

"Yes," Nathaniel said firmly. "I would have us wed before I march against my father. I need to know Rose is safe, and if fate takes me, that all I possess will be hers."

"Very well," the Duchess replied with warmth. "We shall plan your union. It would honor me to host the celebration, though preparations will require some time."

"I need very little," Rose said softly. "For nearly nineteen years, I have lived with the simplest of things. A dress and a chaplain will suffice."

"Nonsense," the Duchess countered, smiling. "My granddaughter shall have only the finest. And please, call me Grandmother. Tell me, child, why did your father not arrange your marriage years ago? When were you born?"

"Well, Grandmother," Rose answered, "I begged my father not to marry me off. I longed to wed for love, as he and my mother had. He was also ill, and I tended to him. He honored my wish, and I worked the farm while caring for him. I was born in winter, and in a month and a half, I shall come of age again."

"Then we shall celebrate both your wedding and your birth," the Duchess declared happily. Rising, she embraced Rose. "How lovely! I have much to prepare, so I shall let you rest. We will speak again soon."

Rose hugged her back, tears pricking her eyes. When the Duchess departed, she turned into Nathaniel's arms, sobbing tears of joy.

"I am sorry I lied about us being engaged," Rose whispered. "I did not know what to say when she asked what you were to me."

"You did not lie," Nathaniel replied gently. "I told you already, I want you as my wife. My intent has never changed."

"I thought you were supposed to ask," Rose said shyly. "But perhaps that is not the way of the world. Marriages are arranged; permission is not asked for."

Nathaniel's lips curved in a smile. "Oh, Rose. You want your knight in shining armor to ask properly, don't you?"

Her brows knit. "I do not see the humor in this. My parents had love. He asked her for her hand in marriage. I only wished for the same."

Nathaniel gazed into her eyes, then lifted her hand. "Rose, will you give me your hand in marriage? Will you be mine, and no other's, until death parts us?"

Tears shimmered as Rose smiled. "Yes. I accept your proposal, Nathaniel. My hand, and my heart, are yours."

***

Dominique surfaced from the convulsions, her breath ragged. Strong arms carried her, voices blurring around her; Melissa's sharp and angry, a man's just as heated. Before she could make sense of it, she was lowered into a seat and slipped back into darkness.

She stirred when lifted again, warmth pressed against her side. She burrowed closer, weightless. Melissa's voice pierced through this time, sharp with worry.

"Just bring her back here. She's going to kill me for letting you in her house, her bedroom, no less."

"Melissa, do you ever shut up? She'll be grateful to wake up safe in her own bed."

Pain throbbed behind her eyes as she forced them open. Tim's face hovered close, green eyes flecked with darker specks, his smile soft.

"Welcome back. Melissa found you convulsing at the office. She wanted to call 911, but I stopped her. Hospitals can't help much with seizures. I didn't know you had them." He eased back.

"I don't," Dominique whispered. "I've never had one before. Thank you… both. I just need sleep."

Melissa stepped into view, worry etched across her face. "Okay, Dom. I'll check on you later. I hate leaving you like this, though."

"It's fine. Tomorrow," Dominique murmured, already fading back into unconsciousness.

Chapter 15

Melissa and Tim stepped outside. Tim hesitated, glancing back at Dominique's door.

"Don't even think about it," Melissa snapped. "I didn't want you touching her, let alone putting her in bed. If anyone's staying, it's me."

Tim bristled. "What the hell was that? Has she ever had anything like this before? And quit acting like I crossed a line. She needed help, and I was strong enough to carry her."

Melissa shook her head. "Not that I've ever seen. But this has gone on too long. I'll drag her to a doctor if I must."

"What's been going on too long?" Tim pressed.

"Nothing," Melissa said quickly, covering her mouth. "It's not your business. Just give me a ride back to the club since I drove Dominique's car."

Tim sighed. "Fine. But don't say I never do anything for you."

After dropping Melissa at the club, Tim pulled into his driveway… and froze. Jacob's car waited for him. Great. Just what he needed.

"Tim," Jacob called, stepping out. "I hear you've got a new job. And it's off-limits to us. What's that about?"

Tim kept his voice steady. "The club owner doesn't tolerate drama. I need this job, Jacob. I've already lost too many because of my so-called friends. Just keep everyone away, okay?"

Jacob smirked. "You could work for me again. You were good at it."

"I told you, I'm done with that life. When I met you, I was engaged. I lost her because of everything that happened. Why can't you let me move on?"

Jacob's smile vanished. He grabbed Tim's collar, yanking him close. "Because you belong to me. Maybe you need a reminder. Boys! Show him who's boss."

As Jacob slid back into his car, three men closed in. The beating was brutal, leaving Tim bloodied in the dirt. When it was finally over, he lay there, chest heaving, until he could force himself to crawl inside. No one would ever know how bad he hurt. He just needed rest. Sleep would fix it.

Chapter 16

"Dominique," Tim called as he knocked. "Want a ride today?"

He'd been showing up every morning despite her telling him not to. Dominique couldn't understand it. Why wouldn't he leave her alone? She was still furious, still trying to move on.

With a resigned sigh, she opened the door. Too late, she realized she was in pajamas: shorts that barely covered her, a thin shirt clinging to her curves, and hair a tangled mess from a nap on the couch. Heat rushed to her cheeks as Tim's eyes swept over her.

"Why do you keep coming back? I told you if I need a ride, I'll call Melissa."

"It's just a ride, Dom. I'm not asking you to run away with me. I know I screwed up, but maybe one day you'll let me explain." He stepped closer.

Dominique backed up, his heat caressing her body. She would never forgive the pain he'd caused, but she couldn't deny she still found him attractive.

Then suddenly, Tim inhaled deeply and hauled her against him. She gasped as their bodies collided, his face buried in her hair.

"You smell good. Like sin and desire," he murmured, lifting her by her thighs.

Instinctively, her legs locked around his waist. His mouth claimed hers, his arm steady beneath her while his other hand tangled in her hair, dragging her head back so his lips could scorch a trail down her throat.

Dominique hated that he still knew every spot that unraveled her. Hated even more how her body betrayed her, arching into his hips, grinding into him. She kissed him back until his hand slid under her shirt, cupping her breast.

She broke the kiss. "Tim, stop! Let go of me," she panted.

A low growl rumbled from him as he slowly slid her down his body. Her knees nearly buckled. His eyes were different now: darker, predatory.

"You need to leave. Don't come back," she said firmly.

"I don't get why you fight what you clearly feel. You know I still want you," he said, reaching for her.

Dominique stepped back. "You hurt me in ways I can't recover from. Sure, your body's better than ever, but it doesn't change the past."

"Then tell me what happened after we broke up. Melissa let it slip that there was something else. I'll do anything to make it right. I still love you."

"Love me? Sleeping with other women was love? You broke me! I lost my child. I tried to end my life! Can you fix that? Can you give me my child back? Can you take that darkness from me?" Dominique spat.

"I can't bring back the baby, but we could try again. I always wanted kids. I can't undo the past, but I'll spend every day making it right. I wasn't constantly cheating. Just let me explain. Maybe you can forgive me," Tim said.

"There's nothing you could say to fix this. Go to work, stop coming here. I don't love you or want you anymore."

"That's a lie. I can smell your desire. You haven't been with anyone else, have you?" Tim asked.

"*Smell* desire? And it's none of your business if I've been with someone else," she shot back.

Tim smirked. "Then you're not with Nathaniel. So I still have a chance. And no matter what, I'll keep proving I love you."

Dominique pushed him, trying to force him out. He didn't budge, kissing her hands instead, then drawing her close once more before finally stepping back and leaving. She stood, breathless, then slammed the door.

That man was as frustrating as ever. Being gorgeous didn't matter. She admitted she was still attracted to him. But she wasn't drawn to him the way she was to Nathaniel. Frustration swirled through her at the fact that he had *known* she was feeling that way. And he could smell that? Ridiculous.

Sleeping with him would be a disaster. She knew it, yet the ache remained. Tim always drove her crazy. Restless, she couldn't calm herself. Going to the club was impossible. He'd be there.

She grabbed her phone and texted Nathaniel, jittery but determined to go on the date. Probably not a good idea, but she was doing it anyway.

An hour later, she saw the sun setting. Nathaniel replied that he could pick her up in an hour. She sent him her address and began getting ready. *Oh, the web we weave,* she thought.

***

Dominique heard a car pull up and looked out the window. A shiny black Mustang glinted in the driveway. Nathaniel stepped out, and lust hit her hard. How was she supposed to think of anything else when he was in a dark grey suit that fit him perfectly, hair slicked back with a curl at the top of his shoulders? He carried flowers. Her favorite flowers.

She grabbed her purse and opened the door as he walked up. He smiled, and heat curled in her belly. Nathaniel wasn't as muscular as Tim, but his body was lean and strong. His dark eyes locked with hers, pulling her in.

"Good evening, Dominique," he said, offering her the flowers.

"Thank you. They're beautiful," Dominique said, kissing his cheek.

He gave her a curious look and glanced around the room before returning his gaze to her. Dominique moved to get a vase.

"You can come in, Nathaniel. I'm just going to put these in water before we leave."

He stepped through the doorway. His nose twitched, and his lips curved in a faint grimace. Dominique frowned, sniffing the air. Her house smelled of rose candles, nothing offensive. Still, his eyes darkened, black swallowing out the warmth.

"So, Dominique, what have you been doing lately? I haven't seen you at the club the last few days."

"I've been at home, resting."

"Have you had any other company?" Nathaniel asked.

"I wouldn't call him company. Tim keeps showing up, asking if I want a ride to work," Dominique admitted, cheeks warming at the memory.

Nathaniel's jaw flexed. "Hmmm. Should I worry that Tim knows where you live?"

Dominique bristled. "He wouldn't know if Melissa hadn't told him. He only brought me home because I passed out at work. Melissa couldn't pick me up."

Nathaniel's jaw tightened, and he said nothing for a moment.

His gaze pinned her. "Is he the reason you asked me about tonight?"

"No," she snapped, then softened her tone. "Nathaniel, I don't want Tim. I thought we could hang out. If you don't want to, fine, but don't question me like I'm a child. Now, do you want to go out or not?"

"Yes." His voice lowered. "But understand, I don't wish to fight for your affections. I will be your friend, but I'm a jealous man. I don't like thinking of you with him."

Dominique exhaled, rolling her eyes. "You're sweet, Nathaniel. You'll have to get over the jealousy. We're just friends. If I ever date again, it would be you. But if you find someone else first, I'd understand."

Nathaniel stepped closer, close enough that she caught the spice of his cologne. "I'm not looking for anyone else. I'll wait as long as it takes."

Heat coiled in her chest, but she kept her voice steady. "Okay. Where are we going?"

"La Nobles. Then a movie. And perhaps afterward… a walk."

"Sounds like an all-night event." Her lips curved despite herself. "Your car or mine?"

His lips curved in a possessive smile. "*Mine*."

His arm circled her waist, pulling her flush against him. His mouth claimed hers in a possessive kiss.

Her hands tangled in his hair as their tongues dueled. Breaking the kiss, he trailed kisses along her jaw and down her neck. She pushed him away.

"I can't, Nathaniel. I want to be friends," she said, breath catching. "I can't get wrapped up in someone else right now."

He leaned in again, hunger sparking in his eyes. "I can't help wanting you. You're beautiful. I enjoy our talks. You already know I want more. And when you kissed me back just now… You want more, too."

Her cheeks flamed. "And if I said I was just horny?"

His mouth curved knowingly. "Yes. But if you didn't desire me, it wouldn't matter. You wouldn't kiss me like that. Did you kiss Tim the same way?"

She recoiled. "I didn't kiss him. He kissed me. And I shut it down."

"So, you've been with Tim?" His voice sharpened, edged with anger.

"No!" she stammered. "He came by earlier, grabbed me, kissed me. That's it. I yelled at him, and he left."

Before she could breathe, Nathaniel moved. Faster than she could blink. He grabbed her, rage flashing in his eyes, and crushed his mouth to hers. The kiss was rough, demanding. And yet… her body betrayed her, yielding against him, answering heat with heat.

When she finally tore free, lips swollen, her voice shook. "Wow. I've never been kissed like that."

"I'm sorry," he said, tone softer now, regret slipping in. "But I warned you. I'm a jealous man."

She steadied her breath. "I'm not sorry about the kiss. But I won't deal with jealousy. Either control it, or we're done."

His mouth twitched into the faintest smile. "So be it. I wish to remain your friend. Shall we go?"

"Yes. I think we should let this go."

He extended his arm. She slid her hand into the crook of his elbow. "I hope you can forgive me," he murmured as they walked out to his car.

Nathaniel held the door open, waiting until she slid inside before shutting it gently. He circled, slid into the driver's seat, and the car hummed to life.

At the restaurant, menus were a formality. They ordered quickly, filling the wait with small talk. Dominique ate her food, but Nathaniel's plate sat untouched. He only watched her with a faint smile. She noticed, thought it strange, but bit back the question.

At the theater, he kept his hands to himself this time, no casual arm draped across her shoulders. She wasn't sure if she missed it or felt relieved. Afterward, they drifted toward a quiet park, her mind circling back to what had happened at her house earlier.

"Something weighs on you," Nathaniel said softly. His gaze lingered on her face. "Is it because of earlier?"

Dominique hesitated, then nodded. "Yes. I've never really dealt with jealousy before. I don't like how it felt. You were furious, Nathaniel. It made me wonder just how far you'd go."

"I would never hurt you," he said quickly. "I only ask you to forgive me. Perhaps we can—"

A sharp voice cut through the night.

"Hey, pretty lady!" a man's voice rang across the park, cutting him off. "What's your name?"

Dominique turned. "Dominique," she answered before she could stop herself. "Who are you?"

"Name's Jacob. This is my park. And these are my friends."

Two women and another man flanked him. Dominique stiffened. She knew the women from the bar.

"This is a public park," she said, squaring her shoulders. "The city owns it. And if you think we're scared of you, you're wrong."

Jacob's eyes slid past her to Nathaniel. "You, I'm not worried about. Him? His kind doesn't belong here. Best you two move along."

"His kind?" Dominique repeated, frowning. "He's just like you and me."

Jacob smirked. "Right. Just like you and me. What do you say?" he asked Nathaniel.

Nathaniel's voice stayed even. "We don't want trouble. The lady doesn't understand boundaries."

"Hmm. So she doesn't know. I'll let this one slide. Don't come back here."

Nathaniel inclined his head. "We're leaving." He caught Dominique's hand and tugged her along.

She resisted at first, but his pace quickened until she stumbled. Without a word, he scooped her into his arms and carried her the rest of the way. At the car, he set her down, opened the door, and slid behind the wheel. The tires screeched as he tore out of the lot.

Dominique gripped the seat. "What the hell was that? They can't just claim a public park."

"Trust me," Nathaniel said, jaw tight. "Those are bad people. You don't want to get mixed up with them."

"What did he mean when he said I didn't know?"

His hands tightened on the steering wheel. He didn't answer, only drove faster. Not toward the club. Not toward her home.

"Nathaniel?" Dominique pressed, her voice sharp. "What was he talking about?"

"That man's a menace," Nathaniel said finally. "He's deep into crime. Stay away from him."

"That's not what he implied. He acted like you were the problem. 'Your kind isn't welcome here.' What does that mean?"

"I'm just a businessman," Nathaniel said flatly. "Don't put weight on the words of a criminal. When the time is right, I'll tell you more about myself. But not tonight."

Dominique sank back against the seat, staring out the window. Why was he being so damn secretive? It felt like she'd stumbled into the Twilight Zone. How had her life become so strange?

Nathaniel finally slowed, turning into a familiar field. "We can walk here without visitors," he said. "It's deserted."

He came around to open her door, offering his arm. She hesitated but looped her hand through. They walked in silence at first until he asked how she'd been holding up.

"I'm doing better than I thought," she said. "Lisa, Shane's wife, called yesterday. She's made the funeral arrangements. It's tomorrow at two. If you wanted to go, we could ride together."

"I'm sorry, Dominique. I can't. I have a meeting. But please tell Lisa I'm sorry. If she needs anything, I'll help."

Her heart sank with disappointment. "Sure. Maybe we could do something during the day, then? I'll be back at work this weekend."

"Dominique, I run my business during the day. I can't just take off."

"You can't take a day off?" Dominique asked, incredulous.

"Not right now. I have a lot of important business deals going on. Perhaps later..."

She stopped walking, exasperated. "This feels one-sided. Whenever I ask about you, you shut down. How am I supposed to decide if I want more than friendship if you won't let me in?"

Nathaniel sighed. "You're right. What would you like to know, Dominique?"

"How did you meet your wife?"

His expression shuttered, but after a beat, he answered. "While I was out riding. She was younger than me, the most beautiful woman I'd ever seen. We were young. Too young."

"What drew you to her?"

A small smile tugged his lips. "She was so alive. Fiery temper, but underneath, a kindness I'd never known. Most women in my life wanted one thing. I didn't always say no to that."

"Do you think anyone could bring you as much happiness as she did?"

"Yes." His eyes caught hers, pulling her in.

"Why do you like me?" Dominique asked.

"Because you draw me in. You also have an old soul like me. And you care for everyone around you, never yourself."

Dominique laughed bitterly. "You don't know me. I've been selfish. I put what I wanted above everything, no matter who it hurt."

"I can't see it. Was this just a phase in your life?"

"No." Her voice cracked. "I tried to end it all once. After Tim. The pain... the broken heart... I wanted it gone. Melissa tried, but she couldn't fix me."

Nathaniel's steps faltered. "You tried to kill yourself?"

"Yes." Her fingers lifted automatically to her necklace.

"Dominique, I have to know. What does the necklace symbolize? You always reach for it."

Dominique swallowed hard. "It calms me. You asked me once if I had children. I don't have any kids, but I was pregnant. I lost the baby, had her cremated. The necklace holds her ashes."

Nathaniel's voice dropped. "I'm sorry. If I'd known, I would never have asked." He drew her into his arms, and she wept against him.

When she finally pulled back, embarrassed, she muttered, "Sorry. I probably ruined your jacket."

"The jacket can be cleaned. I'm glad you let me hold you. That you trust me with this."

She gave a weak smile. "I don't know why, but I feel like I've known you forever. Still, you're hiding something. The real Nathaniel stays just out of reach."

"We all have our secrets. You'll know mine in time."

"You already know mine. Those were my biggest ones."

"They may be your biggest," he said gently, "but not all. Mystery remains, Dominique. And I want to unravel it."

"Do you want children, Nathaniel?"

Nathaniel stopped walking. "Sadly, I can't have children."

"Oh." She blinked. "What if you were with someone who wanted them?"

"We would have to discuss it. If she wants children more than me, we would have to part ways. I wouldn't hold it against her if she couldn't have children, but I suppose everyone is different."

"Would you ever consider adopting?"

"No. My life is too chaotic. I wouldn't burden a woman with raising a child alone while I'm consumed with business."

Dominique's chest ached. She'd always wanted kids. Could she give that up for him? He'd never opened up before, so she let it go for now. Those thoughts were for later.

Up ahead, a house loomed. Dominique froze. "I thought you said this field was deserted. Is that house occupied?"

"The field is deserted. The house is not. You didn't see the house the first time, so I saw no need to mention it."

"Do you know the owner? I'd rather not get arrested for trespassing."

Nathaniel laughed. "This is my property. I didn't think you'd be comfortable coming home with me, so we stayed in the field."

She studied the silhouette in the moonlight: a massive Victorian-style house. Exactly the kind of place he'd live. Curiosity burned, but unease won out. "Should we head back?"

"If you wish."

They returned to the car. Dominique's mind churned. The night had been… interesting. And unsettling. She had more questions about Nathaniel than ever. Something was just off about him.

When he pulled up at her house, he walked her to the door. He leaned in, but she pressed a hand to his chest, stopping him.

He sighed. "So no goodnight kiss?"

"No. I appreciate tonight, I really do. But I told you… friends only."

"You're very frustrating, Dominique," he murmured, a small smile tugging at his lips. "Can you honestly tell me that you don't want me?"

Heat rose in her cheeks. "Attraction isn't everything. You know I'm attracted to you. But that can't be all there is. I need to be sure. And your jealousy? That scares me."

"Any man would be jealous where you're concerned. And I'm not the only one." His eyes darkened. "If you think all that binds us is attraction, I'll show you otherwise. For now… goodnight."

Dominique lingered at the door, heart hammering. Was he talking about Tim being jealous? She sighed, grabbed her car keys, and headed out. The bar would be closed by now, but Tim should still be there cleaning. She needed answers about Jacob and those women. And about what they knew of Nathaniel.

Chapter 17

When Dominique arrived at the bar, she asked Tim to meet her in the office once he finished cleaning.

She retreated to her office and waited. An hour later, Tim walked in, dropped into the chair across from her, and studied her. His expression hardened, a deep scowl tugging at his brows.

"Tim, I need to ask about the two women who came in the other night."

"Why? They haven't been back. And why are you dressed up? Weren't you supposed to be resting?"

"That's none of your business. I'm asking about the women."

"So I kissed you earlier, you responded, and now you turn around and go running to someone else?"

"I'm not doing this with you, Tim. My life isn't your concern, and I didn't get with anyone. Just answer the question. Who are they?"

"You say that, but I can tell. You got dressed up, and at the very least, you made out with him. His scent's all over you."

Dominique's jaw clenched. "You're impossible. My life stopped being your business a long time ago. Now answer the damn question."

"They're both loose cannons. Surprised you didn't recognize the blonde. You sure blew up the last time you saw her," Tim said, watching Dominique's face darken.

"She's the whore you cheated on me with?" Dominique hissed.

"I told you before, I never cheated. She wanted me, but I turned her down. I didn't sleep with her until after you broke up with me. Yeah, I drank too much, but it wasn't that bad until I met her."

Dominique's hands clenched into fists in her lap. He'd still been seeing that whore after swearing he hadn't. What did it matter now? They weren't together anymore. She forced in a breath and let it out slowly.

"I don't know why it matters. I'm not with her, haven't been in a long time. She dragged me into trouble, and her sister's just as bad. I told them not to come back here. I meant it when I said I still care about you. I'd cut off my arm if it would bring you back to me," Tim said.

"It won't," Dominique said coldly. "So don't bother."

"Why are you even asking about them?"

"Let's just say I ran into them with some guy named Jacob. He seemed to know Nathaniel. Nathaniel didn't seem to like him much, but all he'd say was that Jacob's a bad guy. I need to know if Nathaniel's mixed up in something."

Tim's face stayed cold, but his shoulders tightened. What was it about this man that riled everyone up? Clearly, Tim knew him, but would he actually say anything now that Nathaniel's name was on the table?

"Nathaniel's right. Jacob's bad news. He runs a gang. Those women are in it. Stay away from all of them. They'll hurt you if they think you crossed them. Where did you run into them?"

"At the park," Dominique said quietly.

"There really are things that go bump in the night, Dominique. Be careful," Tim said before walking out.

Dominique scowled after him. What the hell did that mean? Things don't go bump in the night. And she didn't need Tim warning her. She could take care of herself.

Dominique stepped out of her office and caught up with Melissa. She was mid-sentence about the funeral when Tim appeared beside them.

"I can take you tomorrow, if you want," Tim said.

"Why would you go to a funeral for a man you don't even know?"

"I'm going for you, not him. I'll drive, so if it gets too much, you don't have to handle it alone."

"She's riding with me. You're not needed," Melissa snapped.

"And if you can't drive? Fine. I'll take both of you. Don't worry, I won't hit on her at a funeral. I'm not that much of a bastard."

"Let's agree to disagree on that one," Melissa sneered.

"Fine. Melissa, come by my place tomorrow. Tim can pick us up."

"Seriously? You're letting him back in?" Melissa's gray eyes darkened with anger.

"It's just a ride. Not an invitation back in. I wanted Nathaniel to drive, but he can't," Dominique said.

"Yeah, you can forget him coming to anything like this," Tim said dryly.

"And why would you say that, Tim?"

"I know things about him you don't. Don't ask. I won't tell," Tim replied.

"You know nothing about Nathaniel! A ten-second chat doesn't count!" Dominique snapped, irritated that he was keeping secrets, too.

Dominique shoved the back door open and stormed out, Tim and Melissa trailing. She spotted the blonde perched on Tim's car hood and rolled her eyes.

Their eyes met. The blonde looked away, then back, igniting Dominique's fury. She sneered. Melissa grabbed her, practically dragging her toward the cars. Dominique forced herself to calm down before she did something reckless.

Chapter 18

"Roxy, get off my car. I told you to stay away," Tim said sharply.

"Oh, come on, baby. I just wanted to see you," Roxy purred.

"No. I've said this a million times. It's over between us. Haven't you ruined my life enough?"

"Ruined it? I gave you a gift. A new life. One you've excelled at. You're stronger and faster than ever. You've won your place among us," Roxy said, gaze flicking back to Dominique.

"Whose the chick? Saw her in the park earlier with our enemy. Which is why I'm here. Jacob sent me after you. He doesn't like the possibility of a threat on his doorstep. Bet he'd be interested to know you work for the woman with that thing."

"She's irrelevant. None of your business. Just some girl," Tim said firmly.

"Then why do I smell her all over you?" Roxy pressed.

"Because I work for her. Stay away, Roxy. I mean it."

"You weren't just around her. Dominique. Wasn't she the one who broke you? I was there when she tore you down," Roxy said, pressing close.

Tim shoved her back. "You're why she hates me. I was a mess, I know. But you ruined me. I only slept with you to forget her. I don't want you. Get in your car. I'll go meet Jacob."

Tim waited until Roxy drove off, ensuring she wouldn't follow Dominique. Her vindictive streak worried him; now that she knew Dominique, she could sabotage any chance he had, no matter how slim.

Dominique was still attracted to him. If he could just keep Nathaniel away, he might regain her trust. He growled at the thought of that scumbag. She didn't know how many secrets he was hiding. Tim wanted to tell her his own secret, if only she'd listen.

Tim arrived at Jacob's place and entered. Jacob had called a full meeting, tense over the "threat" Nathaniel posed. No one like Nathaniel had been around in years, but Tim doubted he was a real danger. If he were, Tim would be first.

Was Nathaniel here for Dominique? Or just a coincidence? Tim hadn't believed in soulmates until two years ago. Could Nathaniel truly think Dominique was his?

Tim listened as Jacob briefed everyone to watch Nathaniel. Tim would, too, but not for Jacob's sake. He'd keep Nathaniel away from Dominique if he could.

After the meeting, Tim noticed Roxy pointing at him while talking to Jacob. That was bad. If she involved Jacob in her schemes… trouble. She was with Jacob now, even as she chased Tim.

Did Jacob know? Probably not. He wouldn't tolerate it. Maybe he should tell him, but Jacob might see it as a challenge. Tim didn't want that burden. He headed home to think.

Chapter 19

Tim picked Dominique and Melissa up. He opened the car door for Dominique. She hesitated briefly, then got in. They drove to the funeral, arriving together. Dominique and Melissa approached Lisa.

Dominique saw Tim sitting with Danny as she spoke to Lisa. She watched as he spent time with the little boy, coaxing him from tears to conversation. While the adults focused solely on Lisa, Tim gave him attention, something no one else seemed to think about. Danny was hurting, too.

She was quietly moved that Tim had done the one thing no one else had: brought comfort to a little boy who had just lost his father.

When Tim joined them, she didn't move away. She'd reward his kindness to Danny by not doing so. When the funeral started, the tears came again. Tim drew her close, holding her at his side.

She allowed herself to seek comfort in his warmth. When the funeral was over, Tim held onto her elbow, guiding her to the car. Funerals exhausted her, so she leaned on him for strength. He opened her door, helping her into the car.

He drove them to Dominique's. Melissa left after a short chat; Tim remained.

"Do you need something, Tim?" Dominique asked, keeping her tone civil after his support.

"Yes, but I know I can't have it. Maybe at another time. Could I pick you up later for work?"

"I don't need a ride. I'll drive myself."

"Just humor me for once?"

"No. I haven't had a seizure since the first one. I rested and slept a lot. I'm fine now."

"I thought we made progress today," Tim said.

"I'm being civil, Tim, but there's no excuse for what you did. It's unforgivable. And you still have that… woman. Why chase someone you can't have?"

"I'm not with Roxy. She's crazy, won't leave me alone. Once she's got you, you belong to her, no one else. But she knows I don't want her."

"Didn't seem like she knew that last night, judging by her behavior."

"She knew, but she'll keep trying," Tim sighed.

"Sounds familiar, doesn't it? If you find her annoying, imagine me! You're doing the same to me."

"No. I'm trying to get you back because I know what I lost. I never stopped loving you. Roxy was just a fling after we broke up."

"Yeah, just couldn't wait to get me out of the picture, huh? Bet my side of your bed wasn't even cold before you slept with her, if you didn't do it before I left you. That isn't love," Dominique snarled.

"You're right. I was pathetic. I wasn't thinking about love, just how bad life was. I've made many mistakes, but I've fixed myself. Please, give me a second chance. I just want you back in my life."

"I don't know. I've hated you for so long; I don't know if I can let you back in."

"Would you try? Let me be your friend, maybe eventually I can explain why I was such an ass."

"I don't know. I'll try to be civil, but that's all. I don't see us ever being friends, let alone more."

"How about I pick you up later? Just civility. You let someone care for you, okay?"

Dominique sighed, agreeing. Regret hit immediately. Tim leaned down; she flinched, expecting a kiss.

"Thank you," was whispered against the shell of her ear.

Dominique nodded and went inside, feeling his gaze follow her. Changing, thoughts raced. Nathaniel in the friend zone, Tim wanting the same. She laughed quietly; two hot guys, both friend-zoned. What was she doing with her life?

***

Later that night, Tim picked her up. He tried small talk; Dominique gave curt yes or no answers. This was harder than expected. She turned on the radio; a favorite song played, and she sang along.

At the club, they walked in together. Melissa pounced on Dominique, pulling her away from Tim. Little did they know, Tim could hear every word they said.

"Why did you arrive together? Did he stay at your place after I left?" Melissa asked.

"For a few minutes. Only to ask if he could drive me to work. He wants a second chance, or at least to be friends," Dominique replied.

"You're not seriously thinking of that, are you?"

"I don't know, Mel. We have history. The end was dark, but the beginning wasn't. I can't say if I'd give him a second chance, even as friends. I offered civility. That's all I can give. He claims he has reasons for his actions. Claims he never cheated, but I saw the women he left that bar with. If he wasn't screwing them, then what the hell was he doing with them?"

"Please, don't go back to him. He broke you once. Don't let him do it again."

"I won't, Melissa. I know how to protect my heart. That's why I friend-zoned Nathaniel," Dominique said.

"You did what?!" Melissa exclaimed.

"I don't know if I can risk falling for someone just to be hurt again. If he stays the same, then maybe I can see us being more. But I just don't know. Tim being my only relationship has messed me up mentally."

"Be careful and give Nathaniel a chance. He doesn't seem like that kind of guy."

"Yeah, same thing I thought about Tim," Dominique said, glancing towards Tim, and meeting his gaze.

Nathaniel arrived shortly after. Once open, they went on stage and played.

After playing, Dominique sat at her usual table. Post and Nathaniel joined her.

"So, Dom, when's the final test for the project?" Post asked.

"I haven't thought about it yet, Post. Can we discuss it later?"

"Sure. Just checking if you'd spoken to Melissa about it."

"You're working on a project?" Nathaniel asked.

"Ow!" Post exclaimed as Dominique kicked him. "Why'd you do that?"

"I take it I wasn't supposed to know about this project?" Nathaniel asked.

Dominique sighed. "Only me, Post, and Melissa know. I wanted to keep it quiet until it was ready."

"I can leave if you need privacy. But you've piqued my interest. Would investors be involved?"

"Dom, tell him. If he's interested, he could help, and we could make more," Post suggested.

"Damnit, Post. I wanted to wait. Cat's out of the bag now. Nathaniel, I've created something like VR, but more live, interactive."

"I'd love to see it. Can you show me?" Nathaniel asked.

Dominique hesitated, then led him upstairs to the machines. Nathaniel inspected them, asking questions. Post explained tech details; Dominique covered the software.

"I'd love to test it. Can I?" Nathaniel asked.

Post said, "Yeah, Dominique. Let him do the final test with you."

Dominique's eyes narrowed in anger and suspicion. Was he just helping with funding? Or was he in on hooking her up with Nathaniel?

"What's the final test?" Nathaniel asked.

"A simulation linking both people so they feel each other and interact in the story. Anything you want, but we must test if both can sense each other's actions," Post explained.

"I don't mind if you don't, Dominique," Nathaniel said, smirking, his eyes all predator.

A shiver went down her spine at that look.

Chapter 20

Dominique hesitated at the sight of the simulator. This test felt too intimate, too dangerous. But Post was already prepping the machine, ignoring her reluctance. Nathaniel extended his hand. After a beat, she slipped hers into his.

He stepped into the simulator. Dominique sighed. There was no escaping this. She fitted the helmet over his head.

"We have to picture the same place, or we won't link up," she instructed.

"Your home," Nathaniel said. "You'll be comfortable there."

"Alright. When it starts, watch for the light. Blank your mind, then focus on where you want to be."

He grinned. "See you at your house, Dominique."

With another sigh, she climbed into the second machine, helmet snug. Closing her eyes, she pictured the white waiting room and lowered herself to the floor.

In moments, her front porch materialized around her. Footsteps echoed, and Nathaniel strode up the steps, entering through the door.

"Incredible," Nathaniel murmured, sliding an arm around her waist. "I've seen VR, but this… this is real. It pulls you inside."

He drew her closer and pressed his mouth to hers. A thrill shot down to her toes. Why did he affect her like this? She kissed back until his hands trailed lower, brushing her breasts, sliding toward her hips. She broke away, breath shaky.

"Even here, you pull away," he said, a pout tugging at his lips.

"I said just friends. This isn't that."

"Isn't this machine for living out desires?" he pressed.

"Well, yes, but—" His mouth silenced her.

"Then let's live it. We're not really touching, only imagining. A fantasy, nothing more."

She hesitated. She'd fantasized about him before, but acting it out, even virtually, could change everything between them. No, it wasn't real touch, but still. How could she go back to "just friends" after this?

Nathaniel tugged her close. She swore she could feel his clothes brushing her skin. Glancing down, she froze. She was in a black lace teddy. When she looked up, Nathaniel was grinning.

"You said it's all imagination," he teased. "I like this look on you. How would you like to see me?"

The stray thought of him naked bloomed, and in an instant, he was. She flushed hot. Nathaniel laughed.

"Fair enough," he said, eyes dark with hunger.

His gaze burned with raw lust. He scooped her up, carrying her inside. Yet the scene shifted into a hallway, then a bedroom she didn't recognize. Sliding her down his body, he set her on her feet.

She closed her eyes, savoring his body pressed against hers, hard and ready at her stomach. He stepped back, letting her see him. His form shifted, slightly different than what she had imagined.

"I want you to see the real me," he said.

Her gaze devoured him. Not bulky, but defined. Scars crossed his skin, not a turnoff for her. And when her eyes reached lower, her face flamed. His cock was bigger than she had imagined.

"Will you let me see the real you," he asked softly, "or must I imagine?"

"I-I…" she stammered, torn over letting him see her.

Tim had been the only one to see her fully; every scar, every flaw. Could she let Nathaniel? As if sensing her doubt, he drew her close.

"I don't care about imperfections," he murmured. "What you see as flaws makes you unique to me."

Embarrassment burned her cheeks, yet his words soothed her. She shut her eyes, drew a breath, and released it. She imagined herself bare, stepping back so he could see.

She opened her eyes to find him studying her, as though memorizing every detail. His breath came harder, eyes black as a void yet burning with hunger that sent a shiver through her. Heat coiled low in her belly, tightening.

Nathaniel's toothy grin turned him into a predator as he yanked her close. His kiss stole her breath, and when he finally broke it, his palm lingered warm against her cheek.

"You are beautiful, Dominique. More beautiful than I imagined."

Tears pricked Dominique's eyes. She wasn't beautiful; at least not to herself. A scar marked her stomach from the miscarriage, smaller ones littered her arms, and a white blotch in her elbow crease lingered from a childhood burn. Yet Nathaniel looked at her like she was the most beautiful woman alive.

The next kiss was softer, but his hands claimed her, lifting her off the ground. She wrapped her legs around him, clinging as he carried her to the bed. He laid her down gently before breaking the kiss.

His mouth blazed a trail down her neck to her breasts. Dominique gasped as he took one into his mouth, sucking, tongue flicking, setting her body on fire. He lavished the same attention on the other as her fingers threaded through his hair, loving the silkiness of it over her hands.

Lips trailed down her stomach, lingering over her scar. She moaned as his fingertips skimmed her sides, sliding down to her thighs, teasing until he reached her knees. Then his hands kneaded their way back up, his mouth licking a path to her hips.

His tongue traced circles on her hips before spreading her legs wider. He licked slow, deliberate strokes up her inner thighs, pressing dangerously close to her pussy, making her body spasm with pleasure.

When his mouth found her folds, Dominique gasped. Heat pooled as her belly coiled tight, ready to burst. His hands slid beneath her, lifting her. His tongue moved in fast, tight circles over her clit. Her body shook from the pace of it.

"Nathaniel!" she cried as her orgasm ripped through her, arching her off the bed.

Nathaniel kissed up her body, pressing his length against her. Her hands roamed down his chest, over rippling muscle, until she wrapped her fingers around him.

His groan deepened as her fingers stroked and squeezed. Their kiss burned as she guided him to her opening, desperate to know what it felt like to have him inside.

His hands slid under her, positioning her as he thrust inside. She moaned into his mouth as he filled and stretched her, his slow rolling hips curling her toes.

She met his thrusts eagerly, her belly coiling tighter with each one. His lips brushed her neck, her fingers sliding down his back, until he suddenly stopped. Dominique groaned at the loss.

Pulling out, he flipped her onto her stomach. His tongue glided up her spine, causing a shiver to run down it. Fingers slid between her thighs, entering her with maddening slowness as his tongue pressed into her spine between her shoulder blades. His mouth trailed bites from her shoulders to her neck.

"You have no idea what you do to me, Dominique. You drive me insane," he whispered in her ear.

"I could say the same," she whispered, hips bucking at the growing pleasure.

When his hand slipped away, she grunted, "Nathaniel, please!"

He thrust in, then pulled out, teasing her several times before asking, "Is this what you want?"

"Yes!" she cried.

He thrust harder, grinding into her. "Then show me."

He withdrew, lying back. Dominique climbed atop him without hesitation, kissing and caressing as he had her. His body responded to her touch, groaning as she ground against him.

His hands gripped her hips, guiding himself toward her, but she teased, sliding so he rubbed only against her clit. Panting, she reveled in the torment.

At last, she slammed herself down onto him. He jerked inside her, deliciously. She alternated between grinding hard and nearly pulling free before crashing back down.

Nathaniel thrust upward, rolling his hips in a rhythm that had her nails digging into his chest. He moved so fast her body trembled from the vibrations, then seized her hips to pound into her harder.

"Open your eyes, Dominique. Look at me," he demanded.

Dominique's eyes fluttered open to narrow slits. Nathaniel's hands roamed up her body, cupping her breasts as she rode him. She pressed her hands over his, urging him to squeeze harder, the sharp edge of pain only heightening her pleasure.

Nathaniel growled and pushed upright, capturing her breast in his mouth. His teeth bit down while his tongue flicked over her nipple. His free hand kneaded the other breast, rolling the sensitive peak between his fingers.

Dominique tangled her fingers in his hair, arching to press her breast deeper into his mouth. Tremors rippled through her body as she hovered on the brink of release.

Nathaniel crushed her against him, squeezing until her breath hitched. Bracing on one hand, he drew his knees up against her back, driving into her with brutal leverage. His other hand wrapped around her throat, lightly squeezing until he stole her breath.

Dominique screamed as release tore through her, wetness spilling down her thighs and over Nathaniel. He sank his teeth into her shoulder as he came deep inside her, making her gasp. His fingers tangled in her hair as his mouth crushed hers, tongues clashing, riding out their pleasure.

Nathaniel broke the kiss, resting his head against her chest. Dominique lowered hers onto his and stroked his hair, waiting as her racing heartbeat and ragged breaths slowly steadied.

Dominique pulled back, meeting Nathaniel's gaze as she rose unsteadily to her feet. She shut her eyes, and suddenly they were back on her porch, clothed. Nathaniel drew her close for one last kiss before she vanished from his arms.

Dominique ripped the helmet off, gasping for air. Her body felt spent, yet her heart pounded, sweat clinging to her skin. She couldn't face Nathaniel… not yet. That had been the most intense sex of her life, even though it hadn't really happened. Her body felt it, but her mind knew the truth.

She lingered in the machine, trying to collect herself, until a knock came at the door.

"Are you alright?" Melissa called.

Dominique hesitated. Physically, she was fine. *Mentally?* Not so much. She finally stood and opened the door.

"Finally! I was worried about you! Post told me you hadn't come out of the machine, even though Nathaniel had. He waited a couple of minutes for you, then said he'd see you downstairs. Post thought maybe you were embarrassed about something that happened in there."

"The machine works, Melissa. That was the last test, and it passed with flying colors."

"Great! Now tell me what happened in there. Dish girl! Inquiring minds want to know!" Melissa laughed.

"I am so not going there, Melissa!" Dominique exclaimed.

"Ohhhhh! You two had sex, didn't you? I knew it! That's why you were too embarrassed to come out. Was it hot and steamy? Come on, Dom, tell me. You know I'm going to bug you until you do."

"Melissa, I love you, but you are grating on my last nerve," Dominique ground out.

"That's a yes!" Melissa shouted as she walked away, still laughing.

Dominique shook her head, sighing, as she went back downstairs. She needed a drink. Sitting at the bar, she didn't have to wait long. Tim approached, eyebrows furrowed, sniffing the air.

"You smell strongly of someone who just had sex," he said.

"What?" Dominique asked.

His eyes darkened. "Did you just have sex with Nathaniel? Is that why you took him upstairs?"

"No! I would not have sex with someone in this club, in public!" Dominique exclaimed.

"You obviously did, or you wouldn't smell like sex. But you don't smell like another person. Just your scent of sex."

"Tim, you cannot smell sex on someone or anyone else, for that matter. Just give me a drink. A screwdriver, please," Dominique said.

"Should you be drinking after what happened before?"

Dominique's eyebrows shot up as she scowled at Tim. *The audacity of this motherfucker.*

"I'm not a drunk, Tim. I rarely drink. Back then, I drank to kill pain. Now, I drink for special occasions, or when something happens I need to get over. And since you work for me, you don't get to say no. Now fix my damn drink!"

Tim mixed the drink and set it in front of her, standing close, eyes boring into hers. She shifted uncomfortably, noting the flare of his nostrils, furrow of his brow, and clenched jaw. She'd only seen that look once before… right before he hit her. Dominique stood and moved toward her table.

Nathaniel sat there, gazing at her, so she turned back toward the bar. Tim followed her every movement. She turned around. Could she go over there and face Nathaniel or not? He seemed the safer option.

Biting her lip, she decided to put her big girl panties on and walked over to the table, sitting across from Nathaniel. He smiled, and all she could think about was what he'd done with that mouth in the machine. Heat roared to her face and ears.

"You're enjoying this, aren't you?" she whispered.

"I'm enjoying the pleasure I feel. Your machine works remarkably well. My body responded to what happened, causing me to orgasm in reality as well. I had to clean up. Did you have the same effect?"

"Yes," Dominique admitted, cheeks flaming. "That's the point of the machine. You can do anything and stay out of trouble in real life."

"Well, I must say, you did it. But now I wonder if you'll shut me out after we've had sex?"

"Technically, we didn't have sex. We imagined having sex."

"If we both got off, then I'd say we did. It's like phone sex. You don't touch, but your words affect the other person, and they respond," Nathaniel replied.

"Um… yeah. I'm not sure how I'll act around you now. You already knew I found you attractive, but this is another level. You didn't know my likes, dislikes, or what I look like naked.

Now you know an intimate part of me that only one other person ever did," Dominique said, eyes flicking to the bar.

Tim glared at both of them, scowl darkening, but Nathaniel just smiled. Dominique rolled her eyes at the silent exchange.

Nathaniel's gaze returned to her. "I would love to help you. Would you be interested in having an investor for the machines? I think your idea is fantastic. Since I've tested it myself and know it works, I'd love to invest."

"I… I don't know. I never thought about having an investor. I only have the two machines here."

"That may be true, but they're just the beginning. Imagine a building full of machines, appointments lined up. You'd make money hand over fist," Nathaniel said.

Dominique had never considered opening a separate location for the machines or having a whole fleet of them. Could she really go into business with Nathaniel? What if they stopped being friends, or if a relationship went sour? Could he end up causing problems for her?

"I can tell you're overthinking this, Dominique. There would be contracts, and I'd expect you to read them carefully before signing. I wouldn't do anything to harm a business I'm involved in, no matter what happens between us."

"Wow… you really read my mind. If you draw up the contracts, I'll look them over and see if I'm comfortable with you investing. It all depends on what you want and what you're offering."

"Alright. I'll start the contracts immediately. I think we'll make a lot of money, Dominique. More than you ever imagined."

"I'm not really focused on money. I'm comfortable. That's enough for me."

"There's nothing wrong with having money, Dominique. You can do so much with it. I help people all the time. Without it, I couldn't. Don't assume having money makes you vain or selfish."

"I didn't say that… just…" Dominique began, but her eyes drifted to the two girls back in her club.

Dominique observed them for a moment, trying to gauge if they were there to cause trouble. Tim had warned them not to return last time, so why were they back? Did they enjoy stirring things up?

"Dominique, is everything alright?" Nathaniel asked, following her gaze.

"I don't know… those two girls from the park are back. One even showed up the other night after Tim. I asked him about them; he said they were trouble. The one trying to climb over the bar is Roxy. Tim told her not to return. Excuse me, Nathaniel. I need to handle this."

Chapter 21

"Roxy, I told you not to come back. I don't want trouble. And you're with Jacob now. Always knew you were a whore, but this? Pathetic," Tim snapped.

"Don't you dare call me a whore! I'm just trying to have a little fun. Come on, Tim. It's been a while. Let's get out of here," Roxy said, leaning over the bar, trying to grab him.

"No. I'm working and I don't want you anyway," Tim said.

"Is there a problem?" Dominique cut in, stepping up.

"No problem. Just talking with my friend. Not that it's any of your business," Roxy sneered.

"It is my business. This is my bar. Stay off the bar, or I'll kick you out," Dominique warned.

"You can't make me leave! I'm just talking to Tim." Roxy pouted, batting lashes at him. "Tell her, baby."

"Tim doesn't decide who stays. He works for *me*," Dominique snapped.

"Oh, I know you. You're the one who broke Tim's heart. I picked up the pieces, didn't I, baby?" Roxy purred.

Dominique's eyes narrowed. "And I know you. You're the tramp who slept with my fiancé. I didn't leave him broken. I saw him walk out of that bar with you and plenty of others. He's no saint."

"He wasn't your fiancé when I slept with him. He wouldn't, no matter how much I tried. Just got mixed up with the wrong crowd… us." Roxy laughed cruelly. "What's wrong, didn't know? Tim told me he tried to explain it wasn't what it looked like."

Dominique's eyes flicked to Tim. He stared at the floor, jaw tight, anger simmering. He'd sworn he never cheated, and Roxy had just backed it up, but the crease in Dominique's brow showed she wasn't sure whether to believe it.

He finally lifted his head, shoulders squared, eyes darting between the two women.

"What's wrong, honey? Upset to find out you're the villain?" Roxy taunted.

Dominique's voice was ice. "No. You're still a whore. I'll always be above a barfly. Leave. And don't come back."

"You can't do that! I'll go where I want!" Roxy shouted.

"Keep dreaming, sweetie. I've got the right to refuse service. Come here again, I'll toss you out myself," Dominique smirked.

Roxy shot Tim a look. He only shrugged. Dominique moved toward the door, but Roxy swung back a hand to strike. Nathaniel caught her wrist midair and twisted, breaking it. Roxy shrieked.

Nathaniel bent low, his voice sharp. "You'll heal fast. I know what you are. Next time you won't be so lucky. Come after Dominique again, and you'll regret it."

Tim's lips twitched despite himself. He hated Nathaniel, but hearing him defend Dominique stirred a grudging gratitude.

Roxy bared her teeth. "I'm coming for you. I'll take her out first. And since Tim's one of us, he'll have no choice but to join."

Tim's face darkened. He'd never turn on Dominique. Nathaniel's reply, though, made his blood roar with rage.

"Tim means nothing to me. Killing him would be a pleasure. But I'll be waiting. You won't touch Dominique," Nathaniel promised, releasing her wrist.

"Your pet dies by my hands before this ends," Roxy spat, storming out.

Dominique's eyes flicked to Nathaniel. He only shrugged. Tim prayed she hadn't heard Roxy's threat. Nathaniel strolled back to the bar, and Tim gave him a curt nod.

"You heard her. Where do you stand, Tim? Going to hurt Dominique?" Nathaniel asked.

"I'd never hurt Dominique. Not on purpose. I've hurt her before, but I'm not that man anymore."

"I'll be watching over her. As long as we understand each other, it'll be fine," Nathaniel said flatly.

"I'll be watching over her, too," Tim said firmly. "I don't know what you think you have with Dominique, but I've known her longer, and I love her."

"Someone like you couldn't understand what I feel for Dominique. When the time is right, I'll tell her, and she will understand." With that, he turned and walked away.

Tim's jaw tightened as he watched Nathaniel leave. Who the hell did that guy think he was? He had no claim on Dominique. And what was that cryptic talk about having something Tim "wouldn't understand"? Tim shook it off and went back behind the bar, the motions of bartending steadying his hands.

The hum of conversation slowly returned as the crowd pushed the spectacle aside. Dominique slipped onto a barstool, downing one drink after another. Tim kept his eye on her, concern pulling at him, but he held his tongue. He'd driven them there tonight. No matter how much she drank, he'd get her home safely.

Chapter 22

Nathaniel slid onto the seat beside Dominique. She glanced at him once, then downed the rest of her drink in a single swallow before rising unsteadily.

"Let me take you home tonight," Nathaniel said quietly.

"I don't drink and drive. Didn't bring my car, so I drowned my anger in booze instead. I don't usually drink much. You know why. Tim's taking me home, so I'm fine."

Nathaniel's jaw tightened. "Why let him drive you? Why let him into your home if you're not interested?"

"Because I can spend time with whoever I damn well please. I asked you to take me to the funeral. You said no. Don't get mad because someone else said yes." She turned and walked off.

Tim sauntered over, smirking. "Jealousy doesn't suit you, Nathaniel. Looks like I'm winning."

Nathaniel's glare followed him. The tension between Dominique and Tim burned hotter than ever. Now Dominique was blaming him for not being there. Their earlier intimacy suddenly felt meaningless.

On his way out, Nathaniel scanned the shadows, ensuring the two women were gone. Only then did he leave, the weight of his secret pressing down on him. If he didn't tell Dominique soon, he risked losing her for good.

Chapter 23

Tim stepped into Dominique's office once the club was cleaned up. She was slumped over her desk, face buried in her arms. He touched her shoulder and gave a gentle shake. She only groaned, shifting her head a fraction.

"Dominique, time to go home," Tim murmured.

"Okay… just a minute. I feel awful. Can't remember the last time I drank this much," she mumbled, raising her head sluggishly.

"Come on, I'll get you to the car. You're not steady enough to walk," he said.

"I'll be fine," she insisted, pushing herself upright.

She stumbled as she came around the desk. Tim caught her, her palms flattening against his chest. Her head dropped there, listening to the steady thump of his heart. The pounding in her skull dulled beneath that rhythm, quickening as his pulse raced. Through the haze, she realized she was letting him hold her.

Tim lifted her chin and kissed her. The spark wasn't Nathaniel's, but it wasn't unpleasant. His tongue slid against hers, his hands roaming until they gripped her hips. With a rough pull, he lifted her onto him, holding her tight.

She hooked her legs around him, a groan of nausea slipping out. He ended the kiss and carried her to the couch, settling her in his lap. Her head fell back onto his chest, his racing heartbeat soothing the pounding in her temples.

Why was she letting him do this? She already knew. Loneliness pressed sharply against her ribs, her eyes stinging. Tim's arms enclosed her, strong and steady, his hand rubbing circles on her back. Comfort. Care. It should have been Nathaniel, but he'd left. Tim had stayed.

"You're sad. Lonely," Tim murmured. "I can feel it."

"You can't feel people's emotions. That's not humanly possible."

"Not humanly, no. But I can," Tim said firmly.

"You're losing it, Tim. Don't read into this. I just feel sick and don't want to move," Dominique muttered.

"Fine. I'll take it anyway," Tim replied.

Dominique sighed, fully aware this would give Tim the wrong idea. Regret could wait. His warmth, stronger than she remembered, and the cage of his arms dulled the ache inside her. Pressed against him, she surrendered to the strange safety of his embrace and drifted into sleep.

Chapter 24

Tim held Dominique, drinking in the closeness he'd craved. He knew exactly how things had unraveled, and it was all on him. Losing his job, one of the only steady things in his life, had driven him to the bottle. The bar became his escape, and keeping it from Dominique was his first mistake.

When he started working at the bar, the drinking spiraled. Nights that should have been hers, he gave to the bar. Not telling her about it was mistake two. To admit to the job meant admitting he'd lost the other. Instead of confessing, he drowned himself in whiskey.

Of course, she knew. She always knew his patterns. The late nights, the smell of liquor, the short fuse. Their fights had piled up, each one sharpening the edge of his temper.

His temper finally snapped one night. A fistfight, mistake three, cost him his so-called safe haven.

He'd come home raging, only to find Dominique waiting on his couch. Normally, he would've noticed her car and left, but that night he was too far gone.

The argument, mistake four, burned in his memory. Dominique shoved him, yelling that he was no better than the drunk who'd killed her parents. His fury blinded him, and his hand struck before he could stop it. The crack of impact branded itself into his soul.

The sound jolted him out of his haze. She froze, eyes wide, while his stomach dropped. He'd hit the woman he loved. Before he could stammer out an apology, she stormed out. That was the beginning of the end.

He hadn't even chased her. Just stood there, letting the rage collapse inward. It should've been his wake-up call, but instead he sank deeper, finding another bar to numb himself. Booze became an addiction he wasn't ready to quit.

That bar was mistake number five. Meeting Roxy, mistake number six, was the final blow. The choice that destroyed what was left of Dominique and him. The night that rewrote his life.

Roxy was hot, no doubt. He'd been tempted, but his thoughts had gone to Dominique, and he'd told her no.

As the night wore on, so did his drinking. By the end of the night, he could barely see straight. Too drunk to drive, he accepted Roxy's offer for a ride. But instead of home, she'd dragged him to her place. They didn't have sex. He'd never cheated on Dominique. But what happened there left him unconscious for a week.

By the time he woke and found out what really happened, he knew things with Dominique were over. There was no way he could ever tell her what really happened. Things were too far gone then.

Roxy had dragged him into Jacob's world. His anger, sharpened and twisted, proved useful there. Instead of running, he'd stayed, folding himself into Jacob's darkness. His life had been fucked up ever since.

Now, holding Dominique's sleeping form, regret crushed him. If only he could rewind, choose honesty over booze, courage over silence. If he had, she might still be his.

Tim shifted her gently, easing her into his arms. Cradling her bridal-style, he stood. Sleeping, she looked angelic. He pressed his face into her hair; same shampoo, same familiar scent he'd always loved. A kiss to her temple, then he carried her out of the office toward the back door.

Melissa waited, frowning at the sight. She muttered under her breath as she unlocked the back door. After locking up again, she went to his car and yanked the passenger door open for him.

"Thanks, Melissa," Tim said quietly. "I know you don't like me. I earned that. I was a royal asshole. But I'm trying to make it right."

Tim's jaw clenched as he listened. "You aren't good enough for Dominique. You hurt her so badly she almost ended it all. She didn't think about her family or best friend, only you. For that, I can never forgive you. And I can't see why Dominique ever would either. Be civil if you must, but don't push your luck. If you get back with her and hurt her again, I'll rip your throat out."

Tim lowered his gaze to Dominique, sleeping peacefully. "And I wouldn't blame you. I'll never hurt her again. If I'd just told her the truth earlier, none of this would've happened. That's one of my biggest regrets."

Melissa held out a key. "Take this. You'll need it to get into Dominique's house. I'm not sure if she has her keys or left them in the office. Just don't lose it."

Tim slipped the key into his pocket. "Thank you."

Melissa grunted and walked off. Tim got into his car and drove to Dominique's house.

He arrived and watched her sleep. He hesitated. He might never get another chance to hold or kiss her. Once she was sober, she likely wouldn't want anything to do with him. Today had been the first time she'd let him touch her without pulling away.

With a deep sigh, Tim stepped out and circled to her side. He lifted her in his arms and slammed the door shut behind him. The screen door was awkward with her in his arms. He laid her down on the lounge chair, then snarled as the wind carried a scent—Nathaniel. He had either been here recently or was still around.

Right then, Tim vowed not to leave Dominique alone. Nathaniel might be in the woods, watching. He took the key from his pocket and unlocked the door. Lifting Dominique again, he carried her inside, shut the door with his foot, and locked it tight.

In her bedroom, he slowly laid her on the bed. Dominique groaned but didn't wake up. Tim carefully took off her socks and shoes, setting them beside the bed. She didn't like sleeping in her clothes, so he gently pulled her shirt over her head. The black, lacy bra she wore caught his eye, but he quickly looked away, shaking his head. He moved to her jeans, easing them down slowly.

As he worked, he felt her gaze on him. Glancing up, he noticed Dominique watching him through hazy eyes. He offered a small, sheepish grin and finished taking her jeans off. Kicking off his own shoes, he climbed onto the bed beside her.

"Tim? What are you doing?" Dominique asked, confusion lacing her voice.

"Nothing, babe, go back to sleep," Tim said softly, wrapping his arms around her.

Dominique snuggled into him, her body relaxing. She was too drunk to realize what she was doing. His hands explored her body, unable to stop himself. Even in her sleep, she responded. Her nipples hardened under his touch.

His jeans strained with hardness as he slid lower, hand pressing against her stomach, then her panties. Dominique moaned in her sleep, leg hooking over his hip. Heat radiated through the lace as he rubbed her, her body already responding. Dominique had never been a big drinker, but when she drank, she always got horny. That had been some of the best sex they'd had.

His mouth found her neck, trailing down until his lips closed around a nipple, tongue circling before he bit gently. Her back arched into him. Fingers slipped under the lace, sliding inside. She gasped, pressing down, desperate for more.

The bra strap gave under his hand. Fabric slid away. He covered her breast with his mouth again, sucking hard as his fingers quickened. Her body tightened around him, every clench pulling him deeper.

Her hand dragged down his chest, over his abs, until it closed around him through the denim. His pulse thundered. His eyes flicked to her face. Her eyes were still closed, breath shallow, quick. When she pushed her hand inside his jeans, his restraint fractured. He should stop her.

Her eyes snapped open, hazy and hooded. He growled, crashing his mouth onto hers, rolling her beneath him. In a rush, he stripped his shirt and tugged her panties down, kissing his way along her thighs before rising again. She shoved at his jeans, freeing him. Her feet pushed them to the floor, her slick heat rubbing against him.

He pressed forward, grazing her clit. Her hips bucked. He wanted to fuck her senseless. But he needed to hear her say she wanted this.

He froze, panting. "Are you sure?"

"Yes," she breathed.

The word lit him on fire. He thrust into her, and her cry ripped through him. He gripped her hips, driving her into the mattress with each brutal thrust. Her nails clawed his arms, her body tightening, breaking apart around him. The sound of her moan sent shudders racing down his spine. He needed more.

He rolled, pulling her on top, guiding her into a straddle. His hand pressed between her breasts, forcing her upright as she rode him. Her head fell back, hair spilling, breasts bouncing as she moved faster, harder. God, she was beautiful in the throes of passion.

He growled, rolling her under him again, her legs thrown over his shoulders. The rhythm turned brutal, their bodies slapping together. The sound drove him to madness. She clenched around him, forcing him to thrust harder. He pinned her shoulders down, burying himself deep until release tore through him, his groan rumbling against her skin. She shattered beneath him, intensifying his pleasure.

After, he stayed inside her, chest pressed to hers, skin slick with sweat. Slowly, he shifted, wrapping her close, pulling her into his arms as her breathing evened into sleep.

Tim studied her face as she slept. Seemed impossible, but she was even more beautiful now. Finally closing his eyes, he drifted into a peaceful sleep.

Chapter 25

Dominique woke up later that morning, feeling as if her head was going to split in two. The pounding in her skull was a stark reminder of why she didn't drink that much at once. She instinctively curled into the warmth surrounding her, only to jerk upright when she realized the warmth was coming from an actual body. Panic surged through her.

Her stomach churned violently, nausea and dizziness hitting all at once. Tim, still half-asleep, sat up beside her, and Dominique's heart leapt. It wasn't a dream. What had she done? The nausea took over, propelling her toward the bathroom. She barely made it, sliding onto the floor and vomiting before she even reached the toilet.

Tim's hands were immediately on her, lifting her hair and rubbing her back with gentle strokes. Tears burned her eyes as guilt, shame, and confusion collided. How had she let herself end up in this mess? How could she have thought it was just a dream?

She knew she'd been drunk, but come on. Previous blackouts from drinking binges never led to this. But Melissa had been there in the past to prevent truly reckless decisions. Why hadn't she been there to stop Dominique from going home with Tim? The thought gnawed at her as Tim shifted behind her, continuing to soothe her.

When the nausea finally eased, Tim guided her gently back against him. He pressed a wad of toilet paper to her mouth, then placed a cool rag on her forehead. Dominique closed her eyes, letting herself rest against him for a few moments. She couldn't help but wonder, with everything spinning around her, how she was going to deal with the consequences of this mess.

"Dominique, are you okay? You seemed surprised I was here," Tim said.

"No, I'm not. I was so drunk I thought it was a dream."

Tim's arms stiffened around her. Guilt wracked her. No one wants to hear that. Thinking the other person wouldn't have done it if they had known.

"I asked if you were sure. You said yes," Tim replied, his body still taut.

She shifted carefully, wincing at the pounding in her head. When she turned, her flushed face deepened as she saw his bare skin against hers. Forcing herself to hold his gaze, she swallowed.

"I'm sorry, Tim. I was really drunk. I remember falling asleep on the couch. The rest I thought was a dream. I remember it, but I didn't think it was real."

Tim's eyes dropped. "You regret it."

"I—" Dominique's voice caught.

Her chest tightened as she avoided his gaze. The night still burned hot in her mind, too good to regret, too raw to deny. It wasn't the act she regretted. It was him. The one who'd shattered her before.

"So, you regret it," Tim said, jaw clenched. "But you thought it was a dream. You were dreaming about me, Dominique. That has to mean something." He kept his eyes fixed on the wall, anger and hurt tightening his voice.

"Yes, it was you I dreamed about," Dominique admitted, voice low. "But you were the last face I saw. Attraction was never the problem between us. Letting you back in, even for sex, is. You hurt me, Tim. So much that I nearly ended it all. I can't go back there." Her hand lifted toward him, faltered, and fell into her lap.

"I thought we were moving forward," Tim said, finally meeting her eyes. Hurt darkened his gaze. "I missed you. I regret everything I did, but holding you again, waking up with you, it felt right. Perfect. But all you see is the past."

Dominique leaned in and wrapped her arms around him. The irony wasn't lost on her. He'd been the one to break her, and now she was the one cutting him open. She buried her face against his shoulder, unwilling to add to his pain.

"I'm sorry, Tim. You say it was perfect, but it wasn't. Yes, the sex was great, but that doesn't erase years of pain. Anger doesn't vanish because you're nice for one night. I can't force myself to feel what's gone. I loved you once. I gave you everything, and you tore me apart. I never put myself back together. They say only true love turns to hate, and I loved you with everything I had," Dominique said.

His arms wrapped around her, pulling her onto his lap. He buried his face in her hair, holding so tight she could hardly breathe. His breath shuddered against her. She stayed still. He needed this. And all she could think about was how she'd needed it too when he'd been putting her through hell.

She'd needed him to hold her like this. To be there for her. He could've told her what went wrong. They could've fixed it. Instead, he'd abandoned her.

"I'm sorry, Dominique. Someday, when you're ready, I'll tell you everything. The secrets, the truth. I love you. I always have. But for now, I'll step back. I thought last night meant something, but I see it didn't. Maybe one day you'll see me as more than the asshole I was." Tim eased her off his lap and stood.

He left the bathroom without another word. Dominique stayed on the floor, listening to the sound of him dressing, of the door closing. The cool tile pressed against her burning skin, numbing the pounding in her head. She'd hurt him deeply. And there was no undoing it.

Was she just supposed to forgive and forget? Pretend it was fine? Tears slid down her face. The ache in her chest merged with the throb in her skull until darkness took her, sprawled on the cold bathroom floor.

Chapter 26

Roxy stalked the backroom, heels snapping against the floor. Rage boiled in her chest, hot enough to choke her. Her broken wrist was mended now due to Jacob forcing her to change immediately.

Jacob leaned back in his chair, eyes following her like a predator watching prey. She'd shared information about Dominique and Nathaniel with him, and now he wanted her to keep watch. But all Roxy could think about was the club's door slamming in her face and Nathaniel's grip crushing her bones.

"I'm going to rip that bitch to shreds," Roxy hissed.

Jacob's voice was silk wrapped in steel. "Naive. Why her? What makes this girl worth your fury? Do you know her?"

Her jaw tightened. She couldn't admit the truth… that Tim still wanted Dominique, that jealousy burned her alive. Jacob didn't share. If he knew she was circling back to Tim, he'd kill her.

"She hurt our Tim," Roxy snapped, dropping into Jacob's lap. "She's controlling him, and she's with the asshole who broke my wrist. I want to tear her apart just to watch him bleed inside. Tim would thank me for it."

Jacob's eyes stayed flat. "What happened with Tim is history. I don't give a damn. But the bastard who hurt you? I'll shred him. First, we need his address."

Roxy pouted, fingers tracing Jacob's jaw. "Why not let me play with her a little? I won't kill her… not intentionally."

"No," Jacob said, voice final. "We hit them together. He'll protect her, and that will force his hand. He dies, or he follows us to his torture and eventual demise. Your job is to track her. If she leads us to his place, we make a plan and strike. Tomorrow, I'll deal with Tim. He let that bastard lay hands on you, and he'll pay the price."

Roxy bit back a growl. She wanted blood, not to follow the bitch. Worse, she hadn't meant to put Tim in Jacob's sights. With Jacob, "accountable" usually meant crawling away half-dead… if you crawled away at all.

Chapter 27

Tim trudged to his car, shoulders heavy. Dominique's words clung to him. His heart felt trampled. He'd tested the limits. They'd shattered. He'd give her space, but he couldn't give up.

The attraction was there, better than nothing. But he wanted what they had. Could he get that back after everything?

Pulling into the driveway, he noticed Jacob's car. On the porch, Jacob and Roxy waited. Tim's stomach knotted. Damn it. Roxy no doubt had run to Jacob about the confrontation, even though it was her fault.

Tim climbed the steps. Roxy's eyes flicked to him, guilt and challenge warring. Not a good sign. Roxy sniffed the air, her eyes narrowing on him.

Jacob rose. One long glance, then Jacob's fist slammed into Tim's jaw, sending him sprawling across the porch.

"You let Roxy get hurt. Just stood there." Jacob's boot slammed into Tim's ribs.

Tim gasped, pushing himself up. "Roxy started this. She went for Dominique. He stopped her."

Jacob's eyes blazed. "You should've stopped him. No one lays hands on her. You hear me? Both of you are mine. We protect each other. You'll remember that after this." Fists and boots flew.

Roxy prowled forward, eyes narrowing. "Smells like her all over you. No wonder you let him," she hissed.

Tim staggered to his feet, ribs screaming. Roxy leapt onto his back as he attempted to fight back. Jacob's strength pinned him down as Roxy jumped off him. Pain ripped through his side. Blood trickled from his nose and mouth as his body burned. Jacob stepped back. Tim coughed violently, tasting iron.

Roxy crouched, teeth bared. "I'm going to kill that bitch."

"Roxy, let's go!" Jacob barked.

Silence followed. Each inhale pushed his lungs against his broken ribs. His nose, broken, causing pain with each breath. With labored breathing, he changed, feeling every broken bone reshape. Pain ripped through him as he limped into the woods.

Chapter 28

Dominique woke up shivering, still on the bathroom floor. There was still a dull ache in her head. No dreams. She was grateful for that. Her heart sank as realization hit that she'd slept with Tim and hurt him.

Sighing, she stood on shaky legs. What was she going to do? Was she going to fix things with Tim? Could she? Could she let him back in? And what about Nathaniel? His jealousy had pissed her off last night, and she'd let it.

Something was there with Nathaniel. Not love, but a pull she couldn't deny. And now, after Tim… had she ruined any chance of it?

She shook her head and stepped into the shower, heat rolling over her tight muscles. By the time she dressed, it was already late.

Unable to find her keys or purse, she called Melissa. She had a bone to pick with her anyway.

"Hey, Dom. Feeling any better today?" Melissa asked cautiously.

"No," Dominique snapped. "My head's splitting, and too much shit went down for me to be happy."

"Dom… please tell me you didn't hook up with Tim."

Dominique's grip tightened on the phone. "How the hell did he get into my house, Melissa?"

"I gave him my key," Melissa admitted. "You were out cold, and I didn't know if he grabbed your stuff or not. He was just supposed to take you home and leave."

"Well, he didn't," Dominique growled. "He brought me home, but he didn't leave."

"I'm sorry, Dom. I should've known better than to think Tim was anything but a bastard."

Dominique let out a long breath. "It wasn't all his fault. He asked me if I was sure. I was so drunk, I thought I was dreaming. When I woke and saw him beside me, I bolted and got sick. He held my hair, rubbed my back while I threw up. And then… I crushed him with what I said."

"I can't say I feel bad for him. He had that coming. This kills me to say it…" Melissa hesitated, voice softer. "He still loves you. I saw it last night in the way he looked at you. I'm unsure of why he did all those things, but one thing is for certain. He regrets it."

"I don't know what to do anymore," Dominique whispered. "He apologized for everything. Said he loved me, then just left without a word. So, I guess I need a ride. Can you come get me?"

"Yeah, I'll be there soon. We'll talk on the way to the club," Melissa promised.

She opened a new text for Nathaniel. She owed him an apology, though she doubted he'd respond.

I'm sorry for being curt with you last night. I don't like your jealous streak. We're just friends, or I hope we still are.

Melissa arrived, and they rehashed everything on the drive. Dominique's phone buzzed. Her breath caught, hoping for Nathaniel. Instead, Tim's name lit the screen.

Not feeling well. Taking today off.

Dominique knew damn well he wasn't sick. He'd left her house, angry and hurt.

Frustration built in her chest. Firing him if he didn't come in flicked through her mind. No, she couldn't do that.

Instead, she called him. No answer. Anger settled into her bones.

She shot off a text. **Call me back or you're fired.**

The phone buzzed. She answered. "I know we have issues, but that's no reason to skip work."

Tim's voice cracked, tight with pain. "That has nothing to do with why I'm not coming in."

"Then what is it? Tell me the truth," she shot back.

"I told you… I'm not feeling well. That's the truth. I can't tell you what's wrong, Dominique. Please trust me. I'll be better by tomorrow night, okay?"

Dominique exhaled, sharp and slow. "One night. But you'd better show up tomorrow."

She hung up before he could answer, letting the phone thud into her lap.

Melissa's voice cut through the quiet car. "Trouble in paradise?"

Dominique's reply was flat. "No."

"Sounded like trouble to me."

"Drop it. I don't want to talk. Just get me to work."

Melissa shrugged. "Okay, boss."

They stepped into the club, and Dominique's phone buzzed. Nathaniel.

I apologize for upsetting you. I'm a jealous man. Tim being around you… I can't stand it. Given the chance, he'd be in your bed.

Dominique's lips thinned. He already had.

Dominique: **I'll forgive you this time. But if I choose to sleep with Tim… that's my business. We're not together.**

Nathaniel: **Doesn't mean I have to like it. If you do decide to be with me, I won't be able to handle Tim being in your life. He'll always try to get you back.**

Sliding her phone in her pocket, she went to her office. She couldn't deal with this today. Noticing her purse beside the desk, she grabbed it, taking out some Tylenol. Bartending with a headache wasn't ideal.

Nathaniel didn't come in. His text had said he was working on the contracts and would be in the next night. She wondered if that was the truth.

After closing, Melissa drove her home, both unaware of the shadow trailing them.

Chapter 29

Nathaniel heard movement in the woods. His nostrils flared. The girl from the bar. How had she been able to follow Dominique and Melissa? Hadn't Tim stopped her? Why hadn't he protected Dominique?

He glided across the trees, landing on Dominique's roof without a sound. He watched the woods until Roxy emerged, sniffing the air, checking the trees. When she found him, a howl tore free. Nathaniel's eyes narrowed. Damn Tim. He'd let her track Dominique here.

He'd been here for a while, waiting for Dominique to come home. His thoughts lingered on all that'd happened the night before. Tim had spent the night with Dominique. With his hearing, he knew they'd had sex. His jealousy had flared white hot. Murder had been on his mind.

When Dominique texted him, he wanted to say more than what he did. But he couldn't, not without Dominique knowing he was lurking in her woods night after night.

His secret was still untold. Dominique wasn't ready to hear it yet. He knew it. He felt the tension between the three of them. She was torn. Pushing her any harder than he had wouldn't end well.

His eyes stalked Roxy as she moved beneath the trees. Her low growl dared him to come down. He merely grinned. She couldn't get to him without drawing attention to her presence. They stared each other down until she finally turned to leave. He let out the breath he'd been holding.

He wouldn't be able to watch Dominique during the day. There was only one person who could. One person who knew what was going on. That thought sent him into a rage. No. He wouldn't ask him to watch Dominique.

Chapter 30

Dominique crossed to the bar, eyes narrowing when Tim walked in. His face was marked like he'd been in a fight, though the bruises had the faint yellow of fading wounds. He moved slower than usual, every step careful.

"What the hell, Tim? You call in sick and then stroll in looking like this. Did you go out, pick a fight at some bar, or what?" she asked.

"No. I stayed home. You wouldn't believe me if I told you anyway, so let's not go there. I said I'd be here tonight, and I am. That's all that matters." His gaze met hers, sharp with anger but shadowed by something else — pain, maybe.

Dominique sat, waiting for him to explain. He didn't.

"I'm waiting. Lay it on me and we'll see if I believe it."

"Dominique, can we not do this? You made it clear you don't give a damn about me. So why should it matter what I did or didn't do? I told you I'd back off, and I will. Just… leave me be. I won't be in your business either, okay?" Tim's voice was flat, but his eyes carried a weight that twisted in her chest.

The words stabbed sharper than she expected. Guilt gnawed at her, dragging her down. He was still one of her people. She always made sure her people were okay. So why couldn't she do that for Tim? Why couldn't she see him as just another employee? Why did it have to be this complicated?

She sighed. "Okay, Tim. If that's what you really want, I'll leave you alone. You're right. I told you how I felt. No sense trying to pretend we can be civil. Come in, do your job, and there won't be any problems. Does that work for you?"

"No," he admitted. "But I don't want to be cut open anymore. I told you… When you're ready to hear the truth, come talk to me. I can't promise I'll handle backing off perfectly, but I'll try."

"Fair enough." Dominique turned and walked off, her throat tight.

Later that night, Nathaniel slid into the seat across from her and set an envelope on the table. Dominique opened it. Contracts. Already? He must pay his people well to move that fast.

"How long do I have to look them over?" she asked.

"As long as you need. No rush. Just let me know what you think," Nathaniel replied.

"Alright. Thank you." She set the envelope aside.

His gaze lingered. "You seem distracted. Are you alright?"

"I'm fine. Something happened last night, and I'm not sure how I feel about it. Confused doesn't even cover it."

"Please, keep in mind I'm trying not to show how jealous I feel. Is it about Tim? You've glanced over there more than once since I sat down."

Dominique looked. Had she? She had. Thoughts of him lingered, and she'd been wondering what had happened to him.

His bruises looked old, healing, but the memory of him still weighed on her. She sighed and met Nathaniel's gaze. He was trying so hard to just be her friend, holding back the jealousy he clearly felt.

"Nathaniel, you're sweet, and I really like you. I don't think it's a good idea to talk about this. You've told me you're jealous, and you've shown interest in dating me."

"It's alright. You can talk or not. I won't push," he said, placing his hand over hers.

"Thank you. That means a lot. I guess I'm torn. I like you, but my ex is back, and I hated him for so long. Now he's acting like he did when we first got together, and I fell for him. I can't figure it out. I'll follow my heart eventually, but right now… It's pulling me in two directions, and I hate it."

Nathaniel shifted in his seat, fist tightening under the table. Rage flared white-hot, all aimed at Tim. Why had he come back now, just as Nathaniel was making his move on Dominique? He'd watched her carefully before revealing himself. Now, Tim was wrecking everything.

He needed answers. Why had Tim let Roxy follow Dominique home? Now that she knew where Dominique lived, anything could happen. Sliding his hand over hers for a final squeeze, Nathaniel forced a smile before excusing himself from the table.

Chapter 31

Rose gasped at her reflection. The white gown the Duchess had chosen shimmered like something out of a dream. Tears stung her eyes. She looked like a princess. In the month they'd been here, the Duchess had made her dresses finer than anything she'd ever owned, but this… this was beyond imagining.

The long train spilled behind her, delicate stitching traced patterns across the fabric, and tiny white roses bloomed in the thread. Her hair, woven into several braids twisted into one elegant bun, crowned the look.

When the maids lowered the veil, her breath caught. She hardly recognized the girl in the mirror.

Turning, she found her grandmother quietly weeping.

"Grandmother, what is wrong?" Rose asked.

"Nothing, child. You remind me of Mary. I never saw her marry, never held you as a baby, never watched you grow. But now you've given me the most precious gift. I only hope my wedding gift can compare."

Rose took her grandmother's hand. "Grandmother, you have already given me the best gift. Today I marry the man I love. I never dreamed I would find love, marry a knight, wear a gown like this, or have such a beautiful wedding."

The Duchess smiled and embraced her granddaughter. When she pulled back, a maid placed a bouquet in Rose's hands. Sadness weighed in Rose's chest as the Duchess took her hand to lead her to Nathaniel. She longed for her father to be here, to give her away. She longed for her mother's kiss and blessing.

Her fingers brushed the necklace at her throat, and warmth spread through her. Silly or not, she felt her mother's presence, guiding her toward her union with Nathaniel.

They stepped into the corridor. As they passed, maids curtsied and knights bowed. Rose inclined her head in acknowledgment, a tear slipping free. She was about to live the dream of every little girl.

Her father's words from years ago echoed… *"You will never marry Sir Nathaniel."* A small smile tugged her lips. *"If only you could see me now, Father."*

They stepped into the chapel as the organ swelled. Nathaniel stood waiting, striking in his new breeches and crisp white shirt, dark hair brushing his shoulders with a soft curl. When his eyes found her, his smile lit the room. Rose's chest ached with joy, her heart ready to burst.

The Duchess placed Rose's hand in Nathaniel's, and that familiar spark of fire leapt through her at his touch. She was his… heart, soul, and body. They belonged to each other.

The chaplain spoke the vows, and when he declared them wed, Nathaniel swept the veil aside and kissed her with unrestrained passion. The Duchess cleared her throat, making him chuckle as Rose flushed.

"There's more of that later," he whispered against her ear.

The celebration moved to the great hall, where the feast spread before them. Rose smiled politely at every guest, though her thoughts kept circling back to his promise. The heat in his eyes made her insides twist with anticipation. They had made love every night since arriving, yet each time felt new — longer, more teasing, more consuming.

Life in the castle had been close to perfect, save for the moments she crossed paths with her uncle. His cruelty lingered in sharp words, his disapproval plain. He hated the thought of her being embraced by the Duchess and declared family.

Rose couldn't understand why her uncle bristled so much at her being recognized as family. She wanted no claim to his throne. His line was secure; his heir would inherit. All she wished for was to return to Athalon and live quietly with Nathaniel.

That night, when the last of the festivities faded, Nathaniel led her to their chamber. Her pulse quickened with nerves, though she knew what awaited. The look in his eyes was darker than usual, hungry, possessive, the same as the night he first took her. The memory sent a shiver racing down her spine.

He loosened the laces of her gown, easing the sleeves from her shoulders. His mouth brushed her neck, hot against her skin, as the fabric slid to her waist. She stepped free of the hoop skirt, only to gasp when his teeth sank lightly into her shoulder.

The sharp rip of fabric filled the air as the bodice tore beneath his hands. His palms cupped her breasts, and she melted back against him, breath hitching. In one sudden motion, he swept her off her feet, the ruined dress pooling behind. She gave a startled yelp, her heart thundering.

"You are mine, Rose," Nathaniel growled. "Tonight, I claim you as my wife. You belong to me and no other. Understand?"

"Yes," she whispered, breathless, as he carried her to the bed.

He tore her undergarments away without untying them. Rose's body jerked at the sudden exposure. Swiftly, he stripped off his shirt and undid his breeches, discarding them. He pressed down atop her, capturing her lips in a fierce, claiming kiss.

His hands roamed over her, rough and urgent. Anticipation and a shiver of fear coiled inside her. This wasn't the gentle lovemaking she'd grown used to.

There was no lingering, no teasing tonight. He thrust into her with possession, his dark eyes promising something wilder. Heat pooled in her core, her breath ragged with each demanding movement.

Nathaniel claimed her again and again through the night. By early morning, Rose surrendered to exhaustion, sinking into a deep, satiated sleep in the arms of the man she loved, a contentment she had never known coursing through her.

***

Dominique jerked awake as the dream ended. That was a new one. She swung her legs over the bed and stumbled to her computer, fingers flying over the keys as she recorded every detail. The dreams had stopped for a while. Why had they started again? This one had shown her Rose and Nathaniel's wedding, but was it the end?

Her thoughts drifted to Nathaniel's father. Had the Duchess kept her promise and given him her army? Had he won, or died? Had Rose and Nathaniel truly gotten their happily ever after? Dominique sighed, deciding she'd write it herself if the dream didn't. After all, she wanted that ending for herself, too.

Her mind snapped to Tim, then back to Nathaniel. The pull between them was undeniable, raw. He made her feel things she hadn't expected. She cared for him more than she wanted to admit. They wanted each other. So why couldn't she give him a chance? Was it Tim? Or her own fear of being hurt again?

She knew Tim, or thought she did. The past few days had shaken her assumptions. She'd thought he'd spiraled into a drunk and a womanizer. Roxy claimed he hadn't slept with her until after their breakup. But then why had she seen him leaving that bar with women? What was going on if not that?

And the drinking… When had it started? He'd always been happy, easygoing, and then suddenly, rage and anger had taken over. She'd tried to reach him, tried to talk, but he shut her out, brushing her off or storming away.

He stopped coming to her house. When she stayed at his home, he stayed out until the early hours. When he returned, he was drunk, stumbling. Her own anger hadn't helped — yelling, demanding answers. She should've been softer, more patient, and tried to understand the man he had become.

Dominique returned to her room and lifted the lid off her jewelry box. Her fingers brushed the ring still inside. She'd never had the heart to throw it away. Tim had known she didn't care for traditional diamonds. The turquoise stone at its center, surrounded by real diamonds, wasn't extravagant or pricey, but she'd always loved it.

Knowing she didn't usually wear jewelry, he'd found a ring that had symbolism behind it, making her love it. Dominique slid it onto her finger, and tears formed in her eyes. How had she had it all just to have it ripped away?

She slipped the ring back into her jewelry box. No sense crying over what might have been.

Going to the kitchen, she began fixing food when a knock rattled the door. No car had pulled up.

She peeked through the window. Darkness pressed against it, as if a hand blocked the glass. Dominique backed up, grabbing her phone.

A female voice called out, "Come out, come out, wherever you are. I know you're in there. I can smell you."

She froze. *Smell* her? What the hell? And why the hell was Roxy at her house? How had she even found it?

Dominique dialed Nathaniel. No answer. She hung up and called Tim. He picked up on the second ring.

"Hello?"

"Tim! That crazy bitch is at my house. She's about to beat my door down," Dominique whispered.

"Who's at your house?"

"Roxy. She's yelling for me to come out."

"Shit! Do you still have your dad's gun?"

"Yeah, but it hasn't been fired in years. I don't even know if it'll work," Dominique stammered.

"Go get it. Load it. Shoot that bitch if she gets in before I get there."

"I can't shoot someone," Dominique whispered, but Tim had already hung up.

Dents started appearing in the door. How was Roxy hitting it hard enough for that? Dominique bolted to her bedroom, yanking things off the top shelf until she found her dad's .45. She loaded it, praying it would fire if she had to.

Chapter 32

Tim sped through the streets, praying he'd reach Dominique in time. If a cop stopped him now, it was over. Twenty minutes away. He wasn't going to make it. *God, let her pull the trigger and not miss.*

Roxy was insane, jealous, and furious that he'd been with Dominique.

He should've known Jacob couldn't keep her in check. Nathaniel had told him that Roxy found Dominique's house. He'd been forced to perch on the roof to keep her from getting closer. Furious, Nathaniel had nearly torn Tim's throat out when Tim admitted he hadn't even known she was at the club. He'd been too beaten and battered, still trying to recover, to come to work.

Nathaniel couldn't protect Dominique during the day, but Tim had never thought Roxy would push it this far. No one crossed Jacob without consequences.

He slammed the brakes at the end of her drive, bolted from the car, and tore up the porch. The screen door hung from one hinge. Blood stained the wood. His chest tightened. Too late.

The front door lay inside the house, streaked with blood that trailed deeper in.

"Dominique?" he called, voice hoarse.

No answer. Tim followed the blood trail to the bedroom. Dominique sat on the floor, rocking. Relief crashed over him,

She was alive. He dropped beside her and pulled her into his arms. She screamed at his touch.

"It's okay, Dominique. It's me," he soothed, kissing her forehead, cheeks, and lips.

Her sobs broke against his chest. He held her until they eased, then gently pulled back. The gun shook in her hand. He eased it away, setting it on the floor.

"What happened, Dom?"

"I—I shot her. Is she dead? Did I kill her?" she choked.

"I don't know. She's not here. There's a trail of blood outside. Where did you hit her?"

"I'm not sure. She broke the door down while I was loading the gun. She ran through the house, screaming she'd kill me. That I couldn't have what belonged to her. When she came in here, I just… pulled the trigger. I wasn't really aiming."

Tim cupped her face. "It's okay. You did what you had to. There's no shame in that."

"I have to call the police," Dominique whispered.

"No, you don't. Let me handle this," Tim said firmly. "There's more going on with Roxy than you can imagine. If the police get involved, you'll be the one in jail. She'll spin a sob story about running for her life, and Jacob's connections will make sure you take the fall. I'll take care of it… and you." He pulled her back into his arms.

He had her gather a few things, insisting she stay with him for a while. But even as he said it, dread knotted in his chest. His place wasn't safe either. As much as he hated it, the safest option was Nathaniel. Roxy would expect Dominique at his house. She'd overheard the call; she'd know he was coming.

And if she wasn't dead, she'd be hunting.

Tim clenched his jaw. As much as he despised the thought, he hoped Dominique's shot had finished Roxy. That would spark a war with Jacob, but better that than Roxy coming again. War he could live with. Losing Dominique, he couldn't.

Dominique refused to leave until the blood was gone. Tim helped her scrub it away, then propped the door back in place, though the hinges were twisted from Roxy's assault. He called Melissa, told her to open the bar, and shut down her questions with a curt, "Just open it."

He drove Dominique straight there, ushering her into her office. When Melissa came in, he wanted her gone, but Dominique asked her to stay. Tim said he'd be at the bar and for Dominique to send for him if she needed anything. He didn't want Dominique to tell Melissa what happened. The less she knew, the safer she'd be.

Chapter 33

"Dominique, what happened?" Melissa asked.

Dominique's hands trembled as tears blurred her vision. She'd shot someone, maybe killed them, and now she was hiding it. Why had Roxy come to her house? How had she even known where she lived? And how the hell had she broken the door down?

"I did something awful, Melissa," she whispered, staring at her shaking hands.

Melissa pulled her into a hug. "Tell me. I'm here."

"I don't know what happened. That crazy bitch showed up and beat my door down. How is that possible? How can someone like Roxy do that?"

"What do you mean, beat it down?" Melissa asked, frowning.

"I saw dents forming while she hit it. I tried calling Nathaniel, but he didn't answer. I called Tim. He told me to get Dad's gun and shoot her if she got in. It's like he knew she could break it down. How could he know that?"

Melissa pulled back, eyes narrowing. "Dom… are you saying you shot that woman?"

Dominique looked up, torment etched across her face. Melissa's eyes widened.

"Dom, if you shot an intruder, you need to call the police. You had every right to defend yourself."

"I know, but Tim said not to. He said Roxy's tied to Jacob, and Jacob has people. He said they'd twist it, make it look like I intended to murder her. I'd go to jail, Mel. What am I supposed to do? Tell me what to do," Dominique cried.

"Is she… do you even know if she's alive?"

"I don't know. There was a trail of blood. She ran out so fast… no one with a fatal wound could've moved like that. Tim couldn't find her car, just blood leading up the driveway. He said she must have parked at the top and walked down."

"Holy shit. How did she even know where you live?"

"I don't know. Tim thinks she followed me from the club. Please, don't tell anyone, Melissa," Dominique begged.

"Okay, okay. We need to figure this out, Dom. If she's dead, they'll be looking for her killer. If she hates you that much, she's told people about you. You've got gun residue on your hands that won't be gone overnight. And even if you cleaned, the police can still find blood at your place."

"I know. Tim said to let him handle it. He'll find out if she's alive. If she's dead, I'll turn myself in. I can't live with myself if I killed someone."

"Don't talk like that, Dom. We'll figure this out," Melissa said, hugging her again.

Melissa slipped out to work the floor, leaving Dominique hidden in her office for the night. Everyone kept their distance, making sure no one noticed anything was wrong.

Chapter 34

Roxy staggered toward her car, blood slick on her side. That bitch had shot her. Twice. The first bullet had grazed her, but the second burned deep in her stomach. Her vision blurred as she fumbled for the handle. She needed a doctor to dig the bullet out so she could change and heal. But could she make it in time?

Sliding behind the wheel, she called Jacob with trembling fingers. His clipped response came fast: the doctor would be ready. She floored the gas, pain stabbing with every bump. By the time she screeched to a halt outside, nausea rolled through her from blood loss.

Jacob was already there. He yanked her from the car, cradling her weight as he carried her inside. The doctor didn't waste a second, laying her on the table. Jacob paced like a caged animal as the doctor worked, Roxy's screams echoing in the room.

"The bullet missed her spine," the doctor said, sweat on his brow. "It's lodged in her intestines."

Roxy whimpered as the doctor dug into her.

Jacob's pacing stopped, his voice razor-sharp. "How could you be so damn stupid, Roxy? You were supposed to watch her. Find the bastard she's with. Not go to her house. Not touch her. You've ruined everything."

"Jacob, the bullet's out. She needs to change to heal," the doctor urged.

"No," Jacob snapped. "She won't change. Will she survive if you stitch her up?"

Roxy's eyes went wide. "What? Jacob, no! Please… I need to heal!"

"She'll survive with a transfusion. She's lost a lot of blood," the doctor said.

Jacob's jaw tightened. "So be it. Give her the transfusion, stitch her up, but don't let her change."

"Please, Jacob!" Roxy sobbed.

"No!" he roared, leaning close, his breath hot on her face. "Your punishment is to heal like a human. Maybe next time you'll obey orders. If I find out you changed, I'll kill you myself. Do you understand?"

Roxy's voice was barely a whisper. "Yes… I understand."

Chapter 35

Entering the club, Nathaniel headed straight for the bar. Something was wrong with Dominique. He could feel it. She'd tried calling earlier, and she never called. No voicemail.

"Tim, what's going on? Where's Dominique? She's hurting. I can feel it."

"Not now. We'll talk later, after everyone's gone. She's in her office. She's fine… for now," Tim said.

"What do you mean, for now?"

Tim sighed. "Go check on her. If she wants you to know, she'll tell you."

Nathaniel went to Dominique's office. It was empty. A desk and chair sat against the wall, a couch sat off to the side, and a door near the back. He closed the main door and locked it, ensuring privacy. Moving to the back door, he paused, listening. Soft crying. He knocked. No answer. Trying the knob, he found it was locked.

"Dominique, it's Nathaniel," he called gently. "Please open the door. I saw you tried calling earlier. I'm sorry I missed it. I can hear you crying. Please let me in."

"Please, go away. I don't want to talk to anyone. If you'd been there earlier, you'd know what's wrong. I just want to be left alone."

"Dominique, please," Nathaniel said softly. "I know I wasn't there when you needed me. I can only ask for forgiveness. But I want to be here now. Please open the door."

When she stayed silent, he added, "I'm not leaving. I'll stand here until you open it."

Minutes later, the lock clicked. Dominique stood there, eyes bloodshot. He reached for her, but she jerked back. Stepping aside, he let her pass. She walked around him and dropped into her chair, ignoring his presence.

"The first person I think to call when something goes wrong is you," she said, voice shaking. "And you're never there when I really need you. If we're friends, why is that?"

"I can't always be there, Dominique. I try my best, but it seems it's never enough for you."

"No, it isn't enough," she snapped. "Your work is always more important. You won't even take a day off. You say you're jealous of Tim, but Tim's the one who's been here for me. I was in danger today. He dropped everything and came running, even after I hurt him. He keeps telling me he loves me, and I keep brushing him off. But today? Today, he came for me. He thought that crazy bitch had killed me!"

"What happened, Dominique?" Nathaniel asked, fury tightening every muscle.

"That crazy woman from the other night came to my house and attacked me. She literally beat my door down. I tried to call you, but, like always, you didn't answer. Tim did. He reminded me about my dad's gun and told me to grab it. She rushed me, and I shot her. Twice." Her gaze dropped to her trembling hands. "I don't even know if she's alive."

Nathaniel reached for her. She stiffened, but he pulled her into his arms anyway. If she only knew why he couldn't be there, that he'd been watching over her every night. How could he make her see?

"Dominique, did you call the police?"

"No. Tim said not to. I'm a criminal now. I covered it up. What if she died?"

"Don't think about that right now," he murmured. "You did what you had to do. Tim had his reasons for keeping the police out of it. I understand and agree with him. You'll know everything soon."

He held her tighter as her tears dampened his shirt. Slowly, her rigid frame softened, and she leaned into him. Lifting her easily, he carried her to the couch, cradling her against his chest.

Her head sank onto his shoulder, and sleep overtook her. Nathaniel stroked her hair, rage flickering behind his calm exterior. He imagined ending Roxy himself. Why target Dominique? She'd done nothing to deserve this. He'd protect her at any cost. But he couldn't reveal the truth yet. Not until she loved him. He didn't want a repeat of the past.

Nathaniel shifted, easing back against the couch and settling Dominique between his legs so her back rested on his chest. His plan had been going perfectly… until Tim.

He'd been Dominique's friend. She had come around, feeling the pull between them. For years, Nathaniel had felt the invisible tether that bound him to her. She was his soulmate.

But every lifetime, every rebirth, the women had run. They'd chosen normalcy over destiny, slipping through his fingers before he could make them love him. He'd pushed too fast before. This time, he'd been patient. Had Dominique endured enough loss to be ready to give up a normal life? For him?

He held her for hours, silent and unmoving, until she stirred. She jerked upright, breath catching, fear pulsing from her like a heartbeat. He let go of her. Her head turned slowly, eyes finding his.

Nathaniel stayed still, afraid she'd be upset with him holding her. But she exhaled, the sound shaky, and eased back onto him. For a moment, he didn't touch her, not until she took his hands and guided his arms around her. He tightened them, pulling her close, and brushed a gentle kiss across her hair.

Her voice cracked as she whispered, "I was hoping that nightmare wasn't real. But if you're here, that means I really did shoot someone. You weren't there when I needed you… But you're here now. Thank you for staying. You didn't have to."

"I will never leave you, Dominique. I'd give you every part of me if you'd take it. I know you don't understand why I can't always be here or why I do certain things, but one day you will," Nathaniel said.

"Yeah, yeah, I've heard that before. You and Tim are both so damn secretive. It drives me nuts. Why can't you just tell me already? It's not like I'd tell you to stay away. I care about you," Dominique replied, meeting his gaze.

He studied her for a heartbeat, then pulled her into his lap. His lips brushed hers, soft at first. She hesitated before parting her lips, and his hands slid over her back. Dominique melted against him, threading her fingers through his hair. His palms slipped beneath her shirt, cupping her breasts and drawing a sharp gasp that he caught with another kiss.

A loud knock snapped her away from him. Nathaniel muttered a curse under his breath, already knowing who stood outside. When Dominique opened the door, Tim's sharp gaze swept over her. Nathaniel stayed where he was, amused by the flare of Tim's nostrils and the narrowing of his eyes. Nathaniel was also amused at Dominique's blush from their stares.

"I just came to check on you. Make sure everything's okay. You haven't come out in hours," Tim said.

"Yeah, I kind of fell asleep. Nathaniel stayed with me. I'm fine, Tim. Thanks for checking."

"It's almost closing time. Want to come out and make sure everything's okay, or should I have Melissa do it?"

"No, it's fine. I'll be out in a few minutes."

"Okay," Tim said, shooting Nathaniel a glare.

Nathaniel couldn't help the grin tugging at his lips. Tim's jealousy was obvious, familiar, even. Nathaniel had felt the same when Tim had sex with Dominique. There was no love lost between them, but he had to admit he was grateful Tim had protected her.

A truce crossed his mind, then he dismissed it. As long as they both wanted Dominique, peace was impossible. She'd have to choose eventually, and bringing that up now would only drive her away.

Dominique closed the office door and turned toward him, cheeks flushing again. Nathaniel waited, but she didn't come back to him. Instead, she slipped into the bathroom. The sound of running water hit his ears, disappointment tightening his chest. Damn Tim for ruining the moment. She'd never let him touch her like that before.

When Dominique returned, her eyes were still swollen, but her cheeks had lost their blush. Without a word, she walked past him and out of the office. Nathaniel stayed behind, determined to wait for her return.

Chapter 36

After closing, Tim trailed Dominique into her office. Nathaniel was already there, lounging silently. Tim sat across from her, his expression grim.

"We need to talk about where you're staying for a while," he said.

"I'm going home, Tim. I can't run from this forever. Do you really think she'll come back?" Dominique asked.

"Yes. You didn't kill her, you wounded her. If she were dead, Jacob would've called me by now. You can't stay with me. They know where I live. I'd feel better knowing you're safe. I can't guarantee that at my place, so either we get a hotel or you stay…" His voice faltered.

"She wouldn't be safe at a hotel either, and you know it," Nathaniel cut in.

Tim's jaw tightened. Nathaniel's calm tone only sharpened the tension.

"And what was the alternative you were about to suggest, Tim?" Dominique asked.

Tim's eyes flicked between her and Nathaniel. She glanced at Nathaniel, whose face stayed unreadable, then back to Tim. Realization hit. Tim wasn't seriously suggesting she stay with Nathaniel… was he? Tim hated him. He'd never want that.

But staying with Tim wasn't an option either. They'd already crossed a line, and she'd said things she couldn't take back. How was she supposed to navigate this without making things worse?

"I'm not staying with either of you," Dominique said, voice firm. "And I'm not tucking tail and running. I'll stay in my own home. I'll get the door fixed first thing in the morning. I doubt that crazy bitch will come back tonight."

"If you're staying at your house, then I'm staying too," Tim said flatly. "You don't know these people, Dominique. I do. They won't stop until they get what they want."

"And what is it they want, Tim? I haven't done a damn thing to any of them!"

He looked at her, then at Nathaniel, and back again. She didn't want him to say what she feared. Nathaniel didn't need to know what transpired between them. But of course, he did.

"You and I slept together, Dominique. Roxy thinks I'm hers, even though I haven't been with her in ages. She knows I want you, and that pisses her off. She figured out what we did. She and Jacob were waiting for me that morning. Jacob decided to give me a good old-fashioned beat-down. That's why I didn't come to work. Happy now? Do you understand why I don't want to leave you alone?"

Nathaniel's gaze made her skin crawl. Out of the corner of her eye, she caught him staring, jaw taut, silent. She leaned back, closing her eyes, trying to think.

Jacob really was dangerous. Tim had said he was in a gang. Was Tim part of it? Was that why he'd kept his past hidden? How had he even gotten pulled into Jacob's orbit?

Had Tim finally told her just enough to explain? If he'd been honest before, would she have believed him? The questions twisted in her mind, leaving her unsettled and confused.

Being the shy, awkward kid she'd been, Dominique had never imagined one guy would be interested in her, let alone two. Tim had been there when she needed someone most. But he'd also left her, leaving problems unresolved when she had needed him to step up.

Nathaniel had stayed by her side at night, but when she'd really needed him, he hadn't been there either. Could she really blame him? He hadn't known that crazy woman would attack, hadn't expected her to call at that exact moment. She'd sprung the funeral on him at the last minute, too. Dominique rubbed her face, exhaling sharply.

When she opened her eyes, both Nathaniel and Tim were watching her. She stood and paced, frustration tightening her chest. What was she supposed to do? Give up her house, her business, her life? Hide? How long would that go on for?

"Look, I know you're confused. I'm not asking you to give up your life. Just stay with me. Or let me stay with you for a while, just until Roxy makes another move, or this blows over," Tim said.

"And what if I don't want to stay with you? Or have you stay with me?" Dominique asked.

"Then stay with me," Nathaniel suggested.

Dominique looked at him. "And what if I don't want to stay with you either? What if I just want to be alone to handle this on my own?"

"You can't handle this alone, Dom. You like to think you're a badass, but you don't know these people. They're ruthless. They'll get revenge eventually. Even though it was Roxy's fault she got shot, they won't see it that way. They'll only see you injured one of their own, and they don't stand for that. Plus, Roxy is sleeping with Jacob."

Dominique stopped pacing and looked at Tim. "You mean to tell me that bitch is coming after me because of you, and she's fucking someone else? That's just rich right there!"

Tim shrugged. "I told you she was crazy."

"I think it would be best for you not to go home, at least tonight. If Jacob is going to avenge Roxy, he may come after you. He won't wait. It's only one night. You can stay with me since Tim's residence won't be safe for you," Nathaniel said, finally speaking after watching the exchange.

"As much as it pains me to say this, I agree with Nathaniel. They don't know where he lives. Give me until tomorrow night to figure out what's going on, and then we can go from there, okay?" Tim said.

"Fine, but one night only. Tomorrow I'm going home no matter what. I'll call someone later to fix my door. I still don't feel good about not reporting this to the police."

"Thank you." Tim stood and hugged her.

Dominique hugged him back, grateful he'd been there for her today. Sure, it was partly his fault she was in this situation, but he'd been there and was still trying to protect her. His warmth and strong arms felt so damn good. She was getting pulled back into him, and she didn't like it one bit.

Tim pulled back and kissed her forehead. "I'm going to go get your things out of my car. I'll be right back."

Dominique sat back down. "Okay."

When Tim left the office, Nathaniel stood and walked over to her. He squatted in front of her, grasping her hands, and just looked at her for a long moment before speaking. Dominique didn't know what she could say to him after the revelation of sleeping with Tim.

"Dominique, I'm trying to remain your friend. It's getting harder when I want you for myself. I will not, however, force you to choose between me and Tim. If he is where your heart truly lies, just tell me," Nathaniel said, sincerity burning in his eyes.

Tears pricked her eyes. "I can't tell you that, Nathaniel. I'm confused. I appreciate you not making me choose. No matter what happens, I can't see losing you as part of my life. I don't know why, but I feel drawn to you. It scares the hell out of me. I told you I care about you. I just don't want to be hurt in the end. I thought I was over Tim because I felt such hatred for him, but I guess I still loved him and never really moved on. Now those feelings are resurfacing. He was the love of my life at one point, but if he truly loved me, would he have let us fall apart like he did?"

"I can't say if he would have or not. I can see he regrets his decisions. I told you before, he wants you. I see it on his face when he looks at you. I don't want to admit it because he's my competition, but I believe he truly loves you. Maybe he just didn't know how to handle whatever happened that caused things to sour between you."

Dominique's heart swelled at the thought of Tim still loving her. She'd missed so much of the life they'd shared… the good times.

And here was Nathaniel, offering advice about another man. The realization hit her like a truck. She loved him. They'd spent months together at the bar, texting, getting to know each other.

Nathaniel made her laugh, lifted her spirits on bad days, and even though he wanted more, he had stayed her friend — all because that was what she wanted. He never pushed farther than she allowed. If she stopped him, he backed off. Now, more than ever, she was lost.

Nathaniel stood, pulling her from the chair. He hugged her tightly and only released her as Tim approached. Without a word, Nathaniel took Dominique's things from Tim.

They walked outside. Tim hugged her. "Be safe."

She squeezed him tightly, their lips brushing. She didn't stop him. Stepping away, she got into Nathaniel's car, eyes lingering on Tim as they drove off.

Chapter 37

Tim drove home, replaying the last few minutes with Dominique. The turmoil rolling off her had been impossible to miss. What was she so confused about? Was he part of it? She hadn't resisted when he kissed her, had even hugged him back. Hope flickered in his chest.

Lost in thought, he didn't sense the danger. A grunt escaped as something slammed him to the ground. Hands clamped around his throat. Gasping, Tim struck out and met Jacob's furious glare.

"Roxy almost died! Where is that bitch?" Jacob snarled. "I know you're hiding her. I waited at her house. She never showed. She's not with you, so where is she?"

Tim broke Jacob's grip, dragging air into his burning lungs. Jacob's boots pounded his ribs and skull. Dizziness blurred his vision. He curled into a ball, shielding his head as Jacob straddled him, fists raining down.

"Tell me where she is!"

"I don't know!" Tim shouted.

Jacob could smell a lie. He'd know it was true. Tim had no idea where Nathaniel lived. He'd never asked, deliberately, so he couldn't betray her.

"You'll bring her to me or I'll kill you," Jacob hissed.

"She didn't do anything wrong! Roxy brought this on herself," Tim shot back. "I'm not handing over what's mine just because Roxy thinks she owns me. You'll have to kill me first!"

Jacob shoved his face close to Tim's, fist knotted in his shirt, his voice a deadly whisper. "What did you just say?"

"Which part, Jacob? That I won't bring Dominique to you because she's mine? Or that Roxy thinks she owns me?" Tim's lips curved in a bitter smile. "Oh, wait! You didn't know she's been trying to fuck me this whole time she's been with you."

"I should kill you right here," Jacob growled. "But I won't. I'll find out the truth. If Roxy went after that girl out of jealousy…" His jaw clenched. "I may have to kill her. Still, the girl will pay for what she did to Roxy."

"No. I won't bring her to you. She's mine, Jacob. I've claimed her, and you know it. Roxy smelled her on me. That's probably why she went after Dominique in the first place."

"Damn it, Tim." Jacob's grip tightened. "You could have been so much more. But you've never fully embraced this life. Does she even know what you are?"

"No," Tim admitted. "She wouldn't understand why I never told her… or why I left her."

"Then how can you protect her? This is the same girl you were with before, isn't it?"

"Yes," Tim said, his voice steady. "So if you want punishment, take it out on me. Don't hurt her. She didn't know about Roxy or me. She's mine to protect."

"You really love her if you'd take her punishment." Jacob's tone softened for a beat. "I have no quarrel with her. I only wanted her as bait to get the bastard she's with. But if you've claimed her, she's not with him anymore. Yet I smell him all over her place." He released Tim's shirt with a shove. "So here's your choice: bring her into the pack, make her your mate. Or she dies. Let her fight Roxy and claim what's hers."

"As it stands, she's not yours," Jacob said coldly. "She doesn't know what you are, and the vampire's still hovering. She can't have both, and neither can you. I'll give you until Roxy heals. She's being punished and will heal slowly. Make your choice, Tim." Jacob turned and walked away.

Tim stayed on the ground, gasping. His ribs, barely mended from the last beating, throbbed, broken again. Every breath stabbed his lungs, and a pounding headache flared from the lack of air. Hatred for Jacob burned deep, growing sharper with every heartbeat.

He couldn't bring Dominique into the pack. She'd never want this world. She'd always dreamed of a normal life… marriage, kids, stability. How could he drag her into Jacob's chaos? Especially under a leader like him.

Shifting, Tim bolted into the woods, the change shredding through his pain. Muscles strained as he pushed harder, trying to heal, trying to outrun his thoughts. But the truth chased him… If he didn't kill Jacob and take the pack, he'd never keep Dominique safe. And even if he did… would she stay once she knew what he was?

Chapter 38

Nathaniel pressed a button as he pulled up. A hidden door slid open, blending seamlessly with the three-story house. Dominique's eyes widened. Why did one man need so much space?

The garage swallowed them, gleaming cars lined up like a showroom, each one spotless and expensive.

Nathaniel opened her door, but her gaze stayed locked on the collection. One car stole her breath: a cherry-red 1969 Pontiac Firebird Trans Am, flawless as if it had just left the factory.

"See something you like, Dominique?" Nathaniel asked, amusement curling his lips.

"You have the car I've only dreamed of," she whispered, awestruck.

"And which one is that?" he smirked.

Dominique stepped up to the Firebird, peering through the window. God, it was stunning, restored to perfection, yet every detail looked factory-made. Her mouth watered. Nathaniel strolled over and swung the door open. It wasn't even locked. Was he insane? He gestured to the driver's seat.

"Are you serious?" she breathed.

"Yes. I've never seen you like this. If a car makes you this happy, enjoy it. I collect cars but rarely drive them, just start them now and then."

"Oh my God! How can you let this baby just sit here?"

He shrugged. "I like collecting. My Mustang gets most of the miles. Go on. It's all original, barely driven."

Dominique slid behind the wheel, fingers gliding over the leather. Beautiful didn't even begin to cover it. She'd once checked the price of one and realized she'd never own such a rare '69 Firebird in this condition.

"Want to take it for a test drive?" Nathaniel teased.

She shot him a skeptical brow. He only grinned.

"Are you serious? If you're joking, I might kill you."

"I'm serious. I had no idea you were into muscle cars."

A squeal escaped her as she threw her arms around his neck, then bounced on her toes. "Yes! Let's go!"

"Alright." Nathaniel plucked the key from its box and placed it into her palm.

Dominique stared at it, almost reverent. Nathaniel laughed as she slid behind the wheel and slipped it into the ignition. He climbed into the passenger seat.

Seat belt clicked, engine ready, Nathaniel tapped a button on his key ring. The hidden garage door lifted, revealing the driveway. As she eased the Firebird out, Dominique glanced in the mirror… no sign of a garage behind them. Clever.

She crept up the long drive to the road, palms slightly damp. This wasn't just any car. It was a dream on four wheels, and one wrong move could wreck something irreplaceable. She paused, revved the engine, and felt the vibration hum through her chest.

Nathaniel's smirk met her nervous glance. "You won't hurt it. I'll guide you somewhere you can really open it up."

"Are you sure? If anything happens, I could never replace this car." She bit her lip.

He shrugged, grin widening. "Then pay me for the privilege."

Her brow arched. "What's the price?"

"A mere kiss," Nathaniel said.

Dominique considered it. A kiss? For this car? Easy. She leaned toward him, but he pressed a hand to her shoulder, stopping her.

What the hell? Charge her a kiss, then refuse it?

"Not now," he said, voice low. "When we're back. I want a real kiss, not a drive-by peck. Deal?"

She swallowed a laugh. "Okay… doesn't matter when."

She eased onto the road, following his directions. He steered her toward the highway, but when she guessed his destination, he only smirked. "You don't know," he said, refusing to elaborate.

Once on the highway, she opened the Firebird to seventy-five, the engine's growl vibrating through her chest. A few exits later, Nathaniel pointed her toward a turnoff. A raceway sign flashed past, and he told her to pull in.

He stepped out, disappearing for a minute. When he returned, he waved her through an open gate. The wide asphalt curve of a racetrack stretched ahead.

Holy shit! He had racetrack access. Her pulse spiked.

She guided the Firebird onto the track, fingers tightening on the wheel, heart hammering at the thought of opening it up on real turns.

Nathaniel's laugh rolled through the car. "Alright, Dominique… show me what you've got."

Dominique's heart hammered as she floored the Firebird, the speedometer climbing past seventy-five… ninety… a hundred and ten. The roar of the engine vibrated through her bones. Nausea curled in her stomach on the first sharp turn, and she whispered a frantic prayer not to wreck his car. Each time the wall loomed too close, she eased off the gas and steadied the wheel, forcing herself not to overcorrect.

For twenty breathless minutes, she circled the track, adrenaline flooding her veins. Finally, she slowed, shifted into park, and unclicked her seat belt.

She launched herself across the console and kissed Nathaniel hard. The world felt sharper, brighter. She was more alive than she'd been in years, all because he'd trusted her with her dream car. Nathaniel caught her, dragging her fully onto his lap, their mouths still locked. He deepened the kiss, tongue teasing hers.

A thrill shivered through her; part from speed, part the way his hands slid over her body. Heat coiled low in her belly as she ground against him, desire drowning out doubt. She wanted him badly, even though she'd just been with Tim. The thought flickered, guilt pricking, but it didn't stop the need clawing at her.

Nathaniel groaned, hips rising to meet hers. His hand slipped beneath her waistband, fingers gliding past fabric and sinking inside her. He broke the kiss to trail his mouth along her neck, teeth grazing the pulse at her throat. His thumb pressed and circled faster as his fingers curled, and Dominique rocked against him, palms splayed over his chest, chasing the rush he coaxed from her.

"Nathaniel, I want you."

He kissed her, fingers working faster. Her nails dug into his sides as release crashed through her. He nipped her lip before pulling back and wrapping his arms around her. She rested her head on his shoulder, and for a few quiet minutes, they simply breathed together.

"We need to go, Dominique," he said at last, voice tight. "Please… get back in the driver's seat and take us home."

She blinked at him. "I… I thought you'd want to… you know."

"No. I took care of your needs. Now, please, take us back."

The words stung, but she swallowed the lump in her throat. Without a word, she slid back into the driver's seat, buckled up, and eased the car out of the gate. Nathaniel climbed out to lock it, then returned to the passenger seat.

The ride was painfully quiet, his voice surfacing only to give directions. Once parked, Dominique stepped out, handed him the key, and headed for his Mustang to grab her things. She didn't want to stay. Maybe she'd call Melissa for a ride.

Nathaniel opened a door at the far end of the garage and started up the stairs. She stayed where she was. He came back down, caught her by the arm, and pulled her close. He kissed her, soft, insistent. But Dominique stayed still beneath his lips, offering nothing back.

"I'm sorry, Dominique. I didn't mean to hurt you. I don't want to take advantage of you and have you regret it later. I told you I wouldn't push, and I meant it."

Dominique stepped back. "It is what it is, Nathaniel. I'd like to go to bed now, if that's okay."

Nathaniel sighed and turned toward the stairs. This time, she followed. He pointed out the bathroom and the guest room. The space was beautiful, even for a room clearly meant for visitors. She set her things on the bed.

"There's only one thing I'll ask while you're here. Please, don't go upstairs," Nathaniel said.

Dominique frowned but nodded. What was upstairs that she couldn't see? Was he hiding something? A wry thought flickered… what if he were some serial killer with a torture chamber? She rolled her eyes. Of course not. But he was definitely keeping secrets.

"Dominique?"

"Yes, Nathaniel?"

"May I have that payment kiss as a goodnight kiss?"

She stared at him like he'd grown a second head. Was he serious? He'd just rejected her, claiming it was to avoid taking advantage of her. What kind of excuse was that? And hadn't the kisses in the car counted? Apparently not, since he hadn't seemed to want her then. So why was he asking now?

"You didn't want me a little while ago," she said quietly. "Why do you want to kiss me now?"

Nathaniel stepped forward, yanking her against him. He kissed her hard, grinding into her. She felt his hardness pressing against her. He took her hand and guided it to the crotch of his pants, pressing himself into her hand. Then he broke the kiss and stepped back.

"Wanting you isn't the problem, Dominique," he said hoarsely.

"Then what is the problem, Nathaniel? I don't understand," she whispered.

"I just can't. Not right now. This would only add to your confusion. I want you to come to me knowing you want me… and only me. For now, goodnight. Get some sleep," he said, walking out and closing the door.

What the hell? He wasn't going to push her, yet he'd just made it clear she had to choose him, or nothing. She was frustrated, sexually and emotionally. Sex with Tim had only tangled her feelings more. She wanted Nathaniel, but now he refused her when he'd tried before.

Of course, he hadn't known she'd slept with Tim before. Now he did, and it had screwed things up between them. How was she supposed to fix this? How could she choose? Her heart was torn, wanting both of them.

She lay on the bed, trying to sleep, but her thoughts raced. Being in Nathaniel's house made her feel odd, and that discomfort only pushed sleep further away.

Chapter 39

Nathaniel checked that Dominique was still in the bedroom before opening the hidden door at the end of the hall. He descended the steps and sat on the bed in the secret room. Not on the house's floor plans, built by him, windowless and dark. He undressed, lying down, mind still on Dominique. He hated that he'd hurt her earlier.

The urge to sink his teeth into her burned uncontrollably. Her excitement at the cars, at the track… it had wrapped around him, set him on fire. Her kiss had sent him over the edge, her pulse racing beneath his lips as he kissed her neck. He'd had to pull away.

He'd done the only thing he could for her. Feeling her shatter around his fingers had extended his fangs. Restraint had been all that stopped him from taking her, from tasting her blood.

The hurt lingering in the car had not calmed him.

Coming home, her defiance pushed him further. That kiss, her hand on him… stepping away had been a battle.

She was still upset with him, and he felt it. How could he fix this? He'd waited too long to enter her life, and she'd fallen for Tim. Now, her love had grown again. Her confusion that night made that painfully clear.

He didn't want to give her up, but could he force her to choose? Would she pick him? Could he wait for her to decide later, letting her live a normal life with Tim? No. What if something happened to her while he waited? This was his last chance. She wouldn't have another cycle. He had to make her see she belonged with him.

If he revealed the truth, who and what he was, would she turn away? She'd said she cared for him; she had to love him for his plan to work. He'd moved too fast before. Maybe he could strike a deal if she wanted a normal life, one he could never fully provide.

He'd hate to share her with Tim, but perhaps on his terms… she would have to truly belong to him. A human servant living as long as he did, able to walk in daylight. He'd never considered it before. Would that make her happy? Would she stay? And what of everything else? He couldn't offer what Tim could.

He sighed as dawn crept in, feeling that familiar pull, and was gone.

Chapter 40

Dominique woke late, restless from a morning of tossing and turning. The day before replayed in her mind on an endless loop—Roxy, the gun, Tim, and Nathaniel. Even her dreams had been reruns of blood and chaos. Sleep was pointless.

Her stomach growled, reminding her how long it'd been since she'd eaten. Nathaniel had told her not to go upstairs, but he hadn't said anything about the first floor. She slipped out of the guest room and went hunting for the kitchen.

When she found it, she stopped short. Like the rest of the house, it was spotless; gleaming counters, not a single crumb or coffee ring. No photos, no clutter, no signs of life. Her own place was crammed with snapshots and knick-knacks, while his looked like a model home.

She opened the refrigerator. Empty, and not even humming. Cabinets? Bare. Not so much as a glass. A chill prickled down her spine. Had she ever actually seen him eat? Drink?

Maybe he had another kitchen upstairs? The upstairs he'd specifically told her to avoid. That wasn't an option.

"Well, damn," she muttered. Hunger gnawed at her as she headed back to the guest room. She snatched up her phone and tried Melissa. No answer. Tried Post. Straight to voicemail. With a sigh, she scrolled to Tim's number. Maybe he'd pick up.

She dialed Tim's number, but it rang out. The one person she'd counted on hadn't come through.

Her stomach cramped. Like it or not, she'd have to ask Nathaniel for food. She just hoped she didn't walk in on something private.

At the bottom of the stairs, guilt pricked her. He'd told her not to go up. But she couldn't starve.

She climbed the steps, the old wood whispering beneath her feet. Two doors waited at the top. The first stood open: a bathroom. The next was locked.

"Nathaniel?" she called softly. Silence answered.

Another door, also locked. The next opened to reveal a fully stocked home gym. She blinked. Of course he had one.

The last door opened to an almost bare room, just a desk. She almost shut it again when a splash of color on the far wall caught her eye.

A painting.

She stepped closer. Her breath caught. Holy… Nathaniel stared back at her from the canvas. A blonde woman sat beside him, her painted smile so radiant it reached her eyes. A small boy, maybe five or six, perched on Nathaniel's lap. The woman cradled a newborn in her arms.

This had to be the family portrait Nathaniel had mentioned. The one of his distant ancestor who was his mirror image. The resemblance was eerie, unsettling in its perfection.

Dominique lingered in front of the painting, something about it tugging at her chest. She wanted to know the story behind those faces: the man and woman, the children. But it wasn't her place to pry. Nathaniel had trusted her enough to ask her not to come upstairs, and here she was already crossing lines. With a reluctant sigh, she shut the door and headed downstairs.

"Okay, Dominique," she muttered, pacing the living room. "Use your smarts. How do you get food when you don't know the address and can't leave?"

After a few moments of scrolling on her phone, inspiration struck. MapQuest. She entered directions from "current location" to her own house. Bingo! Nathaniel's address popped up.

She found a local delivery place, ordered food, and wandered down to the garage to wait. The door was sealed tight; no exterior entry she could see. The only exit was the massive garage door, and of course, the opener wasn't obvious.

She scanned the walls, running her fingers along the trim until she spotted a small, camouflaged button near the doorframe. "Paranoid much, Nathaniel?" she muttered.

She waited, scrolling through carpenter listings, dialing for quotes. By the third call, she had a decent price and a promise that someone could come later today to fix her door. Problem was, she had to be there.

That left two options: track Nathaniel down or call someone to come get her. Borrowing one of his cars was out of the question.

The Mustang still sat where it had been last night. Dominique had searched every inch of the house and hadn't found Nathaniel. Two of the upstairs doors had been locked, but surely he would've heard her knocking, or woken when she'd called his name.

Her phone chimed: the delivery was almost there. She hit the garage button and stepped outside to wait. The dense trees pressed close around the property, their shade swallowing what little sunlight filtered through. It gave her the creeps. Her own place was on a dirt road, too, but at least it felt open. This house, with its dark curtains and looming branches, felt suffocating.

The driver was late. Five minutes past the ETA, then ten. When a car finally appeared down the road, relief loosened her chest.

"Sorry it took so long," the driver said as he handed her the pizza. "No mailbox, no address markers. I thought I was lost forever out here."

"Yeah, this place is literally in the middle of nowhere," Dominique replied, forcing a small laugh. She thanked him, hurried back inside, and was grateful she'd remembered to order a drink.

She ate at the spotless counter, leaving the leftovers where they sat since the refrigerator wasn't even on.

Full but restless, she tried to nap again. Sleep wouldn't come. Her mind kept circling back to the painting; the beautiful blonde woman, the children, Nathaniel's impossibly familiar face. Would he tell her about it if she asked, or would he be furious she'd seen it at all?

A sudden unease prickled over her skin. Her muscles tightened, and dread slid down her spine.

No. Not again.

A violent convulsion ripped through her. Dominique's body seized, her mind screaming for control even as the vision dragged her under.

***

Rose had begged Nathaniel to take her when he rode out to face his father, but he'd refused every time. She was not the kind of woman to be left behind. The moment he departed with the army, she kissed him goodbye, then sprinted to the stables.

The scent of hay and horse sweat clung to the cool evening air as she saddled Winter. Metal clinked sharply when she hefted the borrowed battle gear. She pulled the coif over her hair, the rough weave scratching her neck, and dragged the hauberk over her shoulders. The weight pressed into her collarbones, almost enough to steal her breath. With the surcoat hanging loose and the hidden sword in her grip, she looked, at a distance, like another knight. Up close, she felt like an imposter. The blade was heavier than memory promised, but her resolve burned hotter than her fear.

She kept to the shadows, riding the outskirts where the trees whispered overhead and the army's distant torches flickered like fallen stars. Nathaniel would be furious when he learned she had followed, but the thought of him facing death alone clenched her heart tighter than any fear of his anger. If he fell, she would fall beside him; if he triumphed, she would share his victory.

Night deepened, bringing the chill scent of damp earth. Campfires flared ahead, sending sparks into the sky. A knight spotted her silhouette and barked an order for her to dismount and help. The ground jarred her knees when she slid from the saddle, armor tugging at every muscle. Together, they raised a tent beneath a canopy of stars.

When the camp quieted to low murmurs and the distant crackle of flames, she led Winter aside. She hadn't thought far enough ahead to bring her own bedding. Resting her cheek against the saddle's worn leather, she curled up on the hard ground. The smell of smoke and horse filled her lungs as exhaustion dragged her into uneasy sleep.

***

At first light, Rose stood stiff-limbed and resaddled Winter. The bite of morning air stung her cheeks, and every muscle ached from sleeping on the cold ground. Fatigue pressed behind her eyes, and the fear of being discovered gnawed at her stomach. Around her, the camp roused; metal clanked, low voices murmured, and the sharp scent of woodsmoke drifted as the cook stirred breakfast over crackling flames.

She collected her meal quietly, head bowed, lips sealed. All day they rode, hooves drumming a steady rhythm across packed earth until dusk blurred the horizon. By nightfall, tents sprouted again beneath the stars.

When the camp settled into silence and shadows thickened, the cook's heavy steps crunched toward her. Rose stiffened and rose to her feet. Her pulse hammered; if he sounded an alarm, she'd have to flee bareback. Could she with the armor dragging her down like a millstone?

"Fear not, child," the cook said softly, his lined face lit by a stray ember's glow. "I came only to see if my old eyes betray me. M'lady, what are you doing here, dressed like one of the knights?"

She lifted her chin, defiance sharpening her voice. "My husband would not allow me to ride with him. I will not sit idly by while he faces death."

The cook chuckled. "M'lady, this is no place for a woman. Still… you are as stubborn as your mother was."

Her breath caught. "How do you know of my mother?"

"I have been a cook in that castle longer than most knights have drawn breath, M'Lady," the old man said, his voice low and rough as gravel. "I knew of your mother's plans. Caught her once, sneaking food from the pantries under the cover of night. She begged me not to tell a soul."

His eyes softened, memories flickering like firelight. "I could not find it in my heart to betray her. I had seen her steal moments with that boy, and I knew the Duke she was meant to wed; cruel, quick with his fists. She had come to my kitchens often, and I would slip her sweets, watch her eyes light up. I loved her as if she were my own."

Tears blurred Rose's vision. The weight of her lineage, the risk her mother had taken, pressed against her chest. He had helped her mother once. Perhaps he would do the same for her now.

She took a trembling breath. "Will you keep my secret, too? I cannot turn back, and I will not let Nathaniel send me to the castle."

The cook's lined face creased in a gentle smile. "Aye, I will keep it. But to do so, you will need to stay close. Sleep in my tent, and I will see to your meals. Still…" He hesitated, eyes glinting with concern. "The rivers for bathing, the woods for a pot… these things are harder to hide. You will need cunning if you are to remain unseen."

"I have done well enough with the pot so far," Rose said quietly. "Bathing… I have not solved it yet. Perhaps when the others sleep, I will steal to the river. What is your name, good sir?"

"I am called Cook," he said with a shrug. "That is what all the knights call me."

"And your true name? I would know the man who has shown me such kindness."

"My name is George, M'Lady."

"Well then, George, I will call you Cook among the knights, and George when we're alone. But you must not call me 'M'Lady.' If you must address me, call me Rowan."

George's eyes crinkled. "Alright… Rowan. Come. You will sleep in my tent so no one discovers you."

She followed him, and when he closed the flap behind them, she sank onto the ground. George draped his blanket over her, then lay as far from her as he could. Exhaustion claimed her quickly.

By morning, the tent was empty. Voices of knights carried across the field. Rose cracked the flap and, seeing no one nearby, slipped out and made for the trees. The armor's weight dragged at her as she squatted, and she nearly toppled backward; only a tree kept her steady.

Rustling snapped her upright. She hurried to redress and crept toward camp, but a familiar silhouette appeared—Nathaniel. Heart pounding, she ducked behind a tree, holding her breath as he passed within feet of her. Only when he vanished into the distance did she slip from her hiding place and hurry back.

George met her at Winter's side, handing her a bowl. She murmured thanks and perched on her saddle to eat. Worry gnawed at her. How could she stay hidden until Athalon? If she were caught, would George pay the price for her secret?

***

Days slipped by without discovery. They were too far out to turn back now. Too many resources would be wasted if she were found. Rose steeled herself to face whatever consequences might come.

That night, after the knights bedded down, she asked George to take her to the river and stand watch. He nodded and led the way, then drifted off to keep lookout.

She peeled off the heavy armor, laying each piece on the riverbank. Dipping a cloth, she wrung it out and washed quickly before slipping into the cool water. For a brief moment, the current against her skin felt like freedom.

As she swam back toward shore, footsteps rustled through the darkness, coming from the opposite direction of George's post. Panic tightened her chest. She waded silently, hoping the shadows would hide her.

A figure approached the bank, boots crunching near her clothes. Rose ducked beneath the surface, lungs burning as she prayed he'd leave.

When she could hold her breath no longer, she broke the surface for air. Moonless night still cloaked her, but the man stepped forward, sword flashing dully in the starlight. Nathaniel.

"Whoever you are," his voice rang low and dangerous, "announce yourself. Are you friend or foe?"

With no choice left, she swam toward him. Nathaniel stepped back, eyes scanning the riverbank, heart hammering in his chest.

From the trees, George came running, and Nathaniel's head snapped toward him.

"Stop right there, Cook. I know not if this is friend or foe," Nathaniel called.

"They are no foe, M'Lord. Please, come with me, and they will come out of the water," George said urgently.

Nathaniel's gaze sharpened. "What is the meaning of this, Cook? Why can they not come out now? If they are one of us, they should answer when called."

George glanced toward the water, then back at Nathaniel. Something was amiss. Nathaniel snatched the clothes from the bank and strode toward him.

"Tell me, Cook. Do you harbor someone in my army? Speak, or both shall be punished!" Nathaniel's voice was like steel.

"My Lord, I humbly apologize. I promised I would not tell you," George replied, voice steady.

"Then you shall die—" Nathaniel began.

"No! Leave him be. I will come out!" Rose shouted.

Nathaniel whirled toward the water. A woman? With George? His eyes darted to the cook, who avoided his gaze. Nathaniel's anger surged as Rose emerged from the river, the moonless night casting her in shadow, yet she stood there, defiant.

"What in the hell are you doing here?" Nathaniel yelled.

He grabbed George by the shoulders and shook him. What had he been doing down here with Rose? Why had he been anywhere near his wife while she bathed? And what in the hell was she doing here in the first place?

"Nathaniel! Let him go! Please! He has done nothing wrong!" Rose shouted.

"Nothing wrong? Why was he here with you while you were bathing? Why are you here? Did he bring you?"

"No! I stowed away by myself. I rode beside the army until you camped the first night. I asked George to come down to the river to keep watch for anyone coming. It was unfortunate you came from the other direction," she said, her voice steady despite the tension.

Nathaniel's gaze flicked from the clothes in his hand to George, who still avoided his eyes. Rage boiled in him. The man had seen his wife naked, helped her follow them, and said nothing.

"Go back to camp before I change my mind and run you through where you stand," Nathaniel warned.

George backed away and quickly turned to leave. Nathaniel's eyes followed him until he disappeared from sight. If his eyes had lifted at all, he would have run him through.

Then, without hesitation, Nathaniel strode toward Rose. "What are you doing here? I will not ask again."

"I begged to ride with you, but you would not allow it. So, I came by myself. I will not be left behind like a child while you ride into danger," Rose said, her eyes blazing daggers.

"How long has the cook known you were here? And what have you done with him, for him to keep your secret?" Nathaniel demanded, yanking Rose against him.

"The cook realized on the first night. I have done nothing wrong, Nathaniel. I would not betray you," Rose said, her voice steady.

"But you have betrayed me! You snuck out of the castle and followed me. And you were naked while he was here. Have you lain with him, Rose?"

"No! He hid me in his tent. I slept with my armor on. I only undressed once he walked away," she said, lifting her chin defiantly.

"You are in danger here. I cannot send you back with any of these knights. I do not know if they will protect you. And I cannot leave them to take you back," Nathaniel growled.

"Then do not send me back. I love you, Nathaniel. I will follow you to Hell and back if need be. I will not go back. No matter what you do, I will come back to you," Rose pressed, her body tightening against his.

Nathaniel jerked her up and slung her over his shoulder. Rose yipped as the chainmail dug into her stomach. He strode into a narrow alcove by the river and set her down, capturing her lips in a brutal, bruising kiss.

Stepping back, he stripped off his armor, and Rose's eyes followed him, greedy. He pressed her against the cold rock walls, grabbed her hands, and pinned them above her head. His lips found hers again, forcing her against him.

"You are going to be punished for what you did tonight," Nathaniel said, voice low and dangerous.

Chapter 41

"Dominique… wake up. Please, wake up."

A groan escaped her lips as the world tilted. Her skull throbbed, every muscle screaming. Wood scraped under her fingers.

"Dominique, open your eyes. I need to know you're alright," Nathaniel's voice, tight with worry, cut through the haze.

Her lashes fluttered, refusing to lift. She slid her hand over the one pressed to her stomach.

"I'm… okay. I think," she rasped. "Everything hurts. Am I on the floor?"

"Yes," he said, relief sharp in his tone. "You must've fallen. There's a bruise on your cheek, a small cut, and a bump on your temple. Looks like you hit the nightstand."

She forced her eyes open, blinking against the blur. "That explains the pounding in my head."

Nathaniel scooped her up and settled her back onto the bed. He vanished for a moment, then returned with a damp cloth. Gently, he dabbed the blood from her skin, folded the cloth, and pressed it to her temple.

"You need a doctor. Could be a concussion," he murmured. "And I've nothing here for the pain."

Dominique managed a weak, incredulous laugh. "Wouldn't matter. You've got nothing to take it with. The refrigerator isn't even on. Who lives like that?"

Nathaniel perched beside her, guilt flickering across his face.

"I'm sorry. I keep my own stores in a small fridge elsewhere. I didn't think…" His voice trailed off, the unspoken worry heavy between them.

"I—I went upstairs. I'm sorry. I wanted to run to the store, but… I saw the painting."

Nathaniel's shoulders went rigid. He turned his gaze away, jaw tight.

Dominique reached for his hand. He didn't pull back, but he didn't meet her eyes either.

"Are you mad at me?" she asked softly.

"Yes," he said, voice clipped. "Very. I asked you not to go upstairs. Did you see anything else?"

"No. I didn't snoop, even though I wanted to. The painting just… pulled me in. Instead, I tracked down your address and ordered a pizza." She hesitated, searching his face. "But where were you? You didn't hear me knocking or calling?"

"No," he said, the tension in his voice unyielding. "I'm a heavy sleeper. But that bump on your head worries me. You should be checked for a concussion."

"I'll be fine," she said, waving it off. "I just want to go home, grab my things, and deal with my busted door."

"I'll drive you," Nathaniel said. "We'll stop by the store, get you what you need for tonight."

Dominique's chin lifted. "Nathaniel, I don't want to stay here. We agreed. One night. Not two."

"That was *before* you had another seizure and cracked your head," he said, his tone darkening. "If you refuse the doctor, then you're staying here so I can keep an eye on you. Call whoever you need, but you're not leaving."

"Nathaniel, I—"

"No, Dominique." His gaze locked on hers, unyielding. "This isn't up for debate."

She let out a long breath, scanning for her phone. Nathaniel bent, scooped it off the floor, and handed it to her. The screen glowed with missed calls and frantic texts from Melissa, Post, and Tim. Dominique swallowed and hit Melissa's number.

"Where the hell are you? I've been calling and texting."

"Sorry, Mel. I needed a ride earlier, and then I had a seizure."

Melissa's voice softened. "I opened the bar. I'll close tonight. You rest. Tim's here, but he's banged up."

"Thanks. Tell Post what happened so he won't worry."

"Okay. Talk later."

Dominique hung up and texted Tim: **Hey. Are you okay?**

Tim: **I'm fine. Where have you been? I've been calling and texting for hours.**

Dominique: **I had another seizure, fell out of bed. Nathaniel tried to wake me. I'm sorry I worried you. I called earlier for a ride but couldn't answer after the seizure.**

Tim: **The danger at my place has calmed down. Roxy's alive. You can stay with me if you want.**

Dominique: **How do you know she's alive?**

Tim: **I just do. Don't ask. It'll be okay. Tell me if you want me to come get you. I've got to go. I love you.**

Dominique exhaled and let her phone rest on the pillow, the screen still glowing.

Nathaniel said, "Do you want a shower and to get dressed? We can swing by your place and the store."

"I'm leaving in the morning. I need to get my house in order. The door can't be fixed unless someone's there. I'll grab my car and meet you back here."

"No. I don't want you driving. Let me monitor you tonight, then take my car tomorrow."

"I'm not taking your car… that's your baby."

"I wasn't talking about the Mustang. I meant the Trans Am. Would you feel better if I gave it to you?"

"Gave it to me? What does that even mean?"

"As a present. Would that make you happy?"

Dominique sat up, blinking at him.

"I can see you don't believe me," Nathaniel said. "If you promise to stay tonight and not drive until I'm sure you're okay, the car's yours. Your excitement makes me happy."

Dominique threw her arms around him. His embrace tightened, his lips brushing the bruise on her cheek. They stayed like that, silent and close.

"There's one more favor I need," he said quietly. "I hate it, but take Tim with you tomorrow. I want you safe."

"Why can't you just come with me?"

"You know I can't. Please don't be angry. Just have Tim go with you."

"Fine," she said, pulling back.

He hugged her again and left the room. Dominique gathered her things; the room suddenly cold without him. In the bathroom, she turned on the shower, hoping hot water would soothe her pounding head… and maybe wash away the sting of Nathaniel not being there tomorrow.

She cranked the shower as hot as she could bear. Steam wrapped around her, the pounding heat easing her sore muscles and dulling the ache in her head. When she stepped out and wrapped herself in a towel, the soft cotton felt like a sigh against her skin.

The door swung open, releasing a cloud of steam. Nathaniel leaned against the wall, watching. Her grip on the towel tightened.

He pushed off the wall, took two quick steps, and pinned her against the wall.

Dominique's breath caught. His pupils had swallowed the brown of his eyes. Her knuckles whitened around the towel.

His mouth crushed hers; bruising lips, teeth grazing, tongues tangling.

"Nathaniel?" Her voice was a shaky whisper.

"Yes, Dominique," he murmured against her neck, kissing a trail down her skin.

"Are you okay? You're like the big bad wolf after Red Riding Hood."

His low chuckle vibrated against her throat. "Unfortunately for Red, I can't keep pretending to be the sheep."

Heat coiled in her stomach. He'd haunted her thoughts since rejecting her.

He slipped the towel from her hands, fingers tracing her curves. She tugged at his shirt; he pulled it over his head and stepped back, eyes devouring her nakedness. That smoldering look sent a shiver through her core.

She reached for his pants, but he caught her wrists, gently pushing her hands away before sliding the fabric down himself, revealing lean muscle and the faint scars she remembered.

Then he pressed her to the wall again, kissing her hard. Her palms mapped his back, following every scar. Nathaniel's hand slipped between her thighs as his mouth closed over her breast.

Sliding her hand between them, she caressed his velvety length, then encased it with her fingers. His groan hot on her breast sent heat pooling to her stomach. Her fingers glided in fast strokes along his length.

He broke away, kneeling before her, spreading her legs. His mouth claimed her, tongue teasing her clit as he cupped her butt, pulling her forward. Heat bloomed through her, heaviness building.

Fingers plunged inside, drawing a strangled cry. Nathaniel sucked her clit, relentless. She gripped his hair, rocking against his mouth, and her orgasm ripped through her.

He kept lapping at her until she sagged against the wall, trembling. Soft kisses marked a path up her body before Nathaniel rose, towering over her. A shiver rippled through her as he slid his fingers into his mouth, sucking them clean.

She spun him, slamming his back into the wall. His chuckle broke into a groan when her fingers gripped him hard. A sly smile curved her lips as wet kisses trailed down his chest and abs, her descent deliberate until she knelt before him.

Her mouth slipped over him, her hand squeezing the base of his shaft. His fingers dug into her shoulders, groans spilling as he brushed the back of her throat. Her tongue curled around the velvety smoothness, gliding up and down. Sucking the tip, she cupped his balls and squeezed gently.

Nathaniel's fingers tangled in her hair, hips thrusting. Tightening her mouth, she sucked hard, tongue flicking the tip.

His hand wrapped in her hair, tugging her head back, releasing his cock with a wet pop.

She didn't stop. Taking him back in, her pace quickened. Her tongue bathed him, suction grew tighter, Nathaniel's hips thrust faster.

"Dominique…" he growled.

But still she didn't stop. Her tongue lavished every inch of velvety hardness, hand squeezing his balls, mouth tugging with each upward pass. He groaned, his grip in her hair tightening. His cum splashed across her tongue to the back of her throat as she drank him down.

Slowly, Dominique rose, locking eyes with Nathaniel, his gaze dark, unfocused with need. In a sudden motion, he pulled her against him, lifting her effortlessly. She wound her legs around his waist as he carried her to the bedroom, laying her gently on the bed.

Nathaniel sank his mouth to her nipples, sucking and licking as they hardened. He squeezed one breast, bit and drew on the other, lavishing attention.

Then he flipped her onto her stomach. Fingertips trailed down her spine, making her body jerk. His tongue followed, pressing soft kisses to her neck before sliding back down, brushing her ribs. Light kisses dotted her shoulder blades, tongue flicking along her spine. She moaned, hands clutching the sheets.

His cock rubbed along her slit as her body bucked, pressing warmth against him.

He hovered close, his breath hot against her ear. "Are you ready for me, Dominique?"

A trembling whisper escaped her. "Please, Nathaniel… I need you."

"Music to my ears, Dominique," he said, thrusting into her.

She clenched around him. His slow strokes stretched her to perfection.

She pushed back into him as he pinned her to the bed, tongue lingering over her artery, its pulse beating wildly.

Dominique panted, urging him to go faster. But Nathaniel pinned her beneath his weight, refusing to speed up. The unhurried rhythm was new, thrilling, but she ached for more.

He pulled out, flipped her onto her back, and laced their fingers together, raising her arms above her head as he slid back inside. The slow lovemaking sent a delicious warmth pooling low in her belly. Her eyes fluttered shut.

"Open your eyes, Dominique. I want you to see me while I claim you."

She forced them open, meeting his gaze. His dark eyes pulled her under, an intimate abyss she'd never known. Mesmerized, her soul seemed to reach for his.

Heat built and crested into a small orgasm, but Nathaniel didn't stop. His slow, deliberate pace held her there, drawing her deeper into his eyes. Mini flecks of gold ringed his pupils, the rest a deep blackness, wide with lust. His thrusts quickened, pleasure building again.

On the brink of orgasm, Nathaniel stopped and moved away. She groaned in protest as he sat beside her.

His hoarse voice sent shivers down her spine. "Come, Dominique."

Body heavy, drugged with desire, she crawled onto her knees and into his lap. He gripped her hips, guiding her where he wanted.

She slid down his length, his thrust meeting hers. She exploded, and he kissed her. Slow, gentle thrusts intensified her pleasure.

Nathaniel's hands squeezed and caressed her breasts. Dominique moved faster, matching him, but he grabbed her hips, slowing her down. Frustration bubbled up, a groan slipping free.

He kissed her cheek, lips brushing the shell of her ear. "I want you, Dominique, but I want you for as long as I can have you. I'm going to take my time."

"I've never had someone last this long."

Nathaniel chuckled. "Now you have. I can do this every night if you want."

Dominique met his gaze, drowning in his eyes. Did she want this every night? Resting her head on his shoulder, she kept the slow, rhythmic pace. Being held, being made love to, brought tears to her eyes. Her heart stuttered as love pressed against her ribs.

Nathaniel gripped her and flipped them, sliding his arms under her to hook her legs over his shoulders. His hands locked on her shoulders, pinning their bodies tight.

He slammed back into her, each thrust brutal, their bodies colliding.

Her fingers tangled in his hair, yanking him down for a kiss. Pain and pleasure tangled as she tugged harder, her back arching, a scream ripping free as her orgasm crashed over her. Locked in his gaze, she felt their souls connect.

With one final, deep thrust, Nathaniel released into her warmth. He lowered her legs and kissed her softly.

Rolling them onto their sides, he wrapped her close. She draped an arm and leg over him, snuggling into his heat. Their breaths slowed, syncing.

Happiness swelled in her chest as she drifted into peaceful sleep.

Chapter 42

Nathaniel let Dominique sleep a couple of hours before gently waking her. He shouldn't have, but she'd looked so peaceful, curled against his warmth. Her eyes fluttered open, still hazy. He grinned and kissed her.

"I thought I'd wake you and take you to the store, as promised."

"Mmm. What time is it?"

"Midnight. You slept for a few hours."

Heat crept up her cheeks. "That means you lasted for hours."

Nathaniel's grin turned wicked. "Told you I'd take my time."

A tremor rippled through her muscles as she stretched. "Honestly, I don't think I have a concussion. I feel great."

"You promised you'd stay here tonight."

"I did, but I'm leaving later. Tim said everything's handled. I'm guessing he straightened things out with Jacob."

"I'll talk to Tim. I don't want you mixed up with those people… they're bad news, Dominique."

"Yeah, I figured that out."

She slid out of bed and gathered her clothes. Nathaniel's gaze followed every movement, desire tightening in his chest. Not now. Shaking it off, he stepped into the hallway, dressed quickly, and met her as she emerged.

"Shall we go?" he asked.

"Yes, please. I'm starving."

At Dominique's house, Nathaniel caught her tense profile; lips pursed, eyes fixed on the torn screen door. The front door gave way under her touch, collapsing inward. She exhaled a shaky breath and flicked on the light.

Old blood. And… wolf. The scent was unfamiliar. Tim had said everything was handled, so who had been here?

Nathaniel's hand shot out, gripping her arm before she could step inside.

"Let me check first."

"Nathaniel, the door just fell in. If someone's here, they already know we are."

"Just let me make sure, okay?"

She nodded. "Alright. Go ahead."

He moved down the hall, flipping on lights more for her comfort than his. Each room lay in disarray. In her bedroom, the smell was strongest, closet torn apart, drawers dumped. A gun lay on the floor amid the wreckage. What had they been searching for?

"Nathaniel?" Dominique's voice wavered.

He returned quickly to find her by the doorway, trembling, eyes locked on the dark outside.

"What is it?"

"I—I'm not sure. I heard a noise, looked out, didn't see anything… then something looked back at me. Animal eyes, maybe?"

Nathaniel stepped to the door, inhaling sharply—the same scent: musky leaves and dirt. A crunch of sticks to the right drew his gaze. Bright blue eyes glowed in the dark beneath a mane of blond fur. Werewolf.

Their stares locked. The wolf threw its head back, howled, and vanished into the woods.

"Dominique, grab your things and let's go."

"What is it, Nathaniel?"

"A wolf." He didn't add werewolf.

That wasn't Jacob. So who? Did Tim know Jacob was still watching Dominique? Or was he helping lure her out?

Nathaniel pulled out his phone, fingers flying.

I thought Jacob backed off? Why is there a wolf at Dominique's? She saw eyes but didn't know. She's with me tonight. If you're luring her out, I'll kill you.

Dominique rummaged through the cabinets. He tugged her arm.

"Forget that. We'll hit the store."

His phone buzzed. Tim.

How'd you get my number? And no, I'm not helping Jacob. He gave me a choice… that's none of your damn business. If someone's there, it's because of you. Jacob still wants to kill you. Get Dominique out. Now!

Nathaniel texted back. **I saw your messages with Dominique. We're leaving. She's set on fixing her door, but I made her promise to bring you. If you're plotting against her, I'll know.**

Tim replied: **I'm not. I'll figure something out. Don't bring her back. It's you Jacob wants. The closer you stay, the more danger she's in. I thought I had until Roxy healed before Jacob made a move, maybe a month or two. We'll talk later. Watch Dominique.**

Fury burned through Nathaniel. Tim had kept vital information from him. If he'd known Jacob was still after her, he'd never have brought her here. Was Jacob using Dominique as bait?

He scanned the tree line as they got in the car. No sign of the wolf. But in the rearview mirror, movement, blond fur, bright blue eyes, running alongside through the woods. Nathaniel cursed himself for not being more observant. Whoever it was, they were strong.

At the 24-hour store, Dominique browsed the produce aisle, fingertips grazing apples. A sigh escaped Nathaniel.

"Dominique, just grab enough for a few days."

"I'm only staying until morning, Nathaniel. I don't need much. I could've grabbed things from the house if you hadn't been so impatient."

"What if I told you Jacob's still coming for you, probably for me, and using you as bait? Would it matter? If I'm putting you in danger, maybe I need to stay away. For now, he doesn't know where I live."

Her head snapped toward him. "What?"

"Please, just grab what you need so we can go. We'll talk at home."

A prickle of fear crawled up his spine. The wolf couldn't have followed, but caution never hurt. Dominique tossed a few items into the basket. Nathaniel paid, ignoring her protests, and carried the bags out, eyes flicking to every shadow.

Silence wrapped the car. His body stayed taut, gaze darting to the rearview mirror as he took twisting back roads to lose any potential tail. Dominique glanced out the back glass but asked nothing. He didn't explain.

Pulling into the garage, Nathaniel handed her the Trans Am's keys.

"You'll pick up Tim before you go home?"

"I promise," she said, worry threading her voice. "Nathaniel, tell me what's going on. Please?"

He shook his head. He couldn't tell her, not what he was, not what Tim was. The truth would drag her deeper into a world already too dangerous. How could he keep her safe without shattering her reality?

"I believe someone was at your house tonight. Your bedroom was tossed."

"I tossed things from the closet looking for my dad's gun."

"The whole room was ransacked, not just the closet. Someone was searching for something, information, maybe. I don't know what yet."

"All my things, my memories… the last pieces of my parents are in that house! I have to go back and protect them."

"I get it, Dominique, but you can't go back tonight. You'll return later with Tim. I doubt Jacob will risk anything with Tim there. Tim's part of his…" Nathaniel paused. "Gang."

"Eventually, you're going to tell me what's really happening, right? I can't take much more of this. I need to know what I'm in the middle of."

"I can only tell you my part. Tim will have to explain the rest. And yes, I'll tell you everything when the time's right."

"And when will that be, Nathaniel? You keep saying that, but the time never comes."

He pulled her close, holding her tight. He needed more time to figure out Jacob's next move. Telling her now would be a mistake.

"I can't yet, Dominique. Just give me a little more time. Then I'll explain."

Dominique exhaled sharply. "Fine."

"Thank you."

Nathaniel watched her put everything away, plug in the refrigerator, and fix her food. When she offered him some, he politely declined. He'd long forgotten the taste of food, but the aroma still stirred something in him; the pepper's spicy, earthy bite, the steak's subtle sweetness, the potatoes' warm starchiness.

His thoughts drifted back to the night he'd seen her at the restaurant. He'd followed her there, standing in the shadows, watching. Tim had approached, urging him to move closer. Dominique's frown told him she didn't want him there. Tim's earthy, musky, sour scent crinkled his nose as he came near. It had thrown him that she knew a shifter.

Overhearing their conversation had been his stroke of luck, giving him a way in. Seizing the chance, he'd stepped in, claiming to be Dominique's date. Tim's gaze hardened, eyes narrowing as he caught Nathaniel's scent. But her knowing a shifter gave Nathaniel hope… maybe she'd believe him when the time came to reveal the truth.

Through their conversations, he'd realized Dominique didn't know what Tim was, dashing those hopes. Sliding quietly into her life, she'd never once questioned why he didn't eat or drink. Did she suspect?

Snapped from his reverie, his eyes met hers. She raised an eyebrow, and he smiled. Had he missed something she said?

"I'm sorry, Dominique. I didn't mean to be distant."

"It's okay. I was just wondering what you were brooding over. You looked serious."

"I was muddling a few things over. If I asked what you truly thought of me, would you tell me?"

Dominique coughed, nearly choking on her food.

"Um… want to clarify that?"

"What do you think of me? How do you see me? Am I a good person? Odd? Someone you like being around? I could ask a hundred ways, but it's up to you how you take it."

"I told you I care about you, Nathaniel. Have you pissed me off? Yes. Hurt me? Yes. Made me laugh? Yes. Made me happy? Yes. I can tell you exactly the kind of person I see when I look at you.

"I see a person of mystery because you don't let me in. I also see a good man; sweet, caring, with a jealous streak. Earlier tonight, I swear I was looking into your soul. Our connection is something I've never known," Dominique said, placing her hand over his.

Nathaniel smiled, knowing she'd felt their connection. Her heartbeat had spiked, though she'd been too afraid to admit it. He brushed his lips across her knuckles. She gave a sheepish smile and finished her food.

"Now, since I've told you what I think of you, why don't you tell me what you think of me? I can't figure out why you want me, or get jealous."

"There's so much I need to explain before you fully understand why I want you, Dominique. That part will have to wait until I'm ready. But for now, I'll tell you what I see when I look at you, okay?"

Dominique quirked an eyebrow. "Okay."

"I see a beautiful young woman. She's endured so much yet still smiles, holds her head high, and knows what she wants. Her heart, though battered, remains loving. Shy in love but believing in it, her smile always reaches her gorgeous eyes. Her personality? Amazing… shy yet straightforward, even blunt.

"Her soul shines, radiating beauty to everything around her. Some envy it, but that's their loss. She gives everything and asks for nothing. A darkness lies within her, hidden from the world, too scared to let anyone see it. Afraid they'd tear her apart with no chance of recovery."

"Wow. You really see all of that?" Dominique whispered, tears sliding down her cheeks.

"Yes. I see you, Dominique," he said, squatting before her.

His thumb brushed her tears away. She wrapped her arms around him, resting her head atop his. He held her, letting her cry.

Dominique pulled back. "Thank you for truly seeing me. It's been a long time since I felt anyone has."

"I understand that feeling better than you know, Dominique. I think you should rest now. It's clear you don't have a concussion."

"Will you stay with me until I wake up?"

"I'll lie with you for a while, but then I'll have to go. It's all I can give you for now."

"I'll take it… for now. But you'll have to tell me what's going on soon, or I might not stick around."

"I will, I promise. Just not tonight."

Chapter 43

Dominique woke to an empty bed. Checking her phone—ten a.m. The contractor could come in a few hours. She called Tim.

"Hey. Can I come get you now? The contractor's going to be at my house soon."

"Yeah. You want me to meet you there?"

"No. I promised Nathaniel I wouldn't go without you. Can you be ready in thirty minutes?"

"Sure. I'll leave the door unlocked just in case. Need my address?"

"Yes. Text it to me."

"Okay." Tim yawned.

Dominique got ready, heading to the garage. Excitement bubbled as she gazed at her dream car. Starting it, she revved the engine, closing her eyes as the hum thrummed through her body.

One thing she hadn't considered the night before… the garage door. The only button was on the wall. Getting out was easy enough, but sprinting under the closing door spiked her adrenaline. She'd have to ask Nathaniel for the opener. Shaking her head, she pulled up Tim's address.

His place was secluded like hers, quaint, wrapped in woods. Tall front windows invited reading light, blue trim against white siding. A smile tugged at her lips; she liked the property.

There was no answer when she knocked, but the door was unlocked.

"Tim?" she called, stepping inside.

Still no answer. She glanced around the living room, then froze. On the far wall, a framed collage of photos, her and Tim, younger, happy… in love.

Her fingers hovered, then traced the curve of Tim's smile. His eyes told a story: he'd loved her. The realization tugged at her chest. Why had he displayed these now?

Music drifted faintly. Following the sound, she walked deeper into the house. Hardwood floors gleamed under her feet, paneling warm against the walls, more pictures chronicling a shared past. With each step, the music swelled until she reached the hall's end.

"Tim?"

"Yeah, Dom," his voice called back. "I'm back here. Be ready in a minute. Kinda fell back asleep."

Without thinking, she opened the door to scold him, then stopped cold, the words dying on her lips.

Tim stood naked, towel in hand, drying his hair. Her gaze swept involuntarily from his face, down his chest and abs, over powerful thighs, before landing where it shouldn't. Heat flamed up her neck, and she jerked her eyes back to his stomach, where scars slashed across his skin like claw marks.

Their eyes met.

Tim prowled toward her, movements smooth, predatory, a wicked smile curving his lips; one that promised something dark, maybe dangerous.

"Like what you see, Dom?"

"I—I'm sorry, Tim. I didn't mean to walk in on you."

Dominique's eyes dropped, but his nearness pressed in, his heat mingling with hers. Her gaze flicked back, unbidden, to those scars.

Her thoughts tangled with her body's response; confused. How could she love two men at once? Desire them both?

"I don't mind you being here, Dom. Didn't think you'd walk back here, but since you did, might as well enjoy the show."

"Um, no. I'll just wait in the car. I thought you'd be ready to go when I got here."

Tim smirked. "Oh, I'm ready to go… anytime you want."

Her eyes flicked, against her will, back to his cock.

"That's not what I meant, and you know it. Please put some clothes on."

"Why? You don't mind the view. You'd have to be dead not to know what you're thinking."

"I'm not blind, Tim. You've always been attractive." Her fingers brushed the scars across his torso before she could stop herself. "I don't remember these. What happened?"

His muscles tightened under her touch. Tim yanked her against him, kissing her hard. Breathless, she tore away.

"No. We are *not* going there. I need to get home and fix the door. Are you going to tell me about the scars?"

His voice went flat. "No. I'll get dressed."

She knew she should leave, but couldn't. Watching him pull on his clothes, she felt the warning flare. Today would be trouble if she let her thoughts run loose.

Chapter 44

Tim liked that she stayed, watching him dress. Even if it was only physical attraction, he still affected her; her resistance slipping a little more each day.

In the living room, her gaze lingered on the collage. He'd pieced it together the day after she ended things. When he'd moved here, he'd almost left it packed away. Roxy had always hated it. But he never loved Roxy. She'd been a placeholder until he gained control. After that, he dumped her.

He'd picked up the phone countless times to call Dominique, but never followed through. Instead, he'd rebuilt himself, determined to come back as the man she'd once loved. If she let him, he'd prove he'd changed.

At her house, he set the broken door aside and checked the rooms. Reaching her bedroom, he stopped short, and she bumped into his back.

"What's wrong, Tim?"

"I'm not sure you want to see this. It's a mess."

"I know. Nathaniel said someone ransacked it. I need to see if anything's missing or broken."

He flipped on the light, watching her inhale sharply and exhale slowly. She began picking up the wreckage, and he joined her.

Holding up a pair of red lace panties, he smirked. "Oh la la!"

Heat rushed to her cheeks as he laughed. She snatched them from him and tossed them into a drawer, his laughter still echoing as he doubled over.

"Leave the clothes to me. Just pile everything on the bed and I'll sort it."

"Okay," Tim said, still a little breathless.

He gathered clothes and papers into piles. When he found a stack of photos, he paused, thumbing through them. Smiling faces stared back: Dominique, Melissa, Post, and himself. Moments he didn't even have copies of.

Deeper in the stack, the mood shifted: Dominique's bright smile faded, her eyes turned bleak. The final photo made his heart stutter.

Dominique sat in a hospital bed, face red and swollen from crying, wearing a thin gown. In her hand lay something small and bloody. He flipped the picture over. Scrawled on the back:

Lily Rose followed by a date. Beneath, a note in Dominique's handwriting:

Lily, I only met you this once, but I will never forget you. You will always hold a piece of my heart. This is to remind me of what happens when you lose control of yourself. Rest in Heaven, my sweet baby. I'm sorry.

Tim's chest constricted. She blamed herself, but it had been his fault. His choices had driven her to that lowest point.

Without thinking, he crossed the room, turned her toward him, and pulled her into a fierce embrace.

"I'm so sorry," he whispered, then again, and again.

"Um, Tim… why are you apologizing?"

He stepped back slightly, holding up the photo. Her gaze landed on it, and a sharp gasp escaped her lips. Pain flickered across her face, and as tears welled behind closed lids, the salty scent reached him, twisting his heart.

"Please, put it back in the box. I can't look at it."

"Dominique, none of that was your fault. It was mine. Please, look at me," Tim pleaded.

Her watery eyes met his, anger and grief radiating off her in waves. His breath caught.

"Now you understand," she said, lifting her shirt. "This is from the night I miscarried. When I couldn't dilate, they had to do a C-section. This scar reminds me how hard life can hit. It reminds me that I was saved for some reason. I don't know why yet, but I will. This scar is because of you."

Tim traced it with trembling fingers, feeling her shiver, then pulled her into another hug. He was a royal asshole. How could he have thought she'd think less of him for losing his job? She'd loved him with everything she had, and he'd shredded her heart because of his own pride.

"I'm sorry, Dominique. I know that doesn't make it better. I'll spend the rest of my life apologizing and trying to make up for my mistakes… if you'll let me."

"I loved you, Tim. And that love turned to hate. I appreciate you being here these past few days, but I can't go back. You say you'll make it up to me, but how? You can't give me back that time. You can't give me back my baby. Sure, I could have more kids, but it's not the same. I could be with you, but it wouldn't erase what happened. And now I have Nathaniel. He truly sees me. Every part of me. I need that. I want that. I want someone who sees not just my perfections but my flaws, and loves me despite them."

"Telling you I do won't help. You don't believe me. If that's what you really want, I'll prove that's how I feel. I've always seen who you are, Dominique. I've never found shortcomings in you. I loved every part of you. Still do. And I think you still love me too, even if it's just a little. You wouldn't have kept anything that reminded you of me if you didn't."

"Tim, please don't do this. I want to be happy, and having my heart ripped to shreds again would destroy me. You're saying all the right words, but I've heard them before. Can we please just drop this?"

"How can you say that? You don't know what would happen if you gave me another chance." Tim bent to pick up the fallen photos. "Look at these and tell me you don't still love me, even a little."

As he gathered the pictures, something shiny caught his eye. He set the stack down and picked up the object. When he stood, Dominique's eyes squeezed shut.

"You kept it," he whispered. "After all this time… you kept your engagement ring." He stepped closer, voice rough. "Look at me, Dominique, and tell me the truth—that you don't love me at all. Tell me you don't want me, and it's over. But don't lie. I'll know."

"You know I can't," Dominique whispered.

His heart skipped a beat. She still loved him. He kissed her then, pouring every ounce of passion and regret into it. Hope flared, wild, dangerous, and intoxicating. He should've fought for her before. If he had, they might still be together now, married, with a child.

Breaking the kiss, he held her tight. When she finally hugged him back, crying into his chest, he pressed a tender kiss to the crown of her head. Her pain twisted through him, unbearable.

The air between them vibrated with turmoil, her heart still tied to him, but pulled toward Nathaniel. Fear rolled off her in waves: fear of being shattered again.

A voice rang out, splintering the fragile moment. Dominique pulled away, swiping at her tears. With a watery smile that didn't reach her eyes, she walked out of the room. Tim stood frozen, staring down at the ring glinting in his palm.

Gathering himself, Tim moved to the living room and sank onto the couch. Their voices floated in from behind him, but his focus stayed on the ring as he turned it between his fingers. Turquoise: a symbol of peace, love, and hope. If she'd take him back, he'd slip it on her finger again. He slid it into his pocket.

Dominique sat at her desk once the contractor left to get supplies, typing on her laptop, deliberately distant. His gaze lingered on her until she rolled her shoulders.

"Tim, I can feel you staring at me," she said.

He rose and moved behind her, hands rubbing her tense shoulders. Leaning in, he brushed slow kisses along the nape of her neck. Her heartbeat quickened, and she tilted her head, granting him more access.

His hands slid forward to cup her breasts. She moaned softly as he teased her nipples, then turned her chair and claimed her lips. Their tongues tangled, her fingers threading through his hair.

She broke the kiss, breathless. "No, Tim. I can't do this. I told you that."

Tim exhaled heavily. "Why fight this, Dominique? You still want me. I can feel it. How does sleeping with me hurt you?"

"Because sex with you leads to feelings. You can't be with your ex and not feel something. At least, I can't."

"You didn't deny loving me," he said quietly. "I can't promise I'd stop at just sex, because I wouldn't. I still want you, so I can't stop trying."

"But I can stop you," she said firmly. "And I have. Attraction isn't the problem. I hate admitting I still want you, but you already know I do. The problem is… how can I be with Nathaniel and still sleep with you?"

Tim stood straight, eyes narrowing as anger flared. Nathaniel. Always fucking Nathaniel. She wouldn't touch him because of that bastard. Heat surged in his chest, and he forced himself back down onto the couch before he said something unforgivable.

Dominique sighed, then crossed the room. She squatted in front of him, placing her hands gently on his thighs.

"Talk to me, Tim. Don't shut me out again."

His fists clenched. "Why shouldn't I? You don't want me. I keep trying, and all you think about is Nathaniel. I know you want him, and he hasn't hurt you like I have."

"Okay," she said softly. "I understand why that hurts. But I can't help how I feel. No, I didn't come right out and say I still loved you… because I don't even want to admit it to myself. I loved you. Then I hated you. And all I did with that love was bury it. I even tried to kill my love for you by killing myself. Yet here I am. Is there a reason for that? I don't know. Is there a reason you had to go through what you did? I don't know. Did it change you? Yes. Was there a reason you had to leave and then come back? I don't know. But to say I'm confused is an understatement."

Tim swallowed hard, his voice low. "Have you slept with Nathaniel?"

"Do you really want to know? Would it even change anything?" Dominique's voice was small but steady.

"Yes. It changes everything," Tim said. "If you've slept with him, then you're in love with him. How am I supposed to compete with that? I'm already fighting our past, and now this? But you not saying no…" He exhaled, jaw tight. "That tells me all I need to know."

"I can't apologize for how I feel, Tim. I won't. I don't see a way out of this. My heart wants what it wants."

"And your heart wants Nathaniel. You tried to tell me, but I wouldn't listen."

"My heart wants you both," she whispered. "And I don't know what to do. Nathaniel makes me happy. He makes me feel things I've never felt before. There's a connection between us I can't explain. I'm not trying to hurt you by saying that, but I need you to understand why he matters.

"Then there's you. You were there for me when I needed someone most… and then you broke me. And yet, here you are again. When I called, you came without hesitation. *You* came for me, not Nathaniel. You even told me to stay with Nathaniel for my own safety, even though it killed you. You keep choosing me over your pride. But if I go back to you, I lose him. And if I choose him, I already know I'll lose you."

Tim gathered her into his lap, holding her tight. "You won't lose me. Watching you with him will kill me, but I'll still be here. Always."

"Don't say that unless you mean it."

"I mean it," Tim said softly. "If you love something, set it free. If it comes back, it's yours. If it doesn't… it was never yours in the first place, right?"

Dominique's breath hitched. "I let you go… and here you are, back in my life." Her eyes searched his. "Are you trying to tell me something?"

"You already know I'm yours," Tim said, voice low. "And because I love you, I want you to be happy, even if it isn't with me. But don't think for a second I'll stop trying to win you back. I can't promise you that."

Dominique smiled and kissed him. He pulled her closer, deepening the kiss before trailing his lips down her neck. He knew the battle might be hopeless, but he wasn't walking away.

A polite throat cleared. Dominique blushed and slipped from his arms. Tim scowled toward the sound. Damn contractor. Worst timing in the world.

Chapter 45

Tim's phone vibrated in his pocket. Pulling it out, he saw Jacob's name on the screen. He glanced toward Dominique's room and noted the contractor busy reinforcing the front door, the screen already fixed.

Reluctantly, Tim opened the message.

I saw her with him last night. Better make your move fast, or she's going to get hurt. You're one of mine, but she isn't. And you already know I'm after that bastard. I gave you a chance, but if you aren't going to take it, I can't promise she won't get hurt. I don't give many opportunities. You know that. Make up your mind. I'm watching to see if you've changed her.

Tim's jaw tightened. He quickly typed back:

She's not going to lead you to him. I can't force her into this life. I won't do to her what was done to me.

Jacob's reply came almost instantly:

Your choice. Just remember that when she gets hurt or killed.

Tim exhaled sharply and slid the phone back into his pocket just as Dominique returned to the living room. She shuffled through a stack of papers while he sat brooding on the couch.

The contractor finished the repairs and left after Dominique paid him. She turned and caught Tim's gaze.

"Tim, are you alright? You seem miles away."

"I'm fine, Dom. Just… thinking."

"Want to talk about it?"

"Do you really want to hear it?"

"I wouldn't have asked if I wasn't willing to listen. You asked me to be your friend. I'm willing to try."

He patted the seat beside him. "Will you sit with me while we talk?"

"Um, I don't think that's a good idea. We can't seem to be around each other without… something happening."

"Come on, Dominique. We're adults. If something happens, it happens. But friends can sit together without the world ending," Tim teased.

Dominique rolled her eyes. "I already know I'm going to regret this."

She sat beside him, and Tim's grin faded. Her fingers traced the worry lines on his forehead, the tight frown on his lips. He kissed her fingertips but didn't move closer.

"I told you Jacob was in a gang," he began quietly. "That doesn't even begin to cover it, but I can't tell you everything. Roxy coming after you… that was because of me. I'm mixed up in things that would put you in danger just by being near me. If you chose to be with me, you'd be in the middle of it all. I can't hide you. They already know about you. I can't be with you every second, so how do I keep you safe? And now Jacob's forcing me into a choice… one that could mean losing you."

"Tim…" Dominique's voice softened. "I don't even know what to say because I don't know the whole story. I wish you'd trust me enough to tell me everything, so at least I could try to understand. But… how does him giving you a choice mean you lose me?"

Tim's jaw tightened. "He's after Nathaniel. Wants to hurt him for what he did to Roxy. Nathaniel wasn't lying when he told you Jacob's dangerous. Jacob's done things normal people don't even think about doing. He was ready to come after you for shooting Roxy. I couldn't let that happen, so I told him…" He hesitated, his voice dropping. "I told him you belonged to me."

"You did *what*?" Dominique's voice cracked with disbelief. "How could you tell him I was with you when I'm not?"

"I had to." Tim's voice wavered between anger and desperation. "I couldn't let him harm you! He gave me a choice… either I bring you in and you're protected, or you die. He'll let Roxy kill you, Dom. They won't stop until you're gone. Do you understand? I can't—" His voice broke. "I can't lose you like that. But if I bring you in, I lose you anyway. This isn't a life for you."

Dominique stared at him, speechless for a moment. "I… I don't even know what to say. Why can't you just get away from them? Leave that life behind. You said you were trying to better yourself, to come back for me. How is staying tied to them bettering yourself? You're right about one thing, though… this isn't my life. I want no part of what they do. I'm not like that. And if it comes down to kill or be killed, I'm not going down without a fight. I'll figure something out."

Tim's jaw tightened. "Dom, you don't understand how they work. You will go down, whether you like it or not. I've tried to leave before." He swallowed hard, remembering. "When I broke things off with Roxy, I tried to walk away. They broke my bones and left me bleeding out. The only way out is death. Maybe…" His voice dropped to a bitter whisper. "Maybe I should've let them kill me. At least I wouldn't have to drag you into this."

"Don't say that, Tim." Dominique's voice was quiet but firm. "If I've learned anything, it's that everyone matters to someone. Taking your life doesn't just end your pain… it shatters someone else's world."

Tim gave a small, broken smile. "I don't matter to anyone. You were the only person I ever had, Dom. I had people to party with, sure, but they weren't friends. When I really needed them, they disappeared. I don't have any family. Growing up in a boys' home made that clear. You… you were the closest thing to family I ever knew."

Her throat tightened. "Oh, Tim, that can't be true."

"But it is." His voice softened, almost ashamed. "You know I don't have family. And those people I thought cared? I was too drunk to see how toxic they were. Once I lost you, I lost myself. I'd never been good enough for anyone, so when I lost my job, I felt like I wasn't a real man. Not good enough for you… and I couldn't handle it."

Her eyes shimmered with tears. "Is that why you shut me out back then? Because you thought you weren't good enough?

Tim, I didn't care about money or jobs. I cared about you… the man, not the paycheck. Why couldn't you just see that?"

He let out a shaky breath, fists curling loosely on his knees. "Because all I could see was a failure. A disappointment to the one person who ever gave a damn about me. I've been the screwup nobody wanted my whole life. No one but you. But even your love couldn't break through that wall in my head. You tried. God, you tried. But I couldn't stand the thought of seeing disappointment in your eyes. Not from you."

"Oh, Tim…" Dominique's voice cracked. "I'm sorry. I just wish you'd trusted me enough to talk to me. To believe I wouldn't leave."

His eyes darkened with regret. "But ultimately, you did leave. And I know that's on me. I met Roxy one night, left the bar with her. But when it came down to it, I couldn't sleep with her. All I could think about was you. She didn't like that. I barely made it out alive."

Her breath hitched. "Is that why you disappeared? Why wouldn't you talk to me?"

"Yes." His voice was low, weighted. "How could I tell you? You'd think I slept with her, even though I didn't. And after you finally broke up with me…" He swallowed hard. "I did go to her. I was hurting, angry. If the one person in the world who cared about me didn't anymore, then why even try? So I let myself fall into that life, and I've been trapped in it ever since."

She searched his face, tears threatening. "What about the other women? All those nights you left with someone else?"

His jaw tightened. "I wasn't sleeping with them, Dom. Most of the time, I was their protection. After Roxy nearly killed me, Jacob found me. Offered me a job protecting his people. Men and women. At first, it was just a way to stay alive. But I was so full of rage after losing you… fighting gave me somewhere to put it. I moved up the ranks fast. Should've been his third in command by now. But I wanted out. I wanted you."

Dominique leaned back, rubbing her face with trembling hands. The weight of his words pressed on her chest until she could barely breathe.

"I need time to think about all of this, Tim." Dominique's voice trembled. "I don't even know what I'm caught up in because you won't tell me everything. Nathaniel won't either. Honestly, you're both frustrating. I know you're hiding things, and it's pushing me away."

Tim's shoulders sagged. "I'm sorry, Dom. That's the last thing I want, to push you away. I just… I don't know how to tell you everything. I'm terrified that if I do, you'll walk out for good. I couldn't survive you rejecting the real me."

She held his gaze. "You've told me more about yourself today than you ever have before. And look… I'm still here. I haven't kicked you out."

"That's only because you brought me here," he said with a weak, sad smile.

"That's true," she admitted, a ghost of a smile flickering. "But I could've sent you walking. And I didn't."

Dominique slid her arms around him, and Tim pulled her gently into his lap. He held her there, his chest rising and falling beneath her cheek. The heaviness in him was so palpable, he wondered if she could feel it.

"I'm not going anywhere, Tim," she whispered, pulling back just enough to meet his eyes. "I can't promise what the future holds, but I won't leave you, not again. Okay?"

He managed another small, sad smile. "Thank you. That means more than you know. Even if all you ever are to me is a friend… I'll take it. At least then I'll have one person in this world who truly gives a damn about me."

Dominique cupped his face, her palms warm against his skin, her gaze searching his. Tim felt his own pain echoing back at him through her eyes. She understood more than he'd ever guessed. For a long moment, she just stared, and he wondered if the predator in him was close enough to the surface for her to see it staring back.

Then she leaned down, still holding his gaze, and kissed him. Tim's breath caught. Keeping his eyes locked on hers, he flicked his tongue across her lips, demanding entrance. She shifted in his lap, and a low growl rumbled from his chest, vibrating against her. Her excitement and need were a heady scent in the air.

His grip tightened, crushing her body against his. His lips trailed down her throat as his hands slipped beneath her shirt, fingertips tracing her spine in slow, deliberate strokes. She ground against him, and he unhooked her bra with practised ease, his hands sliding around to cup her breasts. Her soft moan shot through him like fire.

When Dominique pulled back, he held her gaze, letting his wolf surface. His eyes followed the movement of her hands as she peeled off her shirt and bra, tossing them aside. Threading her fingers through his hair, she pulled him down to her breasts, arching her back to meet him.

He flicked his tongue over her nipple, quick and light, earning a gasp. His eyes rolled up to watch her face as he drew her breast into his mouth; eyes closed, lips parted, her back arching even farther, offering herself to him.

Encouraged by her movements, he thrust upward, meeting her hips, starting a slow, deliberate grind. His mouth and hands explored, bites, flicks of his tongue, pinches, and rolls, until her nipples hardened under his touch.

Her fingers traced up his sides, muscles flexing beneath her light caress, then slid back down his chest and abs. When her fingertips brushed his scars, his stomach clenched, heat flooding through him. The way she lingered over them, like they were something to be admired, made his blood boil with need.

"Take the shirt off, Tim," Dominique ordered.

"Yes, ma'am. Anything you want," he rasped.

"Then shut up and take it off." She rose to her feet.

He yanked his shirt over his head, breath quickening. His gaze followed the slow trail of her pants and panties sliding down her legs. Then she stood bare before him, breathing unevenly, chest rising and falling fast.

He drank her in from head to toe, his cock straining against his jeans. Her hips looked even rounder, scar marking her stomach, but everything else was the same. She was still breathtaking. His vision flickered, the wolf in him pressing forward, and he forced it back, gripping for control.

A smile played on her lips before her tongue darted out to wet them. His breath caught, eyes following every slow stroke of her tongue.

Then, a surprise jolted through him, she kissed him. Her mouth trailed down his neck, sucking and licking a path lower. When her tongue flicked over his nipple, a groan tore from his chest.

She lingered over his scars, warm breath ghosting across them before her tongue traced every rough line and curve. His pulse thundered; his breathing quickened. What was she doing to him? Her lips curved in a smile against his stomach, and she pressed a soft kiss just above his waistband.

The slow rasp of his zipper lowering sent a jolt through him. She paused, just for a heartbeat, then surged up to crash her mouth against his, her tongue forcing his lips apart. Their tongues tangled as her fingers slid under his jeans and underwear. He lifted his hips, helping her tug them down. Relief flooded him when his cock sprang free, no longer bound.

She broke the kiss and slid down his body, pushing his jeans to his ankles. His gaze locked on her, sharp and unrelenting, as she tugged off his boots and yanked the denim free. God help her if she was teasing him. His control over the wolf inside him was already fraying.

Her hands glided up his legs to his hips, light and deliberate. Soft kisses trailed up his thighs, each one sparking a twitch in his muscles. When her warm mouth slid over the length of his cock, he jerked, a low growl vibrating in his chest.

Her tongue traced him from base to tip, curling as she climbed back up. She wrapped her fingers around the base, squeezing just enough as her lips closed around the head. Her other hand cupped his balls, thumb stroking lazily over sensitive skin. A groan ripped free of him, his head falling back against the couch as heat coiled hard and fast in his gut.

Blood pounded through him, his cock swelling, ready to burst. Then she stopped. His eyes flew open, locking on hers as she crawled into his lap and straddled him. Her arousal was an undeniable scent in the air.

Tim slid a hand between them, and she shifted back just enough so he couldn't touch her.

"Are you changing your mind again? You don't want me to touch you?" he murmured, voice rough.

Her gaze burned into him. "No, I'm not changing my mind. I don't want you to play with me. I'm turned on, and I'm taking what I want now."

She guided herself down onto him, and heat and pressure consumed him all at once.

He gripped her hips and thrust upward, a low growl rumbling in his chest. She guided his head to her breasts again, and he took one greedily into his mouth, rolling his hips beneath her. She'd pushed him away every other time he'd tried, so he let her set the pace now.

Her rhythm was slow, steady, deliberate. When her eyes found his, he knew exactly what she saw: the wolf slipping through. Her pupils were blown wide with lust, breath coming ragged, arousal in every shaky exhale. The sight made his own control splinter, craving a faster, rougher pace.

"Dominique?" His voice was rough, almost a growl.

"Yes?" she purred.

"I'm trying to let you do your thing, and it feels incredible, but I can feel the urge to take you the way I want, and it's getting damn hard to hold back."

She trembled under his hands, her eyes dilating with a flicker of fear. His wolf had bled through. She licked her lips, and his gaze followed the movement like a predator. Leaning closer, her breath mingled with his.

Her words brushed against his lips. "If you want me, then take me."

Tim groaned, rising to his feet, and her legs wrapped around him, trembling with a mix of desire and fear. He gripped her thighs, urging her to let go, a deep growl vibrating from his chest as her legs slid down his.

Turning her so her back faced him, his hand slid between her thighs. His fingers circled her clit, coaxing her arousal as he thrust back inside her. Dominique moaned, grinding against him, the sound feeding the fire in his veins.

After a few minutes, he pulled away slightly, smirking at the low, frustrated groan that escaped her. She arched, displeasure sharp in her cry as he moved.

Guiding them toward the couch, he pressed on her back, bending her over it. Lifting one leg, he placed her foot on the couch, spreading her further, his pulse hammering with need.

"I hope you're ready," Tim growled, pressing against her back as he shoved himself inside.

He drove into her hard and fast, letting his animal instincts take over. Teeth sank into her shoulder; her cry of pain and pleasure spurred him on. Her hands braced against the couch, holding her taut against his relentless pace.

"Is this what you want, Dominique? Do you want me?"

"Yes. Don't stop!"

"Tell me you want me!" he growled in her ear.

"Yes, I want you!" she shouted.

His hands gripped her breasts, rolling and pinching her nipples, rough and demanding. One hand left her chest and tangled in her hair, pulling her head back as his mouth claimed her neck. She tightened around him, and he drove harder, faster, the sound of their bodies slamming together echoing through the room. Her nails dug into the couch, matching the rhythm of his feral thrusts.

His lips and tongue trailed up her spine, teeth nipping at her shoulder blades. Moans spilt from her lips with every bite. Her arms locked straight, bracing against the couch as his thrusts drove her forward. Her body was taut, moulded under him.

He found her clit, pinching and rubbing tight, perfect circles. Her body shuddered, climax tearing through her, warm release coating him. Her cries and tremors only pushed him harder, driving every thrust faster, milking her completely.

"You're mine," he growled in her ear, losing himself in the moment.

She shivered, slumping against the couch when he let go. Tim lifted her effortlessly, carrying her to the bedroom. She curled against him, breath softening as he laid her on the bed. Sliding in behind her, he wrapped his arms around her, pressing her close, whispering, *I love you*. Her breathing evened as sleep claimed her, his heart full.

Chapter 46

Dominique woke and stretched. Tim's arm tightened around her as she moved, and when she tried to shift away, he pulled her closer, face nuzzling into her hair.

"Don't go, Dom. Stay here with me," he whispered.

"I'll be back, Tim. I'm not freaking out on you, I promise," she said, turning her head to meet his eyes.

His gaze softened, spring green, steady. She kissed him and moved out from under his arm, heading to the bathroom and returned a few minutes later.

Tim sat on the edge of the bed, eyes fixed on nothing. She paused, then pushed him back slightly and settled onto his lap. He wrapped his arms around her, laying his head against her chest, letting out a slow, deep breath. She rested her head atop his, grounding him.

"What's wrong, Tim? You looked so sad a second ago."

"I honestly thought you were regretting having sex with me again. I didn't expect you to come back, let alone touch me," he admitted, voice low.

She brushed her lips against his. "I don't regret it, Tim. I wouldn't have done it if I was going to regret it. I wasn't drunk. I wasn't half-asleep. I knew what I was doing, what I wanted. You… you were the Tim I loved and lost so long ago. It meant more to me than you'll ever know."

"I know I messed everything up between us, Dominique. I can't apologize enough. I know that will never make up for what I did. But… you wanting me in any way, even a little, makes me happy. The happiest I've been in a long time. The only times I've ever truly been happy… it was because of you."

She hesitated. "I don't really know what to say to that, Tim. I'm still so confused by… everything."

"You don't have to say anything," he murmured, tightening his hold on her. "I offered to be your friend only, but I told you I couldn't help wanting you. And I don't just mean… for sex. I want all of you. Every piece. I've thought about you every day, every night, all the things we could've had. Then, when you told me about the baby… it crushed me. I didn't just lose you. I lost the family I could've had. My family. The life I always wanted."

Her hand cupped his cheek. "I can't promise we'd get married or even be together like that in the future… but I will be your family. No matter what. You can call me your family, even if it's just as a friend. Okay?"

"That won't work, Dominique. The way I feel about you… It won't let me see you as just a friend. I'll try, but I don't know if I can. How do you shut off your feelings for someone you love?"

"You can't," she sighed.

"You did. You don't love me anymore," he said, looking away, the ache in his chest sharp.

"I didn't stop loving you. I… I started hating you," she admitted, her voice trembling. "And I know you don't want to hear this, but I met Nathaniel. He… he makes me feel like I've never felt before. We have a connection I can't explain. I was trying to move on."

"But then I came back and… messed it up again," Tim muttered, sliding her off his lap and onto the bed.

Her fingers grasped his hand. He glanced over his shoulder at her, his chest tightening as sadness welled inside him. She looked away, her heartbeat rapid, the turmoil radiating off her in waves.

"Yeah… I guess you could say you messed it up," she said, voice low, almost a whisper. "Because now I'm stuck between two men I don't want to lose. I want you both, Tim. I still love you, and I don't want to, because of everything I went through. But I missed the old Tim, the one who loved me, who was there for me. The one you've been these past few days. I want him. I love him. But I fell for Nathaniel too… and I want him for what I feel when I'm with him. I can't have both, and I can't choose… because I'll lose the other."

"Then I'll make it easy for you. I'm not the old Tim. He's gone. I can never be that guy again… not after everything I've done. And I can't let you get wrapped up in my world. You'd get hurt. So… choose Nathaniel," Tim said, pulling his hand from hers.

He left the bedroom, each step heavier than the last. His chest ached. He'd just sabotaged himself again, but he had to let her go, for her safety, for her peace of mind. He had to accept being just her friend. The thought of seeing her with Nathaniel, fully happy without him, made his stomach twist.

But he couldn't let fear stop him. If Jacob went after Nathaniel, Dominique would be caught in the crossfire. He couldn't allow that. He had to act.

Tim bent to gather their clothes. Turning back toward the bedroom, he froze. Dominique stood there, hands wringing, eyes wide and glistening with unshed tears. That nervous gesture hit him harder than anything else.

He approached quietly and held out the pile of clothes. She took them, her hands trembling slightly as they brushed his. He looked down at her face—vulnerable, beautiful, broken—and felt that sharp, familiar tug in his chest.

"Are you really giving up on me?" Dominique's voice cracked, her eyes wide, vulnerable.

That look shattered him. He could never give up on her, but he couldn't keep ripping her heart apart, putting her between him and Nathaniel. And until Jacob was gone, she would always be in danger.

"No. I'm just letting you move on. I'll always be here for you," Tim said, forcing the words through the tightness in his chest.

He started putting his clothes back on when her hand touched his arm. He looked down and saw her holding her necklace. She stared at it for a long moment before stepping forward and placing it around his neck. She hooked it and stepped back.

"It's Lily's ashes. If I'm going to move on, then I have to leave everything in the past. You keep them as a remembrance of the life you could've had… and remember this choice was yours," Dominique said, walking back toward her bedroom.

Tim froze, the weight of it hitting him like a blow. He'd seen that necklace on her every day, the only thing she had left of their baby, and now she'd given it to him. His chest tightened, heart stuttering as he left the house.

When he reached the woods, he dropped his human form, muscles and bones reshaping, fur rippling across his body. A long, mournful howl tore from his throat, vibrating through the trees, echoing his rage and grief. He seized his clothes in his jaws, claws digging into the soft earth, and launched himself into a flat-out sprint.

He ran as fast as he could, desperate to clear his head. The pain followed him anyway, crawling through his veins, relentless. Dominique had made her choice. She'd decided he was no longer part of her life. That wasn't how he'd meant it to go.

Chapter 47

Melissa slipped into the chair across from Dominique, her frown deepening the longer she looked at her.

"Okay, what's wrong? Tim's out there brooding, and you're in here sulking. And don't you dare say nothing," Melissa said.

Dominique sighed, rubbing her forehead. "Tim broke up with me. For lack of a better explanation."

"What the hell does that mean?"

"He opened up to me more today than he has in a long time. The past few days, he's really been there for me. I slept with him today, and then he held me as I slept." Her voice wavered. "I've been so confused about him and Nathaniel. I told him how I really felt. He said he'd make it easy for me and… took himself out of the equation." Dominique closed her eyes against the tears.

"Well, that's a good thing, right? Now you can go after Nathaniel and not be confused. I can't believe you were even thinking about going back to Tim."

"I can't either. How could I have been so stupid? I let him back in just for him to rip me apart again. Why do I keep falling for it?" Dominique's hand moved instinctively to her chest, only to meet bare skin.

Tears spilled over, and Melissa was at her side in an instant, wrapping her in a hug.

"Where's your necklace, Dom?"

"I gave it to Tim," she whispered. "It's part of my past, just like him. If he's really out of the picture, then I need to move on. I can't do that if I'm constantly living in the past."

"Oh, Dom, I'm so sorry. I wish I knew what to do for you."

"You're doing it right now, Mel. You've always been there for me. Thank you."

"Anytime, bestie."

Melissa held her while she cried, letting her soak her shoulder without complaint. After a while, Dominique's sobs softened to sniffles. She assured Melissa she'd be fine and said she needed to get out to the bar.

Melissa nodded, but as soon as she stepped out of the office and spotted Tim, her sympathy hardened into anger. The bar had started to fill, but she didn't care about the eyes on her. She stormed straight to him and slapped him, hard enough to turn heads.

"What the hell, Melissa?" Tim snapped, startled.

"You bastard!" she shouted. "You hurt her again! If she spirals like she did last time, I swear to God, I'm going to kill you!"

Chapter 48

Nathaniel stepped up to the bar just as Melissa's hand cracked against Tim's cheek. Post appeared from the back, wrapping his arms around Melissa's waist and dragging her, still struggling, into the kitchen. Her fury practically scorched the air.

But beneath the anger, Nathaniel felt something heavier, Dominique's sadness, threading through the room like a cold current. Whatever had just gone down between her and Tim had gutted her deeply enough to set Melissa off.

Nathaniel's voice was calm, but his jaw was tight. "What did you do to Dominique? From the weight of her sadness, I'm guessing Melissa wasn't talking about anyone else."

Tim met his gaze. Anger, regret, and pain flickered in his eyes. His fists clenched, knuckles whitening, but he held them at his sides. Nathaniel arched a brow, silently daring him. The wolf's rage simmered so hot Nathaniel could almost feel it prickle across his skin.

"I slept with Dominique today," Tim said flatly, then smiled just enough to make it a challenge.

Nathaniel's eyes darkened, his voice dropping to a low, controlled growl. "That alone wouldn't hurt Dominique."

Nathaniel's hands curled into fists. He was ready to tear Tim apart himself. How could Dominique make love to him, then turn around and give herself to Tim?

Tim shifted, and a glint of light caught Nathaniel's eye: a necklace hanging against Tim's chest. Recognition slammed into him. Dominique's necklace.

His voice was sharp, deadly quiet. "What did you do to her? And why do you have her necklace? Did you steal it?"

Tim's reply was barely a whisper. "No. I walked away today. Made her choice easier. You won. Are you happy now? She's moving on, leaving her past behind. That includes me… and our daughter. She gave me the necklace."

Nathaniel froze, stunned. He hadn't expected Tim to step aside. Did that even give him a chance now? When Dominique was already breaking?

He drew a slow breath. "I can't say I'm sorry you're out of the picture," he said carefully, "but I never wanted Dominique hurt. I wasn't going to push her. I wanted her to choose, without pain, without forcing her hand."

"Yeah, I know. I'm a bastard," Tim said quietly. "But I love her. I just…want her to be happy."

Nathaniel's jaw tightened. "How can you say you love her and still hurt her like this? You can feel her sadness as clearly as I can. Why not let her figure out what she wants on her own?"

Tim let out a slow, bitter breath. "Because I already know what she truly wants. She's torn because she still feels something for me, what we had before, but like I told her, I'm not that man anymore. And then there's you. She's fallen for you, and you haven't done half the damage I have. I can see it in the way she talks about you, how she says she doesn't want to lose one of us. That tells me everything."

He raked a hand through his hair. "I'll stay her friend, if she'll even have me after this. But after today…" He shook his head. "I'm not so sure."

Nathaniel's voice dropped. "How can you be so sure she loves me?"

"She told me," Tim said simply. "She knew it would gut me, but she was honest. And we were honest with each other. But honesty isn't enough to keep her safe. Jacob's still out there, and I won't let him come near her. So I'm going to do the one thing I swore I'd never do."

Nathaniel's brow furrowed. "What are you talking about?"

Tim met his gaze, unflinching. "I'm going to protect her; her life, and her heart. I'm going to challenge Jacob. With him out of the picture, you'll be safe. She'll be happy. Even if I'm not."

He turned on his heel and walked toward a waiting customer, leaving Nathaniel with the weight of his words.

Nathaniel understood what it meant for Tim to challenge Jacob. If Tim won, the pack would be his. If he lost… he would die. Did Tim truly want to lead? Nathaniel couldn't interfere; the pack's business was their own, but the thought of Tim's blood on the ground and Dominique's grief because of it weighed heavily. That kind of loss would break her far worse than Tim simply walking away.

He shook his head, pushing the thought aside, and made his way toward Dominique's office. She'd texted that she needed to see him. Would she tell him what happened today? Would she finally choose him? Tim's words still echoed in his mind: *She loves you.* For the first time, certainty stirred in his chest. He could move forward now, reveal the truth about himself. This was his last chance, and he couldn't afford a single misstep.

He knocked gently on her door.

"Come in," she called.

He opened it to find her sitting behind the desk, her fingers subconsciously brushing her bare neck. The missing necklace left her looking exposed somehow, fragile. He closed the door behind him and crossed the room, lowering himself into the chair across from her.

"Good evening, Dominique," he said, his voice soft.

"Hey." She slid an envelope across the desk toward him without meeting his eyes.

Nathaniel picked it up, opened the flap, and saw the signed contracts inside, the ones he'd brought her days ago. She'd made her decision: she was going into business with him. A small smile curved his lips. He looked up to see her return it, but the smile never touched her eyes.

He stood, circled the desk, and leaned down to pull her gently into his arms.

"I'm sorry, Dominique," he murmured. "I know what happened today… Melissa kind of attacked and threatened Tim. I asked, and he told me."

"Well, that's just great."

"Tim basically told me I'd won," Nathaniel said quietly. "But I meant what I told you before. I'm not here to pressure you, Dominique. I'm here, whatever you decide."

"Well, I guess it doesn't really matter now, does it? Tim bowed out. I have to put the past behind me. I even gave him my necklace… to remind him. I really thought, after the talk we had today, after all the honesty… that things were finally different. But I guess all it did was upset him more."

"Oh?" Nathaniel tilted his head, careful, probing. "What did he tell you?"

"He told me why he did the things he did before. He still wouldn't say much about what happened with Jacob. Just that he's done things he isn't proud of. He's keeping that part of his life locked away, but… I get it, I guess. He doesn't want me tangled up in whatever danger he's in." Dominique's voice wavered. "But he also said Jacob told him to bring me in, or I'd be in danger. And that they're after you, for some reason I still don't understand."

Nathaniel's brows drew together. "What do you mean, 'bring you in'?"

"Tim said he told Jacob I belonged to him. Jacob told him to bring me into the gang. I guess every guy in a gang has a woman or something? I don't even know what that means."

Nathaniel's stomach tightened. Tim clearly hadn't told her everything. Especially not the truth about the pack. But it wasn't his place to reveal Tim's secrets. Her words sparked unease: Jacob's offer meant Dominique would've been under pack protection, untouchable by anyone else. Tim hadn't offered her that choice. Instead, he'd stepped aside… and now planned to challenge Jacob.

Nathaniel's jaw clenched. Tim wasn't just bowing out. He was preparing for a fight that could get him killed. Nathaniel would need to watch Tim closely, because something about this didn't add up.

"So, you've decided to cut him out of your life?" Nathaniel's voice was gentle, but there was a flicker of tension behind his eyes.

"No." Dominique exhaled, the sound more like a sigh than a word. "He decided that for me."

"If you still want him, why not go after him?"

Her fingers twisted together in her lap. "Because… he was right. He isn't the old Tim I knew, not really. But in some ways, he still is. I'm going to try to move on, live my life, and do what I want for once. If he becomes part of it later… fine. But I can't keep feeling this alone all the time."

Nathaniel's expression softened. "Dominique, you're not alone. You have friends who love you, who care. I love you." He bent down and brushed his lips over hers, unhurried and tender.

Dominique kissed him back, her breath catching. When he pulled away, he cupped her cheek, and the warmth of his palm sent her pulse racing.

"I appreciate you being my friend, Nathaniel," she whispered. "And you're right. I do have friends, like you and Melissa, who love me. That's all I need right now."

"You know that's not what I meant when I said I loved you," he murmured, eyes searching hers.

Her breath hitched. "And if I told you I loved you?"

His answering smile was faint but certain. "You'd make me very happy. I'd love for you to be with me… but I won't push. I'll be here, waiting, whenever you're ready."

Nathaniel's gaze snagged on the flutter of her pulse, a delicate beat just beneath her skin, perfectly in time with the frantic rhythm of her heart. Hunger speared through him, swift and sharp. He forced himself to move, to put space between them before the urge became unbearable. Crossing to the chair opposite her desk, he sat, his hands curling into fists until the craving ebbed.

"Thank you, Nathaniel. I think I just need a few days to process everything," Dominique said quietly.

"Will you still stay with me?"

She gave him a pointed look. "I don't really like having to run out under a closing garage door if I leave."

"Simple enough." His lips curved into a faint smile. "I'll give you an opener. You can come and go as you please."

Her brows rose. "Seriously? You'd trust me at your house? What if you aren't there?"

"I wouldn't mind," he replied without hesitation. "I trust you, Dominique. So… will you come back with me tonight?"

She hesitated, twisting a strand of hair around her finger. "I need a few days, Nathaniel. Just to get myself right after today. I don't know if I can do that while being around you."

Concern shadowed his face. "I'm still worried about your safety. If you'd rather have space, I'll keep to my room. After that, you can go home and only come back if and when you choose."

"Alright," she said after a beat. "But only for two nights. Then I'm going home, okay?"

"Fantastic." His relief showed in the way his shoulders loosened. He picked up the envelope from her desk, his fingers lingering on the edge for a moment before he straightened. "I'll see you later tonight."

Chapter 49

Dominique handed the keys to Melissa. "Lock up for me?"

As she headed for the back door, the air prickled, a pressure on her neck, the unmistakable weight of a stare. She spun and found Tim lingering in the hallway's shadows.

"Why are you following me?" Her voice was sharp, brittle. "You left my house without a word. You told me you were letting me move on. And now here you are."

"I want you to move on and be happy, even if it's not with me." His jaw tightened. "Doesn't mean I don't love you. And I still want you safe. So, yeah, I'm making sure you're okay."

"Tim, I can't do this with you." Heat flared behind her eyes, but she held his gaze. "You ripped my heart out earlier, and it's not even all your fault, because I was stupid enough to let you back in. But I'm not doing this back-and-forth shit anymore. Either you're in my life, or you're not. I'm taking a few days to think it through. Maybe you should, too."

His hand twitched like he might reach for her, but he let it fall. "I don't need time, Dom. I let you go because I'm not the same man I was, and I don't want you stuck choosing between us. But I'm still your friend."

"It's not your choice to make," she snapped. "If I choose Nathaniel, that's on me. If I choose you, that's on me. Taking that choice away didn't protect me… it hurt me. Neither of us are the same people we were two years ago."

"If you're my friend, then act like it. Friends don't trail me everywhere. Friends don't make my decisions. Friends respect me."

She shoved the door open, air rushing in. "I'm a grown woman, Tim. I don't need your protection."

Dominique stepped into the night and let the door swing shut behind her.

Dominique slammed her car door harder than she meant to. Tim, still calling himself her friend, still insisting on protecting her. After walking away like he had? He was impossible. Confusing. Infuriating. She needed distance. Melissa could manage the club for a few days; she'd done it plenty of times.

The drive home blurred past in angry silence. Inside, Dominique locked the door and flicked on the lights. The house felt too bright, too empty. She snatched clothes and toiletries, stuffing a bag without thinking. She just needed to get out, breathe.

She opened the door to leave.

And froze.

Amber eyes gleamed from the tree line.

Her stomach dropped. Dominique slammed the door shut, her pulse hammering in her ears. Nathaniel had warned her about a wolf out here, but those eyes weren't wolf-like. They were… wrong. Too high off the ground. Too knowing.

She edged to the window and eased two fingers between the blinds. Nothing. Just the dark stretch of trees.

A shaky laugh escaped her. "Get a grip, Dom."

But her hands trembled as she reopened the door and stepped onto the porch. The night was still, heavy. No rustle of leaves, no cricket song. Nothing.

"Seriously losing it," she muttered, retreating inside. She locked the door again, tossed her bag into the car, and slid into the driver's seat.

As she shifted into reverse, the eyes flared again, closer now, around the side of the house.

Dominique froze. Fear rooted her in place even as some hypnotic pull locked her gaze on those glowing points. The moonless sky left the yard drenched in shadow, but the eyes burned like coals, unblinking, predatory.

Suddenly, they surged toward her.

Adrenaline spiked. She slammed the car into drive, fingers slick on the wheel. But movement streaked across her peripheral vision, a blur lunging toward the eyes.

She couldn't look away. Black and gray shapes collided, tumbling across the ground in a violent knot. The gray figure staggered toward the trees, then the black mass overtook it with a thunderous howl that split the night.

She slammed her foot on the gas, tires spitting gravel as the car shot up the driveway. Her heart pounded so hard it hurt, each thud echoing in her ears. In the rearview mirror, a flicker of movement.

Something black.

Tall.

Bear-sized.

Bears don't howl.

She didn't think. She swerved onto the road, pedal flat to the floor, engine whining as the world blurred by. She risked another glance in the mirror. Empty.

Then a howl ripped through the night, low, mournful, impossibly close. The sound vibrated through the car's frame and straight down her spine.

Dominique didn't stop until Nathaniel's driveway appeared, her breath coming in shallow, ragged bursts. She threw the gearshift into park but didn't move. Her whole body trembled, fingers white-knuckling the steering wheel. She closed her eyes, tried to steady her breathing.

A sharp knock on the window shattered the moment. She screamed.

Her eyes flew open. Nathaniel. He crouched down, concern etched across his face as he opened her door.

"Dominique, what's wrong?" His voice was low, careful.

"I… I'm not sure," she managed, her words tripping over themselves. She didn't even know what she'd seen, let alone how to explain it without sounding insane. Her legs wobbled as she climbed out, leaning against the car for balance.

"Dominique, you're shaking. Tell me what happened."

She darted a glance toward the shadowed tree line beyond his driveway. The darkness seemed thicker tonight, almost watchful.

"Can we go inside before we talk?" she whispered.

"Sure. Come on," Nathaniel said, sliding an arm around her waist. His touch was steady, anchoring her as he guided her into the house.

Inside the living room, he eased her down onto the couch, then sat beside her. He didn't press her for answers right away. Just wrapped his arms around her and held her. His warmth seeped through her shaking frame until the tremors slowed.

Dominique focused on her breathing—in, slow and shaky… out, slower still. The press of his chest against her back, the steady beat of his heart under her ear, was the only thing keeping her grounded.

When her breaths finally evened out, Nathaniel's voice came, soft but firm. "Are you ready to tell me what happened now, Dominique?"

"I'm not sure what happened, Nathaniel." Her voice cracked. "I went to my house to grab a couple of things since I'm staying here the next few days. When I went to leave, I saw the eyes again. Then… nothing. Then I saw them when I got in the car. I thought I was losing it. They were just… there. But I couldn't see what they belonged to, only a shadow. A big one. And then, it ran at me. Out of nowhere, something else attacked it." She sucked in a deep breath, her hands twisting together.

"And you didn't see what it was?" Nathaniel asked, eyes narrowing.

"Not exactly. It looked huge. Way too big for a wolf, Nathaniel. And the eyes… this set was amber. The other pair I saw before? Blue." She swallowed hard. "One of those shadows followed me up the driveway."

His jaw tightened. "Dominique, I'm pleading with you, stay here for the next couple of days. Not just nights. Days. I don't like whatever was at your house."

"Trust me, I'm not going anywhere," she said, shaking her head. "I was already planning on asking Melissa to open and close the bar for a few days so I could think and get some distance from Tim, but this…" Her voice faltered. "This sealed the deal."

Nathaniel's arms tightened around her again, protective and sure. "I'm glad to hear it, Dominique."

Chapter 50

Tim convinced Melissa to let him leave after Dominique. She agreed, happy to have him gone.

He drove toward Dominique's place but parked his car up the road, out of sight. Slipping into the trees, he stalked through the woods on foot. The deeper he went, the sharper the scent hit him; musky, familiar, dangerous. His gut clenched.

He shifted, paws sinking into the damp earth as his wolf took over, and crept silently toward her house.

Movement flared at the edge of his vision. Karina, a gray streak, barreling straight for Dominique's car.

A snarl ripped through Tim's throat as he lunged. He slammed into her mid-charge, their bodies crashing to the ground in a tangle of fur and claws. They rolled, teeth flashing, the forest echoing with their growls.

Did Jacob back out of his promise to give me time until Roxy healed? Rage burned through him. *And why is Dominique just sitting there? Why hasn't she driven off?*

'Why are you here, Karina?' he snapped through the mental link, his jaws clamped around her shoulder.

'I'm going to kill her,' Karina's voice seethed in his head. 'Roxy can't, but I can. No one hurts my baby sister and gets away with it.'

Tim snarled louder, twisting to pin her. 'Roxy brought that on herself by coming here to kill Dominique. Her stupidity gets her into trouble. I don't know why you keep shielding her from her own mistakes. She has to learn from them eventually. Now, I don't want to kill you. Leave now, and this ends.' He released her throat, letting the threat hang.

Karina's amber eyes blazed. 'No!' she roared through the link.

She sprang to her feet in one fluid motion and bolted toward Dominique, her paws tearing up the earth as she ran.

Tim slammed Karina down again, consequences be damned. He wasn't letting her touch Dominique. Her claws raked his side. Hot pain seared his ribs and tore a howl from his throat. Fury surged; he clamped his jaws around her throat and felt the jugular give beneath his teeth. Karina's body went limp almost instantly.

Breath ragged, he turned toward the road and bolted after Dominique, but by the time he reached the end of the lane, her taillights were gone. He skidded to a halt, frustration ripping a raw howl into the night.

He trotted back through the trees to where Karina's lifeless form sprawled among the leaves. He couldn't leave her here.

Linking Jacob, he growled, 'Karina's dead. I told you I'd protect Dominique at all costs. Either back off and let me handle this, or I'll keep killing your people. Or die trying.'

Jacob's answer was a cold blade in his mind. 'Karina wasn't sent for Dominique. I won't allow you to keep killing my wolves. If I decide to send someone for her, nothing you can do will stop it. You refused to bring her into the pack. Bring Karina's body here. We'll dispose of it properly. Then I'll decide what to do with you.'

The deadly calm in Jacob's tone chilled him more than any roar. Punishment was coming. How, he didn't yet know. Tim shifted back, retrieved his car, and followed Karina's fading scent to her discarded clothes. After dressing her body, he tucked her in the trunk and drove to the pack grounds.

At Jacob's call, the clearing was alive with wolves, every eye fixed on him. Jacob dragged Roxy outside and tossed her onto the ground. Her cry of pain cut through the night.

Tim hauled Karina's body from the trunk and dropped it at Jacob's feet. Roxy saw her sister, screamed, and lunged for Tim, but Jacob snatched her mid-charge and flung her aside.

"Roxy," Jacob's voice carried over the pack, "wanna explain why your sister attacked a pack member's potential mate tonight?"

"She's not his mate!" Roxy shrieked. "She's just some whore he's screwing! One who shot me, and you let her walk away! And she's with a vampire that you keep letting stir up trouble!"

Jacob struck her, the slap cracking through the circle. She flew backward, scrambled up, and snarled in his face. Her claws flashed, slicing his cheek and eye. Jacob's howl split the night.

He shifted in an instant. Instead of killing her outright, he raked his claws across the bullet wound in her side. Roxy screamed and shifted, lunging, sinking her teeth into his leg. The pack whispered in shock.

Jacob jerked free, seized her by the scruff, and closed his jaws on her spine. Her body went rigid, then crumpled. As her form melted back to human, Jacob lifted his head and howled. Around them, fur and claws flashed as the pack shifted and fell on Karina and Roxy's remains, rending them until the clearing stank of blood and betrayal.

Once the pack shifted back to human form, Jacob strode toward Tim. Every muscle in Tim's body tensed. Out of the corner of his eye, he caught Raul, Jacob's Gamma and ruthless enforcer, moving closer. Raul thrived on pain, the perfect man for the job Tim had once declined.

Jacob's voice boomed across the clearing. "Tim has killed another pack member. You are all here tonight to witness his punishment. We don't betray our own kind. Roxy betrayed us tonight and paid with her life. Her defiance cost Karina hers as well. But I gave Tim a chance to bring his potential mate into the pack. Roxy didn't know this, but she still ignored a direct command. She acted without my leave and suffered for it. Make no mistake! My mercy is not weakness. I will not tolerate defiance!"

The pack howled as one, except Tim.

Jacob's hand clamped onto Tim's arm and dragged him to the fighting ring. Tim's stomach sank. He knew what was coming. Jacob nodded to Raul, who stepped inside the circle, rolling his shoulders. Jacob shoved Tim forward.

"Tonight, Tim faces Raul to the death," Jacob declared. "If Tim wins, he takes Raul's place as my Gamma. If anyone interferes, they die where they stand."

Tim had fought and killed in this ring before. The memories clawed at him: blood, bone, the hollow victory of survival. He could've been Raul, could've been Jacob's enforcer. He'd walked away because the cruelty sickened him. But now? Now he'd have to win. Beat Raul. Then maybe challenge Paul, Jacob's Beta. One fight at a time.

Raul smirked, eyes glinting with malice. "When I'm done gutting you, I'll find that whore of yours. Show her who's boss. By the time I'm through, she'll beg for death."

A spark of white-hot rage burned through Tim's veins. One he thought he'd left behind. His vision tunneled.

"You won't touch her!" he snarled, his voice rough with fury.

He lunged, shifting midair, teeth bared. Raul sidestepped. Too late, Tim saw the trap. Silver flashed. Pain exploded in his leg as Raul's blade sank deep. Tim hit the ground, howling, the stink of his own burning flesh filling his nose. Silver. He wouldn't heal fast enough. Raul wanted him to suffer first.

Tim was already limping, each step leaving a faint trail of blood in the dirt. Raul didn't bother to transform. He just danced around Tim's lunges, sidestepping with a predator's patience, his silver blade flashing as he flicked shallow cuts across Tim's flanks. He wasn't trying to kill him yet, just savoring the sight of him bleeding.

Enough. Tim forced himself to slow. He circled Raul deliberately, keeping just out of reach, ignoring the pain throbbing in his leg. He needed Raul to lose his composure.

Raul spat the word like venom. "Coward." He lunged, knife slicing for Tim's chest.

Tim twisted at the last heartbeat and clamped his jaws around Raul's arm. The taste of blood flooded his mouth as Raul roared and drove the knife from his free hand into Tim's side. Pain flared white-hot, but Tim bit down harder until he felt the bone snap. With a violent jerk, he lifted Raul clear off the ground and flung him out of the ring.

Gasps rippled through the watching pack. It wouldn't keep Raul down, but it had the intended effect. Humiliation.

Raul shifted mid-charge as he came back, his broken arm already healed. Snarling, he lunged again. Tim slid aside, seized Raul's hind leg, and crushed the bone with a snap. Raul hit the ground, howling. Before Raul could roll away, Tim seized the other leg and broke it too.

The enforcer staggered, unable to stand, but Tim didn't pounce. He waited. Patience was deadlier than rage.

When Raul tried to scramble up on shattered legs, Tim struck, springing onto his back, teeth closing around the scruff of his neck. He froze. Killing him outright would make Tim no better than Raul.

The hesitation cost him. Raul twisted with sudden strength and pinned Tim beneath his massive weight. Tim growled, tightening his grip on the back of Raul's neck.

Jacob's voice cracked through the air. "Finish him, Tim. Do it now!"

Tim closed his eyes, regret a fleeting ache in his chest. Then he crushed down with his jaws. Bone crunched, Raul's howl curdled to a whine, and with one final, brutal jerk, Tim tore his throat out.

The knife still lodged in Tim's side burned like fire. He staggered back as the pack surged forward to drag Raul's body away, wind stirring, slamming Raul's power into him.

Jacob shifted to human form, his expression unreadable, and barked for the doctor. Tim felt the silver working through his bloodstream, slowing his pulse.

The doctor yanked the blade free. White-hot pain flared, and Tim whimpered low. Jacob's command was firm but not unkind: "Shift, Tim, so they can treat you."

The change washed over him, oddly effortless this time. A wave of Raul's strength, raw power, poured through him, and then darkness took him as he collapsed.

***

Tim woke groggy, the ceiling above him swimming in and out of focus. His muscles ached like he'd been run over, and a deep burn throbbed at his side.

Jacob's shadow moved into view. He wore a smug, easy smile, the kind that never quite reached his eyes. The doctor's hands were cool and efficient as he checked Tim's pulse and muttered, "Vitals are good."

Tim pushed himself upright, a sharp pain stabbing beneath his ribs. He hissed and glanced down. White bandages wrapped his sternum, already spotted faintly with blood. Raul's blade had come close. Too close. The smaller cuts had already sealed over.

"Welcome back to the pack, Tim," Jacob said smoothly. "You're now my third in command. You can feel it, can't you? Stronger already. Faster. Healing quicker." His grin widened. "From now on, when I call, you answer. An enforcer doesn't get to rest."

Tim's jaw tightened. "You knew I didn't want this. So why force it?"

"Because I knew you wouldn't let yourself die," Jacob replied, voice low but firm. "I offered you the job once, and you turned it down. But maybe now—" his gaze flicked, sharp and knowing—"now that the woman you've been pining after has chosen someone else, you'll finally accept what you are. And when we move on the vampire, you'll be with us."

Tim's stomach knotted. "I don't want Dominique hurt."

"That's on you," Jacob said, shrugging like it was the simplest thing in the world. "Your timeline's shorter now. Roxy saw to that. Turn her, or what happens next will be on your head. I won't shield her from the pack."

Tim's fists clenched the blankets. "And if I don't turn her but get her away from Nathaniel?"

Jacob's eyes hardened. "No. She injured one of ours. She replaces Roxy, or she pays the price. If you claim her, I'll forgive her for shooting Roxy. She didn't know who Roxy was, so technically it's excusable."

Tim's voice was like gravel. "And what exactly did Roxy do for the pack besides warm your bed? Dominique's not ending up there."

Jacob's laugh was low and cold. "Relax. I won't move in on your woman. Roxy was a spy, an errand-runner when I needed her. Dominique would do the same. I know she runs her own business, and you work for her. I'll try not to interfere." He paused, his tone softening into something almost respectful. "Raul was a good man, a good fighter. But you're better. I expect great things from you."

"Raul was suited for this because he enjoyed torture," Tim shot back. "I don't."

Jacob's smile turned sharp again. "You used to be good at it, though. I suspect you'll remember how quickly enough." He stepped toward the door. "Finish healing. You've got work ahead... in more ways than one. And don't take too long bringing Dominique into the pack."

The door clicked shut behind him, leaving Tim alone with the echo of Jacob's words and the unwelcome weight of the power coursing through his veins.

The new strength humming through him felt alien, hot, alive, almost electric, but it wasn't victory he felt. It was a weight. Raul's power, Raul's life, now part of him. He rubbed a hand over his face, the faint sting of the healing cuts reminding him of everything he'd lost to get here.

He thought of Dominique. She deserved peace, not the nightmare he'd dragged to her doorstep.

His fists clenched in the sheets until his knuckles ached. He couldn't let Jacob's threats become her future. He couldn't let the pack take her freedom.

Tim exhaled slowly, a low, guttural sound of frustration escaping him. The rage was back, simmering under his skin, but so was something steadier: resolve.

They'd think they'd broken him tonight. But if Jacob wanted to force Dominique into the pack, he'd have to kill Tim first.

Chapter 51

Dominique spent the next two days holed up at Nathaniel's. Daylight hours blurred, half-hearted writing on her laptop, mindless games on her phone. But the third floor kept tugging at her curiosity like a whisper she couldn't shake. Nathaniel had asked her not to go up there, and she'd promised to respect that. Still, the couple in the photograph lingered in her thoughts, demanding answers she didn't have.

With a sigh, she tossed her phone onto the bed and flopped down beside it, staring at the ceiling. Sleep didn't come easily.

Nathaniel kept his word, giving her space. At night, he'd emerge quietly, settle on the couch, and let her lean against him without a word. Sometimes she curled into his side, scrolling through her phone as his fingers drifted through her hair or traced lazy patterns along her arm. He never pushed, never even hinted at more. That restraint after what had passed between them unsettled her more than if he had.

Tomorrow night was band night at the club. She'd have to go back. Tim hadn't reached out once. That stung more than she wanted to admit. Maybe she'd finally set him straight, maybe he really didn't want her in his life.

But she still missed him.

She called herself an idiot for ever letting him close again. Worse, for offering herself to him only to have him walk away. He'd said he loved her, whispered it before they'd fallen asleep. Clearly a lie.

Because if you love someone, you don't leave them behind.

And that excuse… *I'm not the same guy*. What kind of garbage was that? As if she hadn't done things she regretted, too. She still carried the scars.

Her anger dulled to a low ache. Sleepiness crept in, soft and relentless. Dominique curled up on her side, let her eyes slip shut, and drifted under, back into the dreams that never seemed to let her go.

***

Rose rode at the head of the army, always at Nathaniel's side. By day, she kept silent; by night, they shared a tent. Their lovemaking was quiet, a stolen secret muffled by the crackle of distant campfires. Nathaniel didn't want whispers about a woman in his ranks, and Rose didn't want to be heard.

He shadowed her everywhere. The edge of the woods when she slipped away to bathe, the dark trees when she needed privacy, his presence both protective and possessive.

Around the cookfires, the knights muttered. George had shielded her with a lie: her name was Rowan, and she was mute. Still, she overheard their sneers, how Nathaniel had gone soft, saddled with a scrawny, silent squire. They snickered about how the commander never let the boy out of his sight.

That night, Rose told Nathaniel what they'd said. The flicker of the fire sharpened his jawline, and his eyes went cold. She offered him a solution: train her, give the men a reason to believe she belonged at his side. At first, he refused, not wanting her to taste the violence he'd been born into. When she admitted she'd been practicing alone, his anger flared hotter than the flames. Weeks passed, and the whispers didn't stop. Finally, when a knight mocked the ever-present squire, Nathaniel relented.

He spun a story to the men that Rowan was a distant cousin of the Duchess, sent to him for training. Then he put a sword in her hands.

At first, the blade dragged at her wrists, its weight brutal. Nathaniel bested her with humiliating ease. The knights who wandered by snorted with laughter when she tumbled into the dirt or when Nathaniel pressed the tip of his sword to her throat. Heat of shame burned her cheeks, but anger burned hotter.

A week later, her movements sharpened. She still wasn't strong enough to match Nathaniel's power, but she was quicker, darting past the swing of his blade, her smaller frame slipping through gaps in his guard. Her bruises multiplied, a map of purples and blues across her skin. Each ache tempted her to give in, but the laughter in the shadows kept her standing. She wouldn't prove them right. She wouldn't let Nathaniel look a fool for believing in her.

The days blurred together as the army pressed closer to Athalon. Weeks had melted into a month, and Rose had transformed beneath the weight of steel and sweat. The armor that had once dragged at her shoulders now felt like a second skin. The sword no longer trembled in her grip. It swung with purpose.

She had even struck Nathaniel a few times, drawing blood where her blade slipped past his guard. He'd laughed it off, but when she bandaged him later, their lovemaking turned rougher, hungrier. Rose never protested; the fire in him matched the fire he stoked in her. His training grew harsher after those nights, pushing her farther, forcing her to dig into the well of anger and determination she hadn't known she possessed.

One afternoon, her muscles screamed for rest, the sword suddenly felt heavier again, and her lungs burned. Several knights had gathered to watch, their smirks like gnats buzzing at her pride. Nathaniel pressed her relentlessly, knocking her blade aside with infuriating ease.

"Just finish the mute off already and be done with it!" one of them jeered.

The words lit something hot in her chest. Rose straightened, rage burning away her fatigue. She snatched up her sword, fingers tightening around the hilt. Nathaniel circled her, a small, wicked curve to his lips; not mockery, but excitement. Still, it stoked her fury.

"Rowan," he said carefully, using the name that wasn't hers. "We can stop if you're too tired. There's no shame in it. This is only training."

She shook her head once, hard, and dropped into her stance.

Nathaniel inclined his head, and then he lunged.

She met him blow for blow, her anger fueling her strength. Steel rang as their swords clashed, sparks scattering in the afternoon light. She kicked, hard, catching him in the stomach, and used the momentum to shove his blade aside. Another kick sent him stumbling backward.

Before the watching knights could blink, her sword came down, stopping just shy of his throat.

Nathaniel's breath came fast, the muscle in his jaw tight as he stared up at her. Rose's scowl cracked into a wide, incredulous smile, pride radiating from her as victory sank in.

Then his expression shifted. His eyes darkened, pupils narrowing to sharp points. The look he gave her wasn't the playful amusement she expected. It was raw, dangerous, and hungry. A shiver chased down her spine as the camp seemed to fade away, leaving only the sharp tip of her sword and the weight of Nathaniel's gaze.

Rose lowered the blade and planted its tip into the dirt. The knights erupted in cheers, finally impressed with "Rowan." She stepped back as Nathaniel rose, dusting himself off. He moved close enough that only she could hear.

"You will return to my tent. Now. I'll be there shortly."

Her heart fluttered. "Did… did I do something wrong?" she whispered.

"You did exactly what you should have." His voice was low, dark. "I've never seen this side of you before, and I'm not sure I can control myself much longer. Go."

Heat flooded her cheeks as she walked toward the tent, her legs suddenly weak. Inside, she stripped off the heavy armor piece by piece. The air felt cooler on her damp skin, and she splashed water on her flushed face, trying to steady her breathing.

The flap rustled. Nathaniel stepped in and tied it shut behind him. Before she could speak, he pulled her against him. His lips found hers in a hungry, unyielding kiss, the force of it stealing her breath. When he pulled back, his eyes were darker than she'd ever seen them.

"You've driven me past reason," he murmured, his voice a rough whisper. "Seeing you fight, watching that fire in your eyes… it undid me."

Rose swallowed hard, heart hammering. "Then… this isn't anger?"

"No," he said, cupping her face, his forehead resting against hers. "It's desire. Pride. And something I can't hold back any longer."

His words left her trembling. Not from fear, but from the power of the moment, the unspoken darkness in his gaze.

Nathaniel removed his armor, laying it gently aside. Pulling her flush against him, his kiss was crushing, all-consuming. His hand slid between them, fingers slipping inside, drawing a gasp from her lips.

"No sounds, Rose."

His fingers quickened, thumb grazing her clit in tight circles. Biting her lip, she held her sounds as his fingers curled, stroking a spot deep inside her.

Withdrawing his fingers, he lifted her. Her legs wrapped around him as he drew her down onto his cock, hips thrusting forward.

Rose buried her face in his shoulder, teeth grazing his skin, trying to remain quiet.

Nathaniel knelt on the ground, hips thrusting to meet her gentle rocking motion. Gripping her hair, he jerked her head back, exposing her throat, trailing kisses down to her collarbone.

Laying them down, his pace quickened.

Rose pressed her heels into his butt, pressing him deeper, meeting his every thrust, pleasure mounting with the deep strokes.

The taste of iron crossed her tongue as her teeth gnawed at her bottom lip, fighting back the noises threatening to spill from her throat. Her gaze met his, their hearts beating in time.

His hips rolled with each fast, deep thrust, fighting her tightness.

Rose gripped his hair, pulling him down for a kiss as her release crashed through her, a whimper lost between their lips.

Nathaniel's chest rumbled with a contained grunt, burying himself deep in her warmth, spilling his seed.

Nathaniel rested against her for a long moment, their breaths mingling in the quiet of the tent. At last, he shifted slightly, pressing a lingering kiss to her lips before pulling back just enough to meet her gaze.

"We have to get dressed," he murmured, voice low but firm. "If the other knights discover who you are… everything we have done could be undone."

She nodded, her heart still racing, and began to reach for her discarded clothing.

***

Dominique woke up and stretched, the house silent and dark. After a quick trip to the bathroom, she returned to the bedroom and reached for her laptop. Curling up on the couch, she began typing, trying to capture the dream.

She was so focused she didn't hear Nathaniel approach until the cushion dipped beside her.

"What're you doing, Dominique?"

Startled, she froze. "I, uh… I'm writing a story," she stammered, heat creeping into her cheeks.

"Do you mind if I look at it?" Nathaniel asked, his voice soft but curious.

"Um… I'd rather you didn't. I told you, I don't let anyone read what I write."

"Could letting me read just a little be so bad?"

"It's embarrassing. Plus, I've been working on this for months, long before I met you. The story has nothing to do with you," she said quickly.

He raised an eyebrow. "And why are you telling me that?"

"Because…" Dominique hesitated, twisting a strand of hair around her finger. "Because there's a character named Nathaniel. I didn't want you to think I based him on you."

"Fair enough," he said with a small smile. "I won't assume. May I see it, then?"

With a reluctant sigh, she handed him the laptop. She watched his expression shift. First a faint smile, then a shadow darkening his eyes as he reached the part she hadn't finished. He handed the computer back, his gaze unreadable.

"It's quite good, Dominique," he said quietly. "You've poured a lot of feeling into it. It feels alive."

Warmth rose in her chest at the compliment. She turned back to the screen, determined to finish the scene while it was fresh. Nathaniel leaned closer, reading as she typed. She considered asking him to stop, but knew what it was like to need an ending.

When she finally saved her work and shut the laptop, she glanced at him. His expression was distant, almost haunted, as if something in her words had stirred a memory. Then, sensing her gaze, his focus snapped back. Only now his eyes held a smoldering intensity that made her breath catch.

Disappointment flickered when he leaned back against the cushions instead of closing the space between them.

"How do you come up with your stories?" he asked.

"I dream them," she admitted. "If I like a dream, I turn it into a story. This one, though… I've been having these vivid dreams for about eight months. They stopped for a while, then came back with a vengeance. I've even had seizures because of them. It's like… I can't wake up until the scene is played out. When I met you, and you had the same name as the character, it felt… strange. But I can never see his face. I only wake up feeling what Rose felt, like I'm her."

"That's… interesting," Nathaniel said, studying her. "Maybe it's a story you're meant to know. Something that needs to be told."

"Maybe," Dominique murmured. "I've never believed in that kind of thing. But this story… it feels alive. I need to know how it ends. If I don't, I'll write one. After everything they've gone through, they deserve a happy ending."

"You don't believe in all that stuff?" His gaze sharpened slightly. "Do you mean the dreams? The love between your characters? Or soulmates?"

"I don't believe in premonitions," she said after a pause. "I believe in love. I've experienced that. I just don't think it lasts forever. That's… my own baggage talking."

"Are your characters not soulmates?" he pressed gently. "You said they've endured so much to be together. Doesn't that make them destined?"

Dominique's eyes dropped to her hands. "I think they love each other and are fighting for that love. I never thought about soulmates." Her voice softened as she glanced at him. "I believe in love, and in fighting for it, keeping it alive no matter what. That's something real. Not just… meeting someone and instantly knowing they're the only one."

Nathaniel smiled, but it didn't quite reach his eyes. The flicker of vulnerability there made her heart skip. She'd never believed in soulmates until she met him. But she wasn't ready to tell him that.

Chapter 52

Dominique and Nathaniel rode to the club together the next night. Nathaniel opened her door and slipped an arm over her shoulders as they walked inside.

Tim's chest tightened with jealousy as he followed them in. Jacob had given him a week to change Dominique, and the weight of it pressed on him. He still had to defeat Paul before challenging Jacob. And he couldn't let Dominique know any of it.

She didn't so much as glance his way. From across the room, he caught Nathaniel in his usual seat, eyes fixed on her. It grated that Nathaniel got to be so close, where she wouldn't even look at him.

As the songs played through, a few caught his attention. Maybe he could ask Dominique for a dance? Let her listen to the song he'd chosen to dance to? Try to get back in her good graces after screwing up yet again?

When the band played, Tim couldn't take his eyes off Dominique. Every lyric seemed etched across her face as she sang, her expressions carrying the music.

After the set, she turned on recorded tracks and sat with Nathaniel. Jealousy and anger knotted in Tim's chest.

Then *Sorry* by Buckcherry came on. His pulse quickened. He pushed off the bar and crossed the floor.

Without a word, he held out his hand.

Dominique stared at it for a beat, then looked to Nathaniel. When he didn't speak, she placed her hand in Tim's.

He guided her onto the dance floor, holding her close as the song played.

She rested her head on his shoulder, and his cheek rested against the crown of her head. His hand slid down to rest on her hip, her heartbeat thundering against his chest.

When the song ended, he eased back just enough to meet her eyes. The look she gave him splintered his heart, but he wanted to remember it forever just in case she pushed him away.

"I know I'm an asshole, Dom. I've screwed things up yet again. But the song… it says how I really feel, which is why I asked you to dance to it. I wanted to hold you close, even if it's the last time. I'm sorry for everything. I did what you asked and thought things over the past two days. I don't want to lose you again."

Dominique frowned. "You're so damn confusing. How could you get what you wanted and then walk away? I gave myself to you willingly. I thought we were getting somewhere… getting back to us, then you rip me to shreds *again*. I told you I can't do this back-and-forth. I mean, honestly, what is it you want from me, Tim?"

"I want you. *All of you*. I don't want to share you or hear that you're in love with someone else. I want you to choose me, but I'm terrified because you don't know what my life is like now." His arms tightened, drawing her flush against him.

"Then make me understand. You tell me things, make me feel things I've buried for years, and then fucking walk away. You tell me you want me, then say you don't. You don't want me loving someone else, but push me aside right after saying you love me. Why should I deal with that when someone else offers me something simple?"

"Do you really think being with Nathaniel is uncomplicated?"

"Yes! He doesn't make me choose. He doesn't say one thing and then do another. He's evasive about some things, sure, but so are you. You told me to come to you when I was ready for the truth. I thought that's what we were doing, but you still held back and then left. I want the truth, every single detail. When you're ready to tell me everything, I'll be here. If you can't give me that, don't bother saying sorry or trying to get back into my good graces."

Dominique stepped back, anger flickering in her eyes. "You know what? I'm done. When one of you two gets your shit together, come talk to me."

She stomped off to her office, done with their games.

Chapter 53

At the end of the night, Dominique saw everyone out, then turned to her office. Nathaniel was there, waiting.

"Ready to go home?" he asked.

"Yes," she sighed. "More than ready."

To go back to my own home.

As soon as the car stopped, Dominique jumped out and stormed to the bedroom. Anger burned hot in her chest as she shoved her things into her bag.

To hell with Tim and Nathaniel. I need to get away from both of them. They won't tell me what's going on with Jacob. Then, I let them in, and they keep me out. They say they love me, but won't trust me with their truths. What the fuck do they know about love?

She felt Nathaniel's presence behind her but refused to look at him, zipping the bag closed with a sharp jerk. His arms slid around her waist, drawing her against his chest. For a fleeting heartbeat, she let herself sink into his warmth.

When she stepped forward to break free, his grip tightened. His breath brushed her neck.

"Please don't go. I know I said I wouldn't stop you, but… I want you to stay," he whispered.

"I can't. I can't breathe. You and Tim are suffocating me. I'm tired of excuses from you and Tim about yourselves, of being kept in the dark about Jacob."

She turned in his arms, meeting his dark eyes.

"I promised I'd tell you everything when the time was right," he said.

"Which apparently is never. I've given you time. Still, you insist you need more. I've given you all my secrets… the darkest ones. I trusted you with my mind, my heart, my body. And you still hold back. Like I told Tim: get your shit together and talk to me. When you're ready to tell me everything, I'll be here. Until then, I'm done."

Nathaniel's chest tightened.

"All right… If you're really leaving, at least give me tonight. After that, I'll give you space."

"No!" Her voice cracked. "I need space now. I ask for the truth, or I'm done, and all you can do is beg for one more night? Why not just tell me? Do you really think it's so terrible that I won't want you? I'm in love with you, dammit!"

She slapped a hand over her mouth, panic flashing in her eyes. She'd never said she loved him directly before.

Nathaniel gently moved her hand and claimed her lips in a breath-stealing kiss. When he finally pulled back, he rested his forehead against hers.

"I love you too, Dominique."

"Then talk to me," she whispered. "Stop hiding."

"It's because I love you that I hide. You need to see everything first. Only then can I tell you the rest. Then I can reveal myself and you'll understand."

Frustration tightened in her chest as he hugged her. She started to pull away, but he guided her hand to his heart. Its quick rhythm matched her own.

Nathaniel brushed a light kiss across her lips, his eyes locking with hers, pulling her in. A faint pressure gathered at the base of her skull, threading through her mind.

"Sleep," he murmured.

Her limbs grew heavy, eyelids fluttering shut. She sagged against him as consciousness slipped away.

Nathaniel scooped her up and laid her on the bed. The mattress dipped under his weight as he settled beside her, wrapping her in his warmth until her breathing deepened and she sank into a deep sleep, a dream weaving through her mind.

***

As the army drew closer to Athalon, Rose's nerves frayed. Her training with Nathaniel had grown infrequent, less from neglect than from her growing skill with a blade. Only a few days' ride separated them from her village. Nathaniel spoke of marching straight to the castle to challenge his father, but Rose doubted it was possible. A knight would surely spot them long before they reached the gates.

Nathaniel knew his father's army, disciplined but smaller than the force backing him. He'd already decided to leave Rose with the old woman in her village, certain no one would risk angering the witch. George would stay to guard her.

Scouts had ridden ahead to watch the castle. Nathaniel could only hope they returned alive, unseen, and with good news.

A firm shake pulled Rose from sleep. Nathaniel's smile met her bleary eyes as he handed her armor. She dressed quickly, pushing away the fog of dreams.

"We ride tonight," he said. "I will take you to the village. At dawn, I lead the army to face my father. I need you safe before then."

"It is the dead of night," Rose murmured.

"Yes. The darkness will hide us. I cannot bring you with me, Rose, even though I know that is what you want."

"I have trained with you. I can fight. Please, rethink this," she pleaded.

"You promised to stay hidden in the village."

A shout cut through the camp. "Horse approaching!"

Nathaniel threw back the tent flap and sprinted toward the warning. A cloaked rider slowed as the knights bristled.

"Stop and name yourself!" Nathaniel called.

"I am a friend, Sir Knight," came the reply. "I bring a warning. Your father's scouts have seen your army."

"Stand down!" Nathaniel ordered his men, though his hand hovered near his sword.

The rider drew closer, pushing back her hood. Firelight revealed the old woman from Rose's village. Nathaniel's frown deepened. She dismounted stiffly, bowing low.

"Back to your tents," Nathaniel told his knights. "I need counsel with this woman."

Inside the tent, Rose brought a lamp closer. Its glow caught the deep lines of the woman's face, and Rose gasped.

"What are you doing here?" she whispered.

Nathaniel's voice was sharp. "Speak, old woman. What warning do you bring?"

"You are in grave danger," she said. "Your father's scouts watched his lands after you vanished. They have seen your army… and Rose. They burned my village. There is nowhere left for her to hide. I warned you not to bring her back. Now your father plans her death to torment you before your own. She must stay with you. She must fight."

"You lie. My father cannot possibly know about Rose. If his scouts saw my army, they would have only seen her as a squire."

"No, M'Lord. I saw it myself. They spied her without her armor. They know she is here, and now so does your father."

"Damnit!" Nathaniel's shout shook the tent.

He hadn't wanted Rose anywhere near this battle, yet now he had no choice. When he looked at her, there was no fear, only a straight spine, chin lifted, eyes bright with defiance. He frowned, realizing this moment had always been inevitable.

"My spitfire," he muttered, pulling her into his arms. "You will get yourself killed. And for what? Because you refuse to be left behind?"

"No." Her voice was steady. "If I die, it will be for love. I did not come because I feared being left. I came because I love you. I will stand by your side through everything."

"M'Lord," the old woman said softly, "Rose is of the people. Let them see her. The men and boys old enough to fight from our village will recognize her. They will rise against your father."

"I cannot do that. My men will laugh me out of my own army."

"They will not laugh," she said, a sly smile curving her lips. "Not when they realize they have praised a woman's skill. They will laugh only at themselves for not seeing it sooner."

Rose dipped her head in thanks. When she glanced at Nathaniel, a reluctant smile tugged at his mouth. Brave. Loving. Fearless even in the shadow of death. He loved her all the more. He kissed her quickly, then stepped outside.

"Everyone, pack up!" Nathaniel's voice cut through the night. "My father knows of us. We ride straight into battle. Prepare yourselves."

As the knights began tearing down the camp, Nathaniel called Rose out and pulled back the coverings from her head. A ripple of murmurs spread as the men realized the squire among them was a woman.

"Sire, a woman among us? It is bad luck!" one knight exclaimed.

Another stepped forward. "I have watched her train. She will hold her own. You rode beside her without knowing. Why balk now?"

Nathaniel faced his men. "Those who ride with me will be greatly rewarded when this is over. Rose rides with us by her choice, not my command. She understands the danger and still faces death without flinching. So, will you ride with me?"

A roar of cheers erupted, echoing through the camp.

Once packed, they turned their horses toward Athalon. Nathaniel knew fatigue would ride with them, but his men would fight until their last breath. Before they left, he thanked the old woman and offered her a place at the castle when the war was done. He vowed silently that Rose's course would change. That she would not die on this field.

***

Nathaniel halted his army before the dark woods guarding the castle. The old woman's warning echoed in his mind; his father's plan, the villagers armed. Would they truly recognize Rose? Could he send her forward without certainty?

He glanced at her. She only smiled, her long blonde hair lifting in the breeze to reveal her determined face. His frown deepened.

Rose reached for his hand and gently nudged her horse ahead. He understood and matched her pace. Together they rode slowly toward the treeline, leaving the army behind. At the forest's edge, they stopped. Rose dismounted, and Nathaniel's muscles tightened.

"People of the Northern Village," Rose called, voice carrying clear and steady, "I humbly request you come forward. I know Sir Reynald has commanded you to fight for him. Please, I beg you, do not fight us and die in vain!"

Silence stretched until a branch cracked in the darkness. Rose didn't reach for her sword or her horse. She turned toward the sound instead.

"Rose? Is that you?" a voice called.

"Aye, it is," she answered. "Come forward and show yourself. No harm will befall you."

Thomas stepped into the clearing, shield and sword raised. Rose signaled to the archers to stand down. When their bows lowered, Thomas slowly lowered his blade. Other men shifted forward, but he held up a hand to halt them.

"Do you truly mean us no harm? Even though we guard Reynald's castle?" he asked.

"We mean you no harm, Thomas," Rose replied. "We ask that you join us. Help us defeat Reynald, and together we will restore these lands to their former glory."

Pride swelled in Nathaniel's chest. He recognized the boy from her village who had once spoken of her father's death. If Thomas turned, the others would follow.

Thomas approached cautiously. Nathaniel kept watch on the woods as Rose lifted a hand, halting him.

"Thomas, lay down your weapon. I wish no ill will upon you," she said.

Thomas set his sword on the ground and stepped away from it. Nearing her, he knelt and bowed his head. Rose closed the distance, resting her hand on his shoulder.

He looked up, and her smile met his. The villagers began to emerge. Only thirty in all.

"Gather the men, Thomas," Rose said. "You will go into battle, but with us. Any man or boy you deem unready, send them away. I will not have them die for our cause."

Thomas gathered those willing to fight. Rose mounted her horse, and together they turned toward the castle.

The ground trembled as Nathaniel's army thundered through the forest. When he and Rose broke through the trees, all hell erupted.

Chapter 54

Knights clashed everywhere, steel ringing against steel. Rose leapt from her horse, intercepting a charging knight. When he realized she was a woman, others surged toward her, only for Nathaniel's men to close ranks, shielding her. Thomas stayed at her side, Nathaniel fighting just beyond.

Still, enemies pressed in. One knight broke through and swung at her. Her sword caught his, the blades shrieking as she strained against his strength. He wrenched her wrist, pain flaring white-hot. Rose cried out and dropped her weapon. In a blink, he hoisted her onto his shoulder and bolted for the castle.

"Rose!" Nathaniel's roar split the chaos as he carved through foes, bodies falling around him.

One of his knights intercepted the fleeing man, forcing him to drop her. As they fought, Nathaniel cut down opponent after opponent to reach her.

Rose slid a knife from her boot and drove it into the knight's back. He crumpled, and she retrieved the blade, tucking it away before snatching up another sword.

Her wrist throbbed like fire, but she pushed through the pain. She couldn't die here. Couldn't let Nathaniel fall. Skirting the battlefield's edge, she watched castle guards pour out to meet the advancing army. Reynald was nowhere in sight. The coward was hiding.

Clutching her wrist to her chest, she parried another attack. His blade slashed her arm, and she screamed as he shoved her to the ground. A sword suddenly burst through his chest, blood splattering her face. She scrambled back as his body toppled.

Thomas hauled her to her feet. "What were you thinking? Stay close to me or Nathaniel!"

"I need Reynald," she panted. "This war ends if he falls. Nathaniel should not have to worry about me."

"Then you should have stayed with me," Nathaniel growled, striking down another knight.

Rose met his gaze briefly, then pressed forward. The three fought as one, pushing toward the castle. Another enemy lunged for her, and she realized that they wanted her inside. Grabbing her knife from her boot, she slid it into her sleeve. She feigned resistance, letting one seize her while Nathaniel and Thomas battled nearby.

As they neared the gate, Rose palmed her hidden knife. Inside the walls, she drove the blade deep into her captor's back. He grunted and collapsed, his weight slamming her to the ground.

The impact crushed the air from her lungs. She tried to shove him off, but her broken wrist failed her. Agony blurred her vision. As darkness closed in, the world slipped away.

***

The battle had raged for hours. Nathaniel hadn't seen Rose since the knight dragged her away. Rage drove him forward, his blade a blur. No man withstood him.

Bodies littered the ground as he carved a path toward the gate, scanning the fallen for any glimpse of her. Was she in the castle? In his father's hands? Was she already… no. He couldn't think it.

His men were tiring. Beside him, Thomas faltered, his breathing ragged. Nathaniel's fury alone kept him upright. Two knights charged. He cut one down, but the other's blade swung wide, catching Thomas's side. Blood poured.

Nathaniel roared, pivoted, and buried his sword in the attacker's gut. Thomas shoved another foe back, grimacing as he pressed a hand to his wound. Even bleeding, he rose, fighting back-to-back with Nathaniel until his strength finally failed.

Thomas collapsed, crimson spreading beneath him. He'd fought to protect Rose to his last breath. Nathaniel cut down another knight and spared a glance. *I will honor you, brother,* he vowed silently.

The battle surged through the gates now, the castle looming ahead. Still no sign of Rose. Nathaniel gripped his sword tighter. He had to reach his father and end this.

***

Rose gasped as consciousness returned, her breath hitching beneath the weight pinning her. Gritting her teeth, she braced her good hand on the dead knight's shoulder and shoved, wriggling free from under his body. Pain flared in her wrist, dulled only slightly by the brief rest.

She tore a strip from his surcoat, wrapped it tight around her wrist, then slid her knife back into her boot and took up his sword.

The castle loomed silent. Reynald would still have guards inside. Getting to him wouldn't be easy.

Rose eased one of the great doors open. The hall beyond was empty, shadows dancing in the torchlight. She moved quietly, checking each room she passed.

Footsteps echoed. Heart hammering, she slipped into a chamber and flattened against the wall.

A lone figure passed; a maid. Rose lunged, clamping a hand over the woman's mouth and dragging her inside. The maid struggled, teeth scraping against Rose's palm until Rose squeezed her cheeks, forcing her jaw shut.

"Do not scream," Rose whispered. "I will not hurt you. I need your help. Promise you will not scream when I let go."

The maid nodded slightly.

She slowly released her grip and turned the woman toward her. Wide eyes flicked over Rose's bloodied face and tattered surcoat. Recognition dawned.

"Rose?" the maid gasped. "What is happening? Why are you dressed like a knight, covered in blood?"

"Tabitha," Rose breathed, relief washing through her. "There is a battle outside. I am here to kill Reynald. I need to reach him."

Tabitha's expression hardened. "Sir Reynald's drunk, as always. Two knights guard the great hall. They are waiting for his men to bring his son… and the woman he ran off with. You are the woman, are you not?"

"Yes. Nathaniel fights for the throne. Please, Tabitha. I know how Reynald's treated you. Help me end this. I will see you freed."

Tabitha hesitated only a heartbeat before slipping out. She returned with a basin of water, a plain dress, and a wimple. She scrubbed the blood from Rose's skin, bandaged her arm, and helped her into the disguise.

With her head bowed beneath the wimple, Rose followed Tabitha through shadowed corridors to the kitchens. Tabitha filled a glass with mead, then reached into a cupboard and drew out a pouch of white powder. She sprinkled it into the drink and swirled it.

"This puts him to sleep," Tabitha murmured. "It is the only way I have endured him. I will try to lure him, but with the battle raging, I cannot promise he will leave the hall."

"I will take it, Tabitha. I will slip into Reynald's chamber and wait. If we are lucky, the knights will not follow him."

Rose eased through the corridors until she reached Reynald's room. The minutes stretched like hours as she crouched behind the heavy drapes, their folds mercifully pooling over her feet.

The door creaked open. Tabitha's giggle floated through the silence. The bed groaned under the weight. Cloth tore. Rose's stomach knotted. She slowed her breathing, disgust churning as Reynald's drunken grunts and vile whispers filled the room.

At last, the sounds ceased. Tabitha's soft sobs broke the quiet. Rose peeked out. Reynald sprawled motionless atop her. She stepped forward, knife hidden in her sleeve.

"Tabitha, move out from under him. I am sorry you had to do this. Forgive me," Rose whispered.

Tabitha's voice was steady but bitter. "This is not new to me, Rose. But it will be the last."

She shoved Reynald's body aside and rose, clutching the torn dress to her chest. Rose stood over the sleeping tyrant, blade poised.

"Rose, what are you waiting for?" Tabitha hissed.

"I cannot kill him in his sleep. It is not honorable."

"That man has no honor. Let his death match his life."

Tabitha was right. Reynald, a coward, drunkard, tyrant, had earned no better. Rose drove the blade into his heart. His body jerked, blood bubbling at his lips, then stilled. The last beats of his heart sprayed crimson across the sheets when she removed the blade. It was a cleaner death than he deserved.

"We need to go," Rose said. "I have to return to the fight, to Nathaniel, and prove Reynald's dead."

"No one will believe you just by your word," Tabitha warned.

"The horn," Rose replied quickly. "Bring me the horn and his crown. I will meet you at the stables. Be careful. If the knights catch us, it is over."

Tabitha nodded and slipped away. Rose darted through the halls, shadows her only allies. The guards still clustered in the great hall, unaware of their fallen lord. She reached the room where her armor waited, shedding the dress and wimple.

Outside, the clash of steel echoed within the gates. Hugging the castle wall, Rose crept to the stables, forcing the pain down, she saddled a horse, and whispered a prayer for Nathaniel's safety.

Footsteps crunched nearby. She crouched low, heart hammering, knife ready in her hand.

"Rose?" Tabitha's whisper broke the stillness.

Rose rose slowly from her crouch, relief flooding her when she saw Tabitha alone. She stepped from the stall, the horse shifting restlessly behind her. Tabitha pressed the horn into Rose's palm but pulled back the crown, lifting it instead to place on Rose's head. She kissed Rose's cheeks.

"Good luck, m'lady. May God go with you."

"Thank you, Tabitha."

Rose swung into the saddle, heels nudging the horse's flanks. Hooves thundered into the courtyard. She raised the horn to her lips, the sound splitting the night, echoing against stone and sky. Heads turned. Knights froze mid-swing, glancing toward the rider bearing their fallen lord's crown.

She galloped through the carnage—blood-slick stones, broken steel, fallen men. The horse shied at the bodies, the scent of iron in the air, but she tightened her knees and pressed forward.

"This war is over!" Her voice rang clear. "Reynald is dead! Lay down your weapons and you will be spared!"

The remaining Athalon knights saw the crown and, with bitter reluctance, sank to their knees. Rose urged her horse forward, eyes searching desperately for Nathaniel.

At first, nothing.

Then the men parted, and he emerged; each step purposeful, predatory. Blood streaked his armor and matted his hair; his face was carved from stone.

A sob caught in her throat.

But before she could reach him, the Shirely knights began cutting down the surrendered.

"Stop!" Rose's cry tore the air. "These men were promised their lives!"

"Kill them all!" Nathaniel's command cracked like a whip as he strode toward her. "Leave none alive."

She wheeled her horse to block him. "No, Nathaniel! This is not the way. You are not your father."

His gaze held hers. Rage flickered, then wavered. Slowly, he raised his hand. "Stand down."

The slaughter halted. Captives were bound instead of butchered. Rose exhaled a shaky breath. Nathaniel reached her side, pulled her off the horse into his arms, and crushed his lips to hers. When he pulled back, her tears wet his cheek.

"It is over," he murmured, brushing her face with his thumb.

"I thought you were dead," she whispered, clutching his hand to her cheek.

His eyes flicked to the crown. "How did you get my father's crown?"

"I…" She swallowed hard. "I killed him. Two of his knights remain inside."

A shadow crossed Nathaniel's face. "One day, I will have to chain you to my side, Rose. You could have been killed."

"I could not let you bear the weight of killing him," she said softly. "And with everyone thinking me dead, I was free to act."

"When I could not find you, I believed it," he admitted, voice raw. "It filled me with a rage I did not know I had. Do not ever do that to me again. Swear it."

"I swear. I will never do something so reckless again." She removed the crown from her head. "Now, kneel, Nathaniel."

His brow arched, but he dropped to one knee. Rose lifted the crown and set it on his head. The knights roared their acclaim, their shouts shaking the earth.

The prisoners were marched to the dungeons, but two missing knights were later found and cut down when they refused to surrender. Nathaniel stood over Reynald's body in grim silence before ordering it buried. He gathered his fallen men and granted them the honor of a knight's burial. Rose wept quietly for Thomas as his body was laid upon the pyre.

Days later, Nathaniel was formally crowned. Rose became Duchess, seated at his side as their people celebrated long into the night.

Chapter 55

Dominique jerked awake, her body heavy and aching, as if she'd never truly slept. Disoriented, she scanned the room, then froze. Nathaniel's guest room.

What the hell?

The last clear memory was packing her bags and telling him she wasn't staying the night. Yet here she was, tangled in the sheets.

Her phone read one o'clock. She had no idea when she'd passed out. The house was silent.

She gathered her things from the floor, the quiet pressing in around her, and slipped through the hall. The living room was empty. She checked the garage, opened the door, and stepped into the sunlight. Her car waited like an anchor to reality.

She loaded her bags, slid behind the wheel, and started the engine. She didn't look back.

At home, she lingered in the driver's seat, forehead against the steering wheel, trying to piece together her life. Lately, it felt like chaos stacked on chaos.

Inside, she flipped open her laptop. Words spilled onto the screen. The end of Rose and Nathaniel's story. They had earned their happily ever after. They went through all kinds of shit and came out unbroken, together.

Why couldn't her life be like that?

She'd gone through so much, but here she was, trapped between two men who couldn't even be honest with her. What could they possibly be hiding that was so terrible? Tim had been more open than Nathaniel, but even he held back. She knew about the gang, about Jacob's control. If Tim truly loved her, why keep her on the outside? If he thought she'd be hurt, why come back around at all?

Her thoughts circled to the bar Tim used to haunt at the end of their relationship. Jacob's place. Would he tell her the truth if she cornered him? Or would Roxy come for her again?

To distract herself from going there, she searched listings for buildings and machinery costs. Since she wasn't debugging the systems anymore, it would be more cost-efficient to build. Most spaces were overpriced, but one caught her eye.

She called the real estate agent, setting a time to see it, aware she was jumping ahead. The contracts were signed, but nothing yet from Nathaniel. Would he back out now that she'd told him to either step up or walk away?

Only one way to know.

She texted him, knowing he'd be silent until dark. Just another of his secrets.

Chapter 56

Dominique pulled into a sprawling parking lot sitting in front of a cream-colored, two-story building. A blue SUV door opened, and a man stepped out, his movements smooth and assured.

He strode toward her car, hand extended. "Hi, I'm Paul. Lovely to meet you, Dominique."

She shook his hand. "Nice to meet you, too, Paul."

"Let's head inside. I'll go over the specs. See if it fits what you're after."

"Great! I'm so glad you could squeeze me in today."

Paul flashed her a smile. "My pleasure."

Inside, Paul pointed out room ratios, updates, and possibilities. Midway through a sentence, he stopped, realizing she hadn't heard a word. His lips curved into a sly smile.

What luck she'd chosen him out of everyone. Jacob was going to love this.

To anyone else, he was just another professional wearing a suit. When in truth he was Jacob's Beta—survivor of an attack. Normalcy was second nature when you embraced the life. His real estate business was the perfect cover. Keeping Dominique interested in the listing made staying close effortless. Allowed for a private meeting at his home to turn her since Tim hadn't.

No wolf, no mate mark, yet there was a faint trace of Tim's scent. The scent should have been stronger or non-existent. Strange.

He watched as she paced the room, murmuring dimensions.

Intelligent, witty… desirable. He could see why Tim wanted her. She'd be beneficial to the pack.

Pulling out his phone, he shot a text to Jacob.

With Dominique at a listing of mine. Tim still hasn't turned her.

Being Jacob's Beta, orders weren't optional. Enforcing them was his specialty.

If Dominique bought the building, tailing her would be child's play. Tim would scent him near her home, but here was fair game. A cunning grin adorned his lips as his plan fell into place.

"I love the building," Dominique said, excitement lacing her voice. "I see the potential. I just need to talk to my business partner before I commit. Thank you for allowing me time to plot things out."

"No problem, Dominique. It's been my pleasure." Pulling a card from his pocket, he handed it to her. "If you decide you want it, call me directly. My cell's on there."

His eyes lingered on her face a heartbeat too long before he extended his hand. Dominique hesitated, her fear slithering over his skin. His wolf stretched beneath the surface, widening his grin.

At last, she slid her hand into his, voice barely above a whisper. "Thanks again."

He was going to enjoy turning her, having her fear encase his wolf as he ripped into her. She smelled divine—like prey—and that was just from a glance.

His wolf tracked every movement she made until her car pulled away. Inhaling deeply, licking his lips, he devoured the lingering fear before leaving.

Chapter 57

Dominique awoke from her nap, grabbed her phone, turned on music, and got ready for work.

A text from Nathaniel flashed across the screen.

I'll meet you at the club. We can discuss the contracts there.

Her heart slammed against her ribs. Was he pulling the contracts back? No sense stressing until she knew. She forced herself to eat, then left for the club.

Nathaniel didn't keep her waiting long. He strode to the table, sliding into his usual seat across from her. His lips curved in a smile, but sadness lingered in his eyes.

Nausea twisted in her gut.

He brushed his lips across her knuckles. "Good evening, Dominique."

"Hi." Her voice was smaller than she wanted. "I wasn't sure if the deal was still going through, so I wanted to clarify."

His brow arched. "Are you worried I'll back out?"

"Maybe." Her breath shook. "I told you I was done with our relationship until you told me your secrets. So… are we still business partners?"

"I told you before… my personal life and my business remain separate. My lawyer has the contracts and will call you soon. They take time to finalize, but I can give you his card if you wish to speak sooner."

Relief washed through her. "I'd like that. Thank you."

He handed her the card, and she shoved it into her pocket without looking. Silence stretched, thick and heavy, until he broke it.

"Dominique, I hope you weren't serious about being done. I will tell you everything. I meant it when I said I love you."

"And I meant what I said, too." She hesitated, heart pulling in two directions. "I need time to think. I've never been so confused. You and Tim aren't making this any easier. You're both hiding major shit from me. Just… give me space. When I'm ready, I'll let you know."

"I'm not going anywhere." His gaze softened. "But I'll give you time. Contact my lawyer. He'll go over the details. Your company remains under your control. I'm only a silent partner. The decisions will all be yours." His lips tilted into a half smile. "I can't wait to see what you do with it."

He stood, eyes holding hers a beat longer, then brushed a kiss across her cheek.

Dominique turned, lips catching his, hand cupping his face. She rested her forehead against his, chest tight.

Their breaths mingled. "Thank you for giving me time," she whispered.

"Always, my love."

Then he was gone, leaving her gutted.

This should have been simple. Tim kept pulling her back and forth, hot then cold, hiding things behind his walls. It may have been fear of dragging her into his gang ties, but her heart said it was something else.

Nathaniel never pushed her to choose. His keeping secrets from her is what ultimately made her hesitate. Secrets and lies are what destroyed her life two years ago. She couldn't go through that again.

And yet... her connection with Nathaniel ran deeper than anything she'd felt with Tim. However, the connection to Tim was stronger now than it had been two years ago. It was like something was pulling at her soul with Tim, but something far deeper tugged at it with Nathaniel.

Her hand flew to her chest as it squeezed, heart hammering painfully. Breath came in sharp bursts.

Shit. I'm having a fucking panic attack.

She stumbled into her office, slid down the door, and wrapped her arms around her knees. Counting silently, she forced her breaths into rhythm.

This place, the constant tug between two men, the danger was suffocating her. The need to run—to escape—clawed its way through her panic.

Dragging herself to the computer, she clicked into vacation searches, her mind drifting. Running her hands over her face, she sighed. Could she push that on Melissa? Be selfish and just leave?

Groaning, she dropped her head back against the chair. Being responsible sucked.

Walking back into the main area, her eyes scanned for Melissa. The hairs on the back of her neck stood up. She glanced at the bar. Tim was staring at her. A frown graced her lips as she forced her gaze back into the crowd. When her gaze finally settled on Melissa, she pushed her way through the crowd.

Grabbing Melissa's arm, she whispered, "I need to speak to you."

"Now?" Melissa arched a brow.

"Yes." Dominique's tone was flat, urgent.

Once inside the office, door locked, Melissa crossed her arms. "What's going on, Dom? You don't look good."

"I need a vacation." Dominique's voice cracked. "I just had a panic attack. Between Tim, Nathaniel, Roxy, and this damn club… I'm drowning. I need time to get out of my head. I need someone to run the place while I'm gone."

Melissa narrowed her eyes. "Is this your roundabout way of asking me to manage the club?"

"Maybe." Dominique managed a weak smile. "I'd give you a raise."

"How much?"

"A thousand for two weeks."

Melissa blinked. "That's a lot. You sure?"

"I've never been more sure." Dominique's hands trembled. "I need someone I trust. That's you."

Something in Dominique's eyes made Melissa relent. "Alright. I'll do it."

Relief loosened Dominique's chest. "Thank you. Just… don't tell anyone I'm leaving, okay?"

"Okay. But won't people notice you're at home?"

"I won't be. I'm taking a real vacation."

Melissa sighed. "Fine. Just tell me when to start."

Dominique clicked confirm on the screen. "Two days."

Melissa shook her head with a laugh. "Already planned this out, huh?"

Dominique smiled, warmth breaking through her exhaustion. "Thank you, Melissa."

Melissa winked. "You got it, bestie."

When the door shut behind her, Dominique leaned back, breathing deep. For the first time in weeks, the weight on her chest eased.

Two days. Then she'd be gone.

A sly smile curved her lips.

Chapter 58

Dominique called Nathaniel's lawyer and ran through every question she could think of about the contracts.

The money would go into a business account. Once it was set up, she'd come in and sign the papers. The building purchase would go through him, and she'd need to be present for closing. She already knew most of it, but let him prattle on until he ran out of steam.

When he finished, she gave him Paul's contact information so the process could start.

After hanging up, she pulled out her notes and began pricing machines now that the kinks were worked out. Nathaniel had given her more than enough. Enough to buy the building, build the machines, and staff the place without touching her own money.

She leaned back, thinking of the machines she'd already built at the club: the endless nights, the burned-out parts, the debugging. They had saved her life.

After her suicide attempt, Melissa stayed with her. One night, Dominique had confessed she wished she could see her baby. The idea for the machines had sparked. Post could build anything. She'd written the code, then cracked the hardest part… convincing the brain it was real.

Now the machines were ready. They needed to be tested by the public. Tonight.

She called Melissa. Together, they made a banner: *Come visit the world of your dreams.* Hung above the door, it left just enough mystery to lure people inside.

When patrons asked, Dominique explained, hooked them up, and collected feedback after. Their reactions lit her up; pure, unfiltered wonder.

That night, after the bar closed, Tim came upstairs.

"So, what's all the fuss about?"

"I created a machine that takes you anywhere your mind can imagine. You can do whatever you want in your world."

"Can I try it?"

She hesitated but finally nodded, explaining the setup.

"Wanna come in with me?" he asked.

"No." Her tone was flat.

She waited outside. When he emerged, the grin on his face unsettled her. Shaking her head, she powered everything down. *I don't even want to know what he thought about in there.*

"These things are fantastic, Dominique. It feels so real. Congratulations!"

"Thank you. It seems they're going to be a success. Buying that building and making more will be worth it."

"You're going to make more?"

"Yeah. I already talked to a real estate agent. He showed me a building downtown today. I fell in love with it. I've even plotted how I want it set up. I just hope I can get it. Paul was great about the details. I gave his information to Nathaniel's lawyer."

Tim frowned. "Did you say Paul?"

"Yeah. Why?"

"I know a Paul. About six feet, blond hair, blue eyes?"

"That's him. Everything ok?"

"Yeah… It's fine." Tim forced a smile. "I need to get back to cleaning. I'll see you later, Dominique."

She left, excitement buzzing through her. Sleep refused to come, so she packed, loaded her bags in the car, and cranked up the music.

This trip was exactly what she needed.

Chapter 59

Tim walked down to the bar, pulling out his phone.

He wasn't happy that Paul had met Dominique. He wanted to believe Paul didn't know who she was, but the whole pack knew thanks to Roxy. If Jacob had anyone shadowing Dominique, it would be Paul.

If Tim didn't turn her within the week, would Jacob hand her over to him?

Of all the buildings, she had to choose one in Paul's territory. At least she'd said Nathaniel's lawyer would handle the purchase. Maybe that would keep her out of Paul's reach.

Tim clenched his jaw. He had no plans of turning Dominique. She'd hate him for it, and living that close to her while being despised? He'd rather cut out his own heart. For now, at least, he could still be her friend.

He typed a quick message to Jacob, thumb hovering before hitting send.

Is Paul tasked with watching Dominique?

***

Tim woke up to a text from Jacob.

The meeting was accidental. Dominique chose the building herself and called Paul. But if I decided to have Paul bring Dominique over, that's my business. You'll just have to

deal with it.

Tim: **I won't let anyone turn Dominique.**

Jacob: **Then you'd better get it done in the next few days. If not, then all bets are off where she's concerned. I think Paul has taken a liking to her.**

Tim growled.

Tim: **Over my dead body.**

Jacob: **That can be arranged if you don't follow orders.**

"Fuck!" Tim shouted, throwing his phone across the room.

He needed to talk to Dominique, and fast. He'd already pulled himself from the fight for her affections, but losing her to the truth of his world? Unacceptable.

Challenging Paul was the only way. Kill Paul, challenge Jacob. Take over the pack.

His breath shuddered out. No way was he going to let Dominique be forced into this life like he was. Memories stirred against his will.

***

"Hey, handsome. You look lonely. Want a little company?" Roxy purred, leaning into him.

Tim glanced at her. Shoulder-length blonde hair, amber eyes, pouty lips, curves in all the right places. Gorgeous, no doubt. Her smile widened as his gaze lingered.

Dominique's face slammed into his mind. His fiancée. Their relationship was already hanging by a thread, fights piling up, and that one slap still burned in his memory. He shook his head.

"No offense. You're beautiful, but I'm engaged."

"Oh, come on. I've watched you in here every night for a month. If you're engaged, why don't you ever go home to your old lady?"

"I do." The lie left his mouth too easily.

"Sure you do," she snorted. "If you change your mind, I'll be around."

She drifted off but kept circling back, her presence tugging at him as he downed beer after beer. Her words hit harder than the alcohol. Things with Dominique were bad. So bad he'd been afraid to go home, terrified he might lose his shit again. Maybe he should go back, try to fix it.

A shot glass slid in front of him. He raised an eyebrow at the bartender, who nodded toward Roxy. Tim lifted it, knocked it back, the burn trailing fire into his chest.

Minutes later, his head fogged. She slid onto the stool beside him.

"My name's Roxy. What's yours?"

"Tim. Thanks for the drink."

"My pleasure, handsome. Changed your mind yet?"

"No. But I appreciate the attention."

She patted his arm and ordered another round. He downed it, stronger than anything he'd tasted. His head spun. She slid off her stool with a sly smile.

"I'll come back later. See if you want some company then."

He didn't even look up. Whatever she'd ordered was potent. Too potent. But his addiction clawed at him, and he ordered another.

Soon, the world doubled. When he tried to leave, his legs gave out.

"Keys," the bartender demanded.

Roxy was suddenly there. "I'll take him. Come on, honey."

He let her sling his arm over her shoulder, stumbling to her car. The moment he hit the seat, his vision blacked out.

"Wake up, honey. We're home."

Tim groaned. She hauled him out with surprising strength.

"Keys. Right pocket," he slurred.

"You won't be needing those." Keys jingled, but they weren't his.

She steered him to a couch. His bleary eyes darted around. Not his place.

"This isn't my house. I—"

She slid onto his lap. Her finger pressed to his lips. Then her mouth. Tongue teasing, pressing for more.

He jerked back, bile rising. "No. I have a fiancée."

He shoved her off and tried to stand, but staggered.

She yanked him back down, straddling him again.

"Get off!"

Her grin curled, wicked and unyielding, before her mouth pressed to his neck.

With a violent shove, he sent her tumbling to the floor. She hit hard, but before he could rise, she was on him again, fists crashing into his face. The force slammed him back into the couch.

Her lips returned to his throat as her hands clamped his wrists, pinning them to his sides. She was impossibly strong.

When she finally released him, he jerked his hands up to push her away, only for pain to explode across his ribs.

"No one tells me no," she whispered.

Agony cut through his fog. His eyes went wide as her fingers elongated, turning into claws. One hand raked across his chest, the other plunged into his stomach.

A raw scream tore from his throat.

Her claws sank deeper, twisting. His vision narrowed to black, the last sound a maniacal laugh echoing in his ears.

***

He jerked upright, head pounding like a drum. Rubbing his face, he tried to quiet the roar in his skull. *Jesus, what a nightmare.*

Blinking through the haze, confusion clawed at him. This wasn't his place. His gaze caught on framed photos of the woman from the bar.

Shit. Shit. Shit. Did I cheat on Dominique?

He groaned and sank back. His body felt like it had been shoved through a blender.

"Good. You're awake. Means you survived," Roxy said, gliding into the room.

"What did you do to me?" Tim rasped.

"I gave you a gift. You've been out for a week. You'll heal fast now. Rest. When you're ready to change, I'll show you the ropes."

"What the hell are you talking about—change?"

"Into a werewolf, silly." She laughed.

"There's no such thing. Damn, you're crazy. You cut me up," he muttered as flashes slammed into him; hands, claws, blood.

Her hands looked normal now. No claws, no blood.

His chest felt tight as he sat up. His fingers brushed something soft. Looking down, he saw bandages wrapped from chest to hips, clean. Not a trace of blood.

Roxy watched as he unraveled them. Angry claw marks glared back at him. His brow furrowed. Flashes kept coming. Her hands, claws, his stomach ripped open, his screams. How was he alive?

He traced the marks gingerly. No gaping wounds. Just closed cuts.

"I told you. You'll heal fast. Werewolves do. You belong to me now," she cooed.

"I don't belong to anyone, least of all you. I don't know what you did, but you won't get away with it."

Her laugh was low and syrupy. "You'll see. When you're ready, come out and eat. Then I'll take you out and show you how to change."

"What do you want from me, you crazy bitch?"

"I already told you. You're mine. Don't worry, baby, you'll like me. I love fun." She winked and slipped out.

He lay there, trying to piece together the nightmare. His stomach growled. Had he really been here a week? Dominique probably thought he was dead, or worse, had left her.

He rose slowly, finding his shredded shirt and bloodstained jeans. His phone was dead. Pain tightened his torso with every movement. Still, she hadn't locked the door. Did she think he wouldn't run? Call the cops?

Roxy appeared in the doorway. "Follow me."

Hoping for a phone, he did.

At the kitchen table, she motioned to a chair. "Sit."

He sat. She set a plate stacked with sandwiches before him. His eyebrows shot up. He couldn't eat all that. But he did, wolfing them down.

When he finished, she rose. "Come with me."

He glanced around for a phone. Nothing. Standing slowly, pain rippled up his side. He clung to the doorjamb, breath ragged.

Roxy waited in the backyard, an evil smile glinting in her eyes. Then her body bent, reshaped in impossible ways. In seconds, a massive gray wolf stood before him.

His pain forgotten, Tim bolted inside, crashing through rooms toward the front door. He was almost there when a fresh wave of agony seized him. Black spots swarmed his vision. His body crumpled, fingers stretching for the doorknob before darkness took him.

***

When Tim woke again, he knew the nightmares were real. Rage exploded inside him, and the shift tore through his body. He rampaged through Roxy's house, smashing everything in sight.

When the fury finally ebbed, she coaxed him back into human form. He took advantage, beating the hell out of her, rage surging fresh at what she'd done to him.

He yanked on his jeans and shoes and bolted. Her howl echoed after him as he hit the highway. Someone pulled over, pitied him, and gave him a ride to the bar. From there, he drove home.

He never told Dominique. Fear of losing control around her kept him away, sometimes even leaving when he saw her car in his driveway. And yet, he drifted back to Roxy. He had to learn control.

Weeks later, Roxy introduced him to Jacob, their Alpha. Jacob saw the rage burning in him and turned it into a weapon. Tim became an enforcer, hurting anyone who dared threaten the pack. But it didn't stop there. His punishments blurred into torture. And the more his relationship with Dominique crumbled, the crueler he became.

When she accused him of cheating, he snapped. He thought the truth about Roxy had been buried. But Dominique had followed him that night. Followed him on other nights, too. That fight was brutal, and every fight after was only worse.

She never believed his denials. He never told her the truth. Just raged, stormed out, left her alone in his house. Until one day, she snapped first and ended it.

Tim shook his head, shoving the memories back.

Dominique needed to know. All of it. Before Jacob came for her. This time, he'd tell her everything from start to finish.

He went to work, but Dominique never showed. When asked where she was, Melissa only shrugged, claiming she didn't know. Not exactly a lie, but she definitely knew more than she said.

Tim texted Dominique: **We need to talk. I'm ready to tell you everything.**

By night's end, no reply came.

He drove to her house. Empty. No lights. No car. His chest clenched tight.

Remembering he had Nathaniel's number, he fired off a text: **Is she with you?**

Chapter 60

Dominique snuggled deeper into the sheets, burying her face under the blanket. Jet lag had flattened her the night before. She'd barely managed to toss her bag aside before passing out.

For once, the stress stayed at the door. She intended to keep it there.

With a stretch, she flung back the blanket and grabbed her phone. She hadn't even turned it on when she landed.

The moment the screen lit, her notifications exploded. Texts from Tim. From Nathaniel. Even here, they wouldn't leave her alone. With an exasperated groan, she tossed the phone onto the bed and pulled on a tank top and shorts.

The morning was hers.

Shops lined the walkway, their windows full of clothes, trinkets, and jewelry that begged to be touched. At the far end, a smaller store drew her in.

The man behind the counter drew her in, too; tall, bronze-skinned, jet-black hair framing steel-grey eyes. Handsome in the kind of way that demanded attention.

She wandered the aisles, picking out souvenirs for Melissa and Post. Holding a skirt against her hips in front of a mirror, a sharp whistle made her turn.

The clerk leaned on the counter, smirking.

"You'd look gorgeous in that. Bet it would hug your curves in all the right ways."

Heat touched her cheeks. "Thanks."

He chuckled low in his throat. "A woman like you shouldn't blush over a compliment."

Her lips curved. Why not play along? "When it comes from such a *delectable* man, what woman wouldn't?"

"Delectable, huh? I like that." His grin widened. "You're welcome to have a taste anytime you want."

She laughed softly. "Tempting offer… but I think I'll pass."

She turned back to browsing, finding a crop top to pair with the skirt. At the register, his fingers brushed hers a beat too long as he handed over the receipt.

"Come back if you change your mind about that taste test."

Laughter spilled out of her as she stepped into the sun. No chance she was setting foot in there again.

*****

Later that evening, she slipped into the black skirt and teal crop top she'd bought. The skirt brushed her knees, her black heels adding a few inches. A messy bun left strands framing her face, teal shadow made her eyes pop, and ruby lips blew a kiss at the mirror.

Dominique felt sexy and powerful walking into the club. Heads turned. Wanting the full experience, she planned on a little barhopping.

With a drink in hand, she sat at a table and watched. Natural beauties filled the room, men tanned and dark-haired. Several asked her to dance. She declined each one.

"Well, fancy meeting you here," a man whispered in her ear.

Her head jerked. The clerk from the store. Shit. She turned away, ignoring him.

Uninvited, he dropped into the seat across from her.

"Really? Isn't it polite to ask if you can sit down?" Dominique asked.

"No. Our culture is socialization."

"And if the person doesn't want company?"

"Too bad. Tables are shared. Not enough space for everyone to have their own. I'm Devin, by the way. What's your name?"

"None of your business."

"Oh, come on. Now who's being rude?" Devin laughed.

"I'm in a relationship."

"I don't see a ring on that finger."

"Doesn't mean anything."

"Then where's this boyfriend?"

"He's back home. I came here to get away. *Alone*."

"Then let me show you around. This club's okay, but the underground ones? That's where the real fun is."

"Okay, whatever you say. I'm just here to relax. I won't be back tomorrow night."

"You don't come to a club and not dance. At least tell me your name."

She sighed. "Dominique."

"See? That wasn't so hard. So, Dominique, will you dance with me? Dancing's fun. Relaxing." He stood, hand outstretched.

She stared at it. This was supposed to be her break from men, not an invitation.

"It's just a dance." He wiggled his fingers. "No harm in one."

She shook her head, but let him pull her up anyway.

One dance bled into a night of drinking and moving with the music.

"I've had a lovely evening, Devin, but it's time for me to go."

"Wait." He grabbed a napkin, scribbled a number, and handed it over. "Call me if you want to see the real nightlife."

"I'll think about it."

Back in her hotel room, Dominique scrolled through Tim's messages.

We need to talk. I'm ready to tell you everything.

Where are you? I really need to talk to you.

Please text me back and let me know you're okay.

She snorted. *He disappears from my life, wants to play friends, and now he's suddenly worried because I didn't tell him I was leaving? Now he wants to spill everything? When it doesn't matter anymore? What a joke.*

Switching to Nathaniel's message, she read:

I came by the club and noticed you haven't been there the past two nights. Is everything okay?

She typed back quickly: **Everything's fine. Just needed some time away to think. I'll be back in two weeks.**

His reply came almost instantly.

Can I come see you? The past two days without you made me realize I don't want to lose you. I'll answer any questions you have.

Laughter tore from her lungs until they burned. *Fuck, they frustrate me.* Now *they want to talk? I gave them an ultimatum, left, and suddenly they've both found their voices?*

Frustration bubbled as she fired off a reply:

I'm not home, so no, you can't come over. I'll text you when I'm home.

Nathaniel: **Where are you? I can come there.**

Dominique: **No, you can't. I need time away, so I left. No one knows where I am, not even Melissa, so don't bother asking her. Just respect my need for time and space like you said you would, and don't text me again, okay?**

Three dots stayed on the screen for a minute. Then his reply came:

I'll respect your wishes. I love you.

Dominique didn't answer. She tossed the phone onto the nightstand and got ready for bed. Sliding beneath the blanket, exhaustion dragged her under.

Chapter 61

Dominique spent the next week unwinding. She swam the reef, stretched out on the beach, and snapped photos of everything: the turquoise waves, the crowded markets, the sunsets melting over the horizon. Each evening, she curled on her balcony with a book, music humming through her headphones, letting the day slip away with the sun.

She checked in with Melissa a few times, just enough to keep updated. The lawyer called to tell her he'd set up the business account and deposited the money. He was moving forward with an offer on the building. By the time she got home, it might already be hers.

Tim, however, wouldn't stop texting. At first, she ignored him, then finally told him she'd left to clear her head. His replies turned desperate; where was she, was she safe, why wouldn't she just tell him? She answered once more: she was fine, she'd taken a real vacation, one without him and Nathaniel looming over her. He begged her to come see him the moment she got back. She wasn't going to do that. He'd had all the time in the world to talk before. He hadn't.

Nathaniel hadn't either, but at least he'd honored her request for silence. Tim couldn't seem to grasp the concept. Eventually, she stopped replying at all, though the messages kept coming. For him, 'I need space' clearly didn't mean 'leave me alone'.

Sighing, Dominique texted Melissa about the guy she'd met that first night at the club. She hadn't seen him since, though she'd explored plenty of other bars.

Melissa's reply came fast: **You should have a little fun. What's the harm in hanging out with a hot guy on vacation? You don't have to sleep with him. Send me a picture!**

Dominique laughed out loud.

She dug out the napkin Devin had scribbled his number on and finally sent him a message, giving him hers.

If you still want to show me those clubs, I'm in.

His answer didn't take long: he'd love to take her out. They made dinner plans, then a club he promised she'd enjoy.

Staring at the napkin still clutched in her hand, she hesitated. Was she really going to meet up with some random guy she'd only spoken to once? Melissa's voice echoed in her head: *What's the harm?*

Maybe she was right. Maybe a little distraction would help her finally make the decision she'd been avoiding.

***

Dominique slipped into a deep blue dress that hugged her curves just right. After fixing her hair and makeup, she headed for Devin's shop.

As soon as she stepped out of the cab, a sharp whistle split the air. Heat crept up her neck as her eyes met Devin's. His grin made her lips twitch into a hesitant smile.

At dinner, he pulled out her chair before sitting across from her.

"Thank you," she murmured.

"You're most welcome," he said easily.

She folded her napkin across her lap. "Just to be upfront. I'm not planning on sleeping with you."

Devin laughed. "Well, that wasn't what I was thinking about at this moment."

"Most men don't take a woman on vacation out without wanting something," she said dryly.

"You're right," he admitted. "But I know I don't stand a chance since you don't live here. What's the harm in trying, right?"

"I suppose." She gave a small shrug.

He leaned in. "So, Dominique, what do you do for a living? You already know I own my shop."

"I own a club. That's why I want to see the local scene. Might give me ideas."

"Nice. And in your spare time?"

"I write, listen to music, and hang out with friends. You?"

"Surf, swim, hang out with friends." His brows lifted. "Noticed you didn't mention your boyfriend."

"That's… complicated. I like spending time with—" she tripped over the words, "um, well, them too."

"Did you just say *them*?" Devin's mouth curved.

"Maybe," she muttered, trying and failing not to blush.

"So do you really have a boyfriend?"

"That's a long story," Dominique said.

"We have all night." He grinned.

She exhaled. "Fine. I don't actually have a boyfriend. I have two guys I'm in love with, and I can't choose. I want uncomplicated, but they're both complicated."

"Then maybe leave them both alone. Try something new. Something uncomplicated."

"I don't think that would work. I don't want anything new. I want *them*. But one is my ex-fiancé, who just came back into the picture, and the other… he makes me feel like I never have before."

"I'm uncomplicated," Devin said with a playful spark. "You know you won't be here long enough for it to get complicated. Why not see what it's like with someone who won't tangle things up? See if you still want one of them."

"I don't want a fling, Devin. I want a real relationship. I just didn't think it would be like this."

"You don't have to sleep with someone to keep it uncomplicated. I'm yours for the night." He wiggled his brows. "Think of this as a date and see how much fun you can have without the mess afterward."

Dominique laughed. Devin had a charm she couldn't deny. Still, part of her wished she could go out with Tim or Nathaniel like this; just laugh, enjoy without the constant shadow of consequences. But that was impossible. They were always so damn serious, especially after the whole mess with Roxy. Now they hovered more than ever, overbearing and suffocating.

"Okay," she said finally. "We can see how uncomplicated things are tonight. But I'm telling you now, this is not a fling. I'm not sleeping with you."

Devin's grin was maddening. "We'll see. You might change your mind by the end of the night."

"Don't bet on it, Romeo." She shook her head, smiling despite herself.

They lingered at the table, trading stories. Devin shared bits of his childhood and the dreams that had carried him here. Dominique offered glimpses of her own, skimming past the darkest times but giving him a small piece of what her life had been with Tim before it all unraveled. The conversation was easy. No hidden motives, no weight pressing down. Just talk.

After dinner, Devin opened the car door for her and drove them to a part of the island she hadn't seen before. The building didn't look like a club at all. More like an office complex. Inside, a receptionist sat behind a desk, her face blank as she asked, "Can I help you?"

Devin slid a card from his wallet. The woman's eyes flicked down, then back up, her lips curving faintly as she handed it back. Without a word, she crossed to the far wall, pressing a button so subtle Dominique wouldn't have noticed it if she'd been staring straight at it. The wall slid aside, and music thundered out.

Devin laced his fingers through hers and tugged her down a narrow stairwell. At the bottom, Dominique froze. A massive underground club stretched out before her, lights pulsing over a sea of bodies.

Her eyes widened. A hidden club. It was unreal, alive, the kind of place she didn't think actually existed.

Devin led her to the bar, and they ordered drinks, talking a little about the setup. Then the lights cut out. Darkness fell, broken only by the sudden blaze of lasers slicing through the air.

Devin caught her hand again, pulling her toward the DJ booth. He grabbed a set of drums, sliding them in front of her. Other couples were doing the same. Then he uncapped a bottle, pouring liquid across the drumheads.

The moment he started playing, the liquid splattered. Glowing paint erupted across his arms, her dress, the air between them. Dominique burst out laughing. The stuff shone under the blacklight, a riot of neon on skin and fabric.

Devin handed her the drumsticks. She struck a beat, paint flying, and let herself dance with the rhythm.

This place was insane. And she loved it.

Devin snapped a picture while she was playing, catching her mid-rhythm. She was completely in her zone, lost to the beat and the glow of the paint. He slipped up behind her, dancing along, then lifted his phone again. Dominique laughed when he showed her the shot. She couldn't remember the last time her smile had looked so bright, so free.

They danced the night away, beating on drums, streaked with glowing paint until it covered them both. At one point, Devin dipped his fingers into the paint and brushed it across her skin, sweeping a trail from the corner of her eye down her cheek. His palm cupped her face, warm despite the cool slickness of paint, and then he kissed her.

Shock jolted through her, but she didn't push him away. The kiss wasn't heavy, just bold, reckless. The night had been fun, easy, and uncomplicated. Exactly what she wanted from Tim and Nathaniel, but never seemed to get. Why couldn't things ever just be like this with them?

She broke the kiss, turning away, heart tight. No. She couldn't let herself get tangled up in him. She didn't want a fling, didn't want to sleep with someone and then walk away. That wasn't her. She had never had a one-night stand, and she didn't plan to start now. This trip was supposed to be a vacation from romance and secrets, not the beginning of another mess.

Devin came up behind her, his hands trailing lightly down her arms.

"I can't say I'm sorry for kissing you," he admitted, voice low, "but I got carried away. I know you're in love with other guys, and me being around would just complicate things. But you're beautiful, Dominique. And fun."

"I appreciate it," she said softly. "But I think I should head back to my hotel. Tonight's been amazing, and I won't forget it. You showed me what *uncomplicated* can look like." She gave him a small smile.

"All right," Devin sighed. "I'll take you back."

"No. I'll call a cab. Probably best you don't know where I'm staying."

He chuckled. "So that's a no on a good-night kiss?"

"You're impossible. That's a no," she said, already pulling her phone out.

She ordered a cab, then turned back to him. He really was a good guy, from what little she knew. If she lived here, if her heart weren't already torn in two, maybe she could've seen herself dating him. Instead, she hugged him, pressing a quick kiss to his cheek before heading for the steps. The bouncer escorted her out.

Back in her hotel room, Dominique paused in front of the mirror. Neon paint still streaked her skin, glowing faintly under the light. She lifted her phone, snapping a picture; a keepsake of the night. For a long moment, she studied her reflection. Could she ever be this happy in her real life?

Her gaze lingered on the faint handprint Devin had left across her cheek, fingertips tracing her face and arms. She reached up and touched it. The paint had dried, but the warmth of the night still clung to her.

Her phone buzzed. A text from Devin lit up the screen: a picture of himself. She smiled and forwarded it to Melissa. More pictures followed: shots of her in the club, laughing, playing, dancing. The last one was of them together on the floor, both of them streaked with paint.

Devin's next message read: **You should have this much fun all the time. You're a beautiful woman, and it shows in these pictures. If your man doesn't make you feel like this, he isn't worth it. Love shouldn't be complicated. It should come naturally.**

Dominique typed back: **Thank you for a great night and for showing me what uncomplicated looks like. But love is complicated. It isn't easy. You have to put in the work to keep it alive.**

His reply came quickly. **No, you don't. If you truly love each other, then you just want to be with each other. Nothing is complicated because you wouldn't let it be. They'd wait for you, let you come to them, and always make sure you knew they were there.**

She stared at the words, heart tightening. Devin's point echoed the very thoughts that had been twisting inside her. Tim… she loved him, had for years. But he'd broken her so deeply she wasn't sure she could risk it again. And Nathaniel… he was different. Secretive, yes, but he made her feel things Tim never had. She didn't believe in soulmates, not really. Still, if she had one, she liked to think it was him.

If that was true, shouldn't her choice already be clear? Nathaniel had told her he loved her. And she loved him.

Her thoughts flicked to Rose and Nathaniel, and the story she'd wrapped herself in. Was she chasing a dream she'd written for herself? Or had those dreams of Nathaniel come because she was meant to be with him all along?

She read Devin's message again. She wanted to be with Nathaniel all the time. Even when she'd said she needed space, she'd ended up curled beside him anyway. He had never pushed, never forced her hand, only waited, steady and patient. He'd told her he'd wait until she was ready. That whatever choice she made, he'd still be there, even as just a friend.

Tim had said he'd be there as a friend, too. But when she'd finally given in to him, he'd pulled away instead.

The choice seemed simple. Yet love made it anything but.

Dominique sighed, setting her phone aside. In the shower, as the hot water washed streaks of dried paint from her skin, the question still burned in her chest.

Chapter 62

While Dominique was away, Nathaniel had been looking into Jacob. He had a feud with a neighboring pack. Not only had he poached members, but he'd also moved onto their territory with his businesses. Some of his pack dealt drugs, which was not allowed on White Moon pack lands.

The neighboring Alpha had warned Jacob he'd continue killing his people if he found them, but Jacob hadn't reined them in. Every once in a while, he'd have his enforcer make an example, then let it go because it brought him more money. Nicholas had threatened all-out war if Jacob didn't start acting like an Alpha and controlling his pack.

Nathaniel had also researched Nicholas. He knew he couldn't take Jacob and his entire pack alone. But with help, maybe they could be taken down. He didn't think most of Jacob's wolves wanted to fight. From what he found, many were just ordinary people who'd been attacked and survived, trying to live normal lives and forget that side of themselves.

Nathaniel found where Nicholas lived. One night, he crept into the trees on the borderlands, waiting until the patrols were gone. Landing near the front door, he knocked once, then leapt onto the roof. He heard movement inside and knew Nicholas had scented him.

The back door opened, and a pure white wolf stepped out. Nathaniel grinned, eyes tracking as the wolf circled the house.

"No need for that, wolf," Nathaniel said.

The wolf's growl rumbled low. Nathaniel stood, raising his hands, then jumped down to the ground a few feet away. The wolf snarled but held.

"While your fangs are impressive, I have my own," Nathaniel said, baring his. "I didn't come here to fight, but to give you a proposition. I know you're in a feud with Jacob of the Bad Moon pack. I, too, have a problem with him."

Nicholas shifted back into a man and eyed him. "How did you get past my wolves?"

Nathaniel smirked. "Your wolves have never dealt with a vampire. Unlike them, I can climb or leap great distances. They can't track what they can't smell."

Nicholas's eyes glossed, then snapped back to Nathaniel. "I told my wolves to stand down. You'll be safe leaving."

"Thank you. Now, my proposition."

"I'm listening."

"Jacob sees me as a threat because of what I am. I've done nothing wrong except defend the woman I love. His pack member tried to attack her, and I broke the bitch's wrist. It healed easily, but it was meant as a warning. He didn't heed it, and now it's become a feud."

"He's coming after me, and while I might be able to take him, I can't fight his entire pack alone. One of his members loves the same woman and wants to protect her, but Jacob is forcing him to bring her over against her will."

"I'd like to propose that your pack join me. Most of Jacob's wolves are ordinary people forced into fighting. He's a tyrant. You, by contrast, are a fair Alpha. If we destroy Jacob, you can take over his pack."

Nicholas let out a laugh. "So, you and a wolf are both in love with the same woman?"

"Yes. And I don't find it the least bit funny," Nathaniel replied.

"And Jacob is feuding with you over her? I knew he was a stupid son of a bitch, but all that over a woman? No wonder his pack is worthless. He'll use any excuse to start a fight. He thinks the rules don't apply to him. You don't bring someone over without permission. If you can't control them, our secret risks exposure. In my pack, you're born into it. Once in a while, someone mates with a human, but rarely."

"This woman isn't mated to either of us. She's on vacation, trying to get away from both sides pulling her back and forth. She doesn't know what we are, but she soon will." Nathaniel's voice hardened. "I'm asking for your help. It solves both our problems. And now that you know me, you know I'm not a threat to your pack. I've no quarrel with wolves, though we're usually on opposite sides."

Nicholas crossed his arms. "I'll consider it. I won't take my pack into a war lightly. Give me a way to contact you, and I'll decide."

Nathaniel handed him a number and left. He hoped Nicholas would join him. If not, he knew he'd lose when Jacob finally came for him. Jacob would find him eventually. Nathaniel had been careful, but if Dominique ever came over, she wouldn't be.

Chapter 63

Dominique stepped off the plane, stomach churning. Had she eaten something bad on the flight?

She went straight home and crawled into bed.

When she woke, the nausea hit again. Shaking it off, she posted all her pictures from the trip. No more hiding she'd been in the Bahamas.

She texted Nathaniel: **I'm home if you still want to talk.**

His reply came immediately: **Can you come over and talk now?**

She gathered her things and drove toward his house, never noticing the car trailing her until she turned down the dirt road.

Dominique pulled into Nathaniel's garage and hit the button to close the door. She got out of the car and climbed the stairs to the door leading into his living room.

She hesitated. Was she ready for this conversation? She'd thought about it constantly on vacation. She wanted to be with him, but she had to know what he was hiding.

The door opened. Nathaniel stood there, smiling.

Her heart fluttered. His smile always did that to her.

He pulled her close and kissed her. Her fingers slid into his hair. He drew her into the house and kicked the door shut behind them.

"Well, hello to you, too," she said, breathless.

"I missed you. After seeing the pictures you posted, I thought you might not come back," Nathaniel said.

"The vacation was to help me stop going crazy trying to figure out what to do. It was supposed to clear my head so I could make a decision. Why would you think I wouldn't come back?"

"Because of the man in some of the pictures."

"Nathaniel, I went on vacation to get away from you and Tim, because the two of you were so secretive. I didn't go there to find someone else. I just had a good time, that's all."

"How much of a good time?" Nathaniel asked.

"Not that much. I guess you saw the pictures of me in the club."

"Yes. And I didn't like the man hanging all over you."

"It wasn't like that. I came back with a decision. I came back for you. I want to hear the truth from you."

"Alright. Come with me." He took her hand.

Nathaniel led her up the stairs to the third floor. Dominique held her breath, glancing at him. Was he nervous?

Butterflies churned in her stomach. What was up there he didn't want her to know about before?

He led her to the room where she'd seen the picture. The butterflies became a storm.

"You've seen all you need to understand what I'm about to tell you," he said.

"What do you mean, I've seen everything I need to see?"

"The dreams, my spitfire. You've seen enough to know I've come back for you."

"What did you just call me?"

"My spitfire." Nathaniel wrapped his arms around her.

"How did you… How did you know about that?"

"I'm the one who sent you the dreams. I brought you up here to tell you about the picture. This is who you've been dreaming about. I'm who you've been dreaming about."

"What? That doesn't make any sense. You said this photo was of your family."

"And it is. They were my family. My Rose and my children. I have a family tree I've painstakingly written down. Every generation, every branch. They're my family. I've watched over them for almost seven hundred years. I was thirty when I was ripped from my family and put into this existence."

"Nathaniel, you're starting to scare me. Do you honestly expect me to believe you're… what, immortal?"

"I don't expect you to believe me," Nathaniel said softly. "I'm going to show you, Dominique."

With that, Nathaniel gripped her arms and drew her against him. His palm cupped her cheek as his mouth claimed hers. Then the visions slammed into her.

Dominique saw Rose and Nathaniel through the years. Their first baby. Then another. A quiet life was shattered the night Rose's uncle unleashed something worse than an army. A demon who drained blood and life itself.

The creature caught Rose and Nathaniel on a nighttime ride. Nathaniel fought, but she hurled him across the grounds as if he weighed nothing, then stalked Rose, her true target. Rose's uncle had already murdered his own mother. Now it was Rose's turn.

Nathaniel staggered back up as the demon latched onto Rose's neck. Sword in hand, he charged. She flung Rose aside and seized him instead. Stronger than any mortal, she laughed and clamped onto his throat, drinking until he was almost gone.

"All this for love? Fool," she hissed. "Let us see what your love does when you kill her." She bit her own wrist, pried his mouth open, and forced her blood into him before disappearing.

Nathaniel collapsed. Rose cradled his head, tears streaming, while his body convulsed.

"I have to get help. Please hang on, my love."

She leapt onto her horse and galloped for the castle. Nathaniel tried to scream, but couldn't. Breath left him in ragged shudders. His vision fixed on the path where Rose had vanished. She wouldn't make it in time. Darkness swallowed him.

When Rose returned with two knights, she was too late. Her scream tore through the night as they lifted Nathaniel's body onto a horse. Back at the castle, Tabitha tended Rose's wound.

Rose had Nathaniel carried to the tombs. She washed his body, prepared it for burial, and lay beside him one last time, clinging to his cooling frame. She could not bury him, nor watch him burn. Instead, she ordered a place made for him within the walls.

Night fell. In the tombs, the newly awakened Nathaniel rose. No longer a man but a vampire. Hunger ripped through him. He drained the knights dry, then went to find Rose. But he didn't have to; she was already descending the steps.

She stopped, eyes wide. Then she ran to him and threw her arms around him. His thirst had been sated; he found he couldn't drink from her. Her tears wet his shoulder.

"My love!" Rose sobbed.

She drew back, searching his face. His eyes were darker now, the look in them terrifying, yet he was still her husband. With a trembling hand, she touched his cheek. Nathaniel's eyes closed. His arms crushed her against him until she gasped for air.

"You left me to die," he growled. "Left me here to rot."

"No! I went for help. You died! I know you did."

Her words faltered against his grip.

Nathaniel ransacked his memory. Pain. Cold. Her warmth riding away. His body was different, faster, with rage rising. He flung Rose to the ground and bolted up the steps.

In his room, he dressed quickly, pacing. He'd drunk the blood of his own men. What had he become?

Then he heard it. A woman's voice, faint as wind, calling his name. Urging him closer. He moved to the window; the whisper grew stronger.

Nathaniel leapt out. He landed lightly, as if weightless, and sprinted toward the sound.

In a clearing stood a woman, her pale hair and skin glowing under the moonlight. She beckoned. Mesmerized, Nathaniel crossed to her and took the hand she held out.

"Welcome," Eleanor purred, her eyes gleaming. "I see you have changed. Did you savor draining those men?"

Nathaniel's voice was raw. "What are you? What have you done to me?"

She stepped closer. "I am Eleanor. A vampire. And now, so are you, dearie. I turned you to kill your beloved, to please her uncle. But I do not like being used. He slaughtered my people in daylight, left me alive to suffer. Lied, told me Rose was to blame."

Nathaniel's jaw tightened. "Rose would never harm without cause."

"I know," Eleanor hissed, circling him. "I have watched her. She's too sweet, too pure. Sickening. You will be the first in my new line."

He shook his head. "I do not understand."

"My kind, old and strong, can build a bloodline. Mine was destroyed, so I will rebuild. You will kill her uncle. Then, you will kill Rose."

"Never." His voice cracked with fury. "She has done nothing. And I still love her."

Eleanor's smile cut sharply. "Then I will."

She blurred toward the castle. Rage surged through Nathaniel. Rage and love knotted so tightly he couldn't separate them. He hurled himself after her, faster than the wind, catching her on the steps.

Eleanor's claws ripped his chest open. Fire tore through him, but he held ground.

"Stand aside, boy," she snarled. "I will kill you and her both."

"If Rose dies, I have no reason to exist," he growled.

Her eyes narrowed. "What will you give me if I spare her?"

"Anything. Just leave her be."

Her grin sealed his fate. From that night, Nathaniel's soul was hers. He slaughtered Rose's uncle, half his court, and laid the foundation of Eleanor's new bloodline.

***

Nathaniel couldn't stay away any longer. Night after night, he'd watched her from the castle's shadows, but this time, he leapt, fingers catching the stone sill. He slipped through her window, silent, and stood over her bed. Rose slept on, the fire dying low. He brushed a knuckle down her cheek. She stirred, then settled.

He lay beside her, arms sliding around her. Months of her tears had haunted him; his rage was tamed now, but not the hunger. The need to touch her, to feel her again, burned through him.

His mouth found hers, his hands moving over her as before his death. Rose shifted onto her back, stiffening as she blinked awake. Her eyes struggled to adjust to the dim glow. Her mouth opened. He covered it with his palm.

"Please, do not scream, my love," he whispered. "I know this is a nightmare for you. I should be dead. I am… a monster now. I do not blame you if you wish me gone. But I have watched you, night after night. I miss you."

Tears slid from her closed eyes. He felt them on his fingers, breaking him. Slowly, he took his hand away and pressed his lips to hers. At first, she lay still, then a sob escaped her as she kissed him back. He poured every shred of love into that kiss, his body covering hers. When he broke away, his lips found her neck… and her pulse, hammering.

"Nathaniel?" she whispered. "What has happened to you? You died. I felt it."

"I am a bloodthirsty monster, Rose. I cannot be with you, but I cannot let you go."

"How can the man I love be a monster?"

"The man you loved is gone. She turned me into this."

She cupped his face, studying it. Paler skin, yes, but the same eyes. She kissed him softly, resting her forehead against his.

"I still see him. My heart still belongs to you. I do not understand, but I will take whatever time I can have."

"No," he murmured. "I belong to her now. It is the only way to keep you safe."

"You have lain with her?"

"Yes. I am sorry. I could not risk her coming after you. I should not even be here. It puts you in danger."

"I would have given my life for you, Nathaniel. Better to die than to know you no longer belong to me."

Rose tilted her head, baring her throat. Her pulse raced under her skin. She guided his head down, breath quickening. He tasted the beat of her heart with his tongue.

"Take what you want," she whispered. "I have nothing left to lose."

"No!" He tore himself away, pacing the room, hands in his hair.

Rose sat up, watching him. He was right. This wasn't the man she'd loved. That man had lain with another, had given away what she thought was hers. Yet fear wouldn't come. She'd felt dead inside since the night she held his cooling body.

If he were a monster, she would let the monster have her once, and then she would be able to let him go. Live on for their children. The only pieces of him she had left.

Rose rose from the bed and stopped Nathaniel's pacing with a hand on his arm. He froze at her touch, eyes searching hers. Without a word, she slipped the nightgown over her head and let it fall to the floor.

She pressed her bare body against his, lifting onto her toes to kiss him. His growl rumbled against her lips as he gave in, pulling her close. In a rush, he tore his clothes away, and for a moment she saw the man she had always known, unchanged.

They tangled together, kissing, touching, until Nathaniel guided her back to the bed. He lifted her easily, setting her down before crawling over her, his body fitting into hers as if no time had passed. He closed his eyes, savouring the feel of her.

"You will always be my spitfire," he whispered before claiming her.

Pleasure built swiftly inside her, her heartbeat thundering. Nathaniel's control frayed as the rhythm of her pulse consumed him. When she cried out, she turned her head and drew him to her throat. His groan shuddered through her as he gave in, fangs plunging deep. Pain and ecstasy ripped through her together.

Her body softened beneath him as his hunger spiralled. He was drinking too much, too fast. He forced himself away, gasping, blood hot on his tongue. Rose's eyes were closed, her breath shallow. Terror jolted him. He had nearly killed her.

A scream split the night. Eleanor burst through the window, her fury a storm. She struck Nathaniel, driving him down, her voice a snarl. "You belong to me."

When she thought him beaten, she turned on Rose. Her fangs sank into Rose's throat, trying to drain what little life was left.

"No!" Nathaniel roared.

With a surge of strength, he shattered a chair and drove the jagged wood into Eleanor's back. The scream she released rattled the stone walls before her body collapsed into ash.

Nathaniel stumbled to Rose's side, wracked with the searing pain of killing his own sire. She still breathed, faint but alive. He licked her wound, whispering her name as he fought for control. Then, he dressed swiftly, vanishing into the night before the guards arrived.

He survived his sire's death.

But centuries stretched before him in loneliness. Rose recovered, yet when he returned to her, she no longer wept for him. She had moved on, her heart given to another man. He watched her marry, watched her live, watched her die.

And still he remained, cursed to roam without her, his soulmate lost forever. He watched their children grow, then their children's children, and so on through the years. Each name, each birth, each death he inked into his book, a family tree that grew while he stayed the same.

Chapter 64

Dominique came out of the vision gasping, her whole body trembling. Not only had Nathaniel's face appeared to her this time, but Rose's as well. No longer herself as a blonde.

She stared at the portrait. The woman in it was the same one from her vision. The uncanny resemblance of the man to Nathaniel finally made sense.

Nathaniel had sent her those dreams. Wanted her to see a past life.

But why? How?

Nervous energy settled into her bones, yet no fear rose with it. This couldn't be real. Was she dreaming even now?

"Nathaniel?" she whispered.

"You haven't seen it all yet, Dominique." His voice was low, almost mournful. "But now you know the true ending between Rose and me. I left that night and never returned to Rose. I couldn't. I'd almost killed her. Eleanor nearly did because of me. She survived, but it took her a long time to wake from the blood loss. All I could do was watch her and our children from afar." He paused. "You named your daughter Lily Rose. Do you know why?"

"I just liked the name. It came to me."

"No." His gaze pinned her. "It came from your past life. My daughter's name was Lily. Rose chose it, thinking it fitting for our child to be named after a beautiful flower, as she had been. You're more connected to your past than you'll ever truly know."

Nathaniel cupped her face. Her vision went black. Fear prickled her skin before a flood of images swept in. Flashes of women: different heights, different weights, different hair, different eyes, different skin. So many faces. All of them had met Nathaniel. This wasn't the first time he'd come for the soul that called to his.

He had whispered the same words to each one. They were soulmates.

Each time the soul was reborn, he felt it. Waited. Gave them time to grow. Yet none chose him. They wanted what he couldn't give: a life, a family.

His thoughts and feelings poured through her. She felt his mistakes, his fast moves, never giving them time to love him, to know him.

Her soul brushed his, crying out. Each woman had wanted Nathaniel. Love had never been the problem. Fear had. Fear of surrendering their lives, fear of losing themselves.

Pain pulsed from her soul. Hurt. Anger. *Betrayal.*

Rose's soul had fractured with his betrayal. She had never forgiven him, and that scar carried through each life, unhealed.

Nathaniel jerked his hands away, pupils blown wide. Fear coursed through her, but it wasn't hers. It belonged to her soul. She herself didn't fear Nathaniel. She knew he wouldn't harm her.

No anger lingered in his eyes, only pain.

Rose's soul had never been so closely tied to any of the other women. Dominique was the last cycle. She felt it. She knew it.

She was ready. She wanted Nathaniel. Wanted forever. Her eyes met his as she cupped his cheek. A light kiss, then she tilted her head, guiding him to her neck.

Nathaniel hesitated, then sank his fangs into her neck. A groan of satisfaction vibrated against her skin as he drank deeper.

Dominique stumbled, gasping when his fangs tore free. Her hand flew to the wound, covering it as pain pulsed hot through her body.

Her stomach twisted when he whirled into a rage, punching a hole through the wall, scattering papers and books from his desk.

"Nathaniel! What in the hell is wrong with you?"

His eyes snapped to hers, burning with anger. She backed away as he stalked forward, though his gaze never left her neck.

"I'm sorry, Dominique. Please… let me fix this."

Her breaths came in harsh pants as he closed the distance. Gently, he removed her hand and lowered his mouth to the wound, his tongue sealing it.

When he pulled back, his eyes were shut, brows furrowed. "I didn't mean to scare you. I let my anger get the better of me. I've waited so long for you," he whispered, cupping her cheek. "And now I can't have you."

"I don't understand, Nathaniel. I'm giving myself to you. I'll admit I'm scared, but I know what I'm doing."

"No," his voice softened, breaking. "You don't. You're pregnant, Dominique."

Her breath caught. "No, I'm not. I would know if I were."

"I can taste it. Your blood isn't only yours. If I turn you now, you'll lose the baby. Is that what you want? Will you forgive me when it happens? Will you still choose me?"

"I—" Dominique's voice faltered.

Her mind spun. She wasn't careful with her cycle. No birth control, not after two years of abstinence. Then that night with Tim. Twice more since. Her eyes widened. Nathaniel couldn't have children. Tim. They hadn't used protection either time. *Shit.*

"I need to think, Nathaniel. I'm sorry. I have to go."

She turned, but he caught her arm. "Dominique, please. Wait."

She faced him, and he drew her into his warmth, kissing her. Tears slid down her cheeks as her heart fractured. If she was pregnant, she could never truly choose Nathaniel. She wanted a family. Choosing him meant risking her baby… Tim's baby.

Tim had to know. He deserved that much, even if she didn't want him to stay out of obligation.

Could she still be with Nathaniel without being turned? Could she live her life for a while, then let him change her later? Her head swam. She needed air, space, and clarity.

"Please, don't go," Nathaniel whispered. "Stay. We'll figure this out."

"I can't." Her voice broke. "I thought I had this figured out. I love you. I want forever with you, but I can't harm my child. And you know who the father is. He won't let me give the baby up. I need to see if I'm really pregnant, Nathaniel. Please, just give me time."

"Then give me tonight." His words were raw, trembling. "You just came back. I love you, and I don't want to lose you again. If you walk out that door, you'll choose your child, and I'll be left here… alone, forever. I don't blame you, but it doesn't make it hurt less. Just… let me hold you one last time. Can you give me that?"

The pain in his eyes gutted her. She hated that she was the one causing it. Dominique hugged him, holding on until she finally stepped back. Taking his hand, she led him toward the bedroom she'd been staying in.

But Nathaniel tugged her back. He shook his head and went to the wall at the end of the hall. She watched in shock as he touched it and the panel slid open, revealing a staircase.

Her eyes widened. Steps led down into a hidden room. She recognized it from the machine; windowless, buried in shadow. Of course. That was why she could never find him during the day.

He led her to the bed. Nathaniel sat, and Dominique climbed onto his lap, kissing him. His hands slid beneath her shirt, up her back. She broke the kiss long enough for him to lift it away, unhook her bra. She stripped his shirt off in turn, pressing close as heat sparked between them.

Dominique stood, kicking off her shoes while Nathaniel unbuttoned her jeans. She pushed them down with her underwear, stepping free, then urged him back on the bed. Her fingers worked his pants open and tugged them off.

A slow smile curved her lips when she saw him already hard.

That night, she stayed with him, giving herself to him until exhaustion pulled her under. She fell asleep wrapped in Nathaniel's arms.

Chapter 65

Dominique woke trembling, her body ice-cold. Why was she so cold? Her fingers brushed the arms wrapped around her, and memory clicked. She'd fallen asleep with Nathaniel.

Her body went rigid. He wasn't holding her. She was curled against a dead body.

Panic rose in her throat. She fought to slip out of his arms, nausea coiling in her stomach like a fist. When she finally stood, she dared a glance back. Nathaniel looked as if he were only sleeping, but she knew better. A shiver rattled her spine. She snatched her clothes from the floor, dressing with quick, clumsy movements.

Her phone lit up in her hand. A missed call from the lawyer. She'd call back later.

Dominique climbed the steps, searching for the button to seal the hidden door. Finding it, she pressed it and watched the wall slide shut. In the hallway, a fresh wave of nausea hit as her fingers closed on the doorknob. She sucked in deep breaths, trying to steady herself. It didn't help.

She bolted for the bathroom and vomited. One hand gripped the sink; the other drifted to her stomach. Her eyes shut. Pregnant. Nathaniel had said she was, but she needed proof. She added "buy test" to the mental list as she wiped her mouth.

On the way home from the store, she called the lawyer back. The building would be hers as soon as the papers were signed. Paul promised to call later with a time to meet.

Excitement and anxiety twisted together. Her business life was clicking into place; her personal life was a minefield. Every time she solved one problem, another detonated.

At home, she unpacked her food, but her eyes stayed locked on the pregnancy test. Did she really want to take it alone? Should she call Tim, have him wait outside the door?

What if it was negative? Would she have raised his hopes for nothing? Doubt crept in. Nathaniel was so certain. He would know what blood tasted like.

Nathaniel… How would any of this work? A baby, her, and him? He'd said he didn't want a family. Could she wait until the child was older to let him turn her? No. She'd be old by then. She couldn't stand the thought of living forever as an old woman beside a man who looked like Nathaniel.

How would they hide it? Move in together? She snorted mid-bite. Yeah right. Nathaniel, Tim, her, and a baby under one roof. Tim playing Daddy while she played house with a vampire. The laughter bubbled up, sharp and hysterical, until she nearly choked.

Even if she tried, how could she conceal never aging? Never walking into sunlight?

She bit the bullet and took the pregnancy test—the longest two minutes of her life.

Positive.

Tears blurred the little window. She slid down the wall, knees to chest. She'd always wanted children. Now she wanted something else, too—Nathaniel.

She let herself cry, grieve, before pulling herself together. Picking up her phone, she hesitated over Tim's messages. Finally, she typed:

Tim, I need to talk to you. If you get this message in the next few minutes, let me know.

She sat on the edge of the bed, heart hammering, waiting. How could she tell Tim she was pregnant and had chosen Nathaniel?

She definitely couldn't tell him what Nathaniel really was. She barely believed it herself.

Her phone buzzed and she jumped.

Tim: **Hey. I was asleep. I'll get dressed and head over. Be there in about 30 minutes, okay?**

Dominique: **Okay. See you then.**

Dominique paced. Tim probably thought she wanted to hear his story. It didn't matter now. She still loved him, probably always would; he was her first love, but she had Nathaniel now. Her soulmate.

An engine's growl outside yanked her to the window. Tim's car rolled up.

Heart racing, she ran to the bathroom, grabbed the test, and shoved it into her pocket. She tried to steady her breathing as his knock echoed through the door.

"Come in."

Tim walked in, noticing her on the couch.

"Hey, Dom."

She forced a smile as he sat down. "Hey."

His narrowed eyes and tense jaw gave him away. He looked angry, hurt. Could he sense her unease? She shook her head and started before she lost her nerve.

"Tim, I'm sure you know I took a vacation. I did that to clear my head, get away from you and Nathaniel. I needed time to think with no pressure. I know you wanted to tell me everything, but that isn't why I asked you to come here."

"I know you say that, Dom, but I can smell Nathaniel all over you. That tells me everything. You already made your choice. You could have told me you were home, but you didn't. Did you even leave town, or were you just with him the whole time?"

"I went to the Bahamas for two weeks. I came back yesterday."

His frown deepened. "So instead of giving me a chance to talk, you ran straight to Nathaniel? You made your choice. There's nothing more to discuss." He started to rise.

Dominique pushed into his space, stopping him. "Damnit, Tim, would you stop being a hothead for two seconds and listen? Yes, I chose Nathaniel. You told me to. You walked away and said I should be with him. And now you act like a jerk when I do exactly that? What happened to you being my friend no matter what?"

Tim raked a hand through his hair, shoulders stiff. "You're right. I did say that."

Relief softened her voice. "Thank you. I hope you mean it, because I didn't ask you here to tell you I chose Nathaniel. I asked you here because I—" Her voice cracked.

Tim's hands closed around her arms. "Dom? What's wrong?"

She shut her eyes, pulling a deep breath into her lungs. Tears threatened, but she refused to cry. Not over this. She didn't hate the baby. She just hated the timing.

Her eyes flew open. The words tumbled out. "I'm pregnant."

Tim froze. His grip tightened, eyes wide. Then, as shock melted into something else, a grin broke across his face. He pulled her into a crushing embrace and kissed her.

Dominique stiffened at first, stunned, but his joy was overwhelming, infectious. He lifted her, spun her in a circle until nausea made her moan.

He set her down quickly. "Sorry. I wasn't thinking. That probably made you sick. When did you find out?"

She dug the test out of her pocket and handed it to him. "Last night. Confirmed today."

"Dom…" His voice cracked with wonder. "I know you want Nathaniel, but that's my baby. I want to raise it. With you."

"I figured you'd want to be part of its life, Tim. And you should. But I still want Nathaniel. I don't know how this works yet. I need time."

His eyes flicked to her neck. His jaw clenched. "Has he marked you yet?"

"What?"

He brushed her hair aside, exposing the twin punctures. A low growl rumbled from him.

"Did he mark you? Or just drink from you? Is that how you found out you were pregnant?"

"I… I don't know what you mean."

"You don't need to lie. I know what Nathaniel is. Those fang marks say it all. Did. He. Mark. You?"

She shook her head quickly. "No. He only drank from me. He stopped, got angry, said I was pregnant, and he wouldn't change me. Said it would kill the baby."

Tim's mouth opened, but his phone blared Jacob's ringtone. He cursed, glanced at the screen, and shoved it back into his pocket.

"I have to go. Something urgent. But we're not done, Dom. We need to talk more about the baby, and about him. You need to think about how this actually works. How's a vampire going to help you raise a child?"

Her pulse jumped. "How do you know he's a vampire, Tim?"

He hesitated at the door, back rigid. "I just do. I'll explain later. Promise me we'll talk again."

"Okay," she whispered.

The door clicked shut. Dominique collapsed against the couch, hand drifting to her stomach. For the first time since she'd seen those two pink lines, fear coiled in her chest. Not for herself, but for the tiny life inside her.

Chapter 66

Dominique touched her stomach, her palm lingering over the fragile life inside her. This time would be different. No more destroying herself with drinking. She'd take care of her body for the baby.

She tried to picture herself with a swollen belly and let out a laugh. *All in time.*

Sliding into her car, her phone buzzed. Paul had sent her the time and location for tomorrow's meeting. The building would be hers once she signed the papers. Her lips curved into a wide smile as she texted him back. Then she shot Nathaniel a quick message. After all, they were business partners too.

At the club, she lingered in the car. Pregnancy meant she couldn't manage every night. For now, it was fine, but soon she'd have to step back. At least that decision was simple. She already had the perfect person in mind.

Inside, she pulled Melissa into the office, locked the door, and dropped into her chair.

Melissa arched a brow. "What's up, Dom? Why am I being dragged in here without even a hello?"

Dominique hesitated, then blurted, "I have some news. Tim knows. I'm… pregnant."

Melissa shot to her feet so fast the chair toppled. "What?"

"You heard me," Dominique sighed.

"Is Tim the father? Is that why he knows?"

"Yes. Nathaniel can't have kids."

"Dom, I can't believe this. What are you going to do? Are you keeping it?"

Dominique's jaw tightened. "Yes."

Melissa winced. "Sorry. I had to ask. You've been here before. Same guy. Same back-and-forth. I thought you'd choose Nathaniel. Have you told him yet?"

"I know I've been here before," Dominique said evenly. "But last time I didn't know, and I was destroying myself. This time, I'm healthy. Mentally… it was a shock. But I've always wanted a family. And yes, Nathaniel knows. He thinks I won't choose him because of it, but I still want him. It's just complicated."

Melissa softened, leaning on the desk.

"Tim wants to sit down and talk. He wants to be part of the baby's life, and honestly, I want that too. My dad was a good man. Losing him… losing both my parents… left a hole. They'll never see me marry, never meet their grandchild. I don't want that for my child if I can help it."

"I get that," Melissa said gently. "I just hope you end up with Nathaniel. You're different around him, in a good way. You lit up with Tim, too, but it wasn't the same. No matter what happens, I've got your back."

Dominique smiled. "I'm glad you said that, because I actually wanted to offer you a permanent manager position here. With a salary bump. I'll still handle the books, but I don't want to be here every night once the pregnancy progresses. You'd oversee everything, with hiring and firing authority."

Melissa blinked. "Are you serious?"

"Yes. Not right away, but soon. I'll have to hire replacements for you and for the other business anyway."

Melissa's brows shot up. "Other business?"

"Nathaniel invested in the machines. The parts are ordered. I've found a building. Just need to sign the papers. His lawyer's handling the rest. I'm so excited, Mel."

Melissa grinned. "That's amazing! Anything else you've been hiding from me?"

Dominique hesitated, then shook her head with a practiced smile.

Melissa crossed her arms, staring her down. "I know there's something you're not saying. I can feel it."

Dominique laughed lightly. "Well, maybe not a secret, but I want your opinion. If things don't work out with Nathaniel… would it be a mistake to get back with Tim?"

Melissa groaned. "That's loaded. Honestly? I thought it was a mistake the first time. He hurt you, in big ways, small ways. But he is the baby's father. If Nathaniel isn't in the picture, maybe you could try. For the baby. At least then you'd know you tried."

"Thanks, Mel. It means a lot that you'd support me even if you don't agree."

"You know I'm here no matter what. I just don't want to see you hurt again."

Melissa hugged her tightly before heading back to the bar.

Dominique followed her out, catching the daggers Melissa's eyes threw at Tim. Tim just grinned. Dominique shook her head. Hopefully, those two could get along even if it was just for the baby.

Chapter 67

Nathaniel woke to cold sheets. Dominique was gone. He exhaled, not surprised. Waking up wrapped in the arms of the dead would rattle anyone.

He showered, dressed, and headed upstairs. From the fridge, he pulled a sealed pack of blood, warming it with little enthusiasm. The taste was flat, sterile. After Dominique, nothing else compared.

He preferred to linger in shadows, feeding only when necessary. Every so often, he compelled someone to forget, then drank from them. Wolves had the luxury of being born. Vampires were made, and rarely. Four, maybe five, together at most. He'd never cared to build a bloodline of his own.

Once, he'd only ever wanted one by his side. Rose. And she'd died.

The first time he felt her soul return, shock had rattled him to the core. For a century, he'd merely existed, numb. Then she'd come of age, reborn, and yet not. She hadn't chosen him. She'd screamed when she saw what he was. He'd lost control and drained her dry.

It happened again. And again. Each cycle, her soul reborn, each time slipping through his grasp. Each death tore at him, shredding what little soul he had left. He'd gone mad until a witch told him the truth: a soul could only reincarnate so many times before fading forever. Dominique, born in December, was the last. His final chance.

The witch had warned him there was damage between the souls, a rift that must be healed before Rose's soul could settle in its host. He thought it was his leaving her, becoming a vampire. He tried harder with each lifetime, proving his devotion, begging each version to see he'd never abandon her again.

But the truth was worse. The wound wasn't leaving Rose. It was betraying her with Eleanor. He'd felt her anguish, her grief, her fury. That betrayal bled through lifetimes.

Dominique was different. With her, he'd been patient. He'd given her dreams, sparking memories of his, and inadvertently, Rose's. He'd waited. Let her choose. He hadn't stopped her from being with Tim, hadn't forced her hand. Maybe that had been the salve to finally mend the soul.

But what if it wasn't enough? Dominique carried another man's child. She would choose her baby. He knew it, understood it, but the thought of letting her go was unbearable.

Still, she loved him. Had chosen him. Offered herself without fear. He smiled faintly at the memory. So like Rose, defiant even in terror.

He couldn't turn her now, not without killing the child. But perhaps there was another way. Could he bind her to him as a human servant?

His thoughts drifted to Barnaby. It'd been years since they last spoke.

Picking up the phone, Nathaniel saw Dominique's message. A smile curved his lips. She was starting her business. He wished he could be there, but it was daytime. Yet another barrier the women in his life never accepted. Another reason he was considering offering to make her his human servant.

He dialed Barnaby. The voicemail picked up, Veronica's voice spilling through. Nathaniel left a message. Minutes later, the phone rang, Barnaby's cheerful tone filling his ear. Nathaniel's old accent had all but faded now, only a trace left.

"Hello, old friend. It's been a long time."

"Yes, I dare say you forgot about me. I thought you dead, old man."

"No. Although sometimes it felt that way," Nathaniel laughed.

"So, to what do I owe this pleasantry?"

"I'm in quite a predicament. When last we spoke, I told you about the reincarnations, the girl in her last cycle. I had her. She was willing to be with me, but she's torn between two worlds. She's pregnant. I know you and Veronica have been together a long time. I wondered if that might be a solution to my problem."

"I cannot say this would be wise for someone torn between you and a normal life," Barnaby replied. "If she wants that life, she may leave you. Have you spoken to her?"

"No. I wanted to talk to you first. I never learned how to make a human servant. I always hoped she'd become a vampire. But I've been toying with the idea of offering it to Dominique. If she can live her life while her child grows, she could be with me later."

"How can she stay with her child until it's grown? She won't age, Nathaniel. People will notice. Her child will notice."

"She's carrying a werewolf's child. That won't be unusual for the child."

Barnaby laughed. "Chum, you've landed yourself in a mess, haven't you?"

"Yes," Nathaniel sighed.

"I'll help you if you wish to offer it. But you must connect with her mind, body, and soul."

"Thank you, Barnaby. I know I'm asking a lot, but could I speak with Veronica? I want to hear her thoughts on being a human servant before I ask Dominique. I want her truly happy."

"You do know human servants can't run away, don't you?"

"Yes. I know they can't escape their masters. But I still want to know if she's happy. Did you take her as a servant or did she want it?"

"I took her as my servant for eyes and ears during the day. I cared for her then, courted her as I was tempted by her. I happened to fall for her."

"So was she okay being your eyes and ears? Is that what she wanted?"

"I'll let you ask her," Barnaby said. "If she wishes to tell you, she will."

"Thank you."

"Nathaniel, how are you?" Veronica asked.

"I'm well, Veronica. And you?"

"I've been well. Barnaby said you wanted to ask me something. Have you finally found her?"

"Yes, but she's pregnant. I can't ask her to give up her child. She's willing to be with me, but I'm not sure she will after she thinks about it. I want to offer her this option, but I'd like to know what it's like from the human servant's side first."

"I understand, Nathaniel. I'm happy for you. You've searched for a long time. I'll tell you, I was terrified at first. When I discovered what Barnaby was, I was scared. I'd grown fond of him and knew he wouldn't hurt me, but living forever still frightened me. I never wanted children— felt hindered by them. The more I thought about what he offered, the more I liked it."

"Barnaby and I love each other. That makes a difference in whether your human servant will be happy. I know you love her, Nathaniel, or you wouldn't offer this. But does she love you?"

"Yes. She's told me several times. She willingly offered herself to me. That's how I found out she was pregnant," Nathaniel sighed.

"Then I think you'll be okay. If you two truly love each other, you'll make it work. Be part of her life. Let her have that normalcy while she can. Later, she can be with you fully."

"Thank you, Veronica, for your honesty. May I speak with Barnaby again?"

"You're welcome, Nathaniel. Hold on."

Barnaby came back on the line and walked Nathaniel through the ritual to make Dominique his human servant. Nathaniel listened intently, repeating each step back. He couldn't afford mistakes if Dominique accepted. When Barnaby finished, Nathaniel thanked him again and promised to share how it went.

Chapter 68

Tim had been shocked at Nathaniel's restraint. That he'd known the baby wasn't his and still hadn't turned Dominique. He could have eliminated the pregnancy and kept Dominique for himself.

He ran a hand through his hair. He had to tell Dominique everything now. There was a fifty–fifty chance the baby could be a werewolf. With Jacob still pushing to turn her, she needed the full truth.

Jacob's text pinged at the worst possible time. Now here he was, bloody from beating the pack member, chest tight with remorse. This guy was an asshole, but he didn't deserve the beating he got. Jacob pushed debt collection too far. Raul would have reveled in the torture; Tim did not. The sight of the man's gurgling throat turned his stomach.

He rubbed his hands on a towel, grabbed his phone, and sent Jacob a picture. Then:

I need to speak to you about Dominique. It's important.

Jacob: **No time today. Tomorrow at three.**

Tim: **All right. Just give me time. Don't try to turn her.**

Tim swallowed a growl. Jacob had to back off. If Jacob forced a change now, Dominique would lose the baby. He couldn't, *wouldn't* let that happen.

At least now, Tim didn't have to challenge Paul or kill Jacob. He could wait, tell Dominique everything, let her decide.

If she still wanted Nathaniel, he would see her through the pregnancy and proceed with the plan. At least he'd be able to see his baby before possibly dying.

He headed home to clean up and get ready for work. The conversation with Dominique would have to wait until after his meeting with Jacob the next day. This wasn't something to squeeze in after a shift.

***

Jacob's driveway felt wrong — eerily still. Normally, someone patrolled the perimeter. Tim sensed eyes on him but saw no one. Paranoid, he knocked.

"Come in!" Jacob called.

Inside, Jacob stood in front of the bar, pouring a drink like he'd been waiting on Tim.

"Tim! Can I offer you something?" Jacob asked.

"No. I won't be long. I came to talk about Dominique. I need to make sure she's safe."

Jacob shrugged. "We had this talk. Paul's been tasked to bring Dominique into the pack since you refused. Your time's up."

"I didn't refuse. I wanted her to know me first. I'm not going to force her. People forced into the pack become rogues." Tim kept his voice level, but the heat beneath it showed.

Jacob's eyes narrowed. "That can happen. Still, she'll be brought in whether she likes it or not. Have you told her about yourself?"

"No. I wanted to talk to you first. Yesterday, she told me something that changed things. She can't be brought over right now."

"Why not?" Jacob asked.

"She's pregnant. If you bring her over now, she'll lose the baby… *my* baby." Tim's words clipped the air.

"That's bad, Tim. You should've told me yesterday."

Tim's hand shot out, grabbed Jacob's collar, and shoved. "What the fuck did you do?" he snarled.

Jacob smiled, cruel and patient. "Paul set up a meeting today for her to sign a contract on a building. Once the lawyer leaves, he turns her. The meeting started at two-thirty. Maybe you can still get there in time. He had them meet at his house. Now get your hands off me before I decide to kill you where you stand."

"Link Paul. Call him off!"

"Nah. You had your chance to do what you were told. Maybe losing the baby is the punishment you need to understand your place in this pack."

Tim backed away as Jacob shoved him, panic gripping him. Jacob's laugh followed him out the door; it was the kind that left little doubt of the man's relish in Tim's panic.

Jacob had purposefully set up this meeting to start after Dominique's. He'd wanted Tim to be here so Paul could turn Dominique, and he couldn't stop it.

He jumped into his car and floored it. Paul lived fifteen minutes away. Tim had already lost close to an hour since Dominique's meeting began. Traffic blurred as he swerved through lanes, every red light a stabbing risk.

"Please," he breathed to anything listening, "don't let me be too late."

Chapter 69

Dominique sat at the table across from Paul and Mr. Vaughn. After the pleasantries, Mr. Vaughn launched into the contract, outlining every clause in careful detail.

It felt strange being in Paul's house, but he'd explained an unforeseen event had forced him to work from home. At least they were in his office, formal enough to keep things official.

She already knew the terms, but this was Vaughn's job: ensuring she understood, ensuring she still wanted the deal. When they finished, pens scratched across paper. Paul made copies, handing one to her, one to Vaughn, and keeping the last.

By tomorrow, the document would be filed and legalized. Excitement bubbled in her chest. She was about to own multiple businesses. Vaughn had been worth every penny; he'd handled the company name, business account, and purchase agreement in record time. The club deal hadn't gone nearly as smoothly. Of course, it hadn't been a cash purchase either.

Gathering her things, she followed Vaughn toward the door. Paul trailed behind, so close she felt his body heat at her back. The hairs on her neck rose.

Vaughn walked to his car. Paul's hand closed on her arm, halting her. She turned, shuddering at the predatory gleam in his eyes. His smile was slow, calculated.

On the surface, he was gorgeous—tan skin, blond hair, piercing blue eyes. But the look in them made her stomach twist.

"Before you go," Paul said smoothly, "I'd like to show you something. Watching you plot everything out in the building… you'd fit right in with my people. We're creative, outdoorsy. I'd like to put something up so we can meet here once a month. Would you look at the space? Give me some ideas? Then you can see what we're about."

Her anxiety spiked. He hadn't done anything wrong yet, but every instinct screamed that something was off.

"I'm not sure I'd be much help," she hedged.

"I promise the view alone is worth it. Please?" He extended his hand.

Hesitation warred with politeness. Finally, she nodded and followed him out back. Her fingers brushed her purse, closing over the cold metal inside. Since Roxy, she carried her dad's gun everywhere. The thought steadied her. If Paul tried anything, she'd shoot him. Consequences be damned.

The backyard unfolded like a painting—vivid flowerbeds in red, pink, yellow, and blue. A deck stretched toward an in-ground pool. Trees thickened into the mountains beyond, a breathtaking backdrop.

Paul hadn't lied; the view was stunning.

His hand slid to the small of her back, steering her along as he named each bloom: roses, tulips, magnolias, daisies. He stopped at an open patch of grass and spread his arms.

"This is the space. What do you think?"

"A gazebo," Dominique said slowly, vision forming. "Centerpiece here, flowerbeds circling. Hanging plants, a stone walkway, and tiki torches for light. It'd look beautiful."

"I knew you had a creative mind. You should work with us. Be a designer," he said with an easy smile.

"I like my job. And I'm planning to take time off soon anyway."

"Maybe you should start that time off now." His voice dropped. "There's another reason I brought you out here, Dominique."

He stepped closer. She stepped back, hand sliding toward her purse. Another stride and he was on her, grin warping into a smirk as his hands clamped her arms.

Her breaths went ragged. "What are you doing?"

"I've been tasked to bring you in. You'll become one of us. Whether you like it or not."

Fear coiled in her gut. Her fingers closed around the gun. Without thinking, she drew, shoved it against his stomach, and fired.

The blast cracked the air. Paul snarled, clutching the wound. "You shot me, bitch! You'll pay for that!"

Dominique tore free and bolted. She stumbled over a flowerbed, crashing to the ground. The gun flew from her hand. She twisted, landing on her back.

Shit. Shit. Shit. He's going to kill me.

Her scream ripped through the yard as Paul lunged, his body snapping and reshaping mid-stride. A massive blond wolf landed where the man had been.

Adrenaline burned through her veins. She scrambled up and sprinted. His hot breath chased her, close, taunting. He was playing with her.

A sudden blur of black fur cut across her path. Another wolf charged from the side of the house. Her heart seized. Two of them.

The black wolf leapt. Dominique dove, screaming, as it sailed over her and slammed into Paul. The two collided, snarls shredding the air.

She froze, staring wide-eyed. Wolves. Real wolves. This was what she'd seen outside her home that night. *Jesus. Werewolves. Nathaniel's a vampire. And now this? What the fuck have I gotten wrapped up in?*

She staggered to her feet, ready to run, but stopped when she heard a pained whine. The black wolf reeled back, blood streaking down from a gash across his eye.

If Paul was one, who the hell was this other wolf?

They were fighting for her, not against her. Giving her a chance to flee. But Paul was stronger. He was winning.

Her gaze darted frantically across the yard, searching for her gun. One bullet hadn't stopped him, but another could at least slow him down. Give the black wolf a chance.

Chapter 70

Tim pulled into Paul's driveway and killed the engine. Dominique's scream ripped through the air, echoing from behind the house.

He didn't hesitate. Mid-run, his body split, bones snapping, clothes shredding as fur exploded across his skin. He rounded the corner, eyes locking on Dominique, sprinting toward the porch, terror written all over her face. Paul trailed just behind, deliberate in his pace, feeding on her fear.

Tim launched himself, praying she'd duck. She dropped, crashing into the dirt with a ragged scream that tore through him.

He slammed into Paul, both of them rolling, claws and fangs flashing, blood spraying. Tim scrambled to his feet and leapt onto Paul's back, teeth sinking into the side of his neck, the copper taste of blood filling his mouth as his claws gouged Paul's ribs.

Paul roared and, with a brutal twist, flung him off. Tim hit the ground hard, dirt exploding around him. Rage surged, burning hotter than pain. If Paul tried to turn Dominique now, she would lose the baby. Their baby. And there was no guarantee she'd even survive.

He'd kill Paul for putting Dominique in danger. For the fact that she may have a miscarriage from throwing her body onto the ground. He'd kill him because he wanted to. The rage he'd carefully controlled now snapped. No more restraint. Paul had threatened what was his.

'Fool!' Paul's voice snapped through the mind-link. 'You were warned. She will be changed. You can't stop it.'

Tim dug his claws into the earth, bracing. 'She's pregnant. With my child. Touch her, and I'll rip you apart.'

He launched. His jaws tore into Paul's side, ripping flesh and spraying blood across the grass. Paul howled, twisting, and his teeth clamped around Tim's hind leg. Bone cracked, the sound sharp and final.

Agony lit him up, but worse followed. Paul's claws slashed across his face, blood blinding one eye, hot rivulets running down his muzzle.

Tim faltered. Paul seized his shattered leg, snapping it again. Another sickening crunch echoed. White-hot pain stole his balance, and he collapsed with a thud.

Paul turned on Dominique.

Fuck! Run, Dominique! Run! Tim roared in his head.

She screamed, stumbling backward into the grass. Paul loomed over her, tongue sliding across his lips as though he could already taste her fear.

Tim struggled, forcing his ruined body to move. His wolf surged up, savage and uncontrollable, drowning out thought. Vision bled red. He pushed to his feet, running towards Dominique, just as a thunderous boom split the air.

Chapter 71

Dominique saw a silver glint in the yard. She ran, grabbing the gun right before Paul turned on her. Her eyes caught the black wolf struggling to stand on a mangled hind leg.

Paul charged. Feigning a fall, she threw herself on the ground, a scream ripping from her throat. The gun pressed to her back, secure in her grip.

Her heartbeat drummed out everything but the ragged pulls of her own breath. Paul's shadow covered her, his tongue licking his lips like he tasted her fear. His breath hit her face, hot and coppery. His bright blue eyes stood out against the bloody, matted blond fur.

His jaws split wide, plunging for her stomach. Adrenaline took over. Yanking the gun forward, she fired into his mouth. Blood splattered across her face, his deafening howl vibrating her bones.

Paul reeled back just as the black wolf lunged, slamming into his side. They crashed to the ground, the earth splitting beneath them. The black wolf stood on three legs, massive jaws locked onto Paul's throat. Razor-sharp teeth sank deep, and the wet tearing of flesh filled her ears. Blood sprayed in chaotic arcs. Paul gave a gurgling whine before collapsing; his blond-haired wolf lay still.

The black wolf turned. Blood and saliva dripped from his muzzle, spattering red froth on the ground. His dark green eyes, speckled with light green, assessed her.

She scrambled backward, eyes wide, as a hot wind tore through Paul's body, slamming into the black wolf, rustling his fur. The wind wrapped around her, boiling her blood. The wolf closed its eyes, the wind settled, then disappeared, like it had absorbed it.

Goosebumps prickled her flesh as she looked from the blond wolf reknitting into Paul's corpse back to the black wolf as his chest heaved, leg reknitting itself.

Gun forgotten on the ground, she got to her knees. The black wolf opened his eyes. Dark green eyes speckled with bright green around the pupil pulled her in. His eyes shifted, the dark green disappearing into a spring green color that seemed too familiar.

Limping but steady, he stepped toward her. Every nerve screamed to run, yet her body stayed rooted. Unlike Paul, this wolf gave no ill intent to harm her. Still, fear iced her veins.

Her mother always said curiosity killed the cat. Was she the cat in this situation?

Forcing her hand to the ground, her fingers slipped around the gun. Gripping it, she slowly pulled it forward.

The wolf stopped, sniffing the air before his gaze landed on her hand. His eyes shifted back to her face. The familiarity drew her back in, but she wasn't going to die here.

She lifted it, only to freeze as the wolf lowered himself to the ground, bowing, throat bared. Submission. To her.

Shakily, she stood, gun tight in her hand. His head stayed down. Her hand hovered, then stilled as his gaze rose, locking with hers.

Her chest clenched. Sadness poured from his eyes and sank into her bones. She licked her dry lips; his gaze flicked down, following the motion.

Her hand trembled as she reached out and brushed his bloodied muzzle.

"You saved me," she whispered, her voice breaking. "I don't know why, or what just happened, but thank you. I keep waiting to wake up and find out this is just another nightmare."

The wolf stood, forcing her to step back. Black fur clung to him in clots of blood. Paul's or his, she couldn't tell. That strange wind… had it healed him? He still limped as he crept closer.

"If you're a man, like Paul, then why don't you change?" she asked.

Hunger and pain in his eyes pinned her where she stood. He pressed against her, shuddering as he inhaled deeply. Her hand slid down his body and found open wounds. His low whine tore at her chest.

"I'm willing to help you, but you have to change. I don't know how to help you like this. As a man, at least I can treat your wounds. Let me see who you are. I won't tell anyone your secret."

She sank to the ground, eyes fixed on him, gun set beside her.

Those spring-green eyes stirred a memory… Tim, when she'd been lost in his gaze, dark flecks glinting in that same green. Her breath caught. No. It couldn't be.

The wolf eased down, resting his head in her lap. Pain swam in his upturned eyes.

"Tim?" she whispered.

His eyes closed. Flesh rippled, fur retracting until a man lay in front of her. A man she knew. A man she loved.

Tears burned her eyes as Tim's bloody body rose and fell with shallow breaths. The thick scents of iron, sweat, and musk filled her nose.

Some wounds had scabbed, but most still bled freely. She hooked her hands under his arms and tried to lift him. He was too heavy.

"I'm so sorry, Tim. I can't move you. You're too heavy. Can you stand?"

His voice cracked. "I'll try."

She wrapped an arm around his waist, bracing him as he staggered upright, his arm heavy over her shoulders.

He squeezed her as they shuffled forward. "We need to get out of here. Jacob's on his way. We can't go back to your place or mine. He'll look for us there."

"Tim, you need a hospital."

"No. Take me somewhere and patch me up. Please, Dominique. You're in danger here."

"Okay… okay. I know where to go."

She loaded him into her car, grabbing a set of clothes from his, grabbing her purse and gun from the yard. Laying her suit jacket over his lap, she jumped behind the wheel, engine roaring as she reversed hard out of the driveway and onto the highway, praying they wouldn't be caught.

Eyes flicking to the rearview mirror, she wove through back roads until Nathaniel's house came into view. She closed the garage door behind them, sealing them in.

Helping him out of the car and into the bedroom nearly broke her knees under his weight. As soon as they reached the bed, Tim collapsed, unable to hold himself up.

Desperation clawed at her. She filled a bowl with warm, soapy water, grabbed every towel Nathaniel owned, and hurried back. One by one, she cleaned his wounds, pressing towels to the worst gashes on his side and stomach.

Remembering the first-aid kit in her car, she sprinted for it. The roll of gauze inside looked pitifully small. Tim, barely conscious, tried to sit up to help her. She wrapped his torso as best she could, then had him roll onto his stomach to keep pressure on the wound.

Stripping off her shirt, she tore it into pieces, binding his arms and legs.

"I'm sorry, Tim. I don't have what I need to treat you. I wish you'd let me take you to the hospital. Since you won't, I'll run to a store for bandages and come back as quickly as I can."

"Don't go," he whispered. "I'll be fine. The bleeding will stop. I'll heal. A hospital will wonder how I'm healing so fast. My secret will be out. Just… lay here with me, Dom. Please."

Tears stung her eyes. How could she just lie here and watch him bleed?

His eyes closed, breathing evening out. She looked down and saw the bandages already soaked in red.

Climbing onto the bed, she curled around his body, pressing against him to slow the bleeding. Her tears pooled on his shoulder blade.

What the hell had happened today? Paul was a werewolf. Tim, also a werewolf. Tim had protected her, risked his life for her. How had he even known where she was? This was his big secret. Not a gang. A pack.

A shiver ran through her as his cooling blood seeped against her skin. Paul hadn't planned to kill her. He'd planned to make her part of the pack. Her thoughts raced as she held Tim, keeping pressure on his wounds.

Chapter 72

Jacob stumbled; the tether to Paul snapped. Rage surged hot and immediate. Fucking Tim. The coward hadn't even challenged Paul, just taken advantage of the situation. Killing Paul should've made Tim his beta, but not a chance. Jacob would kill him first. No one challenged his authority and lived.

He drove to Paul's house. Tim's car sat in the driveway. The sharp tang of iron hit him as he stepped inside, stronger as he followed it out back. Paul lay in the grass, throat ripped out. Jacob threw his head back and let out a mournful howl.

Cutting Tim off from the link, he called to the pack. Paul's body would be dealt with first. Then the hunt for Tim would begin. Judging by the wreckage in the yard, Tim was badly hurt. He'd better hope death found him before Jacob did.

The pack arrived, and together they disposed of Paul's body. No corpse left for the police to find. The report would claim an animal attack. It paid to have an officer in the pack.

Jacob torched Tim's car, his fury feeding the flames. Tim wasn't home. A scout checked Dominique's home. Nothing. Jacob's frustration spiked. Where the fuck had that bastard gone?

***

By nightfall, the pack had crowded Jacob's yard. He paced the length of the porch, rage pulsing under his skin. There was only one place Tim could have fled: the vampire's house. Tim hated the vampire, or so he'd thought. Now the pieces fit. Tim had chosen the vampire.

Tim had stolen Jacob's beta from him. Jacob would return the favor and make them both watch. He would drag Dominique apart in front of Tim, tear into her stomach, and kill the unborn child. He would leave her mangled and broken, then dole out every humiliation he could dream up until she begged for death.

And when he was finished scarring her for life, he'd finish Tim. Rip him limb from limb and leave nothing.

He turned slowly, meeting every face in the gathered pack. Most of them were not fighters; most wanted only peace. A few obeyed blindly. A few tried to shirk. He kept them all in line with fear; respect was a luxury he didn't need.

"Today one of our own was murdered," he said, voice cold and hard. "Paul was killed while carrying out my orders. The gamma, Tim, has given up his right to be called pack. He didn't challenge Paul. He betrayed us and sided with the vampire."

A ripple of shock and low curses ran through the crowd. Jacob lifted a hand, and the noise cut off.

"Prepare for war. Tomorrow night, we strike the vampire's home. We flush him and Tim out, and we kill them. Bring Tim and the girl to me alive. If you fail to show, don't ever show your face to me again. I'll kill you too. No one disobeys my orders."

The pack answered with a long, rising howl. Jacob watched the ones edging toward the back, the slackers and the faint-hearted. He'd make examples of them later.

"Rest," he snapped. "Tomorrow will be a bloodbath."

Chapter 73

Nathaniel's eyes snapped open. Fear gripped him, sharp and sudden. Dominique. She was close. Too close.

The moment he opened the door, her scent hit him—sweet, familiar, twined with Tim's and the sharp tang of iron. His chest constricted.

He hurried down the hall, flung open her door. Dominique was curled protectively around Tim, his body swathed in crude bandages. Raw, untamed power rolled off Tim, the second time Nathaniel had felt it. Who had he fought?

His gaze swept Dominique. Blood streaked her skin, soaked her clothes. Not hers. Tim's.

"Dominique?" Nathaniel whispered.

She stirred, and Tim shifted with her, arm tightening around her even in sleep. When she tried to move, his muscles flexed, unwilling to let her go. She relented, nestling back into him. Nathaniel stepped closer, brushing her hair from her face.

"What happened? Why bring him here?"

"He saved me," she breathed. Her voice trembled. "I went to Paul's house to sign contracts. It was a trap. Tim… Somehow, he knew. He fought Paul, killed him. He was bleeding so much… we couldn't go to his place, or mine, or the hospital. This was the only place left. I didn't know what else to do."

Nathaniel's jaw tightened, though his voice softened. "He'll recover. He's stronger than you think. You, though… Are you hurt?"

Her eyes fluttered closed as his fingers brushed her cheek. "No. Just shaken."

"You need food. So does he. It'll help him heal." He held out his hand. "Come with me."

Tim growled in his sleep when Nathaniel pried his arm loose. Nathaniel chuckled at the sound, but Dominique hesitated. She bent, pressing a kiss to Tim's forehead, her hand lingering against his cheek.

"I'll be back soon," she whispered.

A jagged stab of jealousy cut through Nathaniel. He forced his face blank as she turned to him, sighing before wrapping her arms around him. He held her tighter than he should, breathing in her warmth before leading her away.

In the bathroom, he set fresh towels on the shelf. "Shower. I'll make you something to eat. Don't worry about clothes. I picked up a few things for you last night. Just in case."

Her lips parted. "Nathaniel, we need to talk about what's happening."

"Not now, love," he said softly. "When it's calmer."

She nodded, reluctant.

He left her to her privacy and busied himself in the kitchen. It had been too long since he'd cooked, but a sandwich was simple. Plate on the table, he waited.

When she appeared, damp and wrapped only in a towel, his restraint nearly snapped. Water traced the curve of her throat, gliding down to her chest. She slid her hand over his, smiling slowly.

His voice came hoarse. "Your clothes are in the dresser."

"I'll change in a bit," she said, settling across from him. "I want to eat first."

His lips twitched. "I can't tell if you're teasing me or just starving."

"Maybe both," she teased, laughter bubbling through the tension.

His phone rang. The unrecognized number flashing on the screen made him frown. He muttered an excuse and stepped away.

Nathaniel lowered his voice so Dominique wouldn't overhear. "Hello?"

"Is this Nathaniel?" a man asked.

"Yes."

"This is Nicholas."

"Hello, Nicholas. Have you decided?"

"Yes. We'll help you. Jacob has lost his mind. I've heard rumors that he's going after a woman because one of his members refused to turn her. I can only assume it's the woman you're protecting. I can't stand by and watch him force people into this life anymore."

"He sent one of his wolves after her today. The woman in question is Dominique. She's here now, along with the wolf who refused to turn her."

"Alright. I'll gather my warriors tonight, and we'll set out a plan of attack. I'll call you tomorrow."

"Thank you, Nicholas."

"I'm not doing this for you, Nathaniel. I'm doing this for my pack. For the wolves. Our secret must stay buried."

"I'll take it however I can."

"Goodbye, Nathaniel."

"Goodbye."

He ended the call and turned back to the table. Dominique was gone. He sighed. This had just gotten more complicated now that Tim had played the hero.

In her room, Dominique was dressed and bent over Tim, carefully cleaning his arms and legs. Pink, shiny skin covered wounds that had been ragged before. The raw pulse of power in Tim told Nathaniel he'd fought someone high-ranked in the pack.

When she struggled to lift Tim, Nathaniel moved to her side and scooped him up with ease. Dominique unwound the bandages from his torso and gasped. Tim's side was covered in that same glossy pink skin, still healing but far beyond what a human body could do.

"How is this possible?" she whispered.

"Wolves and vampires heal faster than humans," Nathaniel said, laying Tim back on the bed. "The stronger the power, the faster the healing. Do you know who Paul was to the pack?"

"No. Until today, I didn't even know werewolves existed, let alone that Tim or Paul was one. To me, Paul was just the real estate agent for the building I bought."

"When I first met Tim, he had power, but not like this. He's fought someone else and gained more strength. I didn't think it would be enough to defeat someone with Paul's power."

"Paul mangled Tim's leg. Tim was fighting through it, but he was down. Paul came after me, and I shot him. Tim took advantage and killed Paul." Dominique's head snapped up, eyes narrowing. "So, you two have known about each other this entire time?"

"Yes," Nathaniel admitted.

Her eyes flashed. "So neither of you thought to tell me? Neither of you had the decency to tell me what you were. Did you think I couldn't handle it? Was I not good enough to know your secret?"

"It wasn't like that for me," Nathaniel said quietly. "I can't speak for Tim. I *was* afraid you'd run. You've seen what happened before when your soul returned. I couldn't risk losing you again. I was told there was damage between our souls, something I had to repair. I didn't even know what that meant until the other night. You're so much like Rose. Her soul has finally settled with you, found peace. That's why I waited. Make no mistake: I never thought you weren't good enough."

He drew a breath. "It's always been my intention to tell you. To let you choose a life with me, forever. I love you, Dominique. That won't change. I've waited a very long time, and I'll keep waiting if that's what you need. If you want to talk about this now, we can. But let's get Tim settled first."

Dominique exhaled slowly, trying to steady herself. "Okay. Can you lift him off the bed?"

Nathaniel picked Tim up. Dominique quickly changed the sheets and cover, then he laid Tim back down. She slid boxers onto him, pulling the blanket over his body. Her hand brushed Tim's face. Jealousy tightened Nathaniel's chest like a fist.

Dominique settled onto the couch and took Nathaniel's hand. His lopsided grin faltered, half-hearted at best. After watching her care for Tim, he wasn't sure he wanted this conversation. She'd chosen him before… but now? Now it felt like Tim might have his chance after all.

"Nathaniel," she began softly, "I love you. I want to be with you. But you were right when you said I'd choose my baby. I can't let you turn me. I've thought about it constantly since the other night. Even if I waited until after the baby was born, I'd miss everything… the games, the recitals, the life my child would have. I could wait until they're grown, but then I'd be much older than you, and I don't want that either."

"This isn't a decision you have to make right now," Nathaniel said, exhaling. "I have another option. I never intended to offer this because I wanted you to choose me, a life with me as a vampire. But things have changed. I can offer you a life where you never age. You'd live like a human but live forever. You could still be killed, but you wouldn't lose time. My question is… are you changing your mind about being with me?"

She hesitated. "Before I answer, would you wait for me if I did choose Tim? Would you still offer me that choice?"

He schooled his expression into neutrality. "I told you I'd wait for you if I had to. It doesn't make me happy. I've waited so long to be reunited with my soulmate. My heart aches at the thought of more time without you. But I'll still give you this choice, no matter what you decide."

Dominique crawled into his lap, resting her head on his shoulder. He pressed his cheek to her hair and held her tight. Contentment warred with heartbreak inside him. The fact that she'd even asked that question meant she was reconsidering her choice.

Wanting a life with her child, he understood that. But she didn't need Tim to have it. Tim wouldn't live forever. He'd already waited hundreds of years. What were a few more if it meant having her for eternity?

He leaned back, thoughts spinning. Would she come back to him after Tim died? Their bond as master and servant would keep her tethered, but would she return willingly? Would that connection poison her and Tim's relationship? Would she resent him for it?

Dominique sat up and surprised him with a kiss. She pulled back, eyes searching his. He tried to smile but couldn't summon one that reached his eyes.

"I want to talk to Tim," she said. "Find out what he wanted to tell me before all this happened. I want to be with you, but I also want to be with my child. I know Tim will be part of my life. I just don't know how big a part yet. So I'm not going to say anything more on this right now."

He swallowed his frustration. "I can't say I'm thrilled hearing this. But if you love someone, you're willing to do anything for them. Even put your own wants and needs last."

"I love you, Nathaniel. You'll never be last, okay?"

He kissed her, his heart aching with loss even though she sat in his arms.

She stayed with him for the rest of the night, checking on Tim periodically. The dark circles under her eyes told him she needed rest.

"You should sleep," he murmured.

"Yeah. I'm getting tired, but Tim's in the bed."

"You can sleep in my room. I'll stay on the other side of the bed. I know you didn't take it well waking up next to me."

"I'm not going to lie. I freaked out waking up next to a cold body."

"I'll lie on top of the cover. You can stay under it and be warm."

"I think I'd still rather stay with Tim so I can make sure he's okay. We can talk tomorrow night."

He watched her walk away, gutted. Tim had wormed his way back in. Nathaniel slipped into the night to hunt, needing to burn off his pain and anger.

Chapter 74

Dominique woke to someone shaking her lightly. Blinking against the blur of sleep, she let her eyes focus. Nathaniel's house. A loud sigh slipped out. Why couldn't she wake from a nightmare instead of waking into one? At least dreams ended. Reality… didn't. She looked up to see Tim sitting up.

"You're awake. That's a good sign. How long have you been up?"

"About five minutes," Tim said, his voice low, rough. "You were tossing, so I woke you. My side and stomach are still tender, but I'll be okay by tonight."

"We need to talk, Tim. I want to know what you were going to tell me before, and after all this, you definitely owe me an explanation. But first, let me get you something to eat. Maybe you'll feel better."

"Food will help me heal faster," he admitted. "I need meat. Protein works best."

"Okay. I'll find something. I know there's sandwich stuff here. Not sure what else Nathaniel bought. I'll be back in a bit. Just stay here and rest."

Dominique rose, but Tim's voice stopped her. "Dom… I can wait on food. Stay with me a few more minutes?"

She hesitated. "Um… I guess."

He held out his hand, and she slipped hers into it. In one motion, he pulled her onto his lap, a grunt escaping as his arms closed around her. He pressed his cheek against her hair, breathing her in. His body was tense, coiled tight beneath hers. She tried to hold her torso away from him, but he drew her flush against him, refusing distance.

For a moment, she let him. He needed it.

She pressed a quick kiss to his cheek and slid off his lap. His stare burned across her as she walked out. Food first. Explanations after.

Tim had said he needed protein. Judging by the shiny pink skin knitting across his wounds, his body was already doing the impossible. Still, she couldn't shake her amazement at how fast he healed. She cooked steak and eggs, poured a glass of orange juice, and carried it back.

Tim was lying down when she entered. She set the plate and glass on the nightstand. His eyes opened, nostrils flaring. His stomach growled, but he didn't move. Just watched her.

"Do you feel like sitting up to eat?"

"Yeah, I can."

She handed him the juice first. He drank, then gave it back. She picked up the plate for him.

"You didn't fix anything for yourself?" he asked.

"No. I'll fix something later. I wanted to make sure you ate. Nathaniel made me a couple of sandwiches last night, so I haven't been without as long as you have."

Tim speared a piece of steak and held it out. She shook her head, but he kept it there until she opened her mouth. A blush crept up her neck as he watched her chew.

Each time he took a bite, he fed her one. When she handed him the juice, his eyes stayed locked on hers as he turned the glass, putting his mouth where hers had been. Heat climbed her face. Too intimate.

"Mmmm…" His voice dropped, almost a growl. "Tastes like you."

She tried to break the moment. "You're being weird. Are you ready to tell me what's going on now?"

Tim exhaled hard. Dominique took the plate and glass and set them on the nightstand. He held his hand out, and when she took it, he pulled her onto his lap.

His kiss hit her like a storm, hungry and passionate, stealing her breath. He held her tight for a heartbeat, then eased her back just enough to meet her eyes.

"I'll start from the beginning, even though you've heard some of it," he said, voice rough. "I've always had a temper. You know that. I mouthed off at my boss one time too many. He fired me. Said he was done with my temper. I didn't want to tell you. I couldn't stand the thought of you seeing me as a failure. You've said a paycheck didn't matter, but it wasn't about the money. It was about control… and losing it.

"When I was with you, my temper was never out of control, until the heavy drinking started." He glanced away. "I started going to a local bar every night. Drinking more. Eventually, I took a bartender job there. Learned the ropes, got discounts on drinks, which just meant I drank more."

He swallowed hard. "When I stayed out all night closing and drinking, we'd fight. That made my temper worse. So I just… stayed away. One night, a guy got in my face at the bar. I snapped. Got into a fight. Lost the job. Lost my only place to hide. That was also the night I hit you. Usually, I noticed your car and left before you could see me. That night, I was too far gone on whiskey and rage.

"When you accused me of being just like the drunk who killed your parents, I lost it. And then I just stood there like an idiot instead of chasing you down. That's when we really started to fall apart. But even then, alcohol was my addiction. My only way to function."

He let out a bitter laugh. "The more you tried to hold us together, the more I pulled away. That led me to another bar. Same faces, same false comfort. One night, a woman—Roxy—approached me, asked if I wanted company. I told her I had a fiancée. She said if I did, I wouldn't be there every night. It hit me hard. I almost came home to you right then."

His eyes flicked to hers. "Roxy bought me a drink—a strong one. Later, I learned it was something that hits wolves harder. Being human, it hit me ten times worse. She tried again to get me to go home with her, but I turned her down and ordered another round. By then, I was dizzy, disoriented. The bartender refused to let me leave, but Roxy offered me a ride. I accepted.

"Things were already so strained between us, I didn't think you'd come get me. I didn't want to fight again. I fell asleep in the car. When I woke up, I was at her house, not mine. Too drunk to do anything about it.

"She sat me on the couch and crawled into my lap, kissing my neck. I pushed her off and tried to stand, but she yanked me back down and climbed on again. I shoved her harder, knocking her onto the floor. That's when she snapped. She punched me, slamming me back into the couch. Stunned, I barely moved before she crawled back onto me, this time digging her claws into my sides, then my chest, then my stomach. That's when she twisted my insides.

"I passed out from the pain. When I woke a week later, I thought it was the next day." He faltered. "That I'd cheated on you. But she was a werewolf. Her claws had infected me. She was almost gleeful that I'd survived, claimed I was hers. I didn't believe her until she showed me.

"I tried to run, but blacked out. When I came to, rage ripped through me, and I changed. She said I needed to learn control. I beat the hell out of her and ran. Some guy picked me up and took me to my car. I went home, but I'd lost any shred of control over my temper. It wasn't long before I went back to Roxy. Not to sleep with her. I swear I never cheated on you.

"I didn't speak to you that week because I couldn't. For another two weeks, I stayed away. That rage… I couldn't risk unleashing it on you. She started teaching me control and introduced me to Jacob. He saw my rage, saw a potential enforcer. His Gamma had died, so he groomed me to take his place.

"With my temper, it didn't take long to rise through the ranks. I learned enough control to keep from shifting around you, but the rage… it still burned. One day, you'd finally had enough. You ended it as soon as I opened the door. That night I went to the bar. Roxy found me. I unleashed everything—pain, anger, doubt—on her. She let me. Let me cut her up, fuck her however I needed. I was her new toy.

"Jacob had already given me a job protecting his people. Some got out of line when they drank. I'd take them home. Those were the women you saw, pack members, drunk on were-liquor. Once I moved up the ranks, Jacob had me enforcing his punishments. It became too much. I quit. I worked odd jobs, always getting fired because of Roxy and Karina. I think Jacob had them do it to punish me.

"Eventually, I got myself together. Raul became Gamma, and I started working my way back to you. I never meant for any of this to happen. Roxy got jealous and went to hit you when you kicked her out of the bar. Nathaniel broke her wrist. Jacob's been after him ever since.

"Roxy was ordered to leave you alone, but she didn't. She smelled your scent on me after that first night we slept together. When you shot her, Jacob wanted you dead. I wouldn't give you up. I told him to punish me instead. That's when he gave me the choice—turn you, make you my mate, and have you fight Roxy, or you die. He gave me until Roxy healed. Without shifting, that should've taken months.

"The night you went home and sat in your car in the driveway, I was fighting off Karina, Roxy's sister. She'd come to kill you. I killed her instead. When I brought her body to Jacob, he brought Roxy out. She attacked him, so he killed her.

"Unfortunate for me, because that moved my timeline up to change you. Something I never intended to do. This wasn't a life for you. Then I was forced to fight Raul, the torture demon and Gamma of the pack. It was a fight to the death.

"Jacob knew I didn't want that, but he forced it on me. I won, and then I planned to kill Paul and Jacob, too. Anything to keep you and Nathaniel safe. It was the only way. That's why I kept going back and forth. I wanted you, but I knew what it might cost to protect you. I couldn't do that to you. And judging by the way you always brought up Nathaniel, I knew you'd choose him. So I tried to protect your heart.

"When I didn't turn you, Jacob ordered Paul to do it. Then you snuck off to the Bahamas, which enraged Jacob. I didn't know about the meeting Paul had set up at first. I'd asked Jacob to talk about the situation when I found out you were pregnant. He told me we'd talk the next day. Now I see that was a ploy to keep me away from you. But Jacob, in his sadistic way, gave me a chance to save the baby. I honestly think he wanted me dead. He didn't think I'd beat Paul.

"Now you know everything. What are you thinking?"

Dominique drew a slow, shaky breath. So much. Two years wasted, angry, depressed, and hurting over his stupidity. He'd gone from the man she loved—handsome, sweet, loving—to a monster in every sense. He'd made her feel like she meant nothing, then vanished, lost to fights and vicious words.

All because he hadn't trusted her. Because he'd thought she'd leave, when it was his actions that drove her away. And now, here he was again, wrecking her life. And she was pregnant. Again.

Anger surged, squeezing her heart. Rage churned and spilled out with her words, her eyes spitting fire.

"I'm angry. You should've told me. Our relationship ended because you lost your job? Because you had so little faith in me? Everything happened because you couldn't just man the fuck up and tell me something simple."

She tried to slide off his lap, but his hands tightened on her hips, holding her there.

"It wasn't that I didn't have faith in you," he said quietly. "I didn't have faith in myself. I don't blame you for being angry. I was an idiot, and I know it. I've thought about what I did every day. Wishing I could change it, go back, have enough faith in us to work things out. I've wished every day that I didn't let my past poison me. That I didn't feel like I wasn't good enough for you. I made you leave anyway with what I did."

"You're a royal asshole," she spat. "I was in pain. Tore myself down every day. Depression set in, and I couldn't fight it. Couldn't drown it, no matter how much alcohol I drank. I downed a bottle of pills and a bottle of booze. If Melissa hadn't been checking on me, I'd be dead right now. And for what? Because of your fucking pride? This just tells me you didn't have any faith in me, in us. Instead of being there when I needed you, you burned our lives to ashes."

"I know, Dom. Believe me, I know. The one thing that hasn't changed through all of this is my love for you."

She scoffed. "If you loved me, you wouldn't have given up over something so trivial. You fucked up both our lives."

"Dom, you haven't lived my life. You had loving parents, a brother, and friends. I had a string of foster homes with people who didn't want me, just the paycheck I came with. You hung out with people, celebrated holidays, and went to a good school. I celebrated if I didn't get a beating from a bully or a foster parent.

"My failures were carved into me—mentally and physically. Before I met you, I'd never had someone look at me with love in their eyes, compassion in their hearts, gentleness in their touch. I hid who I truly was because I didn't want you to see the broken man, the loser who couldn't take care of you. I know it doesn't excuse what I did, but it's all I've ever known."

"Oh, Tim…" Her anger softened. She cupped his face, thumbs brushing his jaw. "I never would've thought that. Everyone makes mistakes. It's part of being human. I've done stupid things I regret, but I never thought you'd love me less because of it."

"You've always been perfect in my eyes, Dom. My mistakes, though… they were life-altering. Even now, I can't stop doing stupid things to push you away. I love you, and that's never going to change. All I can do now is keep showing up, proving it, even if you'll never choose me."

"I know what you want, Tim. I'm just not sure if I can give it to you. I told Nathaniel I needed to talk to you before I made my decision. The baby… It's changed things."

"That's something else we need to talk about. Even though I was turned, there's a good chance the baby will be a werewolf. Even if you don't choose me, the baby needs me so I can teach it."

She closed her eyes, taking a steadying breath. "I'm not giving my baby up for anyone. Whether we're together or not, that won't change. You can help raise it. I won't stop you from coming over whenever you want as long as you tell me first. But I'll never give up custody."

"Can we compromise then?" His voice softened. "Even if you choose Nathaniel, can we be roommates? Or at least live on the same property?"

"We have time to figure that out, Tim. Just give me time to think things through."

Tim pulled her into a kiss. She didn't know how she felt about it. She wasn't technically with Nathaniel, but she had chosen him. Nathaniel had offered her a way out, but could she take it? If she did, could she keep Tim so close and resist the pull of what they had? Could she resist Nathaniel?

Tim rested his forehead against hers. "Just think about it, and we'll talk later when everything settles. I should go. I'm sure Nathaniel doesn't appreciate me being here."

"He helped me take care of you. He knows you're here. He gave me an option I need to think about, too." Dominique sighed. "This whole thing with your pack has gotten out of control."

"I know. I kept trying to stall Jacob. I wanted to tell you everything, give you a choice. I wasn't sure how you'd take the news of Nathaniel being a vampire and me being a werewolf. You took it better than I thought you would."

She shrugged. "I don't know why, but I feel like this is where I belong."

"Nathaniel's awake and heading this way."

"You can feel him?"

"Yes. Just like I can feel you. And he can feel us." Tim glanced toward the door. "Let me get dressed so I can leave."

"Don't leave. It's not safe out there. I'll talk to Nathaniel. He'll let you stay."

"No one is leaving," Nathaniel said, stepping into the room.

Chapter 75

Nathaniel's gaze landed on Dominique in Tim's lap, and his lips curved into a deeper frown. She'd asked him what he'd do if she chose Tim, but he'd hoped she wasn't actually changing her mind. He'd waited centuries for her. He would continue to wait if he had to, but his patience was wearing thin.

Dominique slid off Tim's lap, preparing to stand, but Nathaniel's hand lifted, telling her to stay. Nathaniel's eyes locked with Tim's. On the surface, Tim's face was calm, but Nathaniel felt the jealousy rolling off him, as potent and bitter as his own.

"Your pack is on its way," Nathaniel said, his voice flat. "If they haven't already arrived. Nicholas, the White Moon Alpha, called while I was out. I asked for his help while Dominique was gone. He's been at war with Jacob for years, and he's ready to remove him as Alpha."

He didn't give Tim time to respond. "According to his informant, Jacob has gathered the pack and called for our deaths. They know you and Dominique aren't at either of your houses. They checked the club too. Someone followed Dominique when she came here before, so their next logical step was here."

Nathaniel stepped closer to Dominique, kissed her cheek while watching Tim's fists ball up in his lap, and smirked.

"Who was Paul to your pack?" Nathaniel asked.

"Jacob's Beta," Tim replied.

"I suspected as much. And who'd you kill before that?"

"Raul. Jacob's Gamma."

The two men inhaled sharply at the same time. Smoke. It was faint, but it was there. Nathaniel turned toward the door. The fire hadn't reached them yet, but it wouldn't be long.

Tim stood, grunting as he lifted Dominique. "Your pack's here. They've set the house on fire. We need to get to the third floor, near the windows. I'll call Nicholas. Hopefully, his pack gets here in time."

Nathaniel already had his phone out, dialing while guiding Tim toward the stairwell. Nicholas answered on the first ring.

"Nicholas, Jacob's pack is here. They've set the house on fire. Our only way out is a window, but if I open it, a backdraft may hit."

"My scouts followed Jacob. They're already on your property, staying back, waiting for us. We'll be at the rear in ten minutes," Nicholas said.

"We don't have ten minutes. We'll have to jump."

"Even if you get out, they'll swarm you," Nicholas warned.

Nathaniel cursed under his breath. "We'll do our best to hold out. Get here fast."

He hung up, stuffing the phone back into his pocket. Flames were licking up the opposite end of the house. Jacob was funneling them into a trap. They couldn't wait any longer.

"Tim," Nathaniel snapped, "we move fast. As soon as I open the window, you run. I'll be right behind you."

Tim nodded, tightening his grip on Dominique. Nathaniel threw the window open. The two men burst out onto the balcony as fire roared down the hall behind them. Smoke didn't bother Nathaniel, but Dominique was coughing, her head against Tim's shoulder. He could grab her and leap, but her weight plus Tim's was a risk even for him.

Tim leaned over the railing, scanning the tree line with Nathaniel. Wolves were spilling from the woods like ghosts.

Then Tim's eyes locked with Nathaniel's. Nathaniel shook his head. *Don't do it.*

Tim hugged Dominique tighter, kissed her hair, and shoved her into Nathaniel's arms.

"I love you, Dominique," he said, then vaulted over the balcony.

Chapter 76

Dominique screamed as Tim hurled himself off the balcony. For a heartbeat, her world went still. Then his body twisted midair, fur rippling where skin had been. He landed hard, a sickening crunch muffled by dirt. A whine rose from below, high and broken, and carried to her on the wind. He was hurt.

Nathaniel's arms locked around her, iron and unyielding, as wolves poured from the treeline like a living tide. They descended after Tim in a snapping frenzy.

"Dominique," Nathaniel's voice was a low growl in her ear. "We have to go. Tim's giving us a distraction to get you out."

"We can't just leave him!" Her hands clawed at Nathaniel's shoulders. "He'll die—"

"If we stay, we'll all die. He knew I could get you down. Don't let his sacrifice be for nothing. Hold tight."

Nathaniel's grip shifted, cradling her closer. She wrapped her arms around his neck and squeezed her eyes shut. Then the world tilted. Wind roared past her face as Nathaniel vaulted into the night.

Too fast. Her stomach lurched. Wolves howled behind them, the sound impossibly close. She risked a glance over his shoulder. A massive wolf surged from the underbrush, claws reaching, when another wolf came out of nowhere, slamming it sideways. Teeth and claws shredded earth and fur. Dirt flew. The snarls faded as Nathaniel's speed increased again.

She pressed her face into his chest, swallowing against the nausea.

"Nicholas said some of his wolves were nearby," Nathaniel said between leaps. "Either they're already fighting or he's just arrived. Pray it's the latter."

Fear spiked through her—raw, jagged. Not for herself. Not even for the baby. But for Tim. For Nathaniel. Dying wasn't the worst thing. Losing her baby would be hard, but she'd survived one miscarriage. Losing the loves of her life? She'd never survive that.

"Nathaniel, put me down," she gasped. "If you weren't carrying me, you'd be faster."

"I'm not leaving you." His voice cracked, but stayed fierce. "If I die today, I'll die knowing I had a second chance with my soulmate."

He glanced down at her and tried to smile. Tears streaked her cheeks. She buried her face in his chest again, gripping his shirt like it could anchor her.

A howl echoed ahead of them. Nathaniel veered, his body twisting midstride. Branches snapped. Wind burned her skin as another wolf's claws raked the air where she'd been an instant ago.

Nathaniel pushed harder. His muscles bunched under her hands as he launched upward, landing on a branch that cracked and fell away behind them. Again, he leapt, higher this time. The world blurred, then steadied. Finally, he crouched on a massive limb high above the ground.

"Dominique," he said, breathless, "I have to leave you here. Jacob's below, trying to climb. This is the safest place I can put you."

He set her down. Her knees buckled, hands clutching at his shoulders. When he tried to pry her loose, she wrapped her arms around his waist, trembling so hard he staggered.

Something wet smeared across her palm. She pulled back. Blood. The wolf had missed her only because Nathaniel had swerved and taken the blow himself. The claw marks cut deep.

"Nathaniel, your side. We need to get it bandaged."

"No time. We're in a war." His voice was iron, but his face had gone pale. "Stay here and wait for me. If I'm not back soon, please slide to the next branch, then the next. Slowly."

"I can't." Her voice broke. "I'm afraid of heights. If I try to climb down, I'll fall. Please… don't leave me up here."

Tears blurred everything. Like a fool, she looked down. The ground spun. Her teeth chattered, her head swam, and she slumped against his chest, dizzy and shaking.

Nathaniel tore Dominique's arms from around his neck, ducked under, and shifted in front of her. He guided her arms back over his shoulders before straightening.

She clamped onto him, arms and legs locked tight, screaming into his back as he leapt from the branch. Wind whipped her hair as a wolf's howl split the air below. Panic clawed through her. Her fear was going to get them both killed.

"Nicholas," Nathaniel breathed.

Dominique cracked one eye open. Through the blur of motion, a pack of wolves surged through the trees, a massive white wolf leading them.

Nathaniel jumped for another branch. It snapped under their weight. Dominique's heart lurched as they dropped. He caught another limb, muscles straining, bark splintering under his grip.

"Dominique," he gritted out, "I can't hold us both. Crawl up my back. Get on the limb."

"I can't." Her voice broke. "I'm shaking too bad. I'm slowing you down. I'm sorry."

"Listen to me." His tone turned hard, commanding. "You have to. I can't haul us both up. I know you're scared, but I don't have enough grip to haul us both up. If I try for another limb, you may be injured."

Her forehead pressed against his back. Every breath came ragged. Seconds slipped away.

"I love you, Nathaniel."

She braced her feet against his hips. He grunted, blood slick beneath her shoe. Her foot slipped. She yelped, glanced down, and lost her grip.

She fell.

"Dominique!"

Nathaniel released the limb, streamlined his body, and dove after her. Air rushed between them. He caught her mid-fall, twisting just before they slammed into a lower branch. The impact cracked through him; bark splintered; pain ripped down his spine.

They were still falling. Dominique was struggling for him to release her, panic rising in her chest.

"Either you hold on and let me save us," he shouted over the wind, "or we both die. Is that what you want?"

Her head shook violently. He twisted her around, and she latched onto his back.

He spun his body, snatched another branch, and used their momentum to swing them upward. The world blurred, then stilled as they landed on top of the limb. Dominique clung to his back, gasping for air.

He sat up, yanking her around to the front of him, and crushed her to his chest. She gasped for air.

"Dominique, open your eyes. Now!"

She shook her head. He gripped her chin, forcing her gaze to his.

"I have to fight. I'm joining Nicholas' pack. You will fucking sit on this tree limb until one of us comes to get you. Do you understand me?"

"Y-yes," she stammered.

He eased her forward until her stomach pressed against the limb.

"I'm going to draw Jacob off. Stay put until one of us comes to get you. If you don't…" His tone dropped to a dangerous rumble. "I'll punish you."

Jacob lunged, claws gouging into the trunk. He leapt again, swiping at them. Nathaniel grinned, dropped lower out of reach, and sprang to another tree, taunting him.

Dominique watched them vanish between the branches. Her heart hammered against her ribs as Nathaniel hit the ground running, Jacob on his heels.

She closed her eyes, trying to steady her breathing. Howls echoed through the night. Branches cracked. Leaves rustled. The metallic scent of blood hung thick in the air. So strong she could taste it.

A howl echoed near the tree, low and mournful. Dominique's eyes flew open, scanning the shadows below. A black wolf, slick with blood, was being chased by two others. Her breath hitched. Tim. Was it his blood, or someone else's?

One of the wolves leapt onto his back, and they tumbled to the ground. She screamed as teeth tore into Tim's flesh. Bite after bite. Snarls and wet sounds filled the air. He flung one off, but the other lunged again.

Tim looked up. Their eyes locked. A broken, guttural howl left his throat just before the gray wolf slammed him into the base of the tree. The trunk shuddered violently.

Dominique screamed, arms flailing, barely catching the branch before she slipped. Bark bit into her skin as she clung to it, heart pounding.

The gray wolf staggered upright and looked up at her. His muzzle twisted into something almost human—a grin. Fear slithered down her spine.

Then a white-and-gray wolf exploded from the trees, slamming into the cream-colored one attacking Tim. A tawny wolf crashed into the gray wolf at the base of the tree. Wood cracked beneath her. She prayed it would hold.

Fur, blood, and motion blurred together. She couldn't tell who was winning. Tim's black wolf lay still on the forest floor. She squinted, trying to see if his chest rose. Blood glistened around him.

More wolves charged past. She couldn't tell friend from enemy anymore. A distant howl carried through the forest. The others echoed it, then sprinted toward the sound.

Silence fell, broken only by her ragged breaths. Tim lay below, bleeding out. She needed to move, to do *something*. Finally, she forced herself upright. Nathaniel would just have to be angry.

A flicker of white caught her eye. A white wolf nosed at Tim's body.

"Get away from him!" she screamed.

The wolf lifted his head. Crystal-blue eyes met hers. He looked down at Tim again, then back at her. His gaze glazed over. When he stood on his hind legs, she pressed back against the trunk.

"If you think I'm coming down, you're insane," she said, voice shaking. "I don't even know who you are."

He stared for a long moment, then turned toward the noise of approaching paws. Three wolves burst through the brush and shifted into human form.

"You need to come down," one said. "We have orders to retrieve you if necessary. Our Alpha has a truce with Nathaniel. No matter what happens to him, we guard you with our lives."

The white wolf took off into the woods. The three men approached. One cupped his hands while another boosted upward, pulling himself onto the branch.

"We're not here to hurt you," he said gently. "But we have to move. Now. Is that your wolf down there?"

"Yes." Her voice was barely a whisper. "Is he… still alive?"

"Barely. But if we go now, we might save him. The pack doctor's waiting in a clearing nearby. Please, come. I'll lower you to Tobias. He'll take you."

He reached for her. She hesitated, then placed her trembling hand in his. He lowered her toward Tobias, and the moment he let go, she screamed and fell into Tobias's arms.

Her feet hit the ground. She wobbled, heart hammering.

"I'm shifting," Tobias said quickly. "Get on my back and hold tight."

Snarls and crashing grew louder behind them. Tobias shifted, fur rippling, and crouched low. When she didn't move fast enough, he growled. She scrambled up, grabbing his scruff, pressing close.

He lunged forward. The forest blurred into streaks of green and brown.

Moments later, they burst into a clearing. The metallic tang of blood and antiseptic hit her. Warriors lay everywhere. Hands passed tools and gauze in a frantic rhythm.

Tobias lowered himself, and Dominique slid shakily off his back. The ground felt unsteady beneath her. She stayed there, trembling, nausea burning her throat. Panic clawed up her chest.

Tobias shifted back into human form, muscles flexing as he stood over her. Heat rushed to her cheeks.

He chuckled. "You've seen a werewolf before, haven't you?"

"Just Tim," she said, voice trembling. "Paul was killed when he shifted back. I'm… not used to your world."

His laugh deepened. She scowled, which only made him laugh harder until he finally straightened, expression hardening.

He offered his hand. She hesitated, then took it. His grip was strong, grounding. Together, they crossed to a makeshift tent.

"Your man's on his way here," Tobias said. "He's shifted back, but he's unconscious. He's bleeding heavily. Still, the power rolling off him… If he fights, he'll make it. The Alphas are clashing now." A grin curved his lips. "Nicholas is toying with Jacob."

Dominique blinked. "How do you know all that?"

"I'm Beta," he said simply. "I hear my pack's thoughts. My Alpha charged me to protect you."

Before she could reply, pain ripped through her abdomen. She gasped, clutching her stomach as the world tilted. Vomit burned her throat as she fell to her knees.

"Hey—" Tobias dropped beside her, holding her hair back.

Her vision blurred with tears. The pain deepened, twisting inside her. *Please, not the baby.*

"Are you alright?" he asked, alarm sharpening his tone.

"I'm pregnant," she choked out. "Not far along, but… I think I'm miscarrying."

"Shit."

He scooped her into his arms and sprinted for the nearest tent. The world blurred past. Inside, he lay her on a cot and disappeared. Pain flared through her abdomen, sharp and deep. Her chest tightened as she curled onto her side, breath shallow.

Moments later, a doctor rushed in. His eyes swept over her, quick and assessing. "Get the IV ready," he barked at the nurse. He helped her onto her back, his hands cool against her skin.

"Miss, I need you to calm down," he said gently. "I'm giving you something to help you rest. Your body's under stress. I have to check you, alright?"

Dominique managed a faint nod, her eyelids heavy. They undressed her from the waist down. The doctor's hands pressed against her abdomen, clinical but steady. The nurse pushed medication into her IV.

Warmth spread through her veins, dulling the pain. Her body went heavy, consciousness slipping away.

Please… don't take my baby.

Darkness claimed her.

Chapter 77

Nathaniel hit the ground running, Jacob right on his heels. He vaulted over fallen logs, branches whipping at his face. For a heartbeat, he thought he'd shaken Jacob until a line of wolves emerged ahead.

Shit. A trap.

He veered left, but pain exploded through his leg as Jacob's teeth clamped down. The world spun as Jacob shook him like prey. Snarling, Nathaniel caught Jacob's head and slammed his fist between his eyes.

The grip loosened. Nathaniel pried Jacob's jaws apart and tore his leg free just as more wolves charged from the trees. He twisted, shoving Jacob's body between himself and the pack.

A chorus of howls split the air. Out of the shadows came Nicholas's wolves, colliding with Jacob's like a storm. The ground shook beneath them. Nicholas' massive white wolf slammed into the nearest enemy, sending fur and blood flying.

Jacob lunged again, claws raking deep across Nathaniel's ribs. Pain burned hot, but he didn't falter. He grabbed Jacob's hind leg, yanking until the joint snapped with a wet crack. A smile curved his lips. Jacob howled, and Nathaniel struck, fangs sinking deep into his neck.

Blood flooded his mouth, thick and metallic. Power surged through him, wild and intoxicating. His torn flesh began to knit, the pain fading into savage exhilaration.

Jacob reared back, throwing his weight against a tree. Bark splintered. The impact ripped Nathaniel free, sending him crashing to the dirt. He rolled, caught his footing, and leapt into the branches above.

"Nicholas!"

The white wolf looked up mid-fight, eyes locking with his.

"Go east! Dominique's in a tree. Get her out! I'll hold Jacob!"

Nicholas let off a short howl and took off.

Nathaniel stayed high, watching Jacob pace below, blood matting his fur. He taunted him with low growls, buying time for his wounds to seal.

Then Dominique's scream ripped through the woods.

Adrenaline surged. He dropped from the tree, landing squarely on Jacob's back. His fangs found flesh again, ripping into the same artery. Jacob thrashed, his movements slowing as Nathaniel drank deeper.

Wolves closed in from all sides. Nathaniel tore free, blood dripping down his chin, power burning in his veins. He turned on them, feral and precise—snapping necks, crushing ribs, moving through the chaos like a living weapon.

Nicholas's pack swarmed around him, efficient and lethal. One by one, Jacob's wolves fell.

Then claws tore down Nathaniel's back. Hot, searing pain stole his breath. He staggered forward as flesh ripped away.

Before he could recover, a white blur flew past. Nicholas slammed into Jacob, toying with him. He'd promised to leave Jacob alive for Nicholas to kill.

Nathaniel stumbled to a tree, pressing his back to the rough bark. Blood soaked his side. His body convulsed as his healing burned through what little energy he had left. He gritted his teeth, forcing the cry of pain back down. There wasn't enough energy to completely heal him, just stop the bleeding.

Chapter 78

Dominique woke to a light shining in her eyes. She tried to bat it away, but a firm hand caught her wrist and pressed it back to the bed. When the blinding glare finally vanished, she blinked, waiting for her vision to focus.

A man stood over her, clipboard in hand, checking her vitals. He nodded to the woman beside him, and she slipped quietly from the room.

"Welcome back," he said gently. "Your name's Dominique, right?"

Her throat felt raw. "Yes."

"The nurse will bring you some water soon. You've been asleep for two days. How are you feeling?"

Her eyes widened. "Two days?"

He nodded. "We had to sedate you. Your body needed rest. You had some bleeding and cramping, but—" he smiled faintly, "—no miscarriage."

Tears flooded her eyes. "My baby's okay?"

"Yes, Dominique. The baby's fine."

Relief washed through her, loosening the ache in her chest. When she finally found her voice again, she asked softly, "Where am I?"

"In the pack hospital. You're safe here."

Safe. The word felt foreign, almost fragile.

"What happened after I passed out?"

"Nicholas killed Jacob. Any wolves loyal to him are dead. Your wolf is down the hall. He took a beating, but we stitched him up. He's stable, though still unconscious."

"And Nathaniel?" she asked, her voice trembling. "The vampire. Is he… alive?"

"I believe so. We moved him to a dark room so the sunlight wouldn't harm him. But I haven't checked on him since. I don't know how vampires heal."

Her heart clenched. "Can you take me to him? Or bring him here?"

He frowned. "I'm not sure that's a good idea. What if he's still dangerous?"

"He won't hurt me. Please. Is it day or night?"

"It's close to dusk."

"Then he'll be awake soon," she said firmly. "Take me to him."

Moments later, the nurse returned with water. After helping her drink, she assisted Dominique into a wheelchair. They moved quietly down the corridor until they stopped outside a locked door. Dominique frowned. The nurse unlocked the door and pushed it open, then stepped back.

The room was dark.

Dominique leaned forward, peering into the shadows. Suddenly, a hand shot out of the darkness, seizing her arm and yanking her from the chair. She collided with a hard chest.

Behind her, the nurse screamed.

The overhead light flicked on, and pain exploded through her neck.

Nathaniel's fangs were buried deep.

She cried out, pounding his chest. "Nathaniel! Stop!"

But he didn't hear her. His body trembled as he fed, his grip tightening. Panic clawed up her throat. He was going to drain her dry.

Footsteps thundered in the hallway. Shouts blurred around her. Fear for her baby and for Nathaniel tangled in her chest until she could hardly breathe.

She screamed again, weaker this time. "Nathaniel! You're killing me!"

Her fists grew heavy. Her vision dimmed. She sagged against him.

Then his tongue swept across the wound, sending a shiver down her spine. The pain faded into a strange, electric pull. He drew back just enough for her to see his face. His eyes glowed, starlight against darkness, swirling with something ancient.

He raised his wrist to her lips. Blood smeared across her mouth, the metallic tang flooding her tongue. She tried not to swallow, but her body betrayed her.

As their eyes met, the room dissolved. Her heartbeat synced with his. Something unseen pulled at her, energy twisting, binding, merging. The noise around them vanished into silence.

Nathaniel kissed her, and warmth surged through her veins. The world went still. Emotions crashed over her in one overwhelming wave. Pressure built behind her eyes. Then the dam broke.

Nathaniel's voice drifted through the silence, low and steady.

'Don't be afraid, Dominique. You are mine. Forever. We are connected. We are one. You feel weak because I am weak. You hunger because I hunger. You feel pain because I feel pain. You heal faster because I heal faster. You will be harder to hurt, but can still die. Just remember, whatever happens to me happens to you. Whatever happens to you happens to me.'

Then the weariness came, and darkness claimed her.

Chapter 79

Nathaniel's home had been reduced to ashes, and the fight had left him weak. Nicholas ordered him taken to the pack hospital, ensuring he arrived before daybreak.

He woke the following night, disoriented, lying on a hospital bed. The moment he tried to stand, pain shot through him. He hadn't fully healed before dying for the day. His body trembled with hunger. He needed blood.

Stumbling to the door, he grasped the knob and twisted. Locked. He slammed his fist against it. "Open the door!" No answer. He rammed his shoulder into the metal, but his strength was gone.

Sliding down the wall, he let his head fall back against it. Nicholas had a peace treaty with him. Why lock him up like an animal? He understood the wolves feared him, but surely Nicholas would've told them to tend to him.

Closing his eyes, he reached through the darkness until he felt Dominique's soul. It pulsed faintly, steady and alive. Relief loosened his chest. She lived. That was all that mattered.

He stayed like that until dawn crept in and death took him again, unsure if he'd ever wake.

***

Nathaniel was going mad. Voices rose in the silence. Shadows moved in the corners of the room, twisting into familiar faces. Ghosts from his past.

Rose. She appeared again and again, her voice coaxing him to follow.

Without blood to heal his wounds, his body and mind began to break. Words tumbled from his mouth; nonsense, conversations with people long dead. Then Eleanor appeared.

She drained him, fed him her blood, and left him in the dark. Rose left him.

Cold, shaking, alone, his body convulsed.

Then the scent hit him.

Rose.

She'd come back for him. And he was going to kill her.

He dragged himself upright and followed the scent. When the door opened, he lunged, grabbing her, yanking her close. A scream cut through the haze as his fangs sank deep into her neck.

Her fists hammered his chest. His name tore from her lips.

Bloodlust consumed him, thick and intoxicating. His mind screamed to stop, but his body refused to obey.

"Nathaniel! You're going to kill me!"

Her voice weakened. Her heartbeat slowed. Shouts echoed from the hallway.

Then the taste hit him—wrong, familiar—and the fog shattered. His vision cleared, and he gazed at the woman in his arms.

It wasn't Rose.

It was Dominique.

Horror slammed into him. *Shit. I almost killed her.*

He sealed the wound with his tongue, but it wasn't enough. She was fading.

He bit into his wrist and pressed it to her lips, forcing his blood past them. She tried to turn away, but he held firm, eyes locking with hers as his life force pushed into her soul, binding them.

Her eyes widened in fear as his life force swirled inside her, opening the dam of emotions between them.

He kissed her, sealing their energies together, bonding them as master and servant.

He shoved into her mind.

'Don't be afraid, Dominique. You are mine. Forever. We are connected. We are one. You feel weak because I am weak. You hunger because I hunger. You feel pain because I feel pain. You heal faster because I heal faster. You will be harder to hurt, but can still die. Just remember, whatever happens to me happens to you. Whatever happens to you happens to me.'

Her body went limp in his arms. Voices spilled into the room.

"What has he done to her?"

"He's taken over her mind, I think."

"Do we attack?"

Nathaniel ignored them, lifting Dominique and laying her gently on the bed. Nicholas pushed through the crowd.

He glanced from Nathaniel to Dominique, sighing.

"Everyone, stand down. Return to your duties, and fetch Benjamin."

When the room cleared, Nicholas turned to him. "Isn't this the woman you love?"

"She is."

"Then why attack her?"

"Because your people left me to die," Nathaniel hissed. "I was never given blood to heal. Every time I woke, I was weaker. Not feeding causes bloodlust. Bloodlust drives a vampire mad, especially when his body drains itself to heal. Dominique had the misfortune of being the first person to come to the door. The madness had set in when her scent hit me, and I thought she was someone else. I never would've harmed her if your pack had shown even an ounce of care."

Nathaniel sank onto the bed beside her, eyes burning into Nicholas.

"You need to feed then," Nicholas said quietly. "I'm sorry my people didn't take care of you. I should've checked on you sooner." His gaze flicked to Dominique. "Will she live?"

"She'll recover with rest and food, but she needs a transfusion. She's pregnant. Her blood can't replenish fast enough." Nathaniel rose, voice low and strained. "I have to leave. The bloodlust is rising again, and next time I won't stop."

"I can't have you hunting on my land," Nicholas said. "You already make my people nervous. As Alpha, I'll offer you my blood. Can you control yourself enough to take only what you need?"

"I have no intention of harming anyone, Nicholas. I accept your offer, and your power will be more than enough to sate the bloodlust and heal me."

Nicholas nodded, stepping closer and tilting his head. Nathaniel's fangs sank into his neck.

Power surged through him. More potent than anything Jacob had possessed. Heat blazed through his veins, then pain followed, ripping through his body. He released Nicholas, licking the wound closed before the convulsions started. His body hit the floor, jerking violently.

The power was too much, reknitting every shattered cell from the inside out. A scream tore from his throat.

On the bed, Dominique's body arched, matching his movements. Nicholas caught her shoulders, holding her down.

What had he done? He'd bound them together, and now she was paying the price. He'd sealed their fate without her permission. If he caused her to lose the baby, she'd never forgive him.

When the healing finally stopped, both their bodies went still.

"Benjamin!" Nicholas bellowed. "Get in here! Dominique needs a transfusion. When she wakes, make her eat."

Benjamin stormed in, glaring at Nathaniel.

Nicholas's hand shot out, closing around his throat. "I am Alpha here, not you. You will obey my command. Your thoughts are too loud. We have a truce with Nathaniel. He is not to be harmed. Understood?"

"Y–yes, Alpha," Benjamin choked.

Nicholas released him, and Benjamin stumbled, coughing, before wheeling Dominique's bed out.

Moments later, Nicholas's eyes glazed over, and another bed was brought in for Nathaniel. The attendant avoided his gaze and fled the moment Nicholas nodded toward the door.

"I apologize for Benjamin," Nicholas said. "He should've fed you. They were told to bring you here for treatment. I didn't know he hated vampires. He's never met one before."

"I've been in this room for days," Nathaniel rasped. "I shouted, banged on the door. No one answered. It was locked."

Nicholas sighed. "This room's for wolves who can't control their change. It's soundproof, reinforced, locked from the outside."

"It makes no difference now," Nathaniel muttered. "All that matters is Dominique. If she loses the baby, I'll never forgive myself. Even if she doesn't, she may never forgive me for what I've done."

"You marked her somehow, didn't you?"

"Yes. I nearly killed her. Binding her to me as my human servant was the only way to keep her alive. I'd offered before, but she wanted time to think. Then the war broke out, and time ran out."

"She may not forgive you soon," Nicholas said quietly. "But she will. In time."

He paused, then added, "You can stay another day or two to heal, but after that, you need to go. My pack can't risk another attack."

"The bloodlust is gone. I've healed. As long as I have blood bags, I'm no threat."

Nicholas nodded. "We have plenty. I'll bring one myself. Rest now."

"Thank you, Nicholas."

When he was gone, Nathaniel lay back on the bed, reaching through the bond. Dominique's mind was silent, dreamlike, but she wasn't in pain. Relief loosened his chest.

He held onto that fragile connection until dawn came. Then his body went still, frozen in death once more.

Chapter 80

Dominique opened her eyes, confusion clouding her thoughts. She scanned the room and found Benjamin, eyes closed, in a chair in the corner.

Had she dreamed it? Nathaniel's attack, his bite, his blood in her mouth? The memory hit like a wave. Their souls had connected. She'd heard him, but not aloud… inside her mind. She winced as she touched her neck, brushing the bandages there.

He'd said they were one. Connected.

Her eyes widened.

He hadn't. He wouldn't. Not without her consent.

How could he do that to her? What if she didn't want to live forever? Didn't want to outlive her child? What if she didn't want to be his human servant, bound to him under his command?

At least as a vampire, she'd have freedom. Now she was tethered to him, whether she wanted it or not.

Her chest tightened, anger swelling. All of that, and he'd almost killed her.

The baby… was it still alive?

"You're awake. How are you feeling?" Benjamin's voice pulled her back.

"My baby…" she whispered. "Is it…"

"It's alive," he said. "The vampire didn't kill it." His sneer was sharp. "I told you going to him was a mistake. Vampires are our natural enemies."

"Nathaniel isn't dangerous to me. Or he wouldn't have been if you'd taken care of him. Did you leave him to starve for two days just because you hate vampires?"

Benjamin stiffened. "I don't know how they heal or function. Never cared to know. But if I'd realized starving him would cause this, I'd have given him blood. What is that vampire to you anyway? Why do you care?"

"I love him," she admitted, voice trembling. "Even though I'm furious with him right now. I think he made me his human servant."

She tried to sit up, but Benjamin gently pressed her back down.

"Rest a bit longer." His gaze drifted to her bandaged neck. "I thought you belonged to the wolf."

"I'm not with either of them, technically."

"Then who's the father of your baby?"

"Tim," Dominique sighed. "Vampires can't have children. And before you ask, I didn't know what either of them was."

Benjamin nodded slowly. "Most wolves have wolf offspring. It's rare for one to be human. Your wolf… he was turned, not born, right?"

"Yes. One of Jacob's pack turned him after he rejected her. Does that matter when it comes to the baby?"

"Chances are still high the baby will be a wolf, but there's a slim chance of having a human baby. Don't take the chance on it when it comes to your prenatal care. If your prenatal tests come back strange, the government will get involved. See me for your appointments. I'll handle your care, and when it's time, deliver here."

"Alright," she said softly. "You mentioned your Alpha killed Jacob. What happens to his pack now?"

"They'll either go rogue or swear loyalty to Nicholas. They'll be fine if they follow his rules. Or Nicholas will appoint a new Alpha, and they'll follow them."

"What if they don't want to join his pack?"

"Rogues are on their own," Benjamin said. "But we won't let them expose our kind. If there's any risk of that, they'll be killed. Your wolf is strong for someone who's been turned. Not as powerful as a pureblood, but strong enough to challenge one of our ranked members if he wanted."

"Tim hates being a werewolf. I doubt he'd challenge anyone," Dominique replied.

"Maybe because he's never known a real pack," Benjamin said. "Jacob was a cruel Alpha. Nicholas isn't. He rules firmly but fairly. We live in peace unless someone crosses a line. And even then, we get a second chance to prove our loyalty. Jacob just killed anyone who disobeyed… or had his enforcer torture them until they wished for death. Nicholas punishes, yes, but only when it's deserved. Everyone here has a place, and he doesn't disturb that balance."

"Maybe Tim would like being part of Nicholas's pack," Dominique admitted. "But I can't answer for him. Would he have to live here?"

"No. Most do, but a few of us just live in proximity. Alphas have territories, and that makes it hard for the wolves to really branch out unless they become a part of another pack," Benjamin explained.

"I see. So if Tim joined Nicholas, would he have to move? He lives in Jacob's old territory."

"No. That land will either fall under Nicholas or a new Alpha he appoints. Even if Tim goes rogue, no one will force him out. He just won't have the pack's protection."

Dominique nodded. "I'm kind of hungry. Would it be alright if I got up and grabbed something to eat?"

"I'll get you food," Benjamin said, standing. "We're not cruel here, remember?"

"Didn't seem that way when you left Nathaniel to starve," she whispered.

He sighed. "Nicholas's truce with the vampire extends to you and your wolf. I treated you both, but ignored him because of my own prejudice. I should've done better. You'll find no ill will from anyone here now."

"Thank you. What's your name, Doctor?"

"It's Benjamin. I'll be back with some food for you. Just rest for now."

"Thank you, Benjamin."

He nodded and left.

Dominique's heart suddenly slammed against her ribs. Her breath hitched as her body lurched.

Heat spread through her veins, her pulse syncing to something foreign… something alive.

Her fingers clenched around the blanket. *Nathaniel.*

He was waking up.

And she could feel *everything.*

Chapter 81

Nathaniel woke for the night and immediately reached for the bond with Dominique. She was awake and in no pain. He reached further, brushing against the faint spark of life inside her. Relief flooded his chest.

He needed to speak to her. Needed to know what she thought of what he'd done. Losing her wasn't an option. He pushed on the bond between them, breaking through to her mind.

'Dominique.'

Her anger punched him square in the chest. Her thoughts ran wild, echoing directly through his head.

'I was supposed to have a choice. He said he'd wait for me no matter how long it took. Then he just takes that choice away. He almost killed me. Could've killed my baby.'

'I'm sorry, Dominique. I was crazed with bloodlust and madness. I nearly drank you dry, and I couldn't let you die, so I bonded us. The thought of making you mine was too great a temptation. I gave you no choice, and I don't blame you for being angry. I only hope that one day you can forgive me.'

'I don't know how this works. Do I talk out loud? How do I tell him what I'm feeling? Can I forgive him? He promised not to push, and clearly, he did. This isn't about him pushing me into choosing him, but forcing me to, to be his human servant. Can I even run away from him now?'

A sad smile crossed his lips as her thoughts spilled freely, unaware he could hear every one of them.

'We're connected, Dominique. I can hear your thoughts and feel what you feel. Nicholas doesn't want me to leave this room for now. I'm respecting his wishes, but I needed to make sure you're alright. This was the only way. I want to explain how the bond works.'

'I'm listening,' she replied, bitterness in every syllable. 'Not that I really have a choice.'

'When the bond is open like this,' he explained softly, 'we can hear each other's thoughts. Speak to each other mentally. Feel each other's emotions, like your anger right now. I can close us off, but eventually, I'll need to reopen the link. If one of us is hurt, the other feels it. When we're apart, we'll feel a sense of loss. So, to answer your question, yes, you could run away, but I can call you back to me. You won't have a choice but to answer.'

Her anger flared hotter, licking fire through his veins.

'I promise I won't do that to you," he said quickly. "I want you to come to me willingly. I wanted you to choose a life with me, not have it forced on you. I was a man once, and men make mistakes. Vampires are no different.'

'This isn't a mistake, Nathaniel,' her voice trembled. 'You took my life, my choice, from me. You say you want me to come to you willingly, but according to you, I won't have a choice in the matter. I already feel drawn to you, like I'm supposed to be with you. I didn't truly understand what being your human servant meant. You should've told me everything before binding me.'

'I know,' he whispered. 'And for that, I can never tell you how truly sorry I am.'

'I need time to think, Nathaniel. Stay out of my head.'

Guilt tore through him, heavy and cold. He tried to hide it from her. Tried to bury the sorrow clawing at his chest, but emotion bled through the cracks.

'I love you, Dominique.'

Then he withdrew from her mind, severing the connection between them.

Chapter 82

Dominique closed her eyes, trying to block out the sorrow and guilt flooding her chest. Nathaniel had already sealed off their bond, but it was too late. His emotions had bled through.

Her anger clashed with his pain, creating a storm inside her. When the emotions finally faded, leaving only her fury, silence filled her mind.

Then the thoughts came rushing back.

This wasn't what she wanted. If Nathaniel had explained everything and she'd chosen him anyway, it would've been different. She wouldn't feel this betrayed. She'd known she'd live forever, but not that he could control her.

And then there was the ache in her chest. The constant pull toward him. Would that fade, or only grow stronger? He said he wouldn't call her, but would that change if she chose Tim instead?

Tim.

He'd been there for her, given up everything. He'd sacrificed himself so Nathaniel could get her to safety. He was the father of her baby. He hadn't hesitated to risk his life for them.

Benjamin said he was still alive, fighting for his life. Was he fighting for her? For the baby?

She could've had a normal life with him. A family. But now she couldn't. Not when she was bound to Nathaniel. She'd never grow old. She'd have to watch Tim die. Watch her child die. And she'd stay frozen in the body of a twenty-five-year-old forever.

Sighing, she rolled onto her side, staring at the door. She needed to see Tim soon, to check on him, to decide what came next. This push and pull between them all couldn't go on.

The door opened, and Benjamin walked in with a tray of food. Dominique's mouth watered; her stomach growled. He set the tray down and helped her sit up. As she ate, her thoughts scattered until one hit her like a truck.

Melissa and Post.

Her face went pale.

Fuck! They must be worried sick.

Neither she nor Tim had shown up. Her phone was still at the house. Melissa probably thought she was dead, or that Tim had done something to her. Maybe even that she'd run off with him.

And Post… her only living family. God, how could she do that to him?

There was no way to explain any of this. Benjamin had said no one could expose their kind.

And what about Tim? If he woke up fully healed, how the hell would she explain that?

Oh, he was unconscious and critically injured yesterday. Now he's fine.

She snorted. *Yeah, that'll go over great.*

"Benjamin?"

"Yes?"

"I hope this isn't too much to ask, but can I use your phone? I own a bar, and Tim's my bartender. My best friend handles things when I'm out, but this wasn't exactly… planned. I have a bit of a history with self-harm. Melissa's probably losing her mind. So is my brother."

"Yeah, that's fine," Benjamin said, handing her his phone.

She called Melissa. When she didn't answer, Dominique left a voicemail and called again. On the third ring, Melissa picked up—screaming.

"Where the *fuck* have you been?" Melissa shouted. "Do you know how worried I've been? I called every hospital, morgue, and police station in the *state*! I went to your house and Tim's! Post's been driving around looking for you two!"

Dominique rolled her eyes. "You done yelling in my ear?"

"Girl! Wait until I get my hands on you!"

"Chill out, Melissa."

"*Chill out?* Are you fucking kidding me? Where have you been, Dom?"

"Listen, Tim and I were attacked by his gang. I went to Nathaniel's, but they burned his house down. We barely made it out. I was unconscious for a few days, so I couldn't call. I'm sorry we worried you, but we're okay. Tim's friends have been taking care of us."

"Oh my God! Is Nathaniel okay?" Melissa's voice softened. "The baby?"

"Nathaniel and the baby are fine. One of Tim's friends is a doctor."

Dominique glanced at Benjamin. His brows furrowed, and a frown tugged at his lips. He knew she was lying, but why did he look *confused*?

"Did you call the police? They told me they couldn't give out any info on ongoing investigations."

"No, I haven't called them yet. I only just woke up. But honestly, they won't do anything. Jacob had ties in the department."

"Well, that sucks." Melissa sighed. "Look, I didn't open the bar. With you and Tim missing, I couldn't care less about it. I just focused on finding you."

"Thank you, Melissa. I really appreciate you always being there for me. Everything that's happened just… made me realize how much I value my life, my friends, my family." Dominique swallowed. "Tim's still unconscious. I don't know if he'll wake up."

"Where are you guys? I'll come to you."

"I can't say. Tim's friends are… particular about people knowing who and where they are."

"Dom—"

"No, Mel." Dominique's tone hardened. "This is something you'll just have to accept. I'm calling from the doctor's phone, so don't call it back, okay? Once I get a new phone, I'll reach out again."

Melissa sighed. "Fine. But you'd better keep me updated. It's killing me not knowing what's going on."

"I know. But this man doesn't need to be bothered. I'll call when I get home. I love you."

"I love you too. I'll let Post know you're alive. He's been worried sick."

"Thanks, Mel. I'm tired, so I'm hanging up now."

"Okay. Bye, Dom."

"Bye."

Dominique ended the call and handed the phone back to Benjamin.

He slipped it into his pocket and sat down, eyes fixed on her for a long moment. The silence stretched until she began to squirm.

"You lied to your friend," he said finally. "Why?"

"You said no one could expose you guys. I don't want my best friend to end up dead. I wouldn't even know about any of this if I hadn't gotten mixed up with Nathaniel and Tim. How could I explain what happened without telling her *everything*?"

"So, you lied to keep our secret?"

"Yes."

Benjamin smiled faintly. "You'll fit in nicely with our pack." His expression softened, thoughtful. "But I'm curious. Do you *want* to be with the vampire?"

Dominique hesitated. "Right now? I don't know."

"Do you want to be with your wolf?"

"He's not *my* wolf. And I'm not sure what I want anymore. I just… want a normal life." She let out a small, bitter laugh. "Not that that's ever going to happen."

"You might not think so, but Tim is very much *your* wolf," Benjamin said gently. "Would you ever consider joining a pack?"

"You mean letting someone change me into one of you?"

"Yes. Tim's a wolf, and your baby likely will be too. Wouldn't you want to be like them?"

Dominique shook her head slowly. "I've never thought about it before, but I don't think I'd enjoy it."

Benjamin's gaze sharpened. "I'm curious what the vampire did to you. I ask because I had to give you blood transfusions. All we have here is werewolf blood. With the amount I gave you, you *should've* been infected, but your bloodwork came back clean."

"I'm not sure how it works," she admitted softly. "He bound me to him. Made me his human servant."

Benjamin leaned forward, intrigued. "I wonder if that bond prevents change. I'd like to speak with him, purely for knowledge's sake. But if that makes you uncomfortable, I won't."

"I don't mind. I can't answer your questions anyway. He might mind, though, considering how you treated him." A smirk touched her lips. "Now, about something else, can I see Tim?"

"Of course. If you'd like, I can move you into his room so you can stay with him."

"That would be great. Thank you, Benjamin. You've been very kind."

"It's nothing." His eyes glazed for a second, then refocused. He smiled.

Dominique's curiosity sparked. *Was he talking to someone in his head, too?* This world was definitely going to take some getting used to.

Benjamin pushed her bed into Tim's room and aligned it beside his, lowering the railings so she could reach him.

Dominique looked at the monitors. Tim's vitals were steady. She took his hand; his fevered skin pressed against hers.

"Is he okay? He's so hot."

"Werewolves' body temperatures run higher than humans'. His is even higher now while he's healing. Our Beta donated blood to him, which speeds up the process. I thought he'd be awake by now. But maybe *you're* what he needs for that."

"I doubt that," she whispered.

"Talk to him," Benjamin said gently. "You may be surprised. I'll check on you both later."

He left quietly, closing the door behind him.

Dominique scooted onto Tim's bed. Lifting the sheet, she pressed her body against his, laying her head on his chest. His heartbeat thudded a steady rhythm beneath her palm. Without thinking, words began to spill out.

"So, Nathaniel did something that made me angry," she murmured. "He bound me to him as his human servant. I'll live as long as he does, but I don't know how I feel about it. I chose him before I knew what he was. I thought I could handle it… until I found out I was pregnant."

Her voice trembled. "That changed everything. I thought maybe we could still make it work, but when he offered the bond, he didn't tell me everything. I didn't know he could control me. And now… I don't know if I can get past that."

"I think Nathaniel would help me raise the baby, but only at night. That's not the life I want." Her fingers traced the line of Tim's chest. "I'm sorry I've put you through so much. Our past scares me, and while I know why you did all those things, it doesn't change the fact that they happened. You've changed, Tim. You're not the same man you were. You've grown."

"Tim, I need you to wake up, need you to be okay. I can't have you dying because you put your life on the line for me. The baby needs a father; it needs you. I…" Dominique paused. "I need you."

The words hit her like a shockwave. She'd finally made her choice, and it terrified her.

"Family is everything to me," she whispered. "You never really had one, but you do now. You're going to be a father. And I've always believed family is who you choose… and I choose you. If you'll still have me."

Tears slipped down her cheeks. "Just come back to me, okay? We'll figure it out. Together."

She kissed him softly. His heartbeat quickened under her hand, but his eyes stayed closed.

With a sigh, she rested her head back on his chest, tracing small circles with her fingers. Listening to the steady flutter of his heart, she drifted into sleep.

Chapter 83

Dominique jerked awake to a hand shaking her.

Blinking, she looked at Tim, but he was still asleep. Turning, she found Benjamin leaning over her.

Lying back down, she yawned. Exhaustion still clung to her.

"I hate to wake you, but you need to eat. The baby needs nutrition," Benjamin whispered.

"If you say so," she mumbled through another yawn.

"Come on. Let's get you into the chair. I'm not sure what you did, but Tim's vitals have improved. Having you nearby is good for him."

"I just talked to him like you suggested."

Benjamin helped her from the bed and into the chair. He set a tray in front of her, and her stomach grumbled loudly. She blushed, but Benjamin only smiled.

"I'll be back in a bit to collect your tray. Make sure you eat it all."

"Thank you, Benjamin. I appreciate it."

Dominique dug in. The food was delicious. Real home cooking, not sterile hospital fare.

Halfway through her meal, a knock sounded on the door.

"Come in," she called.

A man stepped inside. She looked him over. Platinum blond hair, striking blue eyes, and full lips curved into a confident smile. Tall, muscular, commanding. There was something about his eyes that tugged at her memory.

"I wanted to check on you," he said, voice smooth and deliberate. "Is our hospitality to your liking?"

"Yes, thank you. And this food," she said between bites, "it's so good."

He leaned casually against the foot of the bed, studying her.

"My name's Nicholas. We've met before. Not sure if you remember. It was a stressful time."

Dominique blinked. "Nicholas… the Alpha of the pack?"

"Yes." His smile deepened. "Who told you about me?"

"Benjamin was answering some of my questions. I needed to know what would happen to Tim."

Nicholas nodded slowly. "Our truce with Nathaniel covers him as well. If he hadn't been fighting Jacob's wolves, we might've killed him without realizing who he was. He's the one you were involved with, correct?"

"Yes."

"Benjamin tells me you're pregnant, and that Tim's the father." A small, knowing smile curved his lips. "I'm glad I brought him here, especially after you yelled at me to leave him alone. It's rare for a human to stand up for one of us. You're… unique in your acceptance. Most humans either want to kill us or join us. But Benjamin says you don't want to be a werewolf. Is that true?"

"Yes," Dominique said firmly. "Tim's a wolf, and I'm pregnant with his baby, but I don't want that life. I'm perfectly fine being human. Tim can teach the baby everything it needs to know."

"Interesting." Nicholas tilted his head. "What if Tim became a ranked member of a pack? Or even an Alpha himself? Would you change your mind then? He'd be more involved in the pack. It could leave you… on the outside."

Dominique shrugged. "That's on Tim. If he chooses that, so be it. I still don't want to be a wolf. I'll help him however he needs, but if he doesn't want that, fine. All I ask is his loyalty to me." She swallowed hard. "If he still wants me."

Nicholas raised a brow. "Why wouldn't he?"

Dominique sighed. "Because I was torn between him and Nathaniel for a long time. I chose Nathaniel, not Tim. Then I found out I was pregnant. Everything got complicated. Before I could make sense of it all, Jacob set Nathaniel's house on fire. And then Nathaniel… did what he did." Her voice hardened. "Why am I even telling you this? It's none of your business."

"Maybe you needed someone to talk to," Nicholas said calmly. "Someone outside of it all."

"Maybe. Not like I can talk to anyone else. I can't expose Nathaniel or Tim."

Nicholas's tone shifted, more measured. "I understand. Still, I needed to speak to you about what comes next. Tim will be part of my pack if he accepts, and I had to make sure you wouldn't expose us. You're no threat to us, so we can move forward."

Dominique stared into his eyes. That color—icy blue. She knew them from somewhere.

Nicholas chuckled. "You still don't remember me, do you?"

She shook her head slowly. "Your eyes look familiar, but I can't place you."

"Maybe you'd recognize me in my wolf form." His smirk was almost teasing. "You're a very stubborn woman. Has anyone ever told you that?"

A sly grin spread across her face. "More than once."

She studied him again. Platinum hair, almost white, electric blue eyes. Then it hit her.

The wolf at the tree. The one who had tried to get her down. Her cheeks flushed.

He grinned wider. "Yes, now you remember."

"Yeah," she said softly. "What difference does that make?"

"None." He chuckled. "But I've been thinking about our situation. My pack works well together, and I don't want Jacob's pack. It would be natural to place my Beta over it, but I don't want to lose him. Wars between packs always bring distress since it's hard to cover up mass disappearances. Then the hierarchy shifts."

"Anyway, I need a strong wolf to take Jacob's pack. Your wolf is strong and loyal. He protected you even though you aren't together. Put his life on the line for you. And even though we could've killed you, you tried to protect him the only way you knew how—by distraction."

"Whether you want to claim the bond or not, you are his, and he is yours. Loyalty is everything to us wolves. We mate for life. There is no greater loyalty than to our mates and our pack. I know you don't feel the connection since you're not a wolf, but you do love him. Being human, you can't be a true Luna, but I believe you could still manage it, from the short time I've spoken to you and from your interactions with Benjamin."

"What I'm about to offer is unheard of in our world. I'm willing to give Jacob's pack to Tim, allow him to run it with you as his Luna, if you want that. Our truce with Nathaniel will hold, and we will form a truce with Tim's pack. There will be peace."

"Peace benefits us all," Nicholas said softly, "but don't mistake this for charity. A strong Alpha nearby keeps my borders secure."

"Wow. I'm not sure what to say."

"One last thing to think about. Should you have a son, he will become the next Alpha. A daughter will become the next Luna. They'll need to be raised in the ways of the wolves and taught to lead. I believe you two are capable of doing this. You have fine traits for leaders—courage, compassion, loyalty."

Dominique was speechless. Nicholas would offer Tim a pack? Wanted her to be Luna?

"I'll leave you to your thoughts. I'll come back in a day or two."

"But Tim hasn't even woken up. He might not. Shouldn't you make sure he does first, and then ask if he wants to be an Alpha? I told Benjamin Tim hates being a wolf."

"It's my understanding that Tim was turned while he was with you and didn't know how to handle it. I don't think he hates being a wolf. I think he hates losing you because he became one. If he can have a life with you, be part of a pack, I think he'll flourish, not only as a wolf but as a leader."

"Jacob's pack was weak, with a weak leader," Nicholas continued. "Tim had to move up the ranks by fighting to the death. Judging by his power, he's fought ranked members before. That kind of strength doesn't come easy."

"He said Paul was Jacob's Beta. He killed him."

"That would explain it. His power will only grow by becoming Alpha. When he wakes, I'll ask him about becoming Alpha, *if* you've chosen him to be your mate."

"What difference does it make if I choose to be with him?"

"Like I said, wolves mate for life. He'll choose you and the baby first every time. If you're with someone else, he'll remain distracted, which makes him useless as an Alpha. I need someone whose loyalty lies with the pack. If you're with him, you'll be pack. And he deserves a mate who'll be there for him. But he's chosen you regardless of who you choose. I'll leave you to think all this over."

"Okay," Dominique whispered.

Nicholas left, and she sat there staring at Tim.

He'd chosen her. That had always been obvious. Her worry was resisting Nathaniel. She was angry now, and that anger kept her grounded, but she knew it wouldn't last forever.

Even now, she longed for Nathaniel. Craved his touch. She'd never cross that line and do that to Tim.

She crawled into the bed with Tim, snuggling into his warmth. His steady heartbeat pressed against her cheek, grounding her in a way nothing else could.

Why couldn't things ever be simple?

Sleep claimed her before she could find an answer.

Chapter 84

Dominique stood in a room, uncertain if she was still asleep or if she'd somehow been moved.

Tim was gone. A bed draped in black, gossamer curtains stood in the center of an all-white room.

She approached slowly, peering through the curtains at the figure lying there. Her hand trembled as she pulled them back.

"Nathaniel? Where are we? And how did we get here?"

"We're in your dream, my love," he said softly. "I projected us here. Nothing bad can happen to you. I just needed to see you… Though I wasn't sure if you wanted to see me."

He drew her into his arms. Sadness washed over her as she hugged him. The pull toward him tugged at her heart. Was this part of being his human servant?

He kissed her cheek and rested his head atop hers, holding her close.

"I can feel you pulling away from me, Dominique," he murmured. "I know I made a mistake binding you to me, but it can't be undone. I'll wait for you as long as it takes. I only hope one day you'll forgive me. I've lost everything—my home, the last traces of my family. You're all I have left. Even if it takes centuries, I'll still be here."

Pain stabbed her heart. He'd lost everything because of her. She'd brought Tim there. Jacob had attacked to reach them.

His family portrait, the book that held his legacy, could never be replaced.

She inhaled deeply. Earth, spice, and iron, *his scent*, wrapped around her like home. This dream felt too vivid. Was it a dream?

"Yes, my love," Nathaniel said, answering her thought. "This is a dream world, but our connection is real. We can feel, smell, and even taste here. I can come to your dreams whenever you wish, but if you don't want me to, I won't."

"I don't know what I want from you anymore," she said quietly. "But I'm not pushing Tim out of my life. He's the father of my baby, and I'm going to be with him… if he'll have me. And when I'm with someone, I'm faithful."

His sorrow swelled inside her, so heavy it felt like her own.

"I love you, Nathaniel," she whispered, "and that makes this harder. Because of the bond, I feel this pull I never had before. When you're gone, it's like something's missing. I don't know how I'm supposed to love Tim when I ache for you."

She closed her eyes, breathing him in.

"Nicholas is offering Jacob's pack to Tim if I'm his true mate," she said. "I don't know if Tim wants that… or me, once he learns I'm bound to you. But I want to give him this chance."

"He'll still want you," Nathaniel said gently. "Because I still want you, even knowing you'll be with him." His arms tightened around her. "You'll stay with him until he dies, but I'll always be waiting. If you change your mind, you'll know where to find me."

His kiss stole her breath.

"We're still business partners," he whispered against her lips. "But if you ever call me in your dreams, I'll come."

Could she resist him if he was always near? What if she dreamed of him again? Could she stay faithful even in her sleep?

"I can hear your thoughts, Dominique," he murmured. "If you dream of me and open yourself to me, I'll come. If you want me only in your dreams, I'll accept that."

She looked into his eyes. So dark, haunted, full of pain. It broke her. She kissed him again, fingers threading through his hair. His grip tightened as he deepened the kiss.

Breathless, she stepped back, tasting him on her lips. Her body trembled, craving more, but she couldn't. She had to end it.

"This is goodbye, Nathaniel. I love you… But I need to live my life with my family. Maybe one day I'll feel differently, but I hope I don't."

Agony tore through her, his and hers, blending until she couldn't tell them apart. It consumed her, stole her breath. Then suddenly, the feelings vanished.

Her eyes found his, calm now, unreadable.

"I've blocked our connection," he said quietly, "so you won't feel my emotions."

"You can do that?"

"Yes. For how long, I don't know. If it slips, I'm sorry. There may be times my emotions break through… or I might invade your dreams. But I'll try not to."

"Thank you," she whispered. "I never wanted to hurt you. But this choice is mine. It may not be the right one, but it's mine."

Something tugged at her consciousness.

"I think someone's trying to wake me up."

"Yes," he said softly. "Then goodbye for now. Since you're well, I'll leave the hospital too."

"Get the key to the club from Melissa," she said. "My office is sealed, no windows. It's the least I can do since I'm the reason you lost everything."

"You're not the reason," he said. "But I'll accept. Thank you."

"Stay as long as you need. I love you, Nathaniel."

The room began to dissolve around her. Nathaniel faded from sight. The floor vanished beneath her, and she fell. A scream ripped from her throat as she jolted awake, eyes flying open to the hospital room around her.

Chapter 85

Dominique's wide eyes turned to the hand shaking her arm.

"Wake up, sleepyhead."

Her gaze shot up to Tim's face. A tender smile curved his lips.

"You're awake!" She kissed him. "How are you feeling?"

"Amazing. How long have I been out?"

"I'm not really sure. I've been sleeping a lot, so maybe three days? I think I was brought in here yesterday. Benjamin said talking to you might help wake you up."

"I thought I was dreaming. It was so real. I had you in my arms, and what you said made me so happy." Tim sighed.

"Yeah? What did I say?"

She traced patterns on his chest, avoiding his eyes.

"You said we'd be together—a family. I want that to be true." Tim's arm tightened around her.

"And if I said it was true?"

"I'd be the luckiest man alive."

She kissed him, and he trailed his hand down her side, gripping her hip. Desire coursed through her as his hand slid inside her gown.

She pulled back. "You've got tubes coming out of everywhere. Don't start something you can't finish."

"My hand is free." He grinned, sliding it back under her gown.

She closed her eyes as his fingertips brushed over her nipple. When she opened them again, she was staring into eyes flecked with dark green. A shiver ran down her spine.

Tim's nostrils flared. "You smell delicious." His voice deepened. "Do you like what you see?"

Dominique was mesmerized by his wolf's eyes.

"Yes. I should be afraid since you look at me like prey, but… it does something to me."

"I tried not to look at you like this. Thought it might scare you off."

"Now you know exactly what it does to me."

His hand slipped between her thighs, fingers teasing her seam. She bit her lip to keep from moaning. He kissed her as his fingers slid inside her. She grabbed a handful of his hair, back arching, heat pooling in her stomach.

His fingers moved faster, curling inside her, only to slow when she was on the edge.

"Are you mine, Dominique?"

"Yes, I'm all yours," she gasped.

"Tell me. You know what I want to hear."

"I belong to you. Please," she begged. I'm all yours."

His fingers quickened again.

"You're marked by another. I can feel it. Are you truly mine, forever?"

"Yes!" Dominique cried out.

His fingers curled deep, his thumb circling her clit until she shattered in his arms.

Tim growled, "Mine."

He ran his nose up her throat, inhaling her scent.

"The things I'm going to do to you when we get out of here," he murmured.

She shuddered as his warm breath ghosted over her ear, his teeth nipping lightly.

The heart monitor began to beep rapidly.

"You're thinking too hard," Dominique chuckled.

"Something's hard, alright," Tim whispered.

She rolled her eyes, snuggling into him.

They lay there in each other's embrace until her thoughts drifted to the future.

"Have you ever thought about being Alpha before?"

Tim sighed. "I thought I was going to have to kill Jacob. That would've made me Alpha, but I never wanted that."

"What if you didn't have to kill anyone for it?"

"I never really gave it any thought. Why?"

"Nicholas mentioned possibly giving you Jacob's pack. He doesn't want to lose any of his people. But he said he wasn't sure about putting you in charge if we're not together. He thinks you'd be distracted if I were with someone else."

Tim stiffened. "Is that why you decided to be with me?"

She sat up and met his eyes—so much hurt there. She cupped his cheek and kissed him softly.

"No, Tim. I didn't decide to be with you because of Nicholas. I'd already decided before he talked to me. I want you to have a family—our family. I choose you. Do you hear me? I choose *you*."

Tim closed his eyes, silent. A single tear slid down his cheek. She wiped it away and kissed him, her heart heavy.

He wrapped his arms around her, kissing her deeply. When he pulled back, he ran his hand across her cheek.

"Thank you," he whispered.

"For what?"

"For choosing us. You're the only person who's ever cared about me. You're giving yourself to me, and I promise to honor you in every way. To protect and love you forever."

"Is it true that wolves mate for life?"

"Yes."

"Am I your mate?"

"It's my understanding that you know when you've found your mate. There's some pull to them. I was in love with you when I was turned. My love never changed."

"So, you're not sure? Is it different now that you're a wolf?"

"I'd have to say yes. Even though we were over, I couldn't stop thinking about you. You were always the one. My wolf took over, and I was never able to love anyone else. I couldn't even bring myself to care about Roxy. I guess he chose you as his mate."

Dominique's heart fluttered. She was his mate. A bright smile curved her lips as she snuggled deeper into his warmth.

They lay there enjoying being together until Tim tightened his grip on her. Someone knocked on the door.

"Come in," Tim called.

Benjamin walked in.

"Welcome back to the land of the living," Benjamin said with a grin.

"Thanks, Doc. I actually feel amazing."

Tim's grip on Dominique eased, his body finally relaxing.

Benjamin checked Tim's vitals, listened to his heart, and then pulled the gown up.

Dominique's eyes traveled over his body. He was completely healed. Their healing never ceased to amaze her. When her eyes met his, his wolf's eyes were on her. She blushed and Tim grinned.

"Well, Tim, you're in perfect health. You'll be discharged today."

"That's good. I have some things to do later," Tim said, smirking at Dominique.

Benjamin cleared his throat. "Dominique, before you go, I'd like to do a quick prenatal checkup. And I want you to return here for your prenatal care and delivery."

"Okay."

Dominique slid onto her bed. Benjamin took her vitals, listened to her heart and lungs, nodded, and walked out of the room.

He came back with an ultrasound machine.

Dominique laid back.

Benjamin pulled the sheet down to her hips, then tucked the gown under her breasts. Benjamin chuckled at the growl from Tim.

"It's okay, Tim. I've done this a lot over the years. I have no intentions to make a move on your mate. You'll be happy in a minute."

Benjamin put gel on her belly, then moved the wand over her stomach. Dominique watched the screen. She didn't see anything but dark space.

"See this?" Benjamin pointed to the screen. "This is your baby. It's small right now, about the size of a pea. You'll be able to see it better later. I just wanted to make sure there were no issues from the other day before I released you. Would you like a picture?"

Dominique's breath hitched. Tears filled her eyes as she whispered, "Yes."

Benjamin nodded and left.

Dominique moved back onto Tim's bed. He hugged her, wiping the tears from her face. She smiled at him and his heart swelled with love.

A soft knock sounded, but before Tim could answer, the door opened. Nicholas walked in, smiling, and handed Dominique the pictures.

Tim's shoulders tensed when Nicholas's hand brushed Dominique's.

Dominique smiled. "Thank you, Nicholas."

"Tim, I'm Nicholas, Alpha of the White Moon pack."

"I know who you are, Alpha. Jacob didn't like you at all. Greetings," Tim said, sitting up.

Tim bowed his head. Nicholas patted Tim's shoulder, but his smile was for Dominique.

Tim was watching her reaction. She shrugged. Nicholas was a good-looking man. Tim would have to get over the jealousy if that was the issue.

"Calm yourself, wolf. I'm not after your mate. I'm here to make you an offer."

"Dominique mentioned maybe taking over Jacob's pack. Why would you want me to do that?"

"I don't want to give my pack members up. You belonged to that pack. You know the members, how they work, and frankly, I don't want more territory. It's a headache. You've already taken out your Gamma and your Beta. Natural order would have been the Alpha next. I've dug into you. You were Jacob's enforcer at one point. I think brutality is too nice of a word for what you did."

Tim glanced at Dominique. She kept her expression neutral. These were things Tim hadn't told her about. Now she knew why.

"You changed, gave up being Jacob's enforcer, and I believe I know why." Nicholas looked at Dominique.

"I never wanted to be Jacob's enforcer, but my anger controlled me back then. I can't lie. I liked the release it gave me. But I had to be better. I couldn't live without Dominique, so I changed."

"This tells me more about you than anything else. You didn't care about power, about ruling. You wanted something far more precious. Loyalty. Love. Those came first for you. These are the markings of a true leader. Anyone can rule through fear; that takes nothing. But to earn respect, to have a pack follow you because of who you are? That's real strength."

Nicholas paused before continuing. "I want a neighboring Alpha I can trust. Someone we can rely on to help protect our borders and our people. You don't drink or use drugs. Your mind stays clear, and that will help you clean out the rot from Bad Moon. Just think about it. Talk it over with your mate, and let me know what you decide."

"Thank you, Alpha. I'll let you know soon."

Nicholas nodded once and left the room.

Tim glanced down at Dominique, curled against his side. He pressed a kiss to the top of her head, and she tilted her face up for another. They stayed like that, wrapped in each other, silent but dreaming of the future, until the nurses came in to discharge them.

Chapter 86

Tim and Dominique sat in the cabin on Nicholas's land. Nicholas had asked them to stay for a few days until Tim made his decision.

Dominique paced the room, checking every corner.

"Dominique, come sit down. Why are you so jittery?"

"Because I don't like being cooped up somewhere I don't know. Why do we have to stay here?"

"Nicholas hasn't officially claimed Jacob's pack yet. If someone steps out of line, he'll be forced to attack and take it. He wants to avoid that until I've decided. Can we just humor him?"

Dominique sighed and sat beside him. Tim pulled her onto his lap, kissing her before burying his face in her hair, breathing her in. Her scent was addicting. Roses and oakmoss. It called to his wolf.

"Have you thought about what you're going to do?" she asked.

"No. All I've thought about is you and the baby. Our future as a family."

"Nicholas said to discuss it with your mate. Do you really want my opinion? I'm just a human. Would anything I say matter to the pack?"

"You're my mate, so it matters. My wolf and I agree on that one. We've chosen you. Besides, you're not just a human.

You're bound to a vampire, and the way you've adapted to our world tells me you were meant to be in it."

"I never thought about it like that."

"Regardless, you belong to me. We're equals. If I'm Alpha, you're Luna. A Luna is a matriarchal leader of a pack, the counterpart to the patriarchal leader of the pack. But, have you thought about what it means for me to lead the pack?"

"No, not really. Why don't you tell me?"

"I'd have to attend meetings that could last for days, which means you'd lead while I'm gone. The Beta would help, but it's still a heavy role. And when members cross lines, there are punishments. I'm not sure you'd want to see that side of me. Then there's the baby. Our child would be next in line to take over one day. Is that what you want for them? For us?"

He watched her think, heart thudding, afraid she might pull away.

"If you lead, I don't think you'll need to punish your members," she said finally. "You're not cruel like Jacob was. I can be a friend to the wolves. I'm with you, whatever you decide. If you want to take the pack, I'll stand beside you. You've always longed for a family. Why can't the pack be part of that?"

"I have all I need with you and the baby."

"But the pack could be like an extended family. Wouldn't you like that?"

"I've always wanted to belong somewhere… but you already give me that."

"Don't you want to feel like you belong to your pack?"

"Yes. My wolf is a pack animal. I always felt like an outsider in Jacob's pack. He craves the connection to the pack, but I only care about my connection to you."

"Then give in to both cravings," Dominique said softly. "I'm here, Tim. I'm not going anywhere, no matter what you decide. And as for the baby… with a strong leader to learn from, they'll become one too."

Tim kissed her, heart full. He was no longer alone, no longer the screwup no one wanted. He held her close, savoring the warmth of her faith in him and the promise of the future they were building together.

Chapter 87

Tim had Nicholas take him to his house, where he retrieved Dominique's engagement ring. Then they went to Dominique's house, where Melissa met them.

"What's going on, Tim? Dominique said you guys were injured, but you look fine to me."

"We're both fine, Melissa. A lot happened, but if Dominique hasn't told you, then I won't either. The only thing I'm going to say is that I plan on marrying Dominique, so you'll have to get over your attitude toward me."

"What?!" Melissa exclaimed.

"Melissa, you're too much of a busybody. Just chill out and all will be revealed to you in time, okay?"

Melissa's eyes narrowed. "I know you didn't just go there."

Nicholas stepped inside, and Melissa went quiet. His blue eyes met hers, and he flashed a grin. She sucked in a breath and held it.

Tim shook his head and walked to the bedroom. He gathered some of Dominique's clothes and went back to the living room.

Nicholas and Melissa were still staring at each other. He cleared his throat, and Nicholas's gaze shifted to him. Tim nodded toward the door. Nicholas threw another grin at Melissa before they left.

"If I'd known all it took to shut Melissa up was to have you come in, I would've done that in the first place."

"Who is she?" Nicholas asked.

"She's Dominique's best friend, a busybody from hell, but she's always been there for Dominique. Why do you ask?"

"I've never met a human I was interested in before. When I looked into her eyes, my wolf spoke to me. He wants her. I wonder what that means," Nicholas said thoughtfully.

"It might mean she's your mate. I'm not going to pretend to know what it means to recognize your mate because I was already in love with mine before I became a wolf. I think my wolf just took that love over. But maybe you've found yours? If it's Melissa, then I feel bad for you." Tim laughed.

"Nicholas, I'm not sure what you're thinking, but Melissa isn't one for games. We don't get along because of what I did to Dominique, but she's a good person. I don't think she could handle being with a werewolf. Think this over carefully.

"You're not Alpha yet, Tim. Watch what you say," Nicholas warned, though his tone was light. "But I am considering carefully. My pack doesn't usually mate with humans. That's why my wolf's reaction surprised me."

"Well, I'll stay out of that one, but at least I told you about her beforehand."

"So, she's a challenge? I like a challenge."

"Oh boy. I didn't tell you that so you'd go after her for the challenge of it."

"No worries. I don't go after women because they're a challenge. That just makes it more interesting. Besides, I can sense what people are really like. If I didn't think she could handle it, I wouldn't bother. I'm looking for something long-term. I no longer want one-night stands."

"I know what you mean," Tim said, pulling the ring from his pocket.

"Are you planning on making Dominique your Luna and wife?" Nicholas asked.

"Yes, I am. I don't know if she'll accept, but I'm not going to stop asking until she does." Tim grinned.

"Will you have a traditional wedding?"

"Well, I think Dominique would like one, but honestly, I have no way of doing that. I don't have any friends. There's no one I can ask to be my best man. Her brother, Post, may do it, but I doubt it. Her parents are dead, so he'll have to walk her down the aisle."

"Tim, you're part of a pack. We have an alliance. I'll gladly stand by your side as your best man. The pack is family and friends. You must learn this if you're to take care of your own. You can have the wedding at my place. It's a beautiful country setting, and the whole pack can come if you wish. When we have the ceremony to make you Alpha and Luna, the pack will definitely be there. Is there anyone you think would make a good Beta?"

"Honestly, no. Jacob's pack was weak. The ones with any real power fought with him, and you killed them. What's left is barely surviving. I need to build it up again. Maybe I can reach out to other packs, find members who want to move up the chain but don't want to challenge their current Alphas. There might be rogues who want to belong somewhere."

"That's a good idea. The first of many you'll have as a great leader. Let's get you back to your mate so you can propose," Nicholas said with a grin.

When they got back to Nicholas's place, Tim walked toward the cabins. He opened the door to find Dominique wasn't there.

She didn't know anyone here, so where had she gone? He stepped back outside and shifted, following her scent to a clearing.

There were wolves everywhere. Mothers sitting on blankets, children playing in the grass. His gaze landed on Dominique. She was running, laughing, as a small child chased her. The sound made his chest tighten.

The child stopped running, bouncing on her feet, while Dominique reached to grab her, both of them laughing.

A woman called the child over, and Dominique followed, sitting with the group of women.

He lingered at the edge of the trees, listening.

"Do you want to become a wolf after the baby is born?" one woman asked

"No."

"How will you become Luna without being a wolf?"

"Tim said I could be Luna regardless. I'm not sure I can become a wolf."

"Do you even want to be Luna of a pack?"

"If Tim wants me at his side as Luna, yes. I'm new to all this, so I think I could use a few lessons on wolves. Would one of you be willing to teach me?"

"I'd be happy to. Who knows? You might decide to become one of us later."

Tim's chest swelled with pride. Dominique was willing to learn about his world. He padded toward the group, and the clearing grew quiet.

Dominique looked around until her eyes found him. She'd seen his wolf before, but never looked at him like this. Her gaze searched over him, memorizing him. Her breath hitched as she met his eyes. He licked his muzzle. Her eyes widened, her breathing quickened.

He nudged her chest with his head. She shivered when he licked her neck. Her fingers sank into his fur, and he ached to mindlink her. Would she be able to hear him once he marked her?

Dominique stood, her fingers trailing down his side. Desire coursed through him. He lay down and huffed.

She raised an eyebrow, and one of the women giggled.

"Child, he wants you to climb on his back," the woman said with a knowing smile. "If you were a wolf, you could run together. For now, he wants you to ride him. We wolves feel things like you do, and some gestures... cause certain reactions."

Dominique blinked between the woman and Tim. Her mouth formed an O shape. His muzzle curved into something like a grin. The women laughed. Dominique blushed.

She swung her leg over his back, gripping his thick scruff.

He stood and howled, and the women joined in. Then he took off toward the cabin.

When they reached it, he lay down so she could slide off. She ran her fingers through his fur again, and he panted, laughing in his wolfish way.

Her blush did him in. He coughed out a rough sound before shifting back.

"Sorry," she said softly. "I didn't realize petting you like that would… cause issues for you."

"No worries. You can touch me all you want. I'm all yours."

Tim scooped her up and carried her into the cabin, heading straight for the bedroom. He laid her on the bed, lifting her shirt and pressing kisses over her stomach. He undressed her slowly, worshipping every inch of skin he revealed.

His mouth found her breasts while his hands explored the rest of her. He trailed kisses down her body until he was between her thighs, tasting her. He teased until she was trembling, on the edge, then stopped.

"Not yet. This time's going to last."

He flipped her onto her stomach, massaging her shoulders and back until she melted beneath his touch.

He rubbed his cock against her, her warmth slick against him. She pushed back instinctively.

His fingers slipped beneath her, rubbing her clit, while his tongue traced her spine. One hand cupped her breast, rolling her nipple between his fingers until it hardened.

Dominique moaned, arching off the bed. "Please," she whispered.

He thrust into her, growling against her back. "So wet for me."

She shivered when he nipped her ear.

"I know you carry Nathaniel's mark. I don't like it. You're mine. My mate. You should bear my mark," he whispered against her skin.

"What does that mean?" Dominique murmured.

He flipped her over, thrusting back in. He licked the hollow of her collarbone.

"My mark would go here. You have no wolf to mark me, but you can bite me in the same spot."

Her eyes fluttered closed as he quickened his pace. When she tightened around him, he slowed.

"Tim, please," she begged.

"I'll mark you when you cum. Do you understand?"

She met his gaze, breathless. "Yes."

He took her harder, faster. When she began to tremble and cry out, he bit down. Her nails dug into his back as her teeth broke his skin.

He groaned, overwhelmed with pleasure as he released inside her. He licked the wound, sealing it, then rested his head against her chest.

'I love you,' he thought.

"I love you, too," Dominique replied.

His head shot up. She raised her brows, smiling. He felt the bond hum between them. Could she hear him?

'Can you hear me?' he asked silently.

'Yes.'

"I can't believe it! You can hear me."

"Well, of course, I can, silly. I'm not deaf," Dominique laughed.

"No, that's not what I meant. You can hear me through the link. I didn't know if you'd be able to since you aren't a wolf."

"Oh! When I heard can you hear me… I thought it was Nathaniel for a moment, because your lips didn't move."

Tim growled. "No," he said, voice flat. "We've completed the mate bond."

"Sorry. I didn't realize." Dominique looked sheepish.

"No more talk about *him.*"

"No. From now on, it's all about us."

Dominique smiled, and he laid his head on her chest, listening to her heartbeat. Her fingers combed through his hair.

"You're happy," she whispered. "I can feel pure joy coming from you."

"Part of the mate bond is feeling each other's emotions."

"I'm glad you're happy."

"You make me happy."

He rolled them onto their sides and held her until they drifted off to sleep.

Chapter 88

Dominique woke up to a grumbling stomach. The rich scent of spices, meat, potatoes, and vegetables filled the air, making her mouth water. At least she didn't have to cook this time.

Her heart skipped, breath quickened, then slowly evened out. Would she always feel Nathaniel wake? The thought unsettled her, a quiet echo of something she wished she could forget. She pushed it aside and got up, stretching away the heaviness of sleep.

Grabbing Tim's shirt from the floor, she slipped it on and padded into the kitchen. Her eyes widened. Tim was naked, packing containers into a picnic basket, muscles rippling with each movement. She leaned against the doorframe, admiring the view.

She'd never been that comfortable in her own skin, but watching him, so effortlessly confident, sent a rush of heat through her. He didn't miss her stare, flashing a sly grin as he worked.

When he finally finished, he walked over and kissed her. She smiled. "Good evening to you, too."

"It's always good when you're around," he murmured.

"So… are you going somewhere?" she asked, eyeing the basket.

"We're going somewhere," Tim corrected with a grin. "I just have to grab a few more things, then we'll be ready to go.

By the way, I like the way my shirt looks on you. Any chance I can convince you to wear just that?"

Dominique laughed. "No way. It's long enough to cover me, but one wrong move and you'll see everything."

"Well, no one's going to see you where we're going. It's private. Come on, humor me." He wiggled his eyebrows.

"Not happening. I'm at least putting on underclothes," she said, still laughing.

"How about just underwear under the shirt?" he teased, wrapping his arms around her.

"You trying to get lucky?"

"I'm already lucky. But sex would be nice too."

"Alright, fine. Just this once, I'll humor you. But if we see anyone, you're in big trouble."

"I'll take it." He turned her around and gave her a playful slap on the butt. "Now go get ready while I grab the rest of the stuff."

Dominique slipped on her underwear and shoes. When she came back, Tim stood in the living room holding two baskets and a coil of rope, still naked. She raised an eyebrow.

He grinned mischievously and walked outside.

"What are you planning?" she asked, following him.

"I'm going to take you somewhere as a wolf. I'll carry these baskets tied to me, and you'll ride on my back. Okay?"

"You're serious?"

"Yes. Don't you want to ride me?" he said, voice dripping with innuendo.

Dominique shook her head at the double meaning.

Tim shifted before her eyes, the transformation both powerful and mesmerizing.

'Take the rope,' his voice echoed in her mind. 'Tie the baskets. One on each side.'

"I can hear you even though you've shifted."

'Yes. You're connected to both of us now through the mate bond.'

She tied the baskets carefully, then climbed onto his back, gripping his thick fur. Tim took off running, and she laid against him, closing her eyes as the wind whipped through her hair.

Joy and freedom flooded her. His emotions flowed through the bond. Her heart swelled. She envied his freedom.

When he slowed, she opened her eyes and gasped. A small river cut through a clearing filled with roses, tulips, lavender, tiger lilies, and daisies. The mingling scents made her dizzy with wonder.

Tim lowered himself, and she slid off, untying the baskets. He shifted back, grabbed a pair of jeans, and spread a blanket.

He lit candles, unpacked dishes and food containers, and poured two glasses of grape juice.

Tears pricked her eyes. Tim had never been the romantic type, but this was beautiful. When he finally sat beside her, she leaned in and kissed him softly.

"This is beautiful, Tim. Thank you."

"Only the best for my mate," he said with a grin.

"How'd you find this place? Are we still on Nicholas' property?"

"Yes. I told him I wanted to do something special for you. He brought me here while you were asleep. I didn't want to wake you."

"Oh," she murmured.

"Are you upset?"

"No. Just surprised. You've never done anything this romantic before. You've really messed up now, though. I'll be expecting things like this all the time."

Tim chuckled. "That won't be a problem. I'm a romantic guy; I just didn't think you wanted the sappy kind. I never really knew how to show it."

"Well, now you know. I like romance and cuddling. You don't have to be afraid with me. I know who and what you are, and I still love you. That's all that matters. With love, anything's possible."

Tim fidgeted with his glass. "I'm glad you said that. There's something I want to talk to you about."

"You seem nervous. That's usually not good."

"It's not bad. I told Nicholas I'm going to take over the pack. The ceremony's in two days. I'll become Alpha, and I want you to be my Luna. If you agree, we'll both be crowned at the ceremony."

"I heard you tell the women that if I wanted you at my side, you'd be my Luna. My Luna is my friend, my confidant, my lover. No one but you could ever fit."

Dominique's stomach tightened. She hadn't thought about what it would mean if someone else stood beside him as Luna.

"I don't want anyone else to be your Luna."

"Good," he said softly, "because I don't want anyone else. I want you to be my Luna… and my wife."

Tim reached into his pocket and slowly dropped to one knee.

"I know I haven't been the best man, but I'm trying every day to be better. To be the man you deserve. I want to be a good husband, a good father, and a good Alpha. I love you, always have."

"The day I saw you still had this ring, I knew you still loved me, too. I knew right then and there I was going to ask you to marry me again. I picked it because it symbolized hope, and I hope you'll spend the rest of your life with me. I want all of you, Dom, and I hope you'll accept all of me, mistakes and all. Will you make me the happiest man in the world and be my wife?"

Tears streamed down her cheeks. She threw her arms around him, her sobs hot against his skin.

"Is that a yes?" he whispered.

"Yes," Dominique whispered back.

Tim laughed softly, stood, and spun her around. He slid the ring onto her finger and kissed her, deeply, tenderly. When he pulled back, he rested his forehead against hers.

Joy and warmth bloomed in her chest, mingling with his emotions through their bond.

"I love you, Dominique," he whispered. "You don't know how happy you've made me."

"Actually," she said, touching his heart, "I think I do. I can feel it."

"I want you to always know how loved you are. How loved you'll always be."

"Then you'll feel the same from me. You'll never doubt that you're loved. You'll never be alone again, Tim. I'll always make things work. That's my promise."

"Thank you. I promise the same. No more secrets."

His words hit her harder than he could ever know.

"Now," she said with a teary smile, "let's eat before it gets cold."

They ate beneath a blanket of stars. When they finished, Tim packed everything away except the blanket.

They walked hand in hand, sharing quiet conversation, before returning to the blanket.

There, under the moonlight, they made love, hearts and souls entwined, no longer fractured but whole.

Later, back at the cabin, Dominique fell asleep in Tim's arms, wrapped in peace she hadn't known in years.

Chapter 89

Tim and Dominique followed Nicholas to the clearing.

Tim wore only a pair of shorts, his chest streaked with war paint. Dominique's shirt stopped just below her breasts, paired with boy shorts. The women had painted moons and wolves across her skin to represent the pack since she couldn't shift.

The closer they got, the tighter her chest became. Anxiety slithered through her veins as her gaze darted over the crowd. There were so many people. Too many.

Tim squeezed her hand. She forced a smile, and he returned it, though a shadow crossed his eyes. She lifted a brow in silent question.

'Dominique,' his voice drifted through her mind.

'Yes?'

'I've never been to one of these ceremonies. Jacob was already Alpha and never took a Luna. Nicholas told me what happens when the Alpha and Luna go through this ritual. Did the ladies explain it to you?'

'Yes. Since I'm not a wolf, I can't do the traditional things. I can't run with the pack, so I'll ride on your back. They said the paint represents the pack assembling under the moon, becoming one.'

'What about the rest of it? Did they go over what happens after the pack run?'

'They said there's a celebration. A claiming of the Luna to show she belongs to the Alpha and no other.'

Her brows furrowed. She didn't quite understand that part.

'If you're going to back out, you need to do it before the celebration begins. Once it starts, all rituals will be observed. I'll apologize now. I didn't know what the rituals consisted of.'

'Why would I back out? It's just a celebration. No big deal.'

Whatever Tim was about to say was cut off when Nicholas gestured to two thrones carved from stone. Once they were seated, Nicholas nodded and stepped forward.

'Dominique, the ritual, it's a mat—'

Tim was cut off by Nicholas. Dominique gripped the stone seat, her pulse quickening. Whatever Tim had been about to say, it sounded like a warning.

"Tonight, we gather to crown the new Alpha and Luna of the Bad Moon pack. We've always observed the passing of leadership through ritual. I killed the Alpha of the Bad Moon pack. It's my right to take or to pass it on. I now forfeit that right to my successor. I, Nicholas Torrain, Alpha of the White Moon pack, relinquish my power over the Bad Moon pack to Tim Lithe."

Nicholas dropped to one knee and bowed his head to Tim.

'Tim,' she whispered through their link. Nothing. No recognition, no answer—just silence.

A howl split the night, echoed by the others. A gust of wind burst between Tim and Nicholas, whipping her hair around her face before slamming into Tim. His body arched, twisting, not shifting but tearing, shredding, until his wolf stood before Nicholas.

Nicholas rose. "Bad Moon pack, your Alpha!" he announced.

He placed a crown of flowers over Tim's ears. The wolf's answering howl sent a tremor racing down Dominique's spine.

Tim's wolf turned to her at the same time Nicholas did. Her palms were clammy and her heart was thudding against her ribcage. She tried the link again, desperate. Nothing. His soft green eyes were gone, replaced with a glowing, dark, unearthly green.

"Tim's solely a wolf until the ritual is complete," Nicholas said quietly. "Once he claims his pack and then his Luna, his consciousness will return. His wolf knows you as his mate, so there's no danger. Are you ready, Dominique?"

She wasn't ready. She was terrified. She swallowed hard and nodded, pushing her fear down.

Nicholas held out his hand, and she took it. He turned her toward the crowd as Tim's wolf pressed against her back, then paced. Nicholas guided her to kneel.

"Bad Moon pack," Nicholas declared, "I present to you Dominique Reed. Your Alpha has chosen her as his mate. Tonight, he will claim her as his Luna!"

He placed a crown of flowers atop her head.

A chorus of howls rose in answer, and a chill swept through her. The word claiming echoed in her mind. Did it mean what she thought it did? Was Tim supposed to claim her body? As a man or… as a wolf?

Her stomach twisted. Sex, she could handle. But not with a wolf.

Was this a public claiming? A private one? When Tim asked if she wanted to back out, she should've agreed right then and there. Those damn women hadn't explained shit to her. They knew and said nothing.

Tim's wolf pressed against her body, drawing her attention to him. Her anxiety skyrocketed looking at the sheer size of his wolf. He licked her stomach, looking at her with his wolf eyes. It sent another shiver down her spine.

There was a pull in the air, a strange, magnetic thread that tugged her toward him. Her hand moved on its own, sinking into his thick fur. Her vision blurred as her fingers slid down his side.

His wolf turned its head, keeping their eyes locked. She licked her lips. His wolf licked his muzzle, his lips peeling back to reveal razor-sharp canines. That grin made her tremble with fear and excitement. Was this what wolves felt from their bond?

"Lower down so I can get on your back," she said, her voice distant, not her own.

His wolf obeyed, crouching low. She grabbed his scruff and swung onto his back, her body moving without conscious thought.

He stepped down from the stone platform and into the sea of wolves. The connection between them pulsed stronger. Her mind wasn't her own anymore.

His howl vibrated through her bones. One tore from her throat in response as the pack joined in, their voices rising in one deafening unity. He ran, the pack, and Nicholas running behind.

'You're mine, Luna,' the wolf's voice rumbled through her head. 'Tonight, you'll become one with me and with the pack. What you feel is natural. It's what your wolf would feel. Tim is gone until I claim you. Once you are my Luna, I'll allow him to return.'

'But I'm not a wolf,' she protested. 'How can you claim something that doesn't exist?'

There was no reply. He only ran faster, wind tearing through her hair.

Desire coiled in her belly, and she couldn't tell if it belonged to her or the beast beneath her.

When they reached the clearing where Tim had proposed to her, the wolf stopped. The pack fanned out around them in a perfect circle.

He lowered himself so she could slide off. The moment her feet touched the ground, he spun, eyes glowing like emerald fire. The predatory look froze her in place.

Her fear seemed to thrill him. She stumbled back, but the wolves behind her blocked her retreat.

Tim's wolf lunged toward her, and she stumbled back, only for the circle of wolves behind her to shove her forward again. Her heart thundered against her ribs. She screamed as his teeth grazed her thigh. Not biting, just catching the fabric of her shorts. The material tore easily, falling away in shreds.

Heat flooded her face. Panic and disbelief tangled inside her. She turned to run again, but he was suddenly there, blocking her path. She collided with his massive chest, the impact stealing her breath.

'Once the ritual starts, it doesn't end until it's complete. You need to submit to your Alpha. Just lie down and it will be over before you know it.'

'Are you insane?' she gasped. 'You're a fucking wolf.'

His eyes softened. 'I promise I won't hurt you, ever. Trust me.'

She laid down, her body tense. He hovered over her, staring into her eyes.

He nudged the shirt above her breasts so she was fully exposed. She closed her eyes, breaths coming quick.

His weight settled on her, but not the weight of a wolf, but of a man.

"Open your eyes, Luna."

She forced her eyes open to find his wolf's eyes staring back at her. He had complete control over Tim's body.

"You're mine, Luna. You will belong to no other. The pack members will obey you. Tim chose to love you, but I chose you as our mate. Whenever you need me, call me through our bond. I will always come for you."

He thrust into her, his pace punishing. His eyes changed, one light green, one dark green, and she knew she was looking into both Tim's and his wolf's eyes.

She blocked out the wolves around them and focused on his eyes.

He kissed her, their tongues clashing for dominance.

His rhythm became brutal. He kissed and licked along her jaw, down her throat, to her collarbone.

She tightened around him, and his teeth pierced her mark. She shattered under him, screaming her pleasure into the night. She bit down on his collarbone, her teeth breaking his skin.

Tim howled as he spilled his seed inside her. The other wolves howled in unison.

A pressure inside her mind broke, and Tim's voice floated through. 'Pack, greet your Luna.'

A chorus of reverent whispers answered.

'Luna.'

'Welcome, Luna.'

Tim hauled her up, wrapping his arms around her until her back pressed against his chest.

"Tim, I'm naked," she whispered.

"We're all naked, Dom. Nudity means nothing to wolves. Animals don't wear clothes, after all," he murmured back.

"That doesn't make me feel better."

He chuckled softly. "Forget about the nudity. Look around you."

He spun them in a slow circle. All the wolves had their heads bowed and one leg bent in a sign of respect. Her eyes caught on Nicholas, and her breath hitched. An Alpha was bowing to *them*.

Tim stopped turning, then shifted. When he lowered himself, she climbed onto his back. He circled the wolves once more until they parted, opening a path.

He walked through to a chorus of howls. He howled in return and took off into a run.

She threw her head back and laughed, wind whipping through her hair. She didn't know what the future held, but one thing was certain. She was Luna now, and carrying the future of the pack.

Epilogue

Dominique fussed with her dress, unhappy with the way it looked on her.

Melissa knocked her hands away and shoved her into the chair. As soon as she started doing Dominique's makeup, Dominique's fingers found the hem of her dress again.

"If you don't leave that dress alone, I'm going to make you go out there naked. Would you enjoy that?" Melissa asked.

Frustration and nerves tightened Dominique's chest.

"No," she murmured. "I just wouldn't go out. The dress doesn't look right, Mel."

"It looks fantastic. Now shut up and let me finish your makeup. Nicholas and I worked extremely hard to plan this wedding. Everything looks beautiful, including you. You're going to go out there and enjoy this beautiful fall night."

A crisp breeze slipped through the open window, carrying the scent of leaves and roses. Dominique wished it would carry her nerves away, too.

"Mel…" she whined.

"No. I wasn't happy when you told me you were marrying Tim, but I accepted it after seeing the change in both of you. I was hoping you'd choose Nathaniel, but that didn't happen. So, you're going to go out there, marry the love of your life, and be happy about it."

Melissa brushed a soft layer of eyeshadow across Dominique's lids. "Tim is like a completely different person nowadays. You're both happy, and he'd probably kill himself if you ditched him at the altar."

"That's not funny. But… Tim has changed since he became a parent."

"Nah. He changed right after the fire. He just kept improving from there. The day I let him into your place, I was ready to kill him when he said he was going to marry you. But when you two came back together after that week? He was more authoritative, more attentive to you, and he even dealt with my bullshit."

Melissa smiled. "The way he was with you during your pregnancy? God help the fool who tried to make you do anything besides sit there and look pretty. He never missed a prenatal appointment, never missed a checkup once Michael was born. And the look on his face when he told us you had a boy? Pure joy."

She pouted. "Still don't understand why you chose to deliver at home and then kept me out."

"I told you I was comfortable with the doctor. He's like a midwife."

"Anyway." Melissa shook her head. "The point is, Tim did a complete turnaround. Did you know he asked me and Post for permission to marry you? For a minute, I thought Post was going to kill him."

Dominique laughed. "I didn't know that."

"Yeah. We grilled him for over an hour. Finally, Post caved because Tim came to him like a man. I caved when he started talking about your future."

Melissa stepped back, satisfied. She placed the veil in Dominique's hair and pulled it gently over her face.

Dominique stood and faced the full-length mirror. Her reflection barely looked like her—radiant, nervous, glowing.

Her dress was an ivory satin A-line with a sweetheart neckline and a lace-up corset leading to a full skirt and long train. Royal blue lines circled the neckline and hem, while roses and Fleur de Lis patterns were embroidered across the fabric.

Melissa's eyes filled with tears. She gave Dominique a watery smile. Dominique hugged her tightly before pulling back quickly.

"Now look what you've done! You made me ruin my makeup," Melissa sniffled.

Dominique laughed. Tim had wanted to get married while she was pregnant, but she'd refused, not wanting to look like a whale walking down the aisle. Once Michael was born, she started planning and getting her body back in shape.

Tim had chased her through the woods every day, exercised with her, cooked, and helped with Michael so she could sleep.

Now, with Michael over a year old, she finally had everything she'd wanted. A family. A future.

Tim had never complained about waiting to marry her. He'd said they were already bound as Alpha and Luna, but she wanted to be Mrs. Lithe too.

Her thoughts strayed to Nathaniel. She'd learned to keep him out of her head when she was awake, but dreams were another story. His presence brushed the edge of her thoughts like a whisper she couldn't silence.

She shook her head. *Today is mine and Tim's day.*

Melissa opened the door. "I think we're ready to go."

Nicholas signaled the band, then held out his arm for Melissa, who cast him a shy smile—an expression that didn't fit her at all.

Dominique wondered if something was going on between them.

Dominique peeked out the door just enough to see Tim under an arch of red and blue roses intertwined with blue calla lilies. She scanned the crowd, but her breath caught when she felt Nathaniel's presence. She couldn't see him, but she knew he was there.

She hadn't invited him, but he knew she was getting married. She prayed he wouldn't cause a scene.

Post offered his arm, and she took it, her heart thudding. The scent of roses and lilies floated through the cool air as her satin slippers glided across the plush grass.

Tim's grin widened as she approached. Tears pricked her eyes.

Under the arch, Post placed her hand in Tim's.

"Who gives this woman away?" the preacher asked.

"I do," Post replied, kissing her cheek before sitting.

Tim mouthed, *I love you.*

The ceremony began.

When it was time for the vows, Tim said,

"Dominique, I've loved you from the moment I laid eyes on you. I haven't always been the best man, but you loved me through it all. You've remained strong, loving, and perfect. I promise to be the best man, father, and husband I can be. Whether we're having good days or bad, I'll love you through them all."

Tears slipped down her cheeks.

"Tim," she began softly, "we've been through so much in the past two years. Things that forced us to change and grow. I've seen you become a better man, a great father, and a true leader. I promise to always love you, stand beside you, and remind you every day that you are my heart. I can't promise forever, but I can promise you the rest of our lives."

They exchanged rings.

"I now pronounce you man and wife. You may kiss the bride."

Tim threw back her veil and kissed her passionately. Cheers erupted. Tim rested his forehead against hers.

"You're so damn beautiful," Tim whispered against her lips. "I didn't know if I'd make it through the ceremony without kissing you."

"You sweet talker." She laughed and kissed him again.

At the reception, Dominique refused wine when the waiter offered it.

"No, thank you."

"Dominique, you can drink," Tim murmured in her ear. "I don't mind."

"It's okay. I don't want any."

"You always have a glass of champagne or wine to celebrate. Just because I don't drink doesn't mean you can't."

"Tim, you're not the reason I'm not drinking."

He frowned. "What do you mean?"

"Do you want part of your wedding gift now?" she asked, teasing.

Tim grinned. "I can wait until tonight."

"Yeah, I can see that look on your face. You're dying to know." She laughed, whispering something to Melissa, who disappeared into the cabin. When she returned, she handed Dominique a small box.

"Open it," Dominique said, handing it to Tim.

He tore off the wrapping. Inside were a pair of tiny baby booties and a pregnancy test with two pink lines.

For a heartbeat, the room went silent. Then Tim grabbed her, kissed her hard, and lifted her into his arms.

"Hey, everyone! Let the toasts begin! Here's to my beautiful wife, Dominique—the mother of my son and our unborn baby! I'm going to be a daddy again!"

Cheers and laughter filled the tent.

Dominique smiled, warmth flooding her chest. Tim looked at her with pure love, his joy spilling through their bond and into her heart.

He pulled her close, his lips brushing her ear. "Thank you," he whispered. "You gave me a son, became my wife, and now you're giving me another child. You've given me everything I ever wanted."

She smiled, resting her hand over his heart. "I'm so glad you're happy about the baby. I love you, Tim."

***

Later that night, Tim and Dominique shared their first dance.

When the band announced the Father/Daughter dance, her heart squeezed painfully. They hadn't been told there wouldn't be one? Dominique blinked fast, trying to hold back tears, when Post appeared beside her and held out his hand.

"I know Dad can't be here to dance with you," Post said softly, extending his hand. "But I have a surprise. May I have this dance?"

Dominique's breath hitched. She placed her hand in his, and Post led her to the floor. The song *My Little Girl* began to play. Then, halfway through, her father's voice joined the music.

Dominique broke. She buried her face against Post's shoulder, sobs shaking her as her father's familiar tone filled the air. She hadn't heard his voice in years.

When the song ended, one last message played: *"I love you, pumpkin."*

Post leaned down, his voice rough. "I know Mom and Dad are looking down on you right now, Dom. They're proud of you, and so am I. I stood in Dad's place and made Tim prove he was worthy of you. Today, I stand here again to give you away. You'll always be my little sister, but if he hurts you, I'll kill him."

Dominique laughed through her tears. "I love you too, big brother. Thank you for the song. That's the best gift you could've given me."

He nodded, stepped back, and handed her off to Tim.

Tim brushed away her tears and kissed her gently before they swayed together again.

An hour later, a familiar pull tugged at Dominique's soul—Nathaniel.

Her gaze swept the crowd until she spotted him. His hair was tied back, his black suit sharpening the icy edge of his eyes. Her heart stuttered. Desire tangled with guilt.

The pack watched Nathaniel warily.

A low rumble vibrated in Tim's chest.

Nathaniel approached. "Tim, Dominique. Congratulations. I hoped for one dance with the bride, if neither of you minds."

Tim's jaw tightened. His eyes met hers, full of warning.

'It's okay,' she sent through the link. 'He won't try anything. One dance.'

His fury burned through the bond, but he stepped aside.

Nathaniel took her hand, pulling her close. "Dominique, I didn't come to ruin your wedding," he murmured. "I've stayed in the shadows all night, but I couldn't leave without a dance. I know you've chosen Tim, but I want you to remember… I'll always be here if you ever need me."

Her chest ached. "Nathaniel, I'm trying to live a normal life with Tim. I can't do that if you're always near. The pull between us will never go away, but I have a family now. I can't tear that apart."

He nodded. "I understand. Congratulations on the baby, by the way. That's my only regret. I would've liked to have a family with you."

"Nathaniel," she whispered, "please don't do this to me today. I'll always feel our bond, but I need time. Eventually, I'll come back. Just not now."

"I'll wait," he promised softly. "But let me hold you one last time. Humor me, and I'll try to stay out of your dreams."

She nodded. "All right. One dance. Then you go home."

He smiled faintly. "One dance."

Nathaniel guided her across the floor, spinning her effortlessly. When he dipped her, their eyes locked. Dark, magnetic, and full of unspoken history.

When he lifted her, she fought the urge to kiss his lips, placing a gentle kiss on his cheek instead. "Thank you," she whispered.

He released her, and by the time she turned, his presence had already begun to fade.

Tim's eyes burned with restrained jealousy. Dominique smiled and sank into his lap, wrapping her arms around his neck. He nipped her bottom lip, making her whimper softly.

When the kiss broke, she murmured, "I think it's time to go. You still need to take off my garter, and I have a bouquet to throw. Then we can leave for the honeymoon. You'll have me all to yourself. For the rest of your life. No need to be jealous over a dance."

Tim sighed. "I know. But I can't help it. You're mine, Mrs. Lithe."

His wolf shimmered beneath the surface, eyes glowing faintly.

"Alpha, control yourself," Dominique whispered teasingly.

His grin turned wolfish. "Until later, my Luna."

His eyes softened back to light green. He kissed her quickly before turning to call the crowd's attention.

Dominique lifted her foot onto a chair. Tim's hands trailed up her leg slowly, deliberately. Their eyes stayed locked as he slid a finger beneath the garter, dragging it down her thigh. He tossed it over his shoulder without looking away.

She laughed when Nicholas caught it, wide-eyed.

Moments later, she tossed her bouquet. Melissa dove for it, knocking over two women to catch it. Dominique shook her head, laughter bubbling out.

***

When they reached the hotel, Dominique slipped out of her dress and into sheer lace lingerie with a red bow on her chest. She giggled at her reflection and crawled onto the bed.

"Okay, Tim," she called. "You can come get your present now."

Tim stepped out of the ensuite, whistling low. He stalked toward her, eyes dark. Leaning down, he tugged gently at the bow. When he reached for the lace, she stopped him.

She laughed as he pouted. "This isn't your gift."

"But I like this one. And it had a bow," he teased.

"You can still have it… later."

She reached for a small box on the nightstand and handed it to him.

"Dom, you already gave me the perfect gift earlier," he said.

"This one goes with it. Just open it."

Tim tore off the paper and lifted the lid. Inside was a journal.

On the inside cover, she'd written:

To my love,

Always remember that you're never alone.

Love,

Dominique.

He flipped the page, and there was a picture of them when they had started dating the first time. They were so young.

She'd written a description under it and how she'd felt about him at that time. He continued to flip the pages, finding more pictures, more descriptions, more thoughts and feelings. It was a journal of their lives. He came to a blank page and realized she'd left him space to continue the journal.

Closing his eyes, he fought back the tears, but he came undone when she wrapped herself around him.

"I love you," she whispered.

"I love you too," he murmured. "This is… perfect. Thank you. I have something for you, too."

He disappeared into the ensuite and returned with a box wrapped in silver paper. His heart pounded as she untied the ribbon. Inside, another box waited—marked Fragile.

Dominique opened it carefully and gasped.

Inside was a glass globe on a wooden base. Encased within was a sculpture of their hands clasped together, holding a gold chain. The gold chain she'd given him years ago that held a locket full of Lily's ashes. On the base was her name, birthday, and engraved words that gleamed softly:

Forever in our hearts, always a part of us.

She remembered Tim asking months ago for a mold of their hands, but she'd thought nothing of it when she never saw the result—until now. Her tears fell.

"It's perfect," she whispered.

"I wanted her to always be part of us," Tim said quietly. "A reminder that even through the pain, we built something beautiful."

He brushed away her tears with his thumbs.

Dominique placed the globe on the nightstand, watching the light reflect off the gold, making it glow—almost as if Lily was saying hello.

She curled against him, listening to his steady heartbeat.

She had gone through hell and back with this man, and together they'd found their way home—to love, to peace, to family.

Dominique smiled against his chest.

She would never forget how lucky she was to live this life.

ABOUT THE AUTHOR

Fantasy started writing when she was in her teens. She got married at eighteen and became a full-time mom shortly after. Due to work, marriage, and kids, she gave up chasing her dream of becoming a writer.

During COVID, when the world was on pause, her best friend talked her into writing out the story she had found a part of from years ago.

That story brought back her passion for writing, and the characters turned on her, altering the story to the way they wanted it.

Now here she sits, looking at her work and wondering how they made her start writing a series. Crimson Under The Moon is the first book of the series, and the characters have all demanded their own story. (Along with her daughter and best friend.)

When she isn't writing, she is constantly listening to an eclectic array of music and reading. Creating her own worlds and living in other people's has always been something she has treasured.

Fantasy lives in Virginia with her two children and numerous pets.

Acknowledgements

I would like to thank all the readers first and foremost. Without you, this story wouldn't matter.

Thank you to my Beta and ARC readers. Without you, I never would have been willing to put this story out.

Thank you to Jennifer for taking my ideas for the cover and bringing them to life. That woman literally plucked them out of my head and drew them up for me. She will never know how grateful I am.

Thank you to M.A. Lay, who has encouraged me not only to publish this book but to keep going and publish the whole series. He has also been a sounding board for chapters in book two and helped me "feel" the emotions needed in them.

Thank you to my engagement group on TikTok. They have supported me, said kind and encouraging words, and some of them even beta-read for me. You guys know who you are! Love ya!

And last, but certainly never least, I want to thank my daughter, and my best friend. My best friend was my sounding board while writing this book. I kept her up so many late nights discussing ideas when I was stuck, and having her read chapters just to get a genuine reaction.

My daughter has been my rock. I've shown her pictures, videos, gone over ideas, had her read bits and pieces of chapters, and give me feedback. She read all of my books in their rawest form and found the beauty in even the roughest of drafts. She also bugged me for everyone's stories, which is what turned this into a series.

I love and appreciate all of you who gave this book and me a chance!

I hope to see you in the next Chapter of the series: Bound By Crimson And Moonlight